INFAMOUS

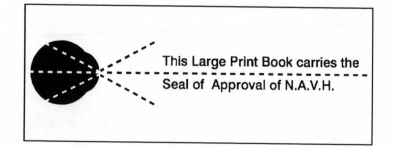

INFAMOUS

VIRGINIA HENLEY

THORNDIKE PRESS

An imprint of Thomson Gale, a part of The Thomson Corporation

Detroit • New York • San Francisco • New Haven, Conn. • Waterville, Maine • London

THOMSON
GALE

Thorndike Press® Large Print Core

The text of this Large Print edition is unabridged.

Other aspects of the book may vary from the original edition.

Set in 16 pt. Plantin.

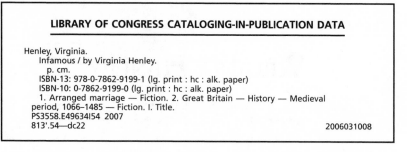

LIBRARY OF CONGRESS CATALOGING-IN-PUBLICATION DATA

Henley, Virginia.
  Infamous / by Virginia Henley.
    p. cm.
  ISBN-13: 978-0-7862-9199-1 (lg. print : hc : alk. paper)
  ISBN-10: 0-7862-9199-0 (lg. print : hc : alk. paper)
  1. Arranged marriage — Fiction. 2. Great Britain — History — Medieval period, 1066–1485 — Fiction. I. Title.
PS3558.E49634I54 2007
813'.54—dc22   2006031008

Published in 2007 by arrangement with NAL Signet, a member of Penguin Group (USA) Inc.

Printed in the United States of America on permanent paper
10 9 8 7 6 5 4 3 2 1

This book is dedicated to my
devoted readers.
You have earned my eternal gratitude.

PROLOGUE

Marjory de Warenne sat in the front pew of magnificent Chester Cathedral watching her brother, Lynx de Warenne, marry the woman he loved more than life. Jane Leslie, the lovely, gentle, flame-haired daughter of the steward of Dumfries Castle, had been handfast to her brother for a year and a day from when he had garrisoned the Scottish castle in the name of King Edward Plantagenet.

Though Jane had given Lynx a son, his heart's greatest desire, she had agreed to marry him only after he had received a wound at the Battle of Irvine that had threatened to prove fatal.

Jory smiled tenderly, remembering how she had pledged her brother's marriage vows because he had been too weak and debilitated to even speak. Then Jane had worked her magic, lovingly nursing Lynx back to life. Now that he had regained his health and been restored to his full fighting strength, he was marrying Jane again here in England, so he could pledge his own undying vows to the woman he worshipped.

Sudden panic threatened to choke Jory. As she stared at the flames of the long, tapered candles ablaze on the altar, she became dizzy. They reminded her of other candles that had burned at another wedding years before.

How extraordinarily strange it seemed that her brother's fortunes had finally flourished with the culmination of those years, bringing him undreamed-of happiness and fulfillment, while her own life lay in heartbreaking, shattered shards!

None yet knew of the disastrous mess she had made of her life. Until now she had managed to hide behind a facade of serene confidence, her emotions buried deep within, safely concealed from the unforgiving light of day that would expose her to a brutal scandal of her own making.

Jory stared at the flames, mesmerized. She had no idea what she would do or where she would go. She was too emotionally distraught to even pray for the help she would need to survive. She swayed as her mind took wing, flying back over the years to the time of that other wedding and the fateful day that had changed her life so completely.

If only, somehow, I had done things differently . . .

■ ■ ■ ■

PART ONE:
THE VIRGIN

■ ■ ■ ■

CHAPTER 1

"Did you *really* do it? Did you lose your virginity?" Marjory de Warenne's wide green eyes glittered with a mixture of excitement and apprehension as she bolted the bed-chamber door and removed Princess Joanna Plantagenet's hooded cloak.

Joanna spun about and stared in amazement at her young friend. Then she began to laugh. "Jory, your innocence staggers me. I lost my virginity more than two years ago, when I was sixteen!"

Jory was visibly shocked. "When you vowed to sow wild oats before your wedding at week's end, I thought as a final act of rebellion you would choose a secret lover for one night . . . and —"

"You thought that tonight would be the first time I'd go all the way with a man so I could experience carnal knowledge? Bless your sweet naïveté, Jory! Though I've never

13

been blatant about it, and never before dared take the chance while Father is here at Windsor, I have indulged in the pleasures of the flesh. What the devil do you think I do when I have a secret assignation?"

As Jory unfastened Joanna's gown, her imagination was limited by the daring things she had done with the opposite sex. "Flirt outrageously . . . perhaps allow him to kiss you?"

Joanna kicked off her shoes, then lay back on the satin bedcover and stretched with sensual abandon. "God in heaven, is that all you've ever done with the male of the species? I thought I had set you a better example than that. The game of seduction goes beyond fluttering your eyelashes and tossing about your silver-gilt tresses. Men's mouths are good for more than kissing and their pricks for more than pissing." Joanna brushed her hand over her mons and moaned with remembered pleasure.

"Do you need a bath?" Jory whispered, as Joanna's words painted a blatant picture of the sins of the flesh.

"Indeed I do." The princess sat up and the corners of her mouth lifted in a self-satisfied smile. "But I won't wash off his male scent or the milky essence of his lust until morning. This was my last night of indulgence. On the morrow my ancient husband-to-be arrives at Windsor."

"Gilbert de Clare, Earl of Gloucester, is England's premier noble. Your father thinks only to honor you, Joanna."

"By marrying me to a man thirty years my senior? Nay! The king thinks only to honor Gloucester, his greatest warrior, who commands more troops than any other earl. In Edward Plantagenet's world, women mean nothing except as rewards, like castles and titles — not even a daughter," she said bitterly. "My appeals to Mother also fell on deaf ears. The queen has always been more wife than mother. She worships him and would never oppose him."

Princess Joanna, the darkly beautiful, sloe-eyed daughter of King Edward Plantagenet had railed for months against her father's plans to marry her to the aging Earl of Gloucester. Her imperious displays of temper, her point-blank refusals, and her melodramatic threats to kill herself had availed her nothing. Her father was implacable . . . always. Not only about this, but about everything in life. Once Edward Plantagenet made a decision, it was final.

"I can manipulate any man in the world . . . any man save Father!"

"That is because you fear him," Jory murmured.

"Aye, I admit it. You should have seen the mad rage he displayed when I objected that Gilbert de Clare was an old man. 'Old?' Father bellowed. 'He is five years younger than I am! Gilbert needs an heir. Your son will inherit all Gloucester's English and Welsh lands and castles. Moreover, the ancient de Clare bloodline makes him one of the few nobles fit to mate with a Plantagenet.'

"When I said Gilbert was too old to give me a son, I thought he would strike me. *'Christ's bones, I'm well into my fifties and I can still sire a son! Do you want me to prove it?'* he roared."

Jory sat on the bed beside her. "I'm so sorry, Joanna. I wish with all my heart you could choose your own husband . . . someone young . . . someone you love." Jory hesitated. "What is his name?"

Joanna looked at her friend blankly for a moment. "You mean tonight? Henry . . . Godfrey . . . or was it Humphrey? Some such name. I don't remember. I'm certainly not in love with him."

Jory was aghast. "You don't remember?"

"Windsor is overflowing with nobles and their sons who are gathering for the royal

16

wedding in five short days. Yesterday when we stood on the ramparts of the Round Tower and watched scores of mounted men ride into the Lower Ward, I selected one of the taller, younger specimens. Since I capitulated and agreed to wed Gloucester, I decided I had earned a reward."

Jory's sense of the ridiculous bubbled to the surface. "Well, by the sound of you, it was certainly rewarding."

"We'll go again tomorrow. This time it will be your turn. Perhaps you will see someone you fancy. Your uncle, John de Warenne, and your brother, Lynx, will soon be arranging your marriage. You'll have no say in the matter, so you might as well indulge in a little dalliance with someone who stirs your blood before they bludgeon you into submission and turn you into a dutiful wife."

"Uncle John and Lynx would never do anything to make me unhappy. I have them wrapped around my finger and they indulge my every whim. Didn't they allow me to become one of your court ladies here at Windsor two years ago?"

"That happened the year after your brother wed Sylvia Bigod, the queen's lady-in-waiting. The Marshal of England's daughter is attractive, but not nearly as exquisitely lovely as you, Jory. Two beautiful females living at de Warenne's magnificent Hedingham Castle, vying for attention, must have given her pause. Sylvia likely got rid of you when you turned sixteen because she didn't want the competition."

Jory fell silent as Joanna stripped off her garments and slid nude beneath the covers. Though on the surface Jory had a sparkling personality and an infectious laugh, underneath, she had a vulnerability that she kept hidden. She did not remember her parents and had never had a home of her own. Her mother had died giving birth to her, and the guilt she carried lay buried deep within. Some months later, her father, Lincoln de Warenne, had died in battle, giving victory to Edward Plantagenet.

Her older brother had inherited their father's castles and lands in Essex, and they had been taken to live with their father's brother John de Warenne, Earl of Surrey, until Lynx came of age. Though her uncle and brother were indulgent guardians who made her feel loved, she had always harbored the belief she was an obligation and a burden that had been thrust upon them, and a secret fear of rejection added to her vulnerability.

Did Sylvia get rid of me by sending me to Windsor to be companion to Princess Joanna?

Jory picked up the discarded gown, hung it in the wardrobe and walked slowly toward the connecting door that led to her own chamber. "Good night, Your Highness."

Joanna sat up. "Come back here! Don't you dare be formal with me. I have dozens of court ladies who bow and scrape and call me Highness, but I have only one true friend."

Jory turned and walked slowly back. "I never dreamed Sylvia wanted to be rid of me."

"She wanted no such thing, Jory, though she should have if she had any brains. I asked for you especially because I wanted a lively companion whose wit and grace outshone every other noble lady I had ever met. And since I'm confessing the truth, I also chose you for your incandescent beauty. Your shining silver-gilt hair and pale green eyes make a perfect foil for the sultry dark coloring I inherited from my mother's Castilian ancestors."

Jory's smile returned as Joanna's words banished her apprehension and restored her confidence. "When we are together, we *do* draw every eye."

"We do indeed. Men gape and women stare with envy. Lord God, Jory, I predict that once you lose your innocence you will exude a sensuality that will be irresistible."

Joanna sighed. "Tonight, you look angelic, as if you've never even glimpsed a naked man."

"I haven't! Wherever would I see men who are naked?"

"Surely you jest? I sneaked into the bath-house when I was about twelve. You had an opportunity last year when we traveled to the Bruce estates in Essex for the ceremony where Bruce passed the Earldom of Carrick to his eldest son. All five Bruce brothers swam naked in the river every day."

Lady Marjory Bruce was Jory's namesake and godmother. "The Bruce brothers are rough boys. Their land runs with ours, so I've known them all my life. Robert Bruce is a wild devil who teased me unmercifully with a ferret and threatened to throw me in the water. I stayed away from the river."

"Ooh, I warrant his ferret was furry!"

Jory dissolved into giggles. "I missed my chance to find out."

"That's better. Now go to bed, and don't wake me before nine."

Princess Joanna stood impatiently for the last fitting of her wedding dress. She was surrounded by the queen's sewing women and the ladies-in-waiting of her own household while the Plantagenet-blue-and-gold gown was adjusted. "I shall scream if you keep me standing here a moment longer. Get me out of the damn thing!"

One intrepid matron protested, "It still needs —"

Jory saw the fury on Joanna's face that preceded an explosion of royal temper and she smoothly intervened. "It is perfect! Even you cannot improve on perfection, madam." She helped Joanna from the yards of rustling blue samite interwoven with glistening gold threads and handed the garment to the head seamstress.

Half an hour later the two friends stood atop the Round Tower, shielding their eyes from the brilliant autumn sunshine as they watched nobles and their retinues enter through the gates and ride into Windsor's Lower Ward.

"There!" Joanna flung up her arm and pointed. "I recognize the de Clare chevrons." She stared hard, trying to pick her future husband from the score of men who rode beneath the banners that displayed the de Clare device. Her eyes focused on their leader. She'd seen Gilbert before while growing up, but paid little heed. "The highest noble in the realm is attired like a common soldier."

Jory looked where she pointed. The rider removed his helmet, but he was too far away to see if he looked like an old man.

"Ha! Gilbert the red is now Gilbert the gray! I wonder if the fiery temper that goes with red hair has faded?" Joanna glanced triumphantly at her friend. "I shall dazzle and beguile him and have him eating from my hand like a besotted lapdog in no time."

Jory did not hear one word of Joanna's vow. Her full attention was riveted on a commanding figure clad in sable breastplate and plumed helm astride a black stallion. A tall black wolfhound stalked beside him, and though his retinue was fewer than a dozen, the other riders in the Lower Ward moved aside to make way for the striking nobleman. His pride of carriage and the power he exuded were obvious, even from this distance. Jory's legs suddenly felt weak and she grasped the stone battlement to steady herself.

Who is he? Jory's eyes lifted to his banner, which displayed a golden bear against a field of black, but her thoughts were in such disarray she could not identify the device. Irresistibly her gaze was drawn back to the man as if she thirsted for the sight of him.

Her heart began to hammer as she watched him wheel his horse in the direction of Gilbert of Gloucester. The earl's attendants fell back as he approached, and Jory wondered if it was respect or fear that compelled them. The thought made her quiver and she licked her lips as her mouth suddenly went dry. The two men spoke, then laughed together, and it was obvious to her that the pair were well acquainted.

"Since de Clare's been traveling for at least three days, the next hours will be taken up with bathing and changing. I won't meet my lapdog until the banquet tonight, so I'm blessedly free of him for now," Joanna said blithely.

Jory's imagination took flight, trying to picture the black knight stark naked as he stepped into a bath of steaming water. Her mind's eye painted a portrait that was vexingly vague and she felt an overwhelming desire to see him in clear, explicit detail.

Joanna sought escape. "I think I'll go for a gallop in Windsor Forest . . . perhaps take a hawk. Will you join me?"

"Your other ladies would jump at the chance. When you favor my company, they feel neglected." Jory searched for a plausible excuse and found one. "I'll stay and watch for Lynx's arrival."

"Family duty be damned. Keep your eyes open for a tempting young lord who will lure you to dalliance."

As Joanna left, the corners of Jory's mouth lifted in a secret smile. She had learned much from the royal princess, not the least of which was how to dissemble, flatter, and manipulate so that she could do exactly as she pleased. She gripped the crenellated wall and gazed downward. She was in time to see the sable-clad noble swing a long, powerful leg across his stallion's rump and dismount in one lithe movement that kept his back ramrod straight and his head erect. A frisson of desire rippled through her belly as he disappeared from her view. *I believe I shall go hunting after all, and I have spotted my quarry!*

Jory returned to the imposing rectangular building in the Upper Ward where Princess Joanna and her ladies resided. Their chambers, which took up the entire second floor, were in disarray.

The ladies had hurriedly changed into their riding dresses and dropped the garments they'd been wearing onto their beds, knowing the servants would pick up after them.

Jory entered Joanna's chamber and swept up the soiled petticoat from last night before the serving women found it. She followed the sound of female voices and found three servants tidying Maud Clifford's chamber. She gave the women a measuring glance, selected one, and took her into her own room. "Dora, you are about my size. How would you like to have this dress I'm wearing?"

"Oh, my lady, it's brocade! Do you mean it?"

"There's a catch. I have need of the plain grey tunic you are wearing. Will you trade with me?"

"Indeed I will, Lady Marjory. I have half a dozen like this."

Jory unfastened her gown and stepped out of it as Dora hurriedly removed her tunic. Then she lifted her gown over the servant's head and fastened the buttons that ran down the back. "Go and look in the mirror at how lovely you are." Jory thanked Dora, hung the grey tunic in her wardrobe, and donned another gown.

She picked up Joanna's petticoat, bundled it with one of her own that needed washing, and made her way to the castle laundry. It was a cavernous place beneath the vast kitchens, where dozens of washerwomen toiled daily over a mountain of soiled clothing and household linen. Boiling water, soap, lye, and starch branded them with red chapped hands, the telltale mark of their trade. The laundry also encompassed drying chambers, pressing rooms, and folding and storage areas for the clean linen.

The head laundress bobbed a curtsy, while her young helpers at their scrubbing boards gaped. "How may I serve ye, m'lady?"

Jory's smile encompassed all. "You do such excellent work and I'm here to thank each one of you. Maud Clifford is responsible for Princess Joanna's personal laundry, but I have a shrewd idea that she passes it off to one of you."

"Mary's the one wi' the gentle hands," the laundress confirmed.

Jory dropped the petticoats into Mary's washtub and smiled her thanks. "I'd love to look around. The vast scale of your operation is astounding. Would you be kind enough to show me?"

The head laundress swallowed the bait and gestured for Mary to accommodate the princess's lady-in-waiting. Jory took the lead immediately and maneuvered her way to the linen press, where the clean garments for all the castle servants were stored. As they walked between the rows of shelves, her eyes searched for things that would serve her purpose. She saw a pile of white linen headdresses and helped herself.

"I've always wondered what the bathhouse women wear when they scrub the noblemen who visit Windsor. They must get soaking wet."

"I'll show you, m'lady." Mary led the way down another aisle. "They wear these cotton smocks that dry quickly."

Jory fingered the material. "Fascinating . . . I'll take one." She lowered her voice to a confidential tone. "When Princess Joanna is wed, she will first move to a splendid country manor house in Clerkenwell, near the Tower. The Earl of Gloucester has more castles and residences than any other noble. If you would like to be part of her household, I will recommend you, Mary."

"Oh, thank you, my lady. I would love to serve the princess."

Jory tucked the garments she'd pilfered under her arm and winked at Mary. "Consider it done."

It wasn't a great distance from the washhouse to Windsor's bathhouse, which was located on the ground floor above the dungeons. The stone edifice was part of the outer wall on the Thames side, where water from the river was piped in and heated. The plan was copied from a system the ancient Romans had built in Britain centuries before.

No lady ever ventured near this strictly male bastion where kings, princes, earls, barons, high-ranking clergy, and the men who held royal office had made their ablutions for over a century. Jory did not dare hesitate about what she intended or her courage would fail her. She had come this far and would not stop now. As she reached the arched entranceway, a cacophony of raised male voices, shouting, cursing, and laughing made her heart pound. She covered her hair with the linen headdress and slipped the cotton smock over her gown. It was such a voluminous garment that it almost drowned her. She gathered its folds about her and stepped inside. When she saw the size of the strapping bathhouse women, she understood why the smocks were so enormous.

She peered through the veil of steam cautiously, realizing that many of the partly obscured figures were unclad males. A matron slapped a wooden tub of soft soap into her hands and pointed. "This is for Gloucester. Make haste!"

She took one step and the woman bawled, "Take the salt." Jory gripped the block of salt the woman thrust at her. "Salt?"

"For the earl's teeth, ye gormless wench."

On what felt like stiff wooden legs, Jory staggered in the direction the matron had indicated and was relieved when a young squire with a Gloucester badge on his tunic took the items from her and passed them to a muscular female. When the squire stepped aside to fill a bucket with water, Jory was presented with an unimpeded view of the naked bridegroom lying full length in a white marble tub. The bathing wench slathered a handful of soft soap onto his chest and reached beneath the water, groping toward his private parts.

Jory stared in amazement. Gilbert de Clare's limbs displayed a few scars and his muscles were ropey and knotted from years of use, but he did not have the body of an old man. The hair on both his chest and head was sparse and grizzled, yet the features of his face were strong. *Joanna, Gloucester is no lapdog!*

"Rinse!" The order from the bath wench brought the bucket of water that the squire held pouring down upon the earl.

De Clare gave a bark of laughter. "You'll

need more water than that to drown me, lad."

The strapping woman hauled up Gloucester's leg and examined his foot. She looked at Jory and ordered, "Pumice stone."

A canvas curtain that hung beside the bathtub was drawn aside. A naked man rose up and stepped from his own marble tub. He handed the bath woman his pumice. "Take mine — I'm done."

Jory stood rooted to the spot and gaped. The male who stood resplendent before her was tall and powerfully built. His broad chest was covered by a pelt of wet black hair and his impossibly wide shoulders rippled with smooth, glistening muscle. Jory did not dare raise her eyes to his face, but looked her fill at the rest of his body. Water droplets trickled down his flat belly and narrow hips. Her gaze followed them as they ran down his long flanks, which bulged with saddle muscles. Her attention shifted to the forbidden place between his legs. His cock and balls were nestled among a heavy thatch of wet black curls that in no way obscured their size. She was shocked at the amplitude of his sex, yet amazed that the male groin could hold her in thrall to such a degree that she was mesmerized.

The spell was broken when the man

picked up a towel and slung it about his hips. The object of her fascination was now covered, enabling her to think more clearly, and it forcefully struck her that she should not be here doing this scandalous thing. Jory backed away slowly, desperately trying to avoid drawing attention to herself, but the two men began conversing and she might have been a block of salt for all the notice they paid her.

As she made her way back to the Upper Ward, she walked as if she were in a trance. Her thoughts were all centered on the powerful naked body she had just witnessed. She had no doubt that it belonged to the compelling noble who had riveted her attention when he rode in this morning, yet his identity was still a mystery. The commanding figure in the sable armor had enthralled her, and now that she had seen him nude, she was completely entranced. Though she hadn't the vaguest notion who he was, she felt his strong magnetic power, which held her in thrall.

Who are you? Who the devil are you? She was bemused that the word *devil* came to mind, yet she knew the reason. He was dark and powerful, sinfully enticing, and he had an aura of forbidden danger about him. Jory sensed all this before she had even seen his face.

She was filled with a driving need to find out who he was. Tonight she would search until she found him. Tonight she would see his face and look into his eyes. Would his visage attract her or repel her? Jory shivered with anticipation.

CHAPTER 2

"I don't wish to wear that head veil." Joanna waved a dismissive hand at her lady as she studied her reflection in the polished silver mirror. "My hair is too lovely to cover." She had already refused to wear the virginal white roses the queen had provided.

Jory stepped forward. "You could wear a jeweled circlet."

"Yes, bring the one that's tiered like a crown. It won't hurt to remind Gloucester that a royal princess stands above an earl."

Jory brought it and stood on tiptoe to fit it into place, as amusement danced in her eyes. "Would you like your ermine cape?"

"I shall save that for the wedding." Joanna's laughter trailed away as her glance swept over Jory. "Why aren't you dressed?"

Jory lowered her voice. "Tonight I have a secret mission."

Joanna slanted a knowing eyebrow. "An assignation?"

"First I must stalk and identify my quarry."

"Happy hunting! Your prey doesn't stand a chance."

Jory waited until the princess and her ladies-in-waiting departed for the banquet. Joanna's chamber was in such disarray that she tidied the room and hung up all the garments that had been strewn about. Jory had a fine appreciation of beautiful clothes and because she'd had the talented services of the royal dressmakers for the past two years, she had developed an elegant fashion sense. She had learned which styles flattered her petite figure and which shades best set off her delicate coloring.

When the room was restored to order, Jory returned to her own chamber and donned the plain grey tunic and white linen headdress. Excitement bubbled inside her as she surveyed her appearance in the mirror to make sure she could pass as a castle servant. She tucked an errant tendril behind her ear and said a quick prayer.

Windsor's Great Hall was packed to overflowing. The earls and barons had come to see and be seen. Those in attendance were obviously in favor with King Edward at the moment. It was a rare chance for the nobles to gather in one place at one time to converse, exchange ideas, air differences, protest taxes, plot intrigues, forge alliances, negotiate deals, and make advantageous matrimonial matches for their sons and daughters.

The attendants who comprised the nobles' retinues were primarily interested in eating, drinking, gambling, and indulging any other vices that slaked their appetites.

By the time Jory arrived, the banquet was well under way. She had stopped in the kitchen and helped herself to some roast fowl and a quince tart. Then she picked up a jug of ale and entered the hall. She put a safe distance between herself and the royal dais, where the Plantagenets, their guest of honor, Gilbert of Gloucester, and the nobles who held high office were seated.

From a dimly lit alcove, her gaze swept the long table. The queen sat on King Edward's left, his son and heir, on his right. Though the youthful Prince Edward was younger than Joanna, there was a strict pecking order. The Earl of Gloucester was seated next to the princess, and Jory smiled, knowing that Joanna thought herself magnanimous to even acknowledge his presence. Gilbert de Clare didn't seem to mind. John de Bohun, the Earl of Hereford and

Constable of England, was seated on his other side and the two military men were deep in conversation.

Thomas of Lancaster, the king's nephew and high steward, was seated next to the queen, and then came Roger Bigod, the Earl of Norfolk and Marshal of England. Jory's eyes widened as they fell on her own uncle, John de Warenne. Though he was the Earl of Surrey, she'd had no idea King Edward held him in such high esteem.

Jory had not been aware of her uncle's arrival, and she now realized her brother, Lynx, and his wife, Sylvia, would be here too. *They must not see me playing the role of serving wench or there will be merry hell to pay!* She cautioned herself to watch out for them and keep a safe distance.

The Great Hall was filled with rows of trestle tables and benches to accommodate the throng of nobles and their attendants. Huge platters of fish, eels, roast fowl, haunches of beef, and whole piglets were placed on every table so the guests could serve themselves, and as Jory glanced around she saw that the dishes were now empty and the bones picked clean. The nobles sat with their own people to eat, but once the tables were cleared, they would be eager to walk about and seek out their friends and allies.

She set off with her jug of ale, ignoring the many tankards thrust at her to be filled. As she nimbly dodged the male hands that reached out to pat her bottom or touch other parts of her anatomy, she scrutinized the badges on the men's tunics. She saw every device and animal imaginable as she searched for a golden bear on a field of jet. She had traversed the entire length of the hall, yet still the badge that she sought eluded her.

A deep male voice echoed in her ear. "Demoiselle, my throat is as dry as an Arabian desert. Will you take pity on one who thirsts?"

Jory whirled around and stared into a pair of eyes so dark they looked purplish black. He was the most handsome man she had ever gazed upon, and pride was stamped in every line of his face. Displaying inbred manners, he arose gallantly and waited for her to fill his tankard. She had to raise her chin and tilt her head back to look up at him, now that he had risen to his full height.

As her avid gaze traveled up his broad chest she saw the golden bear emblazoned on his black velvet doublet and as their eyes met, her brain clicked with recognition and she identified the device. *Warwick! God's blood, the man is the infamous Earl of Warwick! The one they call the Wolfhound.* Jory stood motionless, staring wide-eyed, like a doe poised for flight. Warning bells sounded in her head. She thrust the jug of ale at him and fled.

His attention obviously engaged, the earl set the jug on the table, detached himself from his men, and followed the maid.

Jory's feet did not stop moving until she was outside. She took several deep breaths, filling her lungs with fresh night air.

"Pardon, demoiselle. If you desire some company, you need look no farther. I am Guy de Beauchamp, at your service."

She turned and looked up at him. "Warwick?"

With some amusement he acknowledged, "Aye, I am Warwick." He held out his hand to her.

She tore her gaze from his face and looked at his hand. It was large, calloused, with long shapely fingers, and it was compelling beyond measure. *How can I refuse him? He possesses an invisible force that draws me.* Her impulsive nature willfully banished her trepidation. She placed her hand in his and he curled his fingers about it. She felt his warmth seep into her, and something far more potent: She felt his power.

"What shall I call you, little maid?"

"My name is Mar —" She stopped, appalled that she had almost blurted her true identity. She watched his mouth curve and thought it beautiful.

"Margret? Will you walk with me, Margret?"

"Where, my lord?"

"Wherever you will."

His voice was so deep and lyrical, it insinuated itself inside her. She was acutely aware that Guy de Beauchamp had an innate French charm and gallantry that set her pulses racing madly.

She thought of walking by the river, then with great daring, changed her mind. "I should like to walk in the garden."

His fingers tightened about her hand. "I shall follow wherever you lead, demoiselle."

She knew he was telling her what she wanted to hear. He wasn't blatantly lying, merely blurring the truth. For she knew down to her bones that *he* would do the leading. And she would let him.

Hand in hand they entered the Upper Ward and walked along the terrace that took them past the State Apartments. They went through a stone archway that led to the formal garden. The royal garden was walled and private, but Jory was familiar with a hidden entrance. She slipped her hand from his and with nimble fingers unlatched the gate.

Once they were inside, Warwick did not recapture her hand; instead he slid his arm about her shoulders. His closeness coupled with her own daring sent shivery excitement spiraling inside her, and her senses became drenched with the intoxicating perfume of night-blooming flowers and his potent male scent.

Their footsteps slowed as they came upon an inviting garden seat tucked beneath the cascading branches of a willow tree. The moonlight bathed them in haunting silver and dark shadows. Jory gasped as his power-ful hands encircled her waist and lifted her to stand on the bench, eliminating their difference in height.

His dark eyes studied her heart-shaped face with great intensity. "You are exceed-ingly young, *ma petite.*"

"I am eighteen!" she protested.

His mouth curved. "A delightful age of innocence."

"Yes . . . no! Perhaps," she added provoca-tively.

"An innocence that thirsts for a deeper knowledge and hungers for a wider experience . . . perhaps?"

"Yes, indeed, my lord," she murmured breathlessly.

His long fingers cupped her face, holding her captive. His mouth hovered above hers for a full tantalizing minute before his lips touched hers. She closed her eyes and swayed, intoxicated by the taste of his kiss.

His arms swept about her to steady her; then he lifted her and held her against his hard body. This time he took full possession of her mouth, easily persuading her to open her lips to his questing tongue. He thrust inside the velvet cave of her mouth, tasting her honeyed sweetness. He allowed her body to slowly slide down his until her feet once more touched the bench. Then his hands caressed her back with long, drugging strokes that moved ever lower until he had captured her bottom cheeks.

Held against his powerful body, Jory pictured him naked and was lost, lost in a sea of desire. She was aware of his hard arousal brushing against her soft thighs and felt her mons tingle in response. She gripped his muscular shoulders and arched against him, but because of their disparate size, her woman's center rubbed against his belly.

She moaned softly with frustration.

He lowered himself to the bench, pulled her into his lap, and took possession of her lips. Long, lingering kisses progressed to deeply sensual persuasive ones, and then his mouth became demanding as he ravished her with his tongue.

She could feel his hard shaft beneath her, and shifted her bum to better accommodate his great size. He lifted the hem of her tunic and slid his fingers around her slim ankle. His bold hand moved up her shapely calf, fondled her knee, and then moved beyond her garter to the expanse of bare thigh above her hose. When he began to stroke her naked flesh with his calloused palm, she wanted to scream with excitement.

He nuzzled her ear with his lips. "Open for me, *chéri*."

Jory's eyes flew open as if she had just come out of a trance. She closed her legs tightly, trapping his seeking fingers. "You must stop! This is wrong . . . I should not be here like this."

His dark eyes searched her face. "I will stop, though you cannot deny you invited my advances." His voice held regret. "I have no need to force a woman."

"I did invite your kisses . . . They held me spellbound," she confessed breathlessly. Her breasts rose and fell with agitation over her dilemma. She craved his touch. She desired this man with every fiber of her being, yet at the same time she cursed herself for behaving like a whore. She feared the great Warwick would neither respect nor value a woman who was wanton.

She eased the vice grip of her thighs and felt his palm slide down her leg. When his hand emerged from beneath her skirt, she was shocked to see that his cunning fingers had stolen her garter.

He cocked a black eyebrow. "Just as I suspected. You are no serving wench. Confess the truth and shame the devil!"

Jory was aghast. "How did you know, my lord?"

"Serving wenches are coarse. You are made of finer stuff. I suspect you are a gently bred tiring woman to a noble lady." He grinned. "Does she know you have pilfered her garters?"

Relief flooded over her. *Thank heaven he thinks I'm a servant!*

"No wonder you asked me to stop. You deserve better than a quick tumble in the grass. Will you come to my chamber?"

Jory licked her lips and tasted his kisses. Desire flared up in her for the wicked Warwick, and she knew she must escape before the dangerous devil mesmerized her completely. She slid from his knee. "It's late . . . I must go . . . I have duties . . ."

"My invitation is open." He held her with his dark eyes. "Will you come to my chamber tomorrow night?"

She gazed at him with longing. *He possesses an invisible force that draws me. How can I refuse him?*

His mouth curved. "I know you will not refuse me, demoiselle."

Jory backed away, breaking the spell. Then she turned and ran.

Warwick returned to the hall. He was relieved that the dais was now empty. The queen had retired and the bride-to-be had obviously made her escape. He saw half a dozen earls conversing with the king and decided to join them. He took a tankard of ale from a server's tray and drained it. By the time he had walked the length of the great chamber, he had received three blatant invitations and two that were more subtle from noble ladies who had accompanied their husbands to Windsor for the royal wedding. Guy de Beauchamp was accustomed to female attention. His dark, predatory looks coupled with his reputation as a fierce warrior on the battlefield, were tempting enough. When the dangerous rumors of his dealings with women were added, the more daring matrons were eager to risk playing with fire for the chance to be scorched by Warwick's smoldering passion. He kept walking and ignored the invitations. Over the years he'd had a bellyful of spoiled, highborn noble ladies.

"Why did you not join us on the dais?" King Edward demanded.

"I didn't wish to ruin the celebration of Gloucester's upcoming nuptials by voicing my opposition to the taxes you are about to ask for in Parliament, Your Majesty."

"Damn you, Warwick. What makes you think I'll call Parliament?"

"Since Windsor is so close to Westminster, I warrant you will seize the opportunity while we are all gathered for the wedding."

"And so I shall. Decisions have to be made. My negotiations with Philip of France have come to naught. Hostilities are raging out of control between the sailors of the Cinque Ports and the fishermen of Normandy who sail our waters illegally. I have reports the wily, ambitious Philip will use this as a pretext to seize Gascony, the last of our French possessions."

"Are you contemplating waging war with France, Your Majesty?" John de Warenne asked bluntly.

"I am. I plan to lead an army into Flanders and fight it out. I'll send another army to recover Gascony if he dares touch it."

"Wars cost money, Your Majesty. I am opposed to having my taxes raised," Warwick repeated.

Roger Bigod, Earl of Norfolk, stepped forward. "Now that the subject has been broached, Your Majesty, I also disfavor your calling Parliament. I am in full agreement with Warwick."

"I need money badly, and whether you like it or not, I must take emergency measures to raise it," Edward said emphatically.

"And we are expected to dance to the royal tune." Warwick always had the balls to speak his mind, but tonight he knew the king was on dangerous ground because this means of raising money broke the stipulations of the Great Charter.

John de Bohun, Earl of Hereford, intervened. "Gentlemen, let us keep the peace among us at least until Gloucester here is wed; then we can hammer out our differences at Westminster."

Edward, eager to postpone the inevitable battle of wills until after the nuptials had been performed, called for wine all around. "A toast to the bridegroom." He hoisted his

46

goblet and his earls followed suit. "Gilbert of Gloucester — here's to many fine sons!"

A son and heir was the cherished hope of every noble. Though King Edward had sired four sons, three had died before they reached maturity and only one remained. De Warenne had no legitimate son, and Bigod had only a daughter. All envied de Bohun, the constable, who had two grown sons.

Warwick clapped his friend Gloucester on the back. His dark eyes brimmed with amusement. "The king believes that once you are his son-in-law you will support him in all things."

"Then he is delusional," Gilbert said with a wink.

"I would be hard-pressed to choose which of you has the hotter temper. The Plantagenet rage is formidable to behold, but I've seen yours explode and scorch the earth."

Gilbert stared at him in disbelief. "Your own temper borders on madness — Warwick's reputation is legendary."

"Only when provoked. I have learned to keep the wolfhound in me tightly leashed. It is a matter of pride."

Edward came up behind Gilbert and placed a hand on his shoulder. "I've arranged a hunt tomorrow in your honor. I vow there's nothing better than venison for a wedding feast."

Irony danced in Warwick's eyes as he put his hand on Gilbert's other shoulder. "It's an eat-what-you-kill world, my friend."

Jory drew back the princess's curtains to let in the pale morning sunshine. "It is a beautiful day, Joanna. I hope the banquet met your expectations last night."

"Don't try to be subtle. You mean, did *Gloucester* meet my expectations?" She threw back the covers. "Actually, he turned out better than I thought. When I ignored him, he didn't take offense. He didn't put on any airs and graces; nor did he try to flatter me. Gloucester's still old enough to be my father, but at least he's no toady." Joanna slid her feet into her slippers and donned her bedgown.

"It was what happened after the banquet that bored me to tears and drove me to the edge of insanity. The queen, herding a gaggle of noble ladies, expected me to show them all the wedding gifts on display in the Long Gallery. What should have been ac-complished in ten minutes, stretched to two hours. They took an inordinate interest in every gold cup and silver fork until I contemplated picking one up and stabbing myself for the sheer fun of it."

Jory laughed. "Viewing the costly gifts is one of the great pleasures of attending a royal wedding."

"Your sister-in-law, Sylvia, kept making pointed queries regarding your whereabouts and complaining that you hadn't presented yourself to them yet. I'm adept at avoiding unwanted questions, but now it's your turn to answer a few." Joanna gave Jory back her own words. "Did you *really* do it? Did you lose your virginity?"

Jory smiled her secret smile. "I too am adept at avoiding unwanted questions. I learned the trick from a royal princess."

"You *did* indulge in dalliance! At least tell me his name."

"Gervais . . . Giles . . . or was it Guy? I don't remember."

"Oh, you little hussy, he is *French!*"

Jory rolled her eyes. "He is indeed."

"Do you have another rendezvous planned for tonight?"

"He did invite me," Jory confessed, "but I have no intention of keeping the assignation. I have quite made up my mind. In any case, I shall be far too busy attending the events that Queen Eleanor has arranged in your honor."

"Ah, yes, an al fresco luncheon served in the formal gardens, followed by a sightseeing tour along the Thames from Windsor to London aboard the royal barge. Father has arranged for the men to go on an all-day hunt. Lucky devils!"

"You love going out on the river," Jory protested.

"Yes, I do enjoy it in the company of my own ladies, but certainly not with the queen's uppity attendants, who look down their long, disapproving noses at me. As well, Mother will expect me to remember the name and title of every earl and baron's wife. I cannot tell Countess Cowclap from Baroness Horseface."

"You only pretend you can't tell them apart to amuse yourself."

"You know me so well, Jory."

"Maude Clifford and Blanche Bedford will be attending you this morning, Your Highness. I must go and present myself to Lynx and Sylvia, and my uncle, John de Warenne."

"Don't try to change the subject. The royal barge will be back by nightfall and so will the hunters. That leaves plenty of time for dalliance between sunset and sunrise."

"I shall resist temptation today — I've quite made up my mind."

CHAPTER 3

"Hello, Minx! Where have you been hiding yourself?" John de Warenne, who had come to collect Lynx for the hunt, used her pet name. Lynx and Minx was a jest they had shared with their uncle since they were children. "I swear you grow lovelier each time I see you. Your beauty dazzles my eyes."

Jory dropped him a graceful curtsy. "Thank you, kind sir."

"Don't encourage her, John. Her angelic looks may bedazzle you, but they mask an imp of Satan. I see nothing but devilish mischief dancing in those green eyes."

Jory, used to her brother's teasing, paid him back in kind. "Lynx has forgotten what it's like to be young. He's become cynical and believes all females are spoiled, vain, and shallow."

"You forgot willful," he said pointedly.

"Poor Lynx, I had no idea Sylvia was willful."

"My wife may be spoiled from her days at the Queen's Court, but willful she is not. Only one de Warenne female has a will of iron." His mouth curved. "Marriage will cure you of that."

"Marriage?" Jory wrinkled her nose. "Princess Joanna warned me you would soon be finding me a husband."

"We've searched high and low, but I fear 'tis a futile task."

"Don't tease the child, Lynx." John looked at her with doting eyes. "We had an offer for you not long ago, but turned it down."

Jory's green eyes blazed with indignation. "You gave me no say in the matter? God's bones, Joanna told me it would be so!"

"The offer was from Aylesbury for his younger son. It was out of the question. He must be an earl, or at least heir to an earldom, before we will even consider negotiating a match."

Joanna was right. The men in my life will arrange my marriage and I'll have no say in the matter. "If you receive another offer, please promise you will let me know about it," she begged.

Lynx put a reassuring arm about her. "Trust us to know what's best for you, Jory. We will arrange a good, solid, lasting marriage with a worthy noble family that will bring you security, a title, and provide your children with castles and land."

"But there must be more to marriage than titles and castles. Surely there should be love? You and Sylvia had a love match."

"We had no such thing. The marriage was arranged and negotiated between our uncle, the Earl of Surrey, and her father, the Earl of Norfolk. Our union has proved most amiably adequate in every way, Jory. Love is the stuff of poets and minstrels."

Adequate? Splendor of God, I want more than adequate! "Where is Sylvia?" she asked faintly.

"She was invited to take breakfast with Queen Eleanor this morning. The queen has great affection for her and I warrant she misses my wife's services as lady-in-waiting."

"Is Sylvia with —" Jory bit off her sentence before she uttered the last word. She would know if Sylvia was with child the moment she saw her. She knew Lynx longed for a son and heir and was greatly disappointed that he was not yet a father after almost two years of marriage. She amended her question. "Is Sylvia with the other ladies-in-waiting, or does she dine alone with Eleanor?"

"Lord, I pay no attention to women's affairs." He ran an impatient hand through his mane of tawny hair. "Come, John, we'll be late for the hunt. Try not to commit mayhem today, Minx."

"I cannot promise. You know I am cursed with impulsiveness." She stood on tiptoe and kissed her uncle. When Lynx strode out the door, she gazed up at John with imploring eyes. "You will let me choose my own husband? Promise me I won't suffer Joanna's fate? I have a horror of being given to an elderly noble."

The expression on the flinty earl's face softened. "Sweet child." John caressed her cheek. "You must know that your happiness is paramount to me and to your brother. I give you my word that our choice of a husband will meet with your approval."

Aboard the royal barge, Jory approached Sylvia and took the cushioned seat beside her. Her first glance told her that her sister-in-law was not with child. Her second glance made her wonder why Sylvia covered her lovely chestnut hair with such a matronly head veil. "I'm sorry I missed you this morning when I visited with Lynx and Uncle John."

Sylvia admonished her. "It was your duty

to present yourself yesterday, when we arrived."

"Please forgive me. I had no idea you were here at Windsor. There are so many last-minute wedding preparations that must be attended to. I trust you enjoyed breakfast with the queen?"

"We had a lovely reunion, thank you. Weddings are so exciting. Princess Joanna must be very proud of becoming the Countess of Gloucester. Gilbert de Clare is England's most powerful peer."

"It's an arranged marriage. Joanna was given no choice."

Sylvia looked shocked at her words. "Choice? The marriage of a princess or any highborn lady is always arranged. It would be a sad state of affairs if an eighteen-year-old maiden was allowed to choose her life's partner."

Jory hesitated. "Suppose that you had not wanted my brother for your husband but your father forced you to marry him?"

Sylvia was incredulous. "Not want to marry Lynx de Warenne? You must be mad. He is a handsome, brave warrior whose fighting skills are legend, and he is heir to his uncle's powerful earldom. Through my marriage I will someday become the Countess of Surrey."

"You are most fortunate, but I doubt that most arranged marriages work out so well. What if your father had chosen someone old and ugly? Surely you would have protested?"

"You have seen my father. I would never dare protest a decision he made for me. I'd have done my duty and obeyed him."

Jory pictured the squat, irascible Roger Bigod and was thankful for her Uncle John, who was always extremely indulgent with her. "I intend to choose my own husband. I've quite made up my mind!"

"Marjory, you are being fanciful. Negotiating a suitable match for you is a grave responsibility for the Earl of Surrey and my husband. One they do not take lightly. You must trust them to know what is best for you."

Those are the same words Lynx used. "John assured me that I could choose my own husband," Jory asserted.

Her sister-in-law gave her a pitying glance. "When you act willfully, he tells you whatever you wish to hear."

"He *promised!*"

Sylvia laughed. "You are so naive, my dear. Men's promises are forgotten the moment they are uttered."

Jory found the conversation unsettling. Not only was Sylvia being condescending, she had reminded her that she was a grave responsibility for her uncle and her brother. "Ah, here is Alicia Bolton, one of the queen's ladies. I'm sure you have much to reminisce about. If you will excuse me, I'll return to my duties."

Jory refused to dwell on the things Sylvia had said and for the rest of the day pushed away the disquieting thoughts that tried to intrude. That evening, she ate a light supper in her chamber and then, as she did each night, attended Princess Joanna until she retired.

"There were many empty seats in the hall tonight. Apparently the hunters did not return at sundown as expected. I didn't mind in the least not dining with Gloucester, but I'm sorry that your secret rendezvous has been ruined," Joanna teased.

"You know I had no intention of keeping it!" *Then why did you go to the trouble of locating Warwick's chambers?* her inner voice taunted. She unlaced Joanna's gown and hung it in the wardrobe. "Have you decided which riding outfit you will wear tomorrow?" The hunt with hawks, in the bride's honor, was to include both sexes, and Jory knew the princess wished to look spectacular.

"I have decided on the crimson surcoat so I can wear the ruby-jeweled caul. Don't I have gloves with ruby-embroidered cuffs?"

"You do indeed, and you have jesses and tyrrits to match."

The friends talked until it was late, and Jory laid out everything Joanna had chosen to wear for the morrow's hawking party before she retired to her own chamber.

As she lay quietly abed, the thoughts she had held at bay all day began to intrude. For months she had been so absorbed in Princess Joanna's marriage she hadn't realized her own time was approaching. If there had already been one offer, others would soon follow, and she thanked heaven that she would have a say in choosing her own husband.

Are you sure? her inner voice insisted.

Lynx's words came back to her. *Trust us to know what's best for you, Jory.*

"Uncle John promised me!" Jory whispered fiercely.

Sylvia's voice intruded. *Men's promises are forgotten the moment they are uttered.*

"What exactly did John promise?" *I give you my word that our choice of a husband will meet with your approval.*

"He said *our* choice of a husband, not *your* choice of a husband! Sylvia was right. He told me what I wished to hear just to mollify me. My husband will be *their* choice, not *mine!*"

A full-blown picture of the two men she had seen naked in the bathhouse came into her head. The body of one was so lithe and virile it stole her senses; the other male by comparison was well past his prime and lacked any appeal for Jory.

"Joanna is right! Just like her, I'll have no say in the matter . . . I would be a fool not to seize the opportunity to indulge in a little dalliance with someone who stirs my blood before they bludgeon me into submission and turn me into a dutiful wife!"

She threw back the covers, lit a candle, and padded naked to her wardrobe. As she donned the plain grey tunic and covered her hair with the white linen headdress, her heartbeat danced to the rhythm of one compelling name: *Guy de Beauchamp! Guy de Beauchamp!*

Warwick stood in a wooden tub of water and washed the blood of the hunt from his body. He briskly dried himself and slid his arms into a black bed robe. Then two of his attendants removed the tub from his chamber and his squire carried in a tray of food and a large jug of ale. "Thank you, Will. I'm ravenous."

Warwick poured himself a tankard of ale, but before he had time to drink any, someone knocked. Thinking Will had forgotten something, he strode to the door and threw it open. Surprise mingled with deep pleasure when he saw it was the maid who had taken his fancy the previous night. "I'd given up all hope."

"Yes, I know it's late, my lord."

"Not late at all. You are just in time to sup with me."

A tall black hound with a wiry coat padded forward to inspect the intruder. Its head reached Jory's shoulder.

"This is Brutus. Are you afraid of dogs?"

"Of course not. I adore dogs, especially wolfhounds." Without hesitation she scratched Brutus behind his ears and smiled when he stretched his great length across the door as if he accepted her presence but would guard against any other obtruders.

"Come . . . sit." He held a chair for her at the small table, then took the seat across from her. "I have no wine to offer you, demoiselle. I have only ale, I'm afraid."

"I've never tasted ale, but I'm quite willing to try it."

He watched her closely as she lifted the tankard and tasted the brew. When she licked her lips and seemed to enjoy it he felt inordinately pleased. He lifted the silver covers and served her with a portion of game with walnut stuffing and a mutton pie.

"We should save something for Brutus," she suggested.

"He gorged himself at the hunt. Now he will sleep it off."

Warwick couldn't keep his eyes from her as she ate. Though she had a hearty appetite and relished her food, she had the daintiest manners he had ever seen and he took delight in watching her.

They spoke of food and dogs and hunting and she seemed to enjoy his company as much as he enjoyed hers. He was surprised that she displayed no wariness. "You are not afraid of me, are you?"

She gave him a radiant smile. "Of course not."

Perhaps she has never heard the dark whispers about me.

"Men do not frighten me, my lord. Gentlemen are always extremely courteous and gallant toward me."

He gazed at her heart-shaped face. "That's

because you are ethereal. You look so delicate and fragile, it evokes an urge to protect you . . . even in a brute like me."

Her laughter sounded like silver bells and it enchanted him. She smiled often and it made her look radiant, as if she were lit with an inner glow. Her skin was flawless, and her wide green eyes were the color of pale Chinese jade.

He stood up and held out his hand to her. Without hesitation she placed her hand in his and allowed him to draw her before the small fire that burned in the hearth. Warwick had been able to control his body until she touched him; then his desire ignited, burning hotter than the flames of any fire. He gazed down at her upturned face. She was so very young, perhaps without much sexual experience. "You *should* fear me — I am naked beneath this robe."

"I have already seen you naked, my lord."

His brows drew together. "How . . . where?"

Her laughter floated around him. "I was watching from atop the Round Tower when you rode in. You stood out from all the rest. Even from that great distance you made my knees grow weak. I had an overwhelming desire to see you naked, so I went to the bathhouse. When I gazed at your body, I was mesmerized. I had no idea who you were, but I had chosen you, and I was determined to find you." Her fingers traced the golden bear and the words embroidered on his black velvet robe. *"Non Sans Droit."* She made an attempt to translate the French motto. "Not without honor?"

"Not without right." He immediately breached the ancient chivalric principle of Warwick and took possession of her lips.

The kiss was so profound, almost mystical; it felt as if they had claimed each other. She placed her hands against his chest to steady herself; then her fingers slid beneath the velvet, parting the robe. "I want to see you again," she said breathlessly.

The garment fell to the carpet and she stepped back so that she could view his full naked splendor as he towered before her. The firelight turned his skin to polished bronze, enticing her to touch his flesh to learn if his body was as hard and as strong as it looked. She moved just close enough to reach out and let her fingertips trace the solid muscles that rippled across his powerful chest and shoulders. She feathered her fingers through the black curls, then laid her palm over his heart, feeling its heavy, pulsing beat quicken at her touch to mingle with her own.

Her gaze dropped to his flat belly, then lowered to his groin. She watched his shaft harden and lengthen until it became fully erect. Its velvet head almost reached his navel. Her eyes filled with wonder as she raised them to meet his. "Guy de Beauchamp, you are truly magnificent. I have made the perfect choice."

"I have a towering pride, and value myself above all other men, but you must not delude yourself, little one. Far from being perfect, I am flawed in every way."

To add credence to his words, his bold fingers unfastened the laces of her tunic and slipped it from her shoulders. The loose garment pooled at her feet, revealing that she wore neither petticoat nor hose, but stood before him naked. She glanced down at her upthrust breasts and the laughter that spilled from her was filled with unconcerned delight. "I was abed when I decided to come to you."

"And bed is where I shall take you." His deep voice was husky with desire. He swept her into his arms and held her high against his heart. Her head fell back, the white linen cloth fluttered to the floor, and her glorious silver-gilt hair spilled over his arm.

Warwick stared in disbelief at the exquisite creature he held in his arms. *Splendor of*

God, her hair is like silken moonlight. He thought her weightless as thistledown as he carried his precious burden to the bed, laid her down gently, and spread her shimmering hair across the crimson velvet cover.

He gazed down at her, spellbound, and wondered briefly if he were dreaming — surely she was too unearthly fair to be real. If not a dream, perhaps she was a figment of his imagination, a fantasy come to life. Slowly, he lifted a silvery tendril, and as he rubbed it between his thumb and forefinger, it suddenly curled possessively about his fingers, binding them together, and he rejoiced that she was real flesh and blood.

Her dazzling smile lured him onto the bed and as he gazed down at her, she reached up to touch his face. Her fingers brushed across his lips and then traced the outline of his strong jaw, where the blue-black shadow of his beard showed through his skin. Her fingertips stroked across the arch of his brow, dark as a raven's wing; then she threaded her fingers through his long black hair and pulled his face down to hers. She touched her lips to his and whispered his name. "Guy . . ."

An urge to ravish her flooded over him, but he checked it with his iron will. Instead, he captured her mouth and reveled in its sweet eager surrender. Her kisses tasted like honey, and he couldn't wait to taste the rest of her. His hand stroked down the curve of her throat and his thirsting mouth followed the path of his fingers. He cupped her breast and it filled his calloused palm. Her skin was like alabaster and he hoped he would not mar it with his rough fingers. The tips of her breasts looked like tiny pink rosebuds. When he covered one with his mouth, it swelled and peaked against his tongue.

He kissed her everywhere, the velvety place beneath her breasts, the fine skin that stretched tautly over her delicate rib cage, the soft flesh of her concave belly with its pretty navel. Finally, he came to her plump little mons covered by a hundred tiny gilt tendrils and he groaned with pleasure. She was the most beautifully made female he had ever seen, let alone touched or tasted, and he realized how rare and special she was. "I want to keep you. I want to take you back to Warwick with me."

His words thrilled her. "Make love to me, Guy."

"I want to draw it out all night, little beauty. Indulge me."

"Indulge . . . the evocative word sounds suggestively sinful."

Sins of the flesh! Splendor of God, I want to commit every one with you. Then I'll create some new ones. "Put your arms around my neck and hang on."

She did as he asked, then impulsively wrapped her legs about him too. As she clung to him, he arose from the bed and carried her across the chamber. She pressed her mouth against the muscled cords of his neck, loving the salt taste of his swarthy skin. With every step he took, the crisp curls on his wide chest teased the nipples of her soft breasts, turning them into hard little buds, and with every step she felt his erect cock brush against the cheeks of her bum, exciting her so much she bit his shoulder.

Warwick stopped before the polished silver mirror. "I want to see what we look like together, and I want you to see, too." He lifted her from his marble-hard cock, set her feet on the carpet so that she faced the mirror, and positioned himself behind her.

Though Jory had spent many an hour in front of a looking glass, arranging her hair or admiring the fit of a gown, she had never studied the reflection of herself nude. The contrast between their bodies was startling. It emphasized and exaggerated their many differences. She looked extremely small, soft, delicate, pale, feminine, fragile, and exquisitely beautiful.

Everything about Warwick looked too large, too hard, too dark, too powerful, and far far too masculine. The prideful way he held his head hinted that if the mood took him, he also could be dominant and dangerous. She wanted to scream with excitement.

Her eyes turned dark with desire as she watched his large hands reach from behind her to capture her breasts. He weighed them on his calloused palms and she shuddered at the sensations his touch aroused. She watched his dark head dip down and felt his rough tongue lick a pulse point in her neck. She saw the shiver of pleasure that rippled over her flesh.

She watched, fascinated, as one of his hands moved lower, trailing his long fingers down across her belly until they touched her mons. She saw him separate the gilt tendrils and curl his fingertips into her cleft. With one hand holding her breast and the other cupping her female center, he pressed her back against him and shuddered as the soft curve of her bottom brushed the swollen tip of his cock. Held thus, she appeared to be his captive to do with as he wished, and yet she felt imbued with a beautiful woman's sexual power that made her believe she could sway her captor to do her bidding. "Take me to bed, Guy."

He lifted her and carried her back across the chamber. He drew back the covers and lay down on the snowy sheet, taking her with him. Then with sheer brute strength he lifted her high above him, so that her silvery hair cascaded down across his shoulders and throat as his eyes feasted on her exquisite beauty. Her laughter too spilled over him, drugging his senses and holding him spellbound. He lowered her slowly onto his body, holding her in the dominant position, and when she opened her lips for his kiss, he ravished her mouth with his tongue. Her fragrance intoxicated him and tantalized his memory as he tried to identify the scent.

He rolled her beneath him and rose onto his knees, straddling her thighs. He gazed down with wonder at the ethereal creature who aroused a fierce tenderness in his heart that he had never felt before. He dipped his head to kiss the tempting golden curls upon her mons and he was lost. With a groan, he slid his tongue into her honeyed sheath.

She gasped and moaned with delight at the tantalizing, forbidden thing he was doing to her. She became highly aroused and writhed with sensual abandon. She arched up into his beautiful, wicked mouth and cried out as he thrust deeply.

Instantly, he withdrew his tongue and moved up over her. His black eyes stared down into hers with disbelief and accusation. "You are still virgin!"

"No, Guy, you are wrong —"

"My tongue touched the barrier of your maidenhead." His intense gaze searched her face as if he were seeing her clearly for the first time. It began to dawn on him that the first glimpse of her shimmering silver-gilt tresses had blinded him to reality. He cursed himself for a bloody fool. How could he have imagined her to be a servant? Such a fine-boned, delicate beauty with a vocabulary that matched his own was obviously a wellborn lady. Moreover, she was an eighteen-year-old virgin.

Warwick placed firm fingers beneath her chin and compelled her to look at him. "Who are you? I demand to know your name."

She raised her eyes to meet his. "I am Marjory de Warenne."

"Christ Almighty!" Guy de Beauchamp shot from the bed as if a demon from hell had just skewered him with a burning pitchfork.

CHAPTER 4

"Are you the Marjory de Warenne whose brother is Lynx de Warenne and your uncle the Earl of Surrey?" he demanded.

"Yes," she admitted shyly, lowering her lashes, and crossing her arms to cover her bare breasts.

"It's a little late for that, *Lady Marjory.*" He picked up his black velvet robe from the floor and thrust it at her. "Why, in the name of God, did you pretend to be a serving wench?" He hated deceit with a vengeance and believed that every woman breathing, not just the ones he'd known, indulged in lying and cheating.

Jory slid her arms into his robe and wrapped it about herself. "I do have an explanation, my lord." Though he suddenly found her nakedness highly inappropriate, he seemed unaware of his own.

Silence stretched between them; he said

sharply, "I'm waiting!"

"It's a long story, my lord."

"We have all night. I am not noted for my patience, but in your case, Lady Marjory, I will try to make an exception."

"Please don't call me that . . . My name is Jory." The noise he made in his throat sounded like a growl. She took a deep breath and plunged in. "I am lady-in-waiting to Princess Joanna. I am also her confidante and friend. For months she has railed against this arranged marriage with Gilbert de Clare, but in the end her father's wishes have prevailed and she has no choice but to wed a man who is thirty years her senior."

She watched the impatience mount on his face, but he held his tongue. "Now exactly the same thing will happen to me. The Earl of Surrey and my brother will arrange my marriage and I'll have no say in the matter. I found out that they already received an offer, which they turned down, but others will follow. This large gathering of nobles provides a most timely opportunity to negotiate matrimonial matches."

"Who offered for you?" he demanded sharply.

"Lord Aylesbury, for his younger son."

Warwick's brows drew together in outrage.

"The son of a bitch should be hanged for his temerity!" He strode to the fire and gave it a vicious jab with the poker. "Go on," he ordered.

"My friend Joanna suggested that before they arrange my marriage with someone I don't want and bludgeon me into becoming a dutiful wife, I should choose a tempting young lord who would lure me to dalliance." She sighed deeply. "I chose you."

"I am not young. I am thirty-four years old."

"Truly, my lord? Thirty-four seems a perfect age to me."

"It's not just my age. I am unsuitable in every way."

"Unsuitable for dalliance? You are quite wrong. You set my blood on fire and make me melt with longing."

Warwick flung down the poker with a sharp bark of laughter. He came and sat on the foot of the bed, his eyes filled with amusement. "What the hell am I going to do with you, Jory?"

"I don't know, my lord. I am very willful."

To say nothing of exquisitely beautiful, temptingly innocent, and infinitely fuckable. His cock stirred and he quickly covered it with the sheet.

"You said you wanted to keep me, that you wanted to take me back to Warwick with you."

"That was before I realized you were a highborn noble lady." *The only way I could keep you would be to make you my wife, and marriage is anathema to me!* "Jory, what do you know about me?"

"I know that you are Guy de Beauchamp, the *infamous* Earl of Warwick, but I don't know why you are infamous."

"Are you aware that I am a widower?"

Jory shook her head.

"Are you aware that I have a son the same age as the prince?"

"A son?" she asked with wonder. "Is he here with you?"

"Nay. My son, Rickard, rode with me only as far as Hertfordshire. He has been invited to join Prince Edward's household at King's Langley."

Jory digested the information. Then she gave him a radiant smile. "I now know that you are thirty-four years old, you are the father of a son, and that you had a wife."

"Two wives."

She stared at him; she knew there was more.

"Both died under suspicious circumstances. Dark whispers of murder have swirled about me for years. These rumors are what make me the *infamous* Earl of Warwick. I am beyond redemption."

"Do you deny the rumors, Guy de Beauchamp?" she whispered.

He gazed at her for a full minute, his purple-black eyes unreadable, and then he replied, "No, I do not deny them. Both deaths were rightly laid at my door, and I accept full blame."

Jory sat in his bed, hugging her body, which was clad in his black velvet robe. His stark honesty compelled her to confess something she never said aloud. "I killed my mother. She died giving birth to me. I know what it is like to bear guilt."

Warwick's heart went out to her. He knew better than to diminish the tragedy by telling her it wasn't her fault. What people thought and said about you mattered not one whit. It was the belief buried deep within your soul that counted. "In spite of my blackened reputation, you are still not afraid of me, are you, Jory de Warenne?"

Her glance roamed over the proud face, muscled shoulders and chest, and came to rest on his powerful hands, which possessed enough brute strength to snuff out her life. Yet those same hands had lovingly held the most private and vulnerable parts of her body. "No, I am not afraid of you, Guy. I would willingly place my safety in your hands." She raised her eyes to his and smiled.

The question is: Would you be willing to place your future in my hands? He smiled back at her. He couldn't help it; her smile was infectious and it did strange and wonderful things to his insides. Though he was past thirty, and cynical and jaded beyond his years, this vibrant wisp of a girl made him feel twenty again.

"Let's make a pact that from now on there will always be truth between us. Deceit is the common currency between a male and a female. It is not only uniquely refreshing, it is an aphrodisiac to find a lady who tells me honestly what is in her heart. Candor is a rare and precious thing. Until tonight, I didn't think it was possible to have a relationship without lies and subterfuge. A man usually has to tell a woman what she wants to hear. It is liberating to share my darkest secrets with you, Jory."

"Men have all the power in this world, my lord earl. In order to achieve the smallest fraction of control over her own life, her own destiny, a woman must dissemble, flatter, and manipulate. If needs must, I will delude the entire world, but I promise I will never lie to you, Guy de Beauchamp." She tossed her hair about her shoulders. "I have quite made up my mind!"

You will lie, Jory, but it is pleasant to pretend if only for a little while. "I am honored by your pledge. Come, we must both get dressed and I will take you back." He opened his wardrobe and donned clean garments, while Jory climbed reluctantly from the bed and slipped on the plain grey tunic. She handed him the black robe and he rubbed it against his cheek. "Your fragrance clings to the velvet."

"I always wear freesia."

"The costly scent should have told me you were no serving wench." *I deliberately deceived myself.* He lifted a curl from her shoulder and rubbed its silken texture between his fingers.

"Are you disappointed that I am high-born?"

"Nothing about you disappoints me, Jory." *That was my first lie to you, sweetheart. If you were not highborn, it would be a simple task to make you my mistress and sweep you off to Warwick.*

"I am regretful that there will be no

further dalliance," she said wistfully. She bent to pick up the white linen headdress.

"Splendor of God, I'm not done with you yet — I've hardly begun. There will be no further dalliance tonight, Lady Marjory, but tomorrow I intend to continue my relentless pursuit and explore any and every possibility of a liaison between us."

Her fingers trembled with excitement as she covered her hair. He tucked in a tendril that tried to escape and bent to brush his lips across hers. "Lord God, I intend to do more than woo you." He willfully ignored the emblem on his chest that was doing its damndest to burn a hole in his flesh. *Not without right!*

Though it was long past midnight, no guard challenged the Earl of Warwick as he escorted the young maid through Windsor's Upper Ward. With his wolfhound Brutus stalking beside him, none dared.

When Jory arose, she did not rush to attend Joanna. The royal princess had plenty of ladies to help her dress and make sure she looked resplendent for the planned hawking party. Jory had her own appearance to see to today. She had an overwhelming desire to look beautiful in Guy de Beauchamp's eyes. She put on a soft white underdress with full sleeves gathered at the wrists, then donned a vivid emerald surcoat embroidered with white roses. Rather than cover her hair with a jeweled caul, she braided it with silver ribbon and wound the long plaits about her head to form a regal coronet. Soft green leather boots and gloves completed her outfit.

Jory joined the princess and her other ladies and together they made their way down to the courtyard adjacent to the stables, where grooms waited with their saddled mounts. Since the queen was no longer robust enough to ride, Joanna and King Edward were to host the hawking party, and Gilbert de Clare stepped forward and aided his bride to mount.

The courtyard was crowded, not only with noble lords and ladies, but with attendants, grooms, and falconers. Cadge boys, with wooden frames suspended from their shoulders, held the birds that had been brought down from the mews for today's hunt.

Jory saw her brother and pushed through the throng to greet him. "Good morning, Lynx. Your tawny hair and great height make you easy to spot in a crowd. Oh hello, Sylvia. I didn't see you."

Her sister-in-law, adorned in a drab brown surcoat, stared at Jory's outfit. "You are dressed most impractically for a hunt."

Lynx gave his sister an irreverent wink. "That depends upon what quarry she is after."

Jory threw him a grateful smile, and then her eyes dilated with pleasure as Guy de Beauchamp joined her brother.

"Lady de Warenne." Warwick bowed gallantly to Sylvia and addressed Lynx. "You are surrounded by beautiful ladies. How does an ugly devil like you manage it?"

De Warenne grinned. "This is my sister, Lady Marjory. Allow me to present the Earl of Warwick."

"Not the *infamous* Earl of Warwick?" Jory asked as wicked amusement danced in her eyes. "I already know you by reputation."

Lynx shot her a warning glance. "Lady Marjory has an impertinent tongue and a knack for causing mayhem. I ask that you excuse my young sister, Warwick."

"And I ask that you excuse us both. It would be my pleasure to take her off your hands." He held out his arm. "May I help you choose a falcon, my lady?"

Jory gave him a radiant smile and placed her hand on his arm. "I can think of only one thing I would enjoy more, my lord." As they moved away, she heard Sylvia hiss, "She's incorrigible!"

"God, I hope so," Warwick murmured as he maneuvered them to a less crowded part of the courtyard. When they stopped walking, his black eyes roamed over her, devouring her. "You are a feast for the eyes." He held out his large, closed hand, palm up.

Jory opened his long, shapely fingers one by one and saw that he was offering her a perfect white rose. It filled her with delight to think he compared her with its delicate beauty. As she lifted the fragrant flower to tuck it into her hair, she perceived that its petals had been hiding a small brooch. With a joyous gasp she saw it was a carved onyx wolfhound with an amber eye. "It's Brutus!" Jory immediately tried to pin it to her surcoat.

He grinned down at her. "Let me do that. Are you sure you want everyone to see? It will be like wearing my brand."

"That is what makes it so exciting. It fills me with pride that a powerful earl like Warwick is courting my favor. I want to shout it to the world."

"So it is the power of Warwick that attracts you?"

"I refuse to lie to you. Of course it is the power of Warwick that attracts me. It is also the innate French charm and dark virility of

Guy de Beauchamp. You make my blood sing!"

He slid his fingers into the décolletage of her riding dress and in doing so brushed against her naked flesh just above her heart. When the brooch was pinned securely, their eyes met and Jory quivered at his intimate touch.

"Is this your mount?" Warwick took the reins of the small roan from the groom. "A dainty white palfrey would suit you better."

"Infinitely better, but Princess Joanna rides a white horse and prefers that her ladies own less showy animals."

"She may have her mother's dark coloring, but 'tis rumored her temperament is pure Plantagenet."

Jory laughed. "The rumors are not wrong."

"Rumors seldom are. Come, let me get you a hawk." He looked over the small female birds suited to a lady's hand. "Would you like a merlin?"

"Not really . . . I prefer a kestrel."

He gave her a quizzical glance. "Why would you choose a kestrel over a merlin?"

She lowered her voice. "A merlin preys on songbirds and innocent sparrows that take flight in fear. A kestrel dives to the ground and hunts vermin. I can reward my bird and let her eat what she has killed without pricking my conscience."

"Another secret revealed. You will have a hell of a time surviving in this cruel world with such a soft heart, my beauty."

"I've discovered a hidden vulnerability of yours, too." Her fingers touched the rose he had given her. "Beneath your dark, dominant, and dangerous facade, you are a romantic at heart." She smiled into his eyes. "Your secret is safe with me."

"What heart?" he mocked.

When his hands captured her waist, lifted her high, and set her in her saddle, his brute strength dizzied her senses.

Warwick selected a female kestrel and removed it from its perch. He handed her the creance so she could draw the bird back to her gloved fist. "Here is your fierce predator."

Jory glanced at him playfully. "What makes you think I can handle more than one fierce predator at a time?"

"I'd be willing to wager you are woman enough for anything."

"Warwick!" the king bellowed. "Join us."

"Edward hunts with a goshawk," he told Jory as they approached the king and his party. "I'll take a falcon; they are superior in every way. A peregrine never misses and it kills swiftly."

Princess Joanna gave her friend a sly sideways glance, then rolled her eyes. Jory masked her amusement and threaded the jesses through her gloved fingers.

Joanna introduced her to Gilbert de Clare. "I believe my lord fears falconry is becoming a frivolous and effeminate sport now that ladies are becoming proficient."

Jory smiled at Gilbert. "I doubt the Earl of Gloucester fears anything. We are adept at handling the hawks, my lord, because we have smaller hands that can easily manage to unfasten the jesses and tyrrits from the birds' legs."

Gloucester looked ruefully at his large hand and returned her smile. "I believe you are right, Lady Marjory."

Jory saw Warwick signal the groom, who held his black stallion. She caught her breath and her eyes went wide with admiration as she watched him mount. He balanced the falcon on his gloved fist and swung his leg effortlessly across his horse's rump without ruffling his bird's feathers. He moved with a lithe, sensual grace that aroused her. His eyes, black as his hair, were as piercing as the fierce eyes of the falcon. She decided that Guy de Beauchamp put all other men in the shade, including the king.

Edward Plantagenet held his goshawk high and spurred his enormous horse to plunge forward. He always rode and hunted at full speed, setting the pace and expecting others to keep up with him. His daughter took up the challenge and Gloucester followed.

Warwick drew his horse close to Jory's. "They will hunt on the open ground. My falcon will head to the river, lured by the waterfowl. If you ride into the woods to elude everyone, I will have no trouble seeking you out."

She watched him gallop after the others, closing the distance effortlessly. She saw him stand in the stirrups to cast his falcon and she smiled a secret smile as it circled toward the river. "So this is how assignations are made." She shivered with anticipation.

Jory heard Lynx call out to her, and she had no choice but to join his party. She glanced wryly at Sylvia, who had invited most of the queen's ladies to hunt with her. "Poor Lynx, obviously you share Gilbert de Clare's opinion that the sport of falconry is being ruined by females. Sylvia's father also has a face like a thundercloud. Why don't you and Roger Bigod join John de Bohun and his sons? The ladies will better enjoy themselves without the critical eyes of the men watching their every move."

A look of relief and gratitude came over Lynx's face. He courteously took leave of his wife and joined the men.

Jory hunted with the ladies for an hour before she decided to elude them. It was a simple matter to cast her kestrel toward the woods and then follow the small raptor into the trees.

"How on earth did you find me?" Jory had not been at all confident that Warwick would turn up at the place she had chosen.

"I followed the scent of freesia." He dismounted, perched his falcon on an oak limb, and closed the distance between them. "No, in truth it was horse sense that led me to you. Your little roan instinctively sought a clearing among the trees with a stream nearby. Caesar unerringly ran you both to ground."

"Caesar and Brutus . . . you have a fancy for Roman history."

He took her kestrel, which she had already hooded, and perched it on a tree branch. Then he held up his arms for Jory. "I have a fancy for many things . . . especially green-eyed wood nymphs."

She came down to him in a swirl of white underdress and fluttering petticoats. "Have a care, Frenchman. Mayhap I lured you to this enchanted place to cast a spell upon you."

"Too late, my beauty. You have already done that." He set her feet to the ground and bent his head to steal a kiss. When she offered up her mouth, it led to another and then to a dozen. "Jory, I'll never have enough of you."

He released her and moved away so that he would not lose control of his raging desire. He opened his saddlebags, took out a mantle, and unrolled it on the ground. "If my lady fair will sit, I will feed her ambrosia and tempt her with flagons." He unwrapped a linen napkin that held crusty bread and medallions of cheese and set them down beside a leather wineskin. "I have never wooed anyone before. I'm quite green at the game."

It seemed a most unlikely thing for a twice-wed man in his thirties to claim, yet Jory believed him. She patted the place beside her. "I think we should explore this wooing together." *Guy, I want more than wooing. I want you to court me. I think I'm fall-*

ing in love . . . I want you to beg me to become your wife!

He stretched his length in the grass and picked up the wineskin. "Do you know how to handle one of these?"

"I haven't the faintest notion . . . Will you give me lessons?"

"It would give me infinite pleasure to teach you anything and everything you wish to learn, my beauty."

She licked her lips. "I have a thirst for knowledge." *I have an insatiable thirst for you, Guy de Beauchamp.*

"Better take off your beautiful surcoat. Wine stains are difficult to wash away."

"An ingenious ploy to undress me. If I remove a garment, it is only fair play that you do too." Jory took off her embroidered surcoat, folded it neatly, and set it aside. She watched Warwick shrug from his doublet to reveal a cambric shirt. She could see his black mat of chest hair through the fine material.

He picked up the wineskin. "Come to me."

Without hesitation she accepted his tempting invitation.

He took her hand and pulled her down so that she sat cradled between his legs. His arms reached around her, and he held the wineskin on a level with her mouth. "When I squeeze, it will spurt up like a fountain. You must open your lips and catch it. Are you ready?"

She nodded, opened her mouth like a trusting baby bird, and miraculously managed to capture the arc of bloodred wine. She swallowed it quickly and opened her lips again. After the third mouthful she began to laugh at the absurd game they were playing.

Warwick opened his own mouth and caught a long stream of the potent liquid and managed to swallow it before he too burst out laughing. He fell back into the grass and took her with him. They rolled together, laughing and sharing wine-drenched kisses until they were aflame with desire.

Jory could feel the heat of his body through the cloth of her finespun under-dress. She gazed down into his black eyes, which smoldered with passion, and knew she was madly in love with him.

Warwick realized the game they played was far too dangerous. He wanted her with every fiber of his being. Yet he knew the price he'd have to pay was high and ir-revocable. The price she would have to pay could be even higher. The thought sobered him.

"I believe a little decorum is in order, Lady Marjory. If someone came upon us, your honor would be utterly compromised."

"Blackened beyond repair." She sat up, her eyes glittering with mirth. "A fate worse than death." She picked up a piece of cheese, took a lusty bite, and then held it to his lips. "Will Warwick take the bait?" she teased playfully.

He saw the snare. He had been fully aware of the danger since the moment he had learned her name. It was a trap of his own making and, alas, the bait was irresistible.

He took the cheese and bit her fingers in the process. When she pushed him back into the grass with mock ferocity, he growled fiercely and rolled her beneath him, caging her between his powerful thighs. He gazed down at her with intense black eyes, waging a losing battle with himself. Finally, against his better judgment, he spoke. "Jory, I've never felt this way about anyone before. I have this overpowering urge to court you openly. With my disastrous marital history, I must be mad to even think of wooing another noble, highborn lady, but it seems that I cannot help myself. Even a sinner longs for one last chance at happiness." He paused, hoping sanity would return. When it did not, he threw caution to the four winds. "If I made an offer for you, would you be willing to take the risk and marry me?"

When she gasped with delight, he quickly placed his hand over her mouth. "Don't answer me now. You must think about this long and hard. Your life would be irrevocably altered forever. I am sixteen years older than you and I have a son. Jory, you must be absolutely sure. I will give you all the time you need to make your decision, and whether it be yes or no, I will honor your resolve. Be very cautious before you plunge in over your head. Like crossing the Rubicon, there can be no turning back. The wrong decision could make you hate me with a vengeance someday."

Though Jory knew deep in her heart what her answer would be, she did not say it aloud. Instead, she reached up to tenderly touch his face and smiled her secret smile. *Jory de Beauchamp, Countess of Warwick!*

CHAPTER 5

"Jory de Bohun, Countess of Hereford. It has a nice ring to it, Lynx, and de Bohun's heir will also inherit the post of Constable of England along with his father's earldom. What do you think?"

"I think it an extremely suitable match. As well as Hereford, de Bohun can claim the Earldom of Essex through his mother. I admire Hereford — he is a steadfast man who will stand as a strong father figure to my sister. The contrast between John de Bohun and my irascible father-in-law, Roger Bigod, was quite apparent in the hunt today. Though Sylvia has been wed to me for two years, she still fears her father's authoritarian ways. Jory and young Humphrey de Bohun should deal well together since they are so close in age. Humphrey has just turned nineteen, I understand."

"Aye, your sister does not want to suffer Princess Joanna's fate. She made me promise I would not wed her to an older man."

"At Goodrich Castle in Hereford, Jory would be the undisputed chatelaine, since the earl's wife has been dead these many years and his younger son, Henry, is unwed. My sister would thrive in a household of men and soon become queen of the castle."

"In the hall tonight, we must contrive to seat Jory with the de Bohuns and observe how well they mesh."

"We can try to pin her down, but it won't be an easy task. The minx is as elusive as quicksilver!"

"Jory, I was astonished to see you in the company of Warwick today. Surely you know of his foul reputation?" Joanna stood before the mirror as her friend laced up her purple velvet gown.

"I know nothing of his reputation" — the corners of Jory's mouth went up — "though I am sure you are about to enlighten me."

Joanna's eyes glittered. "What are friends for?" She bent close and whispered, "Warwick's first wife, Isabel, was Gilbert de Clare's youngest sister. Rumor has it that she was poisoned."

Jory caught her breath, and then her eyes met Joanna's. She asked evenly, "If Warwick caused his wife's death, why are he and your husband-to-be such fast friends?"

"Men! Who can explain the bonds that are forged between the rapacious devils? Land, castles, or wealth have always garnered more male loyalty than mere marriage. Why don't you question Gloucester yourself? I believe Gilbert has a soft spot for you."

Jory smiled and changed the subject. If she questioned de Clare, he would immediately inform his friend Warwick. "Will you wear the purple? There is little need to emphasize your royalty again tonight."

"There is every need . . . tonight and every night. De Clare is so blood proud, I have no intention of allowing my bridegroom to forget I am a Plantagenet princess, especially since tomorrow he will lower my rank to Countess of Gloucester."

I am willing to wager that Guy de Beauchamp is tenfold more blood proud than Gilbert de Clare.

"Come, Jory. I intend to eat and drink myself into oblivion since tonight is my last night of freedom and tomorrow I may die!"

Jory winked. "You will survive, Joanna. I am certain of it."

The princess and her ladies arrived late to the hall as usual, and apart from the bride's place of honor beside Gilbert de Clare, there were few empty seats on the eve of the royal wedding.

Jory felt a compelling urge to search out Guy de Beauchamp, but as her avid gaze traveled about the hall, her brother, Lynx, caught her eye and beckoned her to an empty seat between himself and John de Bohun, Earl of Hereford and Constable of England.

The Earl of Hereford rose to his feet. "Lady Marjory, it would be such an unexpected pleasure if you would dine with us."

Jory gave him a radiant smile and took the seat. "My lord earl, the pleasure is mine. Did you enjoy the hunt today?"

"My sons and I enjoyed it so much, we plan to acquire some hunting birds and establish a mews when we return to Hereford. Allow me to present my son Humphrey and my younger son, Henry."

Jory smiled at Humphrey, who sat across from his father, and nodded to Henry on his far side. She was quite used to young men's stares as they appraised her. "You have traveled a long way to attend Princess Joanna's wedding."

When Humphrey flushed at the mention of Joanna's name, Jory was amused. Many young lords were infatuated with the royal princess.

"We didn't journey from Hereford, Lady Marjory. We were at our castle of Midhurst in Sussex," the earl explained.

"The de Bohun land is on the other side of the River Rother, just south of my de Warenne land in Surrey," her uncle John remarked. "We are neighbors for part of the year."

Hereford signaled a server to pour Jory some wine. Then he raised his own goblet and proposed a toast. "Lady Marjory, you are the fairest lady at Windsor tonight. If only I were twenty years younger, I warrant I would seek you for my wife."

"How gallant you are, my lord earl. And if I were a mere five years older, I would accept your proposal," Jory said sweetly.

Flattered beyond belief, John de Bohun lost his heart and immediately resolved to contract Marjory de Warenne for his son and heir, Humphrey, at any cost.

It wasn't until Jory was eating her dessert that she felt eyes upon her and knew someone was watching her. She glanced across the hall and saw immediately that it was Warwick. His intense gaze licked over her like a candle flame, thrilling her to the core. She touched her fingers to her lips and then her heart — two gestures she knew he would understand. When she saw him rise from the table and leave the hall, she was in a fever to follow him. She forced herself to remember her manners and sat politely until all the diners were finished. "My lords, I beg you to excuse me. I must attend Princess Joanna. There are many things that I must see to before the wedding tomorrow."

When she arose from the table, all the men stood too. She bade them good night and as Lynx escorted her partway to the dais, she could not suppress her inner excitement. She went up on her toes and impulsively kissed her brother's cheek.

"You made a most favorable impression on the constable tonight, Minx. I was very proud of you."

Jory's thoughts were so completely focused on Warwick, she did not heed her brother's words. Bursting with happiness she squeezed his arm and confided, "Don't be surprised if you receive an offer for me very soon, Lynx."

He grinned down at her. "You conceited little devil . . . you are convinced you have charmed de Bohun into making an offer, are you?"

"Good heavens no. Guy de Beauchamp is the one I have charmed." As Jory slipped away from Lynx, she did not see the stunned look on her brother's face.

She glanced up at the dais and saw that Joanna was laughing wildly with her brother, Prince Edward. It was quite obvious that the king's son was drunk, and by the look of her, his sister was well on her way to intoxication. The princess didn't seem quite ready to retire in spite of the full day she would have to face on the morrow, so Jory impulsively decided to leave the hall to seek a few stolen minutes with Warwick.

She hurried outside, and her heart sank when she found no trace of Guy de Beauchamp. *I waited too long to seek him. I doubt patience is a Warwick virtue.* Her eyes probed the torch-lit area, but she saw only guards and a few castle servants. *I wonder if he went to the garden?* Jory ran lightly through Windsor's Upper Ward, her heart beating a tattoo of hope and wild anticipation.

When she did not see him inside the garden, disappointment engulfed her. Then he stepped from the shadows of the willow tree. "Guy! Guy!" she cried with delight as she picked up her skirts and ran into his arms.

He held her against him possessively for a full minute before he dipped his head to speak to her. "It's too soon to give me your answer, Jory. You promised me you'd think long and hard about it."

"You came to the garden hoping I'd come to you. How can you deny it?" she whispered joyfully.

"I've learned how impulsive you are, *chéri*. If you had been foolish enough to approach me in the hall, it would have aroused great speculation, so I went outside. Then I realized the garden was the only place that would give us privacy from prying eyes."

"I want you to court me openly, Guy."

"I cannot do that until I get permission from your guardian, John de Warenne, and your brother, Lynx."

Her fingers sought the badge on his velvet doublet. "Not without right . . . you live according to your Warwick motto."

"I try. I do not always succeed, sweetheart."

"I've thought about it quite long enough. If I thought about it for a lifetime, my answer would be the same. With all my heart, I want to be your wife, Guy de Beauchamp." She tossed her hair about her shoulders. "I've quite made up my mind! Will you offer for me?" *Will you offer for me soon?* she begged silently.

He placed his fingers beneath her chin, raised her face, and smiled down at her. "So impetuous . . . so impatient. I will offer for you, Jory, my love." He sealed his pledge with a tender kiss.

"I've imbibed more than my fair share of wine tonight. Can't this wait, Lynx?" John de Warenne held on to his chamber door to steady his balance.

"No, it cannot wait. I have learned something most disquieting. We are about to receive an offer for Jory that is abhorrent." He closed the door firmly and led John to a chair before the fire.

The earl's brow furrowed. "You are mistaken. There is nothing abhorrent about the offer we have received from de Bohun. I assure you the constable is an honorable man, and I am certain I can bring him to a more generous settlement on Jory's behalf."

"I'm not concerned about de Bohun's offer," Lynx said shortly.

"Well surely you're not worried about Jory's reaction. You saw how charming she was tonight. I am almost certain she will be amenable to the match."

Lynx de Warenne gathered his patience. "Where Jory is concerned, I have learned never to be *certain.* The little minx told me tonight we could expect an offer from Guy de Beauchamp."

"Warwick!" John de Warenne sobered immediately.

"It is unthinkable — absolutely out of the question that Jory become the wife of Warwick," Lynx declared.

"I agree wholeheartedly. His reputation with women stinks to high heaven!"

Lynx ran his hand through his tawny mane. "If, or rather when, he comes with his offer, we must be ready. We will have to devise a plausible excuse that will not give offense to the noble earl."

"Absolutely. Under no circumstances must we give offense to such a staunch ally. Christ Almighty, we don't want Warwick for an enemy!"

"Personally, I have always liked de Beauchamp. I've never given a tinker's damn about the dark rumors concerning the death of his wives. What happens in a man's marriage is his own private affair. That is until he proposes to marry my sister. Then it suddenly becomes very much my business."

"It is our duty to protect Jory from a marriage that would prove disastrous to her future happiness. The age difference alone would be insurmountable. Guy de Beauchamp must be at least fifteen years her senior."

"That is not the greatest impediment.

Warwick already has a son and heir. Any child he had by Marjory would receive neither his lands, castles, nor his noble title of Earl of Warwick."

"Marjory would never entertain such a match!"

"We must not give her any choice in the matter," Lynx said flatly.

"You think the idea of becoming a countess might tempt her?"

"God, or perhaps the devil alone, knows the working of a female's mind, and my sister is more of an enigma than most women. There are many temptations out there for an eighteen-year-old, and it's our job to save her from those that could destroy her."

"If — when — he comes, we must treat him with utter respect. We must listen to him and let him know that we are fully aware of the great honor he is bestowing upon the de Warennes."

"And high honor it would be if the happiness of my young sister were not at stake. A connection with the greatly esteemed de Beauchamp bloodline would be advantageous for any noble family."

"Warwick Castle is a magnificent fortalice and Flamstead, which came to him through his marriage to Alyce de Toeni, has the richest pastures in Hertfordshire. Most families would grovel for a chance to tie their fortunes with that of de Beauchamp."

"He may approach you first, since you are Jory's guardian."

"If he does, I will make it clear that I must consult you also in the matter as gravely important as your sister's marriage."

"Yes, that will give us a little time. Perhaps we should let him know from the onset that we have another offer for her."

"But when he learns we have chosen Hereford over Warwick, it could cause bad blood between the earls."

"He is bound to learn of it eventually. We must simply be extremely diplomatic about the entire thing. I'll give it careful thought and hope he doesn't approach us tomorrow."

"Aye. I shall sleep on the matter. I've noticed before that weddings are contagious. A royal marriage seems to overcome men's natural aversion to shackling themselves with a wife."

Joanna Plantagenet's wedding day dawned without a cloud in the sky. Though it had taken an inordinate amount of time to adorn the royal princess in the finery designed especially for her nuptials, she stubbornly refused to be hurried.

"I'm sure it will be taken for granted that I shall be late. How the devil would it look if I arrived before the bridegroom? All would assume that I am overeager to be wed. Being late will put that rumor to rest before it starts."

Joanna's black hair fell in shining waves to her waist, and Jory covered it with the gold tissue veil and then fitted on the princess's new diamond and sapphire coronet to hold it in place. *When I wed Guy, I shan't care if the entire world knows I am eager to become his wife!*

Blanche Bedford returned from the window, breathless with excitement. "There is a huge crowd gathered outside waiting for a glimpse of the bride."

There had been much discussion about how Joanna would get from her royal apartment in Windsor's Upper Ward to the stone chapel in the Lower Ward. Should she be conveyed in a carriage or ride her white horse? Finally, King Edward had declared that his daughter would walk with her attendants so that all who served at Windsor Castle could glimpse the beautiful bride.

Maud Clifford and Eleanor de Leyburn brought Joanna's ermine cloak and held it while the princess slipped her arms through the openings, which were surrounded by black-tipped ermine tails. All four of Joanna's ladies wore identical gowns that were a paler shade of Plantagenet blue than the bridal gown. Jory knew the delicate hue suited her coloring, but did not realize that the wreath of white rosebuds upon her gilt tresses made her look exquisitely innocent and virginal.

Suddenly the queen appeared at the door, pale and breathless. "What on earth is keeping you, Joanna? Your father is pacing about the chapel, working himself into a fine rage. Do you not realize you are showing disrespect to the king and to Gloucester?"

"This is the last day you will have to bear my disrespect, Mother. Tomorrow I shall rule my own household at Clerkenwell. It is the only advantage I perceive in marrying Gilbert de Clare."

Jory blushed for her royal friend's ungracious words.

"Lady Marjory, I leave the matter in your capable hands. Get Joanna to the chapel without further delay," the queen ordered.

When Her Majesty departed, Jory resorted to blatant manipulation. "I believe it is clouding up outside. Perhaps it won't dare rain on such a lovely bride, but the sunshine will make your diamonds and sapphires glitter so brilliantly, you'll dazzle the eyes of those hoping for a glimpse of their royal princess."

"Hurry up, Maud, Blanche . . . I don't want to get wet. All four of you must carefully carry my train so that it doesn't drag on the ground. Where is that damn page boy with my kneeling cushion?"

A great cheer arose from the crowd as Princess Joanna emerged, and in spite of her studied arrogance, it brought a smile to her lips. Jory, too, beamed with delight when applause broke out as the procession of beautiful noble ladies walked with slow measured steps toward the Horseshoe Cloister that led into the Lower Ward.

There was not room enough for all the invited guests in Windsor's Royal Chapel and a crowd of nobles stood beneath the stone arcading outside the entrance to the chapel. Six little girls of noble birth awaited the bride's arrival in the vestry, and they walked down the aisle before Joanna, strewing rose petals, myrtle, and mint, an ancient custom that verily bestowed love, happiness, and fertility upon the couple.

Focusing her attention on holding up Joanna's train, Jory did not see Warwick, who was standing at the back of the chapel in the last pew. Guy de Beauchamp, however, saw Marjory de Warenne in all her youthful innocence.

When the bride and her attendants reached the front of the chapel, Jory and the other three came to a halt at the altar steps and watched Joanna ascend to stand beside Gilbert de Clare, who was attended by King Edward and Archbishop Winchelsey. Jory bent to whisper instructions to the page boy, who then quickly set the velvet kneeling cushion before the bride. When the Earl of Gloucester went down upon his knees, the regal princess slowly followed suit, and the archbishop made the sign of the cross and began the Solemnization of Matrimony.

Jory did not understand the words of the Latin prayer, and her mind began to wander. Her eyes focused on the candle flames of the tall tapers that adorned the altar and in her imagination Jory replaced Joanna as the bride. As she knelt beside Guy de Beauchamp, he took her small hand in his and squeezed it. Her heart overflowed with joy and happiness.

When King Edward Plantagenet stepped forward to give his daughter in marriage to Gilbert de Clare, Jory's attention came back to the royal ceremony. She smelled the incense and heard the muffled noises of the nobles who packed the pews behind her.

Though she felt a great compulsion to turn around and seek out Warwick, she resisted the temptation and smiled as she imagined she could feel his dark, possessive eyes riveted upon her.

Though not often given to introspection, the sight of Jory gave Warwick pause. Her extreme youth and angelic innocence had a profound impact on the earl that was almost akin to a blow in the solar plexus. *What the hellfire am I doing contemplating marriage with a girl of eighteen? Such an act could be deemed the height of arrogance and self-indulgence and rightly so!*

As the ceremony advanced and the couple exchanged their vows, Warwick's mind flew back to the vows he had pledged on two separate occasions. His inner voice spoke again, this time more insistently. *Neither marriage was successful. Are you sure you are ready to risk committing a third disastrous mistake?* The answer came back a resounding yes. He was perfectly willing to take the chance for himself, but he was completely unsure about condemning the exquisitely lovely Lady Marjory to a life of unhappiness. As the beautiful voices of the young choirboys filled the air, Warwick slipped unnoticed from Windsor's chapel.

Guy saddled Caesar, and with Brutus loping before him, he galloped north until he came to the edge of the Chiltern Hills, then turned east, riding through verdant Hertfordshire in deep contemplation. When he became aware of his surroundings, he realized that he was more than halfway to his castle of Flamstead. Warwick suspected that the sanctuary had unwittingly drawn him so that he could make his decision in the peaceful solitude of the lush meadows he used to crossbreed his distinctive and much sought after horses, renowned for their speed and strength.

Guy decided to spend the night at Flamstead, make a firm decision about his future, and return to Windsor on the morrow. He knew what was in his heart, but he needed to come to terms with the cautionary thoughts that filled his head.

to keep our beloved Jory from ruining her life?"

Lynx thought it over and conceded. "Her happiness and well-being must take precedence over my conscience."

The timing of the wedding banquet, which would not begin until late afternoon, helped Jory accomplish many of the last-minute tasks that must be completed before the Earl and Countess of Gloucester could depart for their country mansion at Clerkenwell the next morning. She supervised the servants as they crated up all the wedding presents that Joanna and Gilbert had received. Among the gifts were forty golden cups, forty silver forks, and twenty zones of vibrantly colored silk, many of which were shot through with real silver threads. There were so many hampers, coffers, baskets, and bags, it was difficult to keep track of them all, and Jory made a list, tallying each item as it was carried off to be packed in carts that would be pulled by sumpter horses.

For three days Joanna's attendants had been packing her wardrobe and her vast collection of jewelry, but these were not the only possessions that were to accompany the Plantagenet princess. Her chapel apparatus, her chamber furnishings, pantry stores, table linen, and candles, as well as her kitchen furniture, were all being transferred to Clerkenwell.

Jory, feeling as if she needed to be in three different places at once, somehow managed to pack her own personal belongings and her considerable wardrobe in between her other tasks. Inside, she was bubbling with happiness, knowing that sometime soon, she too would be a bride. In the past week her life had suddenly taken an exciting turn when she had fallen in love with Guy de Beauchamp.

At the evening wedding banquet, Jory kept watch for Warwick. The hall was crowded with celebrants as they dined on course after course, beginning with marinated eel, pickled herring, fresh oysters, and shelled prawns. Next came chestnut-stuffed game birds and lemon venison with fennel. Toasted garlic and thyme custards, huge platters of scallion bread, and roasted potatoes vied with dishes of leeks, marrows, and pure white clusters of cauliflower.

The sweet course was amazing for its diversity as well as its decorative effects. Plates of cream-filled éclairs competed with ginger-walnut tortes. Gooseberry, quince, and blackberry tarts tempted the guests, along with fig and cherry gâteaux with lemon curd. The huge wedding cake was a marvel of decoration, packed with dried fruit and lucky silver bridal charms and covered with a thick slab of almond paste. Royal lions and tiny gilded Gloucester pigs, molded from sugar, sat atop the gigantic confection and elicited smiles from all the noble ladies.

Liveried servants moved about filling goblets with wine imported from Gascony, or cider from Devon. The men who preferred home-brewed ale found their tankards filled again and again. All the while minstrels and musicians strolled among the guests, singing and playing everything from love ballads to rousing epics of valor.

Jory's glance roamed about the crowded hall, hoping for a glimpse of Guy. Surely she could not miss such a striking male if he were present at the banquet tonight. By the time the tables were cleared and pushed back to make room for dancing, she was convinced Warwick was not there. Dancing was included strictly for the ladies. Noblemen from the king on down through the ranks much preferred drinking and gambling to prancing about. King Edward danced with the bride, as did the Earl of Gloucester, but the moment each had performed his obligatory measure, they left the dancing to the younger men.

Both Henry and Humphrey de Bohun partnered Joanna; then Humphrey led Jory into the dance, while her brother and her uncle watched with approval. Jory was totally distracted, watching and waiting for Guy de Beauchamp. She feared he had taken ill, and the moment she felt that she could slip away unnoticed, she left and made her way to the chamber he had been assigned at Windsor. When she found it locked and in darkness, she hurried to the stables, where she saw that Caesar's stall was empty. She was relieved to know he was able to ride, which eliminated his being sick.

Jory laughed at her own vanity. He was an earl with much responsibility who had far more to occupy him than dancing attendance upon her day and night. "He must have been called away unexpectedly . . . perhaps regarding his son at King's Langley." Since it was a distance of less than a dozen miles, Jory told herself he would soon return. "I wonder if he spoke to Lynx before he left?" Jory hurried back to the hall and sought out her brother.

She joined the de Warenne men, who were watching Sylvia dance a lively measure with the elegant Thomas of Lancaster, nephew of King Edward and hereditary high steward of England.

Lynx smiled at his sister. "If you stand beside me, Minx, Lancaster will most likely partner you when he returns my wife."

"I hope not . . . I have no desire to dance with him."

Her uncle John chided her. "Lancaster holds five earldoms and also is heir to his wife's father, de Lacy's earldom of Lincoln. It would not be politic to offend Thomas Plantagenet."

Jory smiled. "I am not in the habit of offending royal gentlemen. Certes I will dance with him if he wishes it." She turned to Lynx and murmured, "Did the earl offer for me yet?"

"Jory, we have received an offer for you, but —"

John cut in before Lynx could tell her who had made the offer. "We are still negotiating and cannot speak of it yet."

"But, Uncle, I leave for Clerkenwell early tomorrow."

"Have no fear. The king has called Parliament, so we shall all be journeying from Windsor to Westminster shortly. We will summon you to Westminster Palace when our negotiations near completion."

Jory smiled radiantly and accepted another

offer to dance from Humphrey de Bohun. When the dance ended, she saw that Joanna was preparing to retire. She told him, "I must attend the bride. She is bound to be apprehensive on her wedding night."

"The princess should not be overly nervous. I warrant she is no untried maiden."

Jory's lashes flew up. *Does the entire Court know that Joanna is no longer a virgin?*

The newly wed bride had chosen a night rail of pale blue silk and a velvet bed gown of deep Plantagenet blue with a band of golden lions embroidered around its wide sleeves. Jory hung up Joanna's bridal gown, then glanced about her chamber to make sure all was in order and the bridal bed turned down. She jumped as a low knock came upon the door. "He's here," she whispered breathlessly. "Remember, there isn't a man breathing cannot be manipulated."

Joanna faced the door and lifted her chin, refusing to admit even to her friend that she was nervous. "Let him in."

Gilbert's eyes smiled into Jory's and he held the door for her until she departed. Without haste he advanced into the chamber. "It has been an exhausting day for you, Joanna. Are you tired?"

"Nay, my lord, though I am glad 'tis over and done!"

Her honesty brought a smile to his lips. "I am glad we can converse plainly, my dear. Flowery phrases do not come easily to me, though a bride as lovely as you surely warrants them."

Joanna poured herself a goblet of wine. "Would you like some?"

"Nay, I've imbibed enough toasts to make even a bishop stagger. Poor lady, do you need to fortify yourself with strong drink to endure an aging husband?"

She gave him a quizzical glance over the rim of her goblet.

He sat down on a love seat before the fire and patted the cushion. "Come, let us talk, Joanna. You can be at ease with me; I have no delusions about marriage."

"*You've* been wed before," she said bluntly. "*I* have not."

Gilbert threw back his head and laughed. "Such irony! Just as you are a wife for the first time, so I am a husband."

"Such a statement intrigues me." She sat down beside him. "Explain yourself."

"Your grandfather, King Henry III, over-eager to honor and impress his Continental half brother, proposed a marriage between de Lusignan's sixteen-year-old daughter Al-

119

ice and myself, because I was the heir to England's wealthiest earldom of Gloucester. I was ten years old. Alice was a fecund bitch in heat who had no intention of waiting years until I was old enough to bed her. Her lover was Prince Edward's best friend and steward, Rodger de Leyburn, or so I thought for a long time. In reality it was the heir to the throne with whom she committed adultery for years."

"My father?" Joanna asked in disbelief.

"I lay no blame at his door. He was a virile, unwed prince of the realm, who took what was blatantly offered. The whore easily seduced him as well as others over the years. I held her in utter contempt. Such seeds of hatred had been planted between us that I never consummated the marriage even when I was old enough."

"You divorced her and sent her back to the Continent."

"Yes, after your father became king."

"Your armies won back the realm from Simon de Montfort, the great baronial warlord, and as a result my father now wears the crown. He owes you a great deal."

"I threw in my lot with Edward Plantagenet, not just because he was the rightful king, but because he was a great warrior who was strong enough to rule justly."

"He thinks to repay you with this marriage."

"Undoubtedly. At the same time he will gather the de Clare castles, landholdings, and wealth into the Plantagenet coffers."

"Only if there is an heir," Joanna said bluntly.

Gilbert took her hand and pressed it between his own. "You are eighteen, Joanna. You will outlive me by decades. If you will be my wife in more than just name for the years I have left, and you are generous enough to give me a child, I will leave you the wealthiest widow in the realm. Then the choice of husband will be entirely yours and you will rule your own destiny."

I thought my life was over, but mayhap it is just beginning.

"Joanna de Clare, if you deal honestly with me and show me respect, from this day forward you may make your own decisions regarding anything and everything that affects your life."

Joanna's eyes widened. "I have not married a lapdog after all, but a real man. I will be your wife in more than name, Gilbert."

He smiled into her eyes and squeezed her hand. "You won't regret it, my love." The bridegroom blew out the candles and led his wife to the bed. In the darkness he removed his bed robe and the first thing he did when they lay naked together was to gently roll her to a prone position so he could massage her back.

It didn't take long for Joanna to relax and become used to the feel of her husband's hands upon her body. Languidness swept over her, which was soon replaced by a feeling of sensuality. When she reached out to touch him, she was not repelled by an aging body. Gilbert was well muscled and hard in all the right places.

The earl's hands were well versed in how to arouse a female, and when he rose above her in the dominant position and thrust into her young body, desire for fulfillment rose up in her. He had great staying power and slowly and steadily brought her to orgasm twice before he allowed himself to spill his seed.

Joanna lay in wonder at the unexpected passion Gilbert had aroused in her. She cupped her own breasts and moaned with pleasure. *That was the best sexual encounter I have ever experienced. My husband is a far superior lover than young de Bohun. The constable's son no sooner began than he was finished!* The newly wed Countess of

Gloucester curled onto her side and smiled into the darkness.

Jory was most reluctant to knock on Joanna's bedchamber door, but when the new Countess of Gloucester had not emerged by nine o'clock, she summoned her courage and rapped lightly.

Much to her relief, she found Joanna abed alone when she entered. "Blanche has your breakfast tray, Lady de Clare."

"Well, I declare!" Joanna punned.

"If I'd known you were alone, I would have knocked earlier."

"Gloucester is a soldier. He arose hours ago."

Jory, her head on one side, glanced at her friend and the tumbled bed. "Your mood seems light and gay this morning."

Joanna smiled slyly. "I came to the marriage prepared to do battle. To my utter amazement, I have no complaints about my new husband. Give me a few days; I'm sure I'll think of something."

"I'm happy you have declared a truce."

"Nay, I surrendered unconditionally the moment he unsheathed his formidable weapon." Joanna laughed delightedly when she saw Jory blush. "His swordplay was masterful."

"Here's Blanche. I'll return when you've eaten."

Joanna swept her hand over the clothes Jory had laid out for her to wear on the journey to Clerkenwell. "Take those away. I've changed my mind. I don't wish to wear Plantagenet blue and gold today. I shall wear the colors of Gloucester and ride proudly beside my husband."

Jory rolled her eyes. *May God give me patience. Gloucester's colors are red and blue, but I have no idea which trunk holds Joanna's red surcoat.* "You wore your crimson riding outfit only two days past at the hunt. Why don't you wear the blue today and I'll remove the gold braid decoration. Your red boots and ruby caul will look striking against your blue surcoat, and the earl will recognize immediately that you are wearing the colors of Gloucester."

Joanna actually smiled. "What would I do without you?"

Jory heaved a sigh of relief. It wouldn't take her long to rip off the ornate gold braid, and the ruby caul was safe in the princess's jewel casket, which hadn't yet been taken to the stables.

It was two more hours before the cavalcade

of the Earl and Countess of Gloucester was ready to depart Windsor. Gilbert de Clare was not the sort of man to exercise patience, especially when women caused the delay, but he spent the morning hours with the king and his fellow earls discussing the Parliament, which he had agreed to attend two days hence. When Joanna and her ladies finally arrived in the courtyard shortly before noon, de Clare held his tongue and helped his bride into her bejeweled saddle.

Jory accepted the assistance of a groom, then took her place with Maud Clifford, Blanche Bedford, and Eleanor de Leyburn behind the Earl and Countess of Gloucester. She held her breath as suddenly she caught sight of Guy de Beauchamp. *He's back!* Jory's first impulse was to dismount and run into his arms, but there were too many eyes to witness such an affectionate display. Instead, she watched him approach his friend de Clare. They exchanged a few words, laughed, and then nodded in agreement. As the cavalcade began to move through the throng of well-wishers, Jory's eyes were riveted on Warwick. Rather than wave, he touched his fingers to his lips and then to his heart. *Two gestures he knows I will understand.* Overflowing with joy, her own heart almost turned over in her breast. *I will think of you every moment we are apart, Guy, my love!*

The de Clare mansion at Clerkenwell was in the countryside. Its closest neighbor was the ancient Tower of London. From the moment Jory rode through the iron gates that were ornamented with the boar device of Gloucester until she fell exhausted into her bed in a chamber she shared with Eleanor de Leyburn, she was busy sorting out Joanna's belongings. It took the entire afternoon and evening to hang the royal gowns and place the shoes that matched them in the wardrobes of the dressing room, which was adjacent to the de Clares' master bedchamber. Then she filled the drawers with Joanna's petticoats, nightgowns, corsets, stockings, garters, gloves, scarves, veils, and handkerchiefs. Last, but not least, Jory took inventory of the princess's vast collection of jewels, to make sure nothing had been pilfered on the trek from Windsor.

She bade Eleanor good night and wondered how she would ever get used to the manor house after living at spacious Windsor Castle. Then she smiled into the darkness. *I shan't be living here long!* A full-blown vision of dark, compelling Warwick filled her head, and her heart yearned for him. Surely she was the luckiest female alive to have captured Guy de Beauchamp's interest. He was a prize beyond her wildest dreams.

The next morning Joanna summoned her four ladies. It was obvious to each of them that she was in an expansive and generous mood. "I truly appreciate your friendship, loyalty, and hard work on my behalf. I have suddenly come to realize my own good fortune that you are in my service. You are all at an age when marriage will take you from me, so before that happens I would like to reward each of you with a token of my affection."

The countess gave a signal, and Gloucester footmen wearing livery carried in the bolts of vivid silk woven with silver thread that she had received as a wedding gift. "The choice is yours."

As the other three ladies pondered indecisively, Jory unerringly chose the bolt of silk that would be most flattering to her delicate coloring. The pale jade green was the exact color of her eyes. "It's the loveliest cloth

I've ever seen. I thank you with all my heart!"

The Earl of Gloucester came into the chamber. "Good morning, ladies." When each curtsied to him, he quickly shook his head. "Be at ease — such formality makes a soldier uncomfortable." His friendly eyes brimmed with secret amusement as they sought out Jory. "Lady Marjory, you have a visitor."

She hurried downstairs to the reception hall, thinking perhaps someone had brought a message from her brother. She almost missed a step as she saw Warwick pacing the room, slapping his riding gloves against his thigh. "Guy . . . I didn't expect . . . Guy!"

He held out his hand to her. "I wanted it to be a surprise. Come, see what I've brought you."

She slipped her hand into his, trying not to feel self-conscious that the servants might see, and matched her steps to his as he swept her from the hall into the courtyard. There stood a beautiful white palfrey with a long silken mane and tail.

"I rode all the way to Flamstead for a mount that is worthy of you, *chéri*. That's why you didn't see me yesterday."

"Such a costly gift . . . Are you sure it is permissible to come and visit me like this, my lord?" she asked breathlessly.

"Certes! Gloucester invited me. He cannot stop laughing that such a jaded swine as myself has finally lost his heart."

"Oh, Guy, I love you so much!" She raised her mouth to his.

CHAPTER 7

Warwick lifted Jory into the saddle, then mounted Caesar. "Come on, let's go for a wild gallop."

"I will have to ask Joanna to excuse me."

"Nonsense," Warwick said firmly. "You won't be in her service much longer. She knows what's in the wind, and if she doesn't, Gilbert will soon explain matters."

Her white palfrey took a couple of steps, sidling away from the huge black Caesar. Tiny silver bells attached to her harness tinkled prettily and Jory was delighted with the effect. "None would ever guess to look at you that you are an incurable romantic, Monsieur de Beauchamp."

"You are in grave danger if you reveal my secret, *chéri.*"

The corners of her mouth went up. "Will you beat me to a jelly? I shudder at the thought. You'll have to catch me first." She touched her knees to the palfrey and it surged forward.

"I'll make you shudder," he vowed, plunging after her.

Seemingly from out of nowhere, Brutus appeared and loped ahead of them as they rode through the flower-strewn meadows down to the river. They drew rein to view the foreign vessels that lay at anchor on the broad Thames.

"I wonder what cargoes they carry?" she mused.

"That one yonder is a Flemish merchantman. Likely it will carry fine English fleeces to Bruges and Antwerp in Flanders."

"We breed many sheep on de Warenne lands. Do you breed sheep?"

He nodded. "At Warwick we do. At Flamstead, I breed horses."

"Like this beauty." Jory stroked the palfrey's silky mane.

"She's a crossbreed. Her dam came from Middleton. The monks of the Abbey of Jervaulx breed pure white horses noted for their hardiness and strength. I brought her sire back from the Perche region of France. He was part Arabian. The result is a very showy female and a most fitting mount for you, my beauty."

"I love her, but didn't I tell you that Joanna rides a white horse and prefers that her ladies ride less showy animals?"

"And didn't I tell you that you will not be her lady-in-waiting much longer? You're about to become my Countess of Warwick."

"If you insist, my lord. Does she have a name?"

"None that I know of, *chéri*."

"Then I shall call her Zephyr."

"A light breeze from the west; a perfect name."

Brutus took off into the trees after a hare, and Guy took Jory's bridle and led her into the wooded copse. He dismounted, fastened Caesar to a young sapling, then lifted Jory from her saddle. They walked together along a path until they came to a pond where large yellow king cups and purple water hyacinths bloomed. The lovely buzz of insects and birdsong filled the air, making it a truly enchanted setting.

His visit to Flamstead had so convinced him that this marriage was right, he had stopped on the way back to tell his son of it. "Will you marry me, Jory?" His dark face was intense.

"Yes, Guy. I've quite made up my mind. I *will* marry you." Her heart was in her eyes.

He gave a whoop, snatched an insect from the air, and held his hand out to her, as he had done the day of the hunt.

She opened his fingers and laughed as a tiny iridescent dragonfly swooped up from his huge palm to reveal a small gold ring set with an emerald. "Guy, you are my magic man!"

She slipped the ring onto her finger and held up her hand so she could admire it.

He brought her fingers to his lips and gazed at her with adoration. "You enthrall me, Jory. I love the way you toss your hair over your shoulder and declare: *I've quite made up my mind.* You say the phrase often, and it has a finality about it that challenges any who would dare question your decision."

"Isn't being in love the most glorious feeling of all time? I want to sing and dance and carry on inordinately. I have the impulse to climb on the de Clare mansion roof and shout to the world that I am madly in love with Guy de Beauchamp!"

"A more calculating female would never tell a man she loved him. It would make her feel far too vulnerable."

"A secret," she whispered. "I've felt vulnerable all my life."

An urge to protect her rose up in him. She had a fragility about her that tugged at his heartstrings. The world was ofttimes cruel to its most sweet and gentle creatures and he silently vowed to shield her with all his strength and power. His arms swept about her and he pressed her to his heart.

They spent the entire afternoon together, riding, talking, laughing, and kissing away the hours. When they returned, Gilbert invited them to sup with him and Joanna, and Guy accepted. The newly wed Countess of Gloucester did not warm to Warwick, but held herself coolly aloof. As a consequence the two earls fell into a conversation about tomorrow's Parliament and the upcoming French wars that seemed inevitable. They also spoke of unrest in Wales, where both men had spent considerable time in the last decade, fighting battles, building castle fortresses, and patrolling the Welsh marches to enforce the peace.

Jory listened intently and it was brought home to her that all the nobles of the realm and their men-at-arms were at the beck and call of King Edward Plantagenet. If war was declared, these two earls, as well as her brother and her uncle, would be in the vanguard of the fighting.

"Whenever men get together, the talk of war is incessant. It is the one thing they love above all else," Joanna declared.

"*Au contraire,* my lady," Warwick replied.

"We can imagine, in the privacy of our thoughts, that war is heroic and honorable — even noble. It is an illusion. But we force ourselves to believe the illusion, denying reality, denying death, regardless of evidence to the contrary. War is bloody, brutal; the enemy is vicious."

Gloucester nodded. "We invade France or Wales out of political ambition or revenge, then try to plant our seeds of law and government in some very harsh soil. Cultures can be changed, but it takes years, not months. Look at Wales — how many years?"

"Most of my life," Guy replied.

"And mine," Gilbert added reluctantly. "And there are rumblings of rebellion once again."

Guy saw that Jory had gone pale. "Do not let our talk of war alarm you, ladies. Gilbert and I would drone on all night if someone didn't stop us." He got to his feet. "I thank you for supper — the food and the company were excellent. Since we must attend Parliament tomorrow, I shall take my leave early."

De Clare rose to his feet. "I shall see you on your way."

Jory longed to bid Guy a private good night, but realized it would be improper for her host, the Earl of Gloucester, to allow it.

He had already turned a blind eye to propriety by allowing the couple to spend the day together. "Kindly give my regards to my brother and my uncle tomorrow, my lord."

Warwick bowed gallantly, amusement dancing in his dark eyes. It was Jory's way of asking him to expedite their marriage plans. "It will be my pleasure, Lady Marjory."

The moment the men left the room, Joanna's knowing gaze swept over Jory. "You haven't given yourself to him yet, have you?"

Jory was startled at the intimate question. "I . . . that is — no."

"That's the only reason the *Wolfhound* is still sniffing round you. He's a notorious womanizer, Jory. Once he takes your virginity, you'll never see the lecherous swine again."

Jory raised her chin. "Guy has asked me to marry him."

Joanna's laugh was cruel. "I cannot believe your *naïveté!* That is what all men promise when they are intent upon bedding a reluctant female. It's *Warwick* for God's sake! You don't honestly believe the infamous earl will make the mistake of shackling himself to a third wife, do you?"

Jory's smile was serene. "He has already

offered for me."

Joanna arched a perfectly plucked eyebrow. "Are you sure? Or is that what the devious devil has told you?"

Jory's mind flew back to the last time she had spoken with Lynx, when she'd asked: *Did the earl offer for me yet?* The answer had been in the affirmative: *We have received an offer for you, but we are still negotiating and cannot speak of it yet.*

Jory answered her with quiet confidence. "My guardian is negotiating the terms. Lynx and the Earl of Surrey will summon me to Westminster Palace when an agreement has been finalized."

"Well, aren't you a sly minx to keep all this to yourself?" Joanna stood up and yawned as if the subject bored her. "I'm going up now. I shan't need you tonight."

Jory stared after her friend. *Surely Joanna isn't jealous?*

She retired to her bedchamber, and Eleanor de Leyburn, who was already abed when Jory opened the door, sat up immediately, bursting with curiosity. "Was that really the Earl of Warwick who visited you today?"

"Yes, that was Guy de Beauchamp."

"Aren't you afraid of him, Jory?" she

asked, wide-eyed.

"No. He is very protective of me. I feel absolutely safe and secure when I am in Guy's company."

"You dare to call the Earl of Warwick by his first name?"

Jory smiled her secret smile. "I'm going to marry him." She tossed her hair over her shoulder. "I've quite made up my mind."

At Westminster, the nobles assembled for the first session of Parliament. Before King Edward arrived, the barons gathered in groups to discuss war and taxes, both of which seemed inevitable. Guy de Beauchamp approached Lynx and John de Warenne, who were conveniently in the same place at the same time today.

"Gentlemen, I ask that you see me in private. There is a personal matter of importance I would like to discuss."

"By all means, Warwick," the earl said affably. "Tonight, after the session, come to my chamber. Lynx?"

Lynx nodded his assent.

"Thank you, Surrey." Warwick greeted the constable and his sons and then nodded to the marshal. Bigod looked particularly irascible this morning, and Guy anticipated that the session would likely exacerbate tempers. The barons were intensely jealous of their rights, particularly when the king attempted to trample on their feudal privileges, and Warwick was no exception.

Within the hour Edward arrived, and with a minimum of pomp and ceremony the session began. John de Bohun, Earl of Hereford, in his capacity of Constable of England took the floor.

"On behalf of the barons, I have been asked to make a formal objection to the forty-shilling tax on wool. Such an amount is a heavy imposition and we respectfully request it be rescinded."

Since Edward had called Parliament to get more money, not less, he refused the request. "Unfortunately, the Crown is in no position to rescind the wool tallage at this juncture. However, we pledge to address this tax at a future time when the defense of England and her territories has been accomplished."

"Your Majesty, we the barons are collectively determined to prevent the Crown from levying further taxes at will."

"I need money to fight the belligerent King of France!"

"We respectfully suggest you get it from the Church and the wealthy merchants."

The king made a dramatic appeal. "I am

going to meet danger on England's behalf, and when I return, I will give you back all that has been taken from you."

Roger Bigod, Earl of Norfolk and Marshal of England, got to his feet. "You intend to lead the army into Flanders, Your Majesty?"

"I do indeed. And you shall lead an army to recover Gascony."

Bigod became truculent. "With you, Sire, I will gladly go. As belongs to me by my hereditary right, I will ride before you."

Edward saw Bigod's dour expression and his stiff back. He hung on to his temper and said in a silky tone, "But without me, you will of course go with the rest."

"Gascony is five hundred miles farther south. I am not bound to go," asserted Bigod. "And go, I will not!"

Edward Plantagenet's temper flared. He drew himself up to his full height and stared down at the squat figure of the marshal. "By God, Sir Earl!" he cried. "You shall go or hang!"

"By God, Sir King!" Bigod spat. "I shall neither go nor hang!"

Though King Edward was in a white-hot rage, he did not explode into violence. He was in no position to quarrel with his baronage now that a French war was looming and Welsh rebellion was threatening to flare up on the home frontiers. Edward also knew that calling Parliament to raise money broke the stipulations of the Great Charter. The king swallowed his bile and excused the hereditary marshal from his duty, on condition that Bigod appoint a temporary substitute.

Warwick leaned close to his friend Gloucester. "That was a close battle of wills."

"All told, the earls and barons here today have with them fifteen hundred men-at-arms."

"That would be open rebellion."

"Aye, and he's not sure you or I would come down on his side."

The king's next opponent was the Archbishop of Canterbury. Edward and Winchelsey had a bitter debate on what the clergy should pay toward the war.

"I go to fight for the people as well as the Church of England." He paused dramatically. "And if I do not return, crown my son as your king."

At his father's words, young Prince Edward broke into tears and his mood communicated itself to the archbishop, who immediately capitulated and raised his hands high to show his loyalty.

Warwick and Gloucester exchanged a

glance of disgust that a prince of the realm would shame himself by weeping like a girl. The son was only a pale and pathetic shadow of his dominant sire.

During the recess, Roger Bigod approached his son-in-law, Lynx, and John de Warenne. After much back and forth over who would pay the lion's share of the costs, the Earl of Surrey agreed to lead an army into Gascony to secure it along with Guienne, from the avaricious Philip of France.

When the session resumed, Bigod announced that he wished to nominate John de Warenne as temporary substitute marshal, if it pleased the king. Edward Plantagenet was more than pleased and immediately appointed Surrey as head general of the army that would go to Gascony.

That evening when the first day's session of Parliament ended, a crowd had gathered outside Westminster Hall. Edward Plantagenet was shrewd enough to address the common people. With his son and heir on one side and Archbishop Winchelsey on the other, he made a speech aimed directly at their hearts. He told them how the French king was usurping territory that belonged to England and vowed to stop the fishermen of Normandy from stealing English livelihoods. The mass of people listened avidly, then cheered when their monarch ended his speech, showing their admiration for his bravery and pledging their complete loyalty.

After supper, Guy de Beauchamp made his way to the Westminster Palace chambers of John de Warenne. He was cynic enough to realize that ambition had prompted the Earl of Surrey to agree to take an army to Gascony, yet he thought more of him, rather than less, for that ambition. Warwick knew it would be expedient to get the matter of Lady Marjory settled without delay. After the two families formed a blood bond, he would not be averse to joining the de Warenne men when they went to fight in Gascony.

When Guy arrived, he was glad to see that Lynx was present.

"Come in, Warwick," the earl invited. "That was quite a session today. Thirsty work — pour us some ale, Lynx."

"Congratulations on your appointment, Surrey. Edward is lucky to get a general with your battle experience." Guy took a chair and half emptied the tankard of ale. "I have come to propose a match between Lady Marjory and myself. I would be deeply honored to make her the Countess of Warwick and have reason to believe the lady is

143

not averse to becoming my wife."

"Lord Warwick, this is indeed a surprise," Surrey replied. "I had no idea you were contemplating marriage."

"I wasn't," Warwick said flatly, "until I met Lady Marjory." He made eye contact with Lynx de Warenne. "Your sister has won my devotion. She is a prize beyond compare."

"A much sought after prize," Lynx said.

"We are aware of the great honor you bestow with this offer," John said quickly. "A union between the de Warennes and the noble house of Warwick would be most advantageous and give us much to celebrate. Though we have other offers for Lady Marjory, naturally yours will take precedence. We will give you our highest consideration, and of course we will consult the lady herself regarding her choice of future husband."

Warwick allowed himself to smile for the first time. "That is all I ask." His heart lifted and he felt supremely happy. He knew he had made the right decision and vowed to cherish Jory. "Thank you, gentlemen. I look forward to negotiating the terms."

After Guy de Beauchamp departed, Lynx said, "I had no idea you were such a skillful diplomat."

"I learned diplomacy in a hell of a hurry

when I negotiated the terms of your marriage with Roger Bigod, the irascible earl!"

"My hat is off to you, John. Sylvia's father can be extremely truculent, as he was today with the king."

"I had the advantage. It was Bigod who wanted you for his daughter's husband — not the other way around."

Each morning when Jory awakened, she hoped that this would be the day that she would be summoned to Westminster Palace. After the third day of disappointment, she became apprehensive. *Perhaps Warwick has changed his mind!* Her fear of rejection made her feel extremely vulnerable. She twisted the ring on her finger, and when she glanced down at the sparkling emerald gem, it reassured her. *No, no, Guy de Beauchamp loves me as much as I love him!*

The Countess of Gloucester's seamstress brought the gown she was making for Jory. "This is the loveliest material I've ever sewn, Lady Marjory, but it is so sheer and delicate. I took the liberty of making you a taffeta underdress to help show off its beauty. Would you like gathered sleeves?"

Jory donned the lustrous taffeta, then tried on the new gown. "Oh, it's exquisite! You have done a superb job." She twirled before the mirror, thrilled that the pale green silk floated about her like gossamer. "I think I'd like trailing sleeves, please." *I love it so much! This will be my wedding gown.* She twirled about, then curtsied to her reflection. *Marjory de Beauchamp, Countess of Warwick!*

When morning turned into afternoon, Jory's doubts crept back. As she laid out the clothes that Joanna would wear to dinner that night, she sought to reassure herself. "Is Parliament still in session? It's been four days."

"Yes, they'll be at it for some time. Gilbert informs me that Father is pressing for money for the French wars, and extracting gold from the barons is like squeezing blood from stone."

"Will the Earl of Gloucester go to fight in France?"

"Nay, Jory. The king relies on Gloucester to safeguard Wales. Gilbert had me in stitches last night. Apparently Roger Bigod and the king almost came to blows. The Earl of Norfolk refused to take the army to Gascony and my father threatened to hang him."

Roger Bigod is Lynx's father-in-law! "Did

the marshal finally agree to do the king's bidding?"

"Nay, the irascible old devil appointed your uncle, John de Warenne, to lead the army instead."

No wonder I haven't been summoned to Westminster. They have been completely occupied with preparing to fight a war in France!

John de Warenne and his nephew, Lynx, paid a late call on John de Bohun, Earl of Hereford. The Constable of England's son Humphrey was with him when they arrived.

"Come in, Surrey; de Warenne. I'm delighted to see you both. Since Humphrey is a party to this match, I warrant he can be present while we negotiate?"

"By all means." Both de Warennes took the chairs they were offered and accepted tankards of ale.

"We have come to advise you that we have received another offer for Lady Marjory. Without revealing his name, I feel it only fair to let you know that the noble is an Earl of the Realm."

De Bohun's brows drew together, and though Humphrey did not frown, the de Warennes saw that they had his undivided attention.

"Marriage with Humphrey will not make Lady Marjory a countess immediately," Hereford conceded, "so let me offer a substantial incentive. I will deed my castle of Midhurst, Sussex, to my heir upon his marriage to Lady Marjory, with the stipulation that it become the legal property of the firstborn child of the union, should my son predecease me, God forbid."

The de Warennes exchanged a guarded glance that was noncommittal and immediately John de Bohun added, "And of course it goes without saying that no dowry is necessary for a lady as highborn as Marjory de Warenne."

"That is most generous, Hereford." Lynx turned to Humphrey. "I warrant you are an excellent match for my sister. We will inform her of your offer and feel confident that Lady Marjory will happily assent to the union."

The Earl of Surrey softened his flinty demeanor. "A blood bond between the de Bohun and de Warenne families will be advantageous for us all, and for England."

As the pair returned to their own chambers in Westminster Palace, John said dryly, "Lady Marjory will assent to the union, happily or otherwise, only if she receives no other offers."

"Jory is as elusive as quicksilver and more willful than a dozen men-at-arms. If given the choice, she will unswervingly pick the *infamous* Earl of Warwick." Lynx let out a resigned breath. "I warrant you are right. The only way to keep her safe from making a rash decision is to keep silent about de Beauchamp's offer."

CHAPTER 8

Warwick bathed and took special care with his wardrobe. He had often been told that his pride was indelibly etched on his face, and as he glanced into the mirror, he could not deny it. He brushed an invisible speck from his black doublet. *I am what I am, nothing more, nothing less.*

As the fifth session of Parliament had drawn to a close, the Earl of Surrey had asked Guy de Beauchamp to join him after dinner. Warwick bid Brutus, "Stay!" He locked his door and his long strides soon brought him to John de Warenne's chamber. His mood was high; he was actually looking forward to negotiating for Jory.

The first thing he noticed when he entered the room was that Lynx de Warenne was conspicuously absent. *Why is Jory's guardian negotiating without her brother? Do they disagree on terms or do they believe two earls of equal rank will deal better one-on-one?*

Guy took a seat, stretching his long legs to the fire. He knew that a worthy negotiator would point out all the disadvantages to the union in order to gain the upper hand.

John sat down opposite him and cleared his throat. "The de Warennes are most honored by your offer for Lady Marjory," Surrey began, "but I hope you'll not object to my being blunt, Warwick."

He's going to bring up the death of my wives. "By all means, Surrey, let us speak plainly. I would have it no other way."

"My niece is an eighteen-year-old maiden, while you are past thirty. In both age and experience you are worlds apart."

"True. I cannot deny either my age or my experience; nor do I intend to."

"You have been married twice before, which would make Lady Marjory the *third* Countess of Warwick."

Surrey's words set Guy's teeth on edge. "You have a penchant for stating the obvious."

"Forgive me," Surrey said expansively. "All these objections could be overlooked if it were not for one glaring obstacle that can neither be ignored nor changed."

Warwick remained silent. There were numerous obstacles from which Surrey could choose.

"You already have a son, Rickard. Any male issue from a union with Lady Marjory would not be the heir to Warwick."

"Any child of mine, male or female, will be well provided with Warwick castles and land, as will their mother." *Christ, that sounded defensive!*

"But not the title — not the Earldom of Warwick," Surrey said.

"We are back to the obvious." His voice was like silk and steel. "I have made certain that Lady Marjory is aware of all the disadvantages connected with marriage to me, Lord Surrey. I am content to abide by her wishes."

"I am relieved to hear it, Warwick. Lady Marjory has accepted an offer from the Earl of Hereford's heir, Humphrey de Bohun. The Constable of England's son is close to her own age."

Warwick rose to his feet, towering over Surrey. His black eyes blazed with accusation. "This is *your* fucking decision, not Jory's!" He knew he should not lose his temper, the temper that was reputed to be blacker than the devil's own, but in that moment Warwick could not control himself.

"You are quite mistaken. Lady Marjory

has no desire to cause you pain, but her decision to wed Humphrey de Bohun is final. She asked me to tell you that she has quite made up her mind."

Guy felt stunned, as if a stone wall had fallen on him. These were Jory's own words and no others would have convinced him. A picture of her came to him full blown, tossing her silvery hair. Pride rose up in him. It was the only thing that stopped him from committing an act of savage violence upon John de Warenne.

Warwick masked his emotions instantly. "I shall abide by her wishes." He nodded curtly to Surrey and departed.

He unlocked his chamber door and slammed it shut with a force that broke its iron hinge. He emptied the wardrobe and threw everything into his bags. He clenched his jaw and his fists, lusting for vengeance, wanting to kill. His glance fell on Brutus, who sat quietly, watching him with knowing yellow eyes. Warwick went down on his knees and gathered the wolfhound in his arms. He rubbed his face in the wiry coat and, though his wound remained raw, he felt some of his black fury melt away.

"You know she has saved herself from a fate worse than death," he told Brutus. "The full moon stole my senses and turned me into a lunatic." His wolfhound nodded in agreement. Warwick laughed at his own folly.

He went to the barracks where his men were housed and found his lieutenant casting dice. "Pack up; we are leaving."

"Tonight, my lord? I didn't realize Parliament was over."

"It's over for me. We leave for Warwickshire in an hour."

At long last, Jory received the summons from her uncle John to attend him at Westminster Palace. She was so excited that she changed her outfit three times before she was satisfied with her appearance. She wished to appear mature, dignified, and above all, confident that she would fit the role of Countess of Warwick.

The Earl of Surrey had sent a de Warenne escort to accompany her from Clerkenwell to Westminster, and she rode her new white palfrey with great pride. She arrived in the afternoon, and since her uncle was attending Parliament, she decided to visit with Lynx's wife until the session was over.

"Marjory, you are looking very elegant today."

"Thank you, Sylvia. You know why I'm

here, I warrant. It's a momentous occasion for me."

"Indeed. An offer of marriage is very exciting. I remember exactly how I felt when it was my turn."

"Are you enjoying Westminster?"

"Not really. I'm counting the days until Lynx and I can return to Hedingham. I am quite homesick."

Jory searched Sylvia's face. *Does she not know that Lynx will be going to France to fight a war?*

"I thoroughly enjoyed my stay at Windsor and my visit with Queen Eleanor, and the royal wedding, of course. How is the bride? I hope Joanna finally realizes how fortunate she is to be wed to Gloucester, the highest peer in the realm."

"They seem to get along famously. The age difference is no longer a bone of contention." Jory's mouth curved. "I firmly believe that age has nothing to do with happiness. The best husbands are always a few years older than their wives."

Sylvia called for refreshments, and the two ladies chatted amiably as they sipped their wine and enjoyed a variety of fruit tarts. When they were done, it was time for the daily session of Parliament to be over and Sylvia took Jory to her uncle's chamber.

"You must stay with us tonight. I shall order you a trundle bed."

"Thank you. Ah, here comes Uncle John," she said breathlessly.

"Hello, Minx." He gave her an appreciative glance. "You grow lovelier every day."

"It's because I'm happy," she confided.

"Come in, child, and make yourself comfortable. Is there anything I can get you?"

"No, thank you. I had dessert with Sylvia."

John sat down at the table and shuffled some papers on it. "So, my dear, I believe you are quite aware that we have had an offer of marriage for you?"

"Yes. I thought you'd never send for me!"

"Negotiations take time, Mistress Impatience. This is a marriage between two great noble families. All the details have to be laid out clearly before the contract can be signed. I told the earl that I would inform you of the offer, which is just a formality, of course, and assured him I was confident that Lady Marjory would happily assent to the union."

"Most happily! I've quite made up my mind."

"Splendid! You have made a wise decision, my dear. I shall inform the constable without delay, and all that remains is to sign the papers and set a date for the wedding."

"I didn't realize the constable had to be informed."

"It is the Earl of Hereford who has made the offer for you on behalf of his heir, Humphrey de Bohun."

"Oh heavens . . . I had no idea! I'm afraid you'll have to tell him my answer is *no*. It is Guy de Beauchamp's offer I wish to accept, Uncle John."

"We have had no offer from the Earl of Warwick, my dear."

Marjory jumped to her feet. "You must be mistaken! Guy has already asked me to marry him, and I accepted his proposal!"

John de Warenne gave his niece a pitying glance. "Are you sure it wasn't a *proposition,* Jory my dear? A man like Warwick —"

She raised her chin in defiance and could feel the hot blaze of her cheeks. "I assure you that Guy de Beauchamp *will* be offering for me. Any other offers are out of the question! When you have received the offer, I will be happy to return to Westminster."

Jory knew that if she didn't get some fresh air into her lungs, she would suffocate. She was furious with her guardian and left him sitting at the table with his mouth open. She walked briskly along the facade of the old palace and stopped a liveried servant.

"Could you direct me to the Earl of Warwick's chamber, please?"

"Sorry, m'lady, there's scores of nobles here fer Parliament. I don't know which chambers they're assigned to."

Jory next approached a serving woman wearing a smock. "Do you know where the Earl of Warwick is lodged?"

"Sorry, luv. This old palace is like a rabbit warren."

Under the circumstances, Jory knew she could not go back and spend the night with Sylvia and Lynx, so she went to the stables to retrieve Zephyr. One of Surrey's men who had escorted her earlier in the day was in the stables and she asked him if he would see her safely back to Clerkenwell.

On the three-mile-ride home she clung to her anger, knowing instinctively it was the only thing that would keep her tears at bay. When she arrived back at Gloucester's mansion, she thanked her escort, turned Zephyr over to a groom, and then went upstairs.

Eleanor de Leyburn, who was getting ready for bed, dismissed the maid so she could learn all about Jory's exciting summons to Westminster. "You guessed correctly? It was an offer of marriage?"

"I . . . Yes, I did receive an offer of marriage," Jory replied.

"Did you accept?" Eleanor asked breathlessly.

"No . . . I . . . Nothing is settled yet. I'll likely be returning to Westminster in a couple of days." Jory pretended to yawn. "I'm exhausted, Eleanor. Can we talk about this tomorrow?"

Once Jory was abed and the room lay in darkness, her thoughts flew about like caged birds colliding with each other in a panic to escape. *Why did Guy not make a formal offer for me? Perhaps he spoke with Lynx and my uncle doesn't yet know about it? I didn't dream it — Guy did ask me to marry him!* Jory twisted the ring on her finger. *A ring is a promise.* She heard Sylvia's voice: *Men's promises are forgotten the moment they are uttered! No, no, he gave me Zephyr as a gift. Surely the white palfrey wasn't a parting gift?*

Jory's fear of rejection fed on itself as she remembered the things Joanna had said about Guy: *The Wolfhound is a notorious womanizer, Jory. Once he takes your virginity, you'll never see the lecherous swine again. No, no, Guy was too honorable to take my virginity once he knew I was a lady. He lives according to his motto: Not without right!*

Jory conjured his image and gazed intently into his purple-black eyes. *Please, Guy, please!* She saw his fingers touch his lips and then his heart and hope returned. *There is a valid explanation why he hasn't yet offered for me. They will call me back to Westminster very soon.*

As she drifted to the edge of sleep, she slipped into the vulnerable void between a dream and a nightmare. She heard a voice in the distance laughing: *I cannot believe your naïveté. It's Warwick for God's sake!*

Jory opened her eyes before dawn and instantly a feeling of dread descended. She dressed quietly without waking Eleanor and went down to the library. She wrote a brief note that was a cry for help. *Humphrey de Bohun has offered for me.* She put only her initial J beneath the seven words and addressed the envelope to: *Guy de Beauchamp, Earl of Warwick, Westminster Palace, London.*

Jory made her way to the reception hall and waited by the front door. It wasn't long before Gilbert de Clare came into view.

"My lord earl, I know this is presumptuous, but would you kindly do me the service of delivering this to your friend?"

Gilbert read the name on the note. "Lady Marjory, I will gladly deliver your note if Warwick is at the session today. He was absent yesterday." The look of vulnerability on her face prompted him to reassure her. "He'll likely be back today."

She smiled with relief. "Thank you, my lord."

Jory went back upstairs. Her head had begun to ache and she lay down quietly on her bed, determined to ban all thoughts of rejection. She pretended sleep when Eleanor arose and dressed, and she sighed deeply when she heard the chamber door close.

Half an hour later, Eleanor returned. "Jory, thank heaven you are awake. Joanna is asking for you. She doesn't want anyone else." Eleanor lowered her voice. "I think she's ill."

Jory jumped up from the bed, her own plight momentarily forgotten. She encountered Blanche Bedford in the hall outside Joanna's chamber. "She has refused her breakfast. She won't even let me go in there. All she wants is you."

"Thank you, Blanche. I'll find out if anything's wrong."

Joanna was sitting on the edge of her wide bed; a grayish pallor had replaced her usual high color. "Jory, I've been sick." She indicated the chamber pot, now covered with its fancy lid.

"Do you feel ill?" Jory went to the bed

and put her hand on Joanna's forehead to see if she was fevered. "You're not hot." The princess enjoyed good health and was never ill. "Perhaps you had something last night that upset your stomach."

"I was sick yesterday morning, too, after Gilbert left," she whispered. "I think it's morning sickness."

"Oh, Joanna, do you think it possible? It's so soon."

Joanna took Jory's hand and clung to it tightly. "What if it isn't . . . Oh God, what am I saying? Of course it's Gilbert's!"

Jory shivered and her arms became covered with gooseflesh. "Stop, Joanna. You are being fanciful. Stay still until the nausea passes. I'll get rid of this. No one else needs to know."

"Thank you, Jory. What the hell am I going to do without you?"

Joanna continued with her morning sickness and her menstrual flow was late. The two friends concluded that the Countess of Gloucester was indeed with child. The pair of conspirators had an unspoken understanding that the child was Gilbert de Clare's. "I don't want anyone to know until the first month has passed. I hope I can count on you, Jory, to keep my secret."

"My lips are sealed. You alone will decide the time to reveal your wonderful news." Jory took a deep breath. "I have a secret of my own that I don't want to share with anyone but you." She lowered her voice. "Warwick didn't offer for me yet. It was the Constable who made the offer for me on behalf of his son."

"De Bohun?" Joanna's face blanched.

"Yes, they want me to marry Humphrey de Bohun."

Color came back into Joanna's face. "Well, he's certainly a tall, attractive young noble. Most ladies would be ecstatic."

"But he's not Warwick," Jory whispered miserably.

"Dearest Jory, do you really wish to marry a man rumored to have caused the death of, not one, but *two* wives?"

She answered silently, *Yes. I'm hopelessly in love with Guy de Beauchamp, in spite of all the rumors.*

"I don't give a fig about his reputation," she defended. "If he offers for me, I shall accept. I've quite made up my mind."

That night when Gilbert de Clare returned from Westminster, he sought a private word with Jory. "Lady Marjory, it seems my friend returned to Warwickshire

163

two days ago. I immediately forwarded your letter by courier along with one of my own. He should receive it by tomorrow."

Jory's mouth went dry. She licked her lips. "Thank you, my lord earl. That was most kind."

Hope refused to die. *When Guy learns that Humphrey de Bohun has offered for me, he will contact my guardian immediately.*

Two days later when Jory was again summoned to Westminster, her heart lifted with incurable anticipation. She firmly pushed all doubts away, resolutely refusing to acknowledge any uncertainty.

Only when she was face-to-face with her uncle and heard his words, did hope begin to drain away.

"Jory, my dear child, I am afraid you must accept the truth and put away your daydreams. Guy de Beauchamp abandoned Parliament a week ago and returned to Warwickshire. Believe me when I tell you there is no chance that you will become the Countess of Warwick."

The word *abandoned* echoed in her head. The thought of rejection was too devastating to contemplate. She stared straight ahead, her face a cool mask, determined to display no emotion.

"Marjory, Lynx and I are going to France to fight a war. It is our responsibility to get you safely settled before we depart."

Her heart contracted. *I hate being my brother's responsibility.*

"Both of us are convinced the match with Humphrey de Bohun is right for you in every way. The Earl of Hereford would be like a father to you, and his son will make an honorable husband. Can I tell them that you accept?"

"No! No. I don't even know Humphrey de Bohun!"

"That can soon be remedied. I'll tell you what — Parliament should be over tomorrow, so why don't you stay at Westminster for a couple of days so you can get to know him better? If you are still adamantly opposed to de Bohun, I'll give him your regrets."

"I don't believe . . . I need time to think . . . I'm going back to Clerkenwell." Jory saw the sharp disappointment in his face. "I promise I will consider what you suggest, Uncle John, but please don't be upset if I cannot bring myself to do it."

When Jory got back to the Gloucester mansion, the first person she encountered was Blanche Bedford.

"Marjory, I'm so happy for you. Eleanor told me you had received an offer of marriage. How excited you must be."

"I . . . I haven't accepted any offer yet. Please don't say anything to the others."

Blanche giggled. "They all know, Jory."

As Jory tried to hurry past the luxurious sitting room on her way to the stairs, Joanna called her name. "Jory, come join us."

She took a deep breath and entered the lovely chamber. She sent a cool look in the direction of Eleanor de Leyburn, thinking she was the one who had told them she had had an offer.

Maud Clifford clapped her hands together with delight. "Congratulations on your coming marriage to Humphrey de Bohun, Marjory. Someday you will be the Countess of Hereford!"

Jory's accusing glance fell on Joanna. She was the only one who knew the offer had come from de Bohun. *Damn you, Joanna! You knew that was confidential between the two of us. I would never break your trust, no matter how scandalously you have behaved.* Jory quickly protested. "I haven't agreed to the match."

"But you *will*," Joanna said with emphasis. "Just think how close we will be to each other when I go to Gloucester and you go to Hereford. They are only a few miles apart. We can be wives and mothers together, Jory, when our men go off to war. Becoming part of the constable's family is a high honor, and I know the king will thoroughly approve that the de Warennes and the de Bohuns will be bound by blood."

"Oh, Jory, I envy you so much. The constable's sons are extremely tall and handsome, and fair haired like you." Maude Clifford sighed deeply.

"Indeed they are," drawled Joanna. "Young too. To find fault with such a match would brand you a spoiled, ungrateful wretch."

Jory's heart sank. *I realize I am spoiled, as we all are here, but I don't want my brother and my uncle to think me ungrateful.*

"Leave us. I'd like a private word with Jory." Joanna waited until her other ladies withdrew. "You're angry with me."

"How could you? You know I love Warwick."

"If they learned such a thing they would think you daft in the head . . . or worse, they would pity you. You must accept the fact that Warwick didn't offer for you, Jory. I was given no choice. What makes you think your case will be any different?"

Jory swallowed the lump in her throat and lifted her chin.

CHAPTER 9

The dining hall at Westminster was not overcrowded when Jory arrived. Many of the earls and barons had left to ready their men to fight in France or quell the trouble brewing in Wales.

She watched as the newlyweds were seated on the dais with the king. *I warrant he invited Joanna and Gilbert so he could gauge how his daughter is adjusting to marriage.* Jory saw that the Earl of Hereford was seated next to her uncle.

Jory took a seat next to Lynx and his wife, just below the dais. She blushed slightly when she saw that the de Bohun brothers were across the table from them. Her nerves were taut, because the moment the dinner was over she intended to approach the Earl of Hereford and, in the gentlest way possible, tell him she could not marry his son Humphrey.

At last the interminable meal was over and

as the servants began to clear the tables and everyone stood to mingle about, Jory steeled herself to approach John de Bohun up on the dais. She curtsied gracefully to King Edward, then turned to speak to the constable. "May I speak with you privately, my lord earl?"

Hereford beamed at her. "Lady Marjory, my heart overflows with happiness and pride that you have consented to marry my son Humphrey. I pledge that you will be like a beloved daughter to me." His great arms enfolded her and he kissed her on each cheek.

Jory's mouth opened in astonishment, but nothing came out. She was absolutely speechless.

King Edward, who had overheard John de Bohun's triumphant declaration, took both her hands and bestowed a royal kiss upon her. "Lady Marjory, this match pleases me as much as the one between my daughter and Gloucester." The king turned to John de Warenne. "I congratulate you, Surrey. Strong blood bonds between our noble families can only strengthen England."

"Your Majesty . . . please," Jory murmured through bloodless lips.

Edward Plantagenet held up his arms and called for silence. "Humphrey de Bohun, come up to the dais," he ordered.

The tall blond knight strode forward without hesitation, climbed onto the dais, and stood proudly beside the king. Jory wished she could vanish into thin air.

"It is my great honor and my deep pleasure to announce that a marriage has been arranged between Marjory de Warenne and Humphrey de Bohun, son and heir of the Earl of Hereford."

As a great cheer went up, Edward looked down at the small female who looked far too pale and vulnerable. "Your father would be very happy this night, Lady Marjory. He served me well and was taken from us far too soon. My dearest child, I know the de Bohun family will cherish you." The king took Jory's hand and placed it in Humphrey's. "A toast to the happy couple!"

Joanna stepped forward and thrust her own goblet of wine into Jory's free hand. "You are as pale as death. Drink up. There is nothing you can do . . . It is a fait accompli."

Jory's hand trembled as she lifted the cup to her lips and quaffed deeply. Joanna congratulated Humphrey, and his fair skin flushed red. Jory saw and, not for the first time, wondered if he was infatuated with the king's daughter. *Perhaps Humphrey too is being coerced into this marriage.* As she looked up at him, she saw that the bridge of his nose was covered with freckles. *He is impossibly young and boyish compared with Warwick!*

Jory looked at the people below the dais, all drinking a toast to her happiness. Then she saw Lynx. His face had a gaunt, haunted look, as if the heavy responsibility for her future happiness lay on his shoulders alone. Jory's heart went out to him. *He was far too young when Father died. He had no chance to be a boy . . . He had to become a man, burdened by a baby sister.* She turned away quickly before her brother saw tears flood her eyes.

She became aware that her uncle John was watching her and her eyes glittered green through her tears. *You are the one who told de Bohun I accepted the proposal, and you don't even have the decency to look guilty about your lie!*

Jory wanted to rush over and fly at him. Though frustration almost choked her, she knew she would have to wait until she and her guardian were private before she could protest.

Everyone crowded round, congratulating the groom, wishing the misty-eyed bride happiness, and asking the date of the wedding.

"The wedding hasn't been settled yet," she protested firmly, but everyone took that to mean the *date* had not been settled.

"Lady Marjory cannot delay the nuptials too long, under the circumstances," Humphrey declared.

"What circumstances?" Jory demanded.

He looked down at her uncertainly. "War," he murmured.

Dear God, how can someone so young be sent to war? Her own plight receded as she considered Humphrey's. She heard the echo of Guy de Beauchamp's words: *War is bloody, brutal; the enemy is vicious.* Jory's anger flared anew, bringing color back to her cheeks. *War is the reason I never knew my father!*

Her brother enfolded her in his powerful arms and she pressed her face against his heart. "Lynx, I don't want you to go to war."

He tightened his embrace. "It's my duty, Minx. It won't be my first war; nor will it be my last," he said cheerfully.

She looked up at him aghast. "How can you be so nonchalant?"

"You are too emotional and vulnerable tonight, Jory. You must believe with all your heart that I will return. How can I believe myself invincible, if you have doubts?"

"I swear to you I have no doubts about you," she assured him passionately. "My doubts are for myself," she whispered.

I cannot fill his ears with my woes; he has enough on his plate. She swallowed her despair and gave him a radiant smile.

She saw that Humphrey was being toasted by his brother, and she quickly sought out Joanna. "How soon will we be leaving?"

"We are sleeping at Westminster, Jory. I think tonight will be an opportune time to tell Gilbert my news. He will tell Father, and tomorrow I shall be the center of attention. If I ask the pair of them for the moon, they will likely give it to me."

Face it, Jory . . . there is no escape tonight . . . no escape ever. She felt forlorn and helpless. Then suddenly she lost patience with herself. *Stop wallowing in self-pity, for God's sake!*

She pasted a smile on her face, accepted the wine she was offered, and silently prayed for the evening to end. When it was at last time to leave she bade Humphrey good night and took her uncle's arm. "We need to talk," she said through clenched teeth.

The palace steward gave them directions

to the chamber that had been plenished for Lady Marjory, and they walked side by side in total silence until they were inside and the door was closed.

Jory withdrew her arm and set her hands to her hips. "I did *not* consent to marry Humphrey de Bohun!"

John spread his hands in a conciliatory gesture. "De Bohun offered to deed Midhurst Castle in Sussex to Humphrey and thus to the firstborn child of your union. Lynx said: *It is an excellent match. We will inform Lady Marjory of your offer, and feel confident she will happily assent to the union.* The de Bohuns obviously took it for granted that you had accepted their offer."

"You will have to disabuse them of their assumption when you receive the offer from Warwick!"

"And when will that be, my dear?"

"I sent Guy a letter warning him that de Bohun had made an offer for me."

"And what was his reply, Jory?"

She bit her lip and did not answer.

"Exactly," John said quietly.

Why did you not answer my cry for help, Guy?

"You promised you'd consider getting to know Humphrey."

"*Consider!* Do you know the meaning of that word? It means that I will think about it! Instead, the de Bohuns *consider* me Humphrey's bride, King Edward *considers* me Humphrey's bride, and even my own family *considers* me Humphrey's bride."

"Jory, my dear, you have every right to be angry. But not at the people who love you. Your anger should be directed at Warwick. You are not the first woman to suffer at his hands."

"Stop! I will not listen while you catalog his infamy." She laughed, but there was little mirth in it. "Uncle, I am quite aware you think I am making a fool of myself. Indulge me."

"Lynx and I have always indulged you, Marjory."

She suddenly felt very spoiled and demanding.

"Jory, I'll make a bargain with you. If Warwick does not offer for you in the next week, you will let the engagement stand. Shortly, we go to France to fight a war. I want you safely settled as a wife. I don't want you to be left a lonely spinster. Humphrey isn't the villain here, Jory. Cast me in the role if you must, but not Humphrey de Bohun. He is an earnest young knight who does not deserve to be treated shabbily."

A feeling of guilt assailed her. For the first time, she noticed that her uncle looked tired. Jory took a calming breath. "May I sleep on the matter and give you my decision tomorrow?"

"Of course, my dear. I have always found it impossible to refuse aught that you ask of me."

Yes, I have always gotten my own way. Until now. The thought added to her guilt. "Good night, Uncle."

Jory lay abed, wide-awake. Her mind went over everything since the moment she had laid eyes on Guy de Beauchamp, Earl of Warwick. Her heart ached for him and her body lusted for him. After many hours of tantalizing herself, she could taste him and smell him. Yet her longing was tinged with an anguished poignancy. Deep down in her soul she feared that she had been rejected. He did not love her . . . His offer would never come.

Just before dawn she fell into an exhausted sleep and a man dressed in armor came to her. When he removed his helm and his tawny mane of hair fell to his shoulders, she thought it was Lynx. Then she realized it was her father, Lincoln de Warenne.

"My own sweet Jory." He gently stroked her hair. "Silver-gilt tresses." He smiled into her eyes. "You have made me very happy tonight. The de Bohun family will cherish you as a daughter."

"But, Father, the Earl of Warwick proposed to me."

"Dearest Jory, do you really wish to marry a man rumored to have caused the death of, not one, but *two* wives?"

"Are the rumors true, Father?" she pleaded.

The vision of the man in armor began to fade.

"Don't go. Please don't leave me!"

Jory awoke with a start. The first shadowy light of dawn was stealing into the chamber and for a moment she was disoriented. Slowly, she remembered where she was and details of her dream. Her father wanted her to wed Humphrey and was against Warwick.

Did my mind create the dream or did Father really come to me? Jory was unsure. Many people believed in visions and portents.

She drew up her legs, wrapped her arms about them, and rested her head on her knees. Portents aside, it was time to face facts. Warwick would not offer for her. His silence told her louder than any words that he had rejected her. *Damn him to hellfire!*

What John had said was the truth. Humphrey de Bohun was not the villain. He was an earnest young knight who did not deserve her shabby treatment.

Warwick has blinded me to all other males. She knew she must eradicate him from her mind and resolved to do so, starting today. Slowly, she slipped the emerald ring from her finger and put it away. She would not even attempt to disroot him from her heart — the infamous earl with the lethal French charm was there to stay.

Jory dressed and made her way to her guardian's chamber. "I've come to tell you I am ready to get to know Humphrey de Bohun."

"Jory, my dearest, you are doing the sensible thing."

Sensible, yes. "If we clash I will tell you outright that I will not marry him. Otherwise I'll be amenable to the match."

John nodded in agreement. "Fair enough, Jory."

She wanted to scream that life was decidedly *unfair,* but the new Jory held her tongue. She would behave in a mature manner and, in truth, she already felt older and wiser. She had learned the hard way that when a man made passionate promises and then betrayed you, it left you feeling jaded and brittle.

Westminster's Great Hall was abuzz with the news of the expected royal babe. A grandchild for the king and, if the gods smiled on Joanna, she would produce a son and heir for Gloucester. Not only Gilbert, but Edward too exuded male pride today.

Jory greeted Lynx, who was conversing with John de Bohun and his sons. She curtsied to the Earl of Hereford, who stayed her with his hand. "My dear Lady Marjory, there is no need of formality with me." He grinned at Lynx. "We're all family here."

Jory spoke to her brother. "When do you leave for Hedingham?"

"Well, Minx, we have a tentative plan that centers on your joining us. The Earl of Hereford has invited us to view his Castle of Midhurst in Sussex before we return to Hedingham."

"I see," Jory said calmly.

Humphrey bowed formally and took her hand to his lips. "I hope you will consent to join us, Lady Marjory."

"I shall take leave of Joanna and return

tomorrow." *They all look relieved that I am ready to follow wherever they lead,* Jory thought cynically. *I feel like a bloody pawn in a chess game.*

At Clerkenwell, Joanna and her ladies-in-waiting gathered to bid Lady Marjory farewell.

"I asked Gilbert if we could stay here for a month rather than rushing off to Gloucester. I don't relish meeting all those de Clares who think their bloodlines make them superior to Plantagenets. He agreed, so I shall come dance at your wedding."

"I warrant both the de Warennes and the de Bohuns will rush the nuptials so they can get on with the more important things in life, such as their disgusting wars."

"Are you afraid, Jory?" Joanna searched her face.

"Of war, yes; of Humphrey de Bohun, no." She was lying of course. Jory had never felt more vulnerable in her life.

Outside, a baggage cart piled with Jory's belongings stood waiting with a de Warenne escort. She mounted her black palfrey and gazed at Zephyr, who had been placed on a leading rein. *I'll never be able to ride her again without thinking of Warwick.*

The de Warenne escort asked, "Are you ready, my lady?"

Jory stiffened her back and raised her chin. "Quite ready."

Marjory was quite taken with Midhurst Castle when she saw it had a moat and a round tower that gave it a romantic air.

"Midhurst always has guests to entertain when we are in residence," the constable said. "You'll be an invaluable asset, Lady Marjory. The royal family is often at Winchester Castle and the visiting nobles invariably drop in here. We get more than our share of the baronage, too, whenever they travel to the coast."

"I can smell the sea!" Jory exclaimed.

"You can see it from atop the Round Tower," Humphrey told her. He helped her dismount and spoke quietly so the others would not hear. "This is the castle that Father will deed to me upon our marriage, and I will pass it on to our firstborn child."

"It is quite lovely." *If you mean to bribe me, it is working!*

When they entered the hall, Jory was surprised at how shabby the furnishings were, until she remembered it was a household of men.

John de Bohun waved an all-encompassing

arm. "All needs refurbishing. It sadly lacks a woman's touch. I hope you're willing to take on the task. Portsmouth will provide anything you fancy. Spare no expense. Same goes for our castle in Hereford."

Jory, who already felt affection for the fatherly de Bohun, lost her heart to him in that moment. "You indulge me, my lord."

"It's been a long time since the de Bohuns have had the luxury of indulging a lady. I forgot how good it feels."

At sunset, Humphrey came to find Jory. "Would you like to go up to the tower roof, Marjory? I think you'll enjoy the view."

She had been about to change her gown for dinner, but was eager to ascend the tower and view the landscape. As they climbed the circular stone steps, Humphrey held a protective arm behind her as if he expected her to fall. *I wish he wouldn't do that — I'm agile as a bloody monkey.* To prove it she ran lightly up the steps and waited for him to catch up. Together they walked to the crenellated wall and Jory caught her breath as the setting sun turned the water of the moat to molten gold.

Humphrey pointed across the lush landscape. "There is the coast and the town of

Portsmouth. You can see a blue ribbon of sea and beyond is the Isle of Wight."

"Your castle is lovely. I have taken a great fancy to it."

"Marjory, I never did actually ask you to marry me — it was taken for granted and more or less arranged by the two earls. So I'm asking you now. Will you marry me?"

Humphrey looked so painfully anxious, she wanted to put him out of his misery. Though she was not in love with him, the marriage had begun to appeal. She would not just be taking on Humphrey, but also his family and this castle. The de Bohuns made no secret that they *wanted* her. There was not a hint of *rejection* from any of them and it warmed her heart.

"Yes, Humphrey. I will be honored to marry you." She smiled at him in the fading light, and she knew he would kiss her.

His movements were slow, gentle and, to Jory, the kiss seemed a long time coming. Humphrey's lips brushed hers tentatively, softly, touching her as if he were afraid she would break. The kiss in no way offended her. In fact, she decided it was a nice kiss. Her pulses however did not begin to race. *Don't start to compare him — don't you dare compare him to that infamous swine!*

■ ■ ■ ■

The date was set for three weeks hence because, in one month's time, King Edward wanted John de Warenne to gather his army and lead it to France to wrest Gascony from King Philip's clutches.

The de Warennes bade the constable and his sons farewell. It was agreed that the de Bohuns would arrive at Hedingham the day before the wedding celebration. Jory was relieved that there had been no time for her and Humphrey to linger over their good-byes. They had shared a gentle kiss and a rather awkward embrace before he lifted her into her saddle.

Sylvia sent invitations only to those in the closest counties, since most nobles were oc-cupied readying their men-at-arms. She did however invite the king and queen; Joanna and Gilbert; her father, Roger Bigod; and the bride's godmother, Lady Marjory de Bruce.

A messenger arrived with Joanna's ac-ceptance and the following day a letter came from Queen Eleanor advising that King Edward was on his way to Flanders. The queen however accepted the invitation and would bring a few of her ladies. Sylvia was in a flutter of excitement and Jory sought escape at the stables.

She intended to saddle her horse to take a ride when she caught sight of Zephyr. Memories came flooding back to her, bringing anger with them. The little horse was a constant reminder. She went to the white palfrey's stall and gently rubbed her nose. "Beautiful Zephyr. It's not your fault but, under the circumstances, I really cannot keep you. You are a gift I cannot accept and I must return you." *I want nothing from him!*

Jory was about to summon one of Lynx's men and ask him to return the palfrey to Flamstead when she thought better of it. All the de Warenne men were busy shoeing their warhorses or mending armor, and she could not in good conscience take a man from his duties to do her bidding. She saddled Zephyr then put a bridle and leading rein on her own horse. She led them both outside and mounted Zephyr. "I shall return you myself. Flamstead is only a few miles away in the next county and it will give me a chance to ride you one last time, my beauty."

The lands she rode across in Essex belonged to the de Warennes and when she crossed into Hertfordshire some harvesters directed her to Flamstead. She knew she had arrived when she saw the horse pastures. The guard gave her no trouble entering the bailey, and she wondered if it was because she was a female, or because she arrived with two horses. Jory headed toward the stables and when she saw a groom currying a large gray, she dismounted.

"Good day, sir. I am Marjory de Warenne. Most likely you recognize this lovely palfrey that was bred here at Flamstead. She was a gift from the Earl of Warwick that I am returning." *He's staring at me like a lunatic. Does the man have no tongue in his head?* "Would you help me put my saddle on my own mount?"

"Certainly, my lady." The groom immediately did her bidding.

Two men emerged from the stables and Jory caught her breath in panic. *You bastard! I thought you were in Warwickshire!*

Guy de Beauchamp's heart lurched, and then he narrowed his eyes at the vision before him. She was more exquisitely lovely than he even remembered and her hair, like a silver-gilt cloud, caressed her shoulders. *You aging fool, don't let the little bitch wound you again.* He spoke to the steward who stood beside him. "Fetch the lady some ale, Mr. Burke — she has a taste for it."

He watched her chin lift and knew she was angry. It gave him satisfaction that she had to look up at him.

"I didn't expect you to be here. Since you are, I can return your gift in person. In the circumstances I cannot keep it."

The insult to his pride was massive. Returning the beautiful white palfrey that he had bred himself was like flinging it in his teeth, as if the animal were tainted, like him.

"I got your note that de Bohun had offered for you." The thought of her marrying another filled him with black fury, yet his face remained impassive, his voice indifferent.

Her green eyes glittered with defiance. "Humphrey de Bohun is an *honorable* young noble, unlike others of my acquaintance."

Warwick could mask his indifference no longer. "A gullible young fool you found easy to manipulate, I warrant."

"What the devil does that mean?" she challenged.

"It means you are a spoiled little courtesan — a cock-teasing little bitch. I hope he can

188

stomach a highbred noblewoman who amused herself before she wed by trying to lose her virginity to the infamous Earl of Warwick."

Jory was stunned. She also was furious at the brutal insults he hurled at her. Determined to match him in cruel barbs, she gave him a brilliant smile and swept a graceful hand to encompass their surroundings. "Flamstead is magnificent. Acquired through one of your late wives, I understand? A gullible young woman you found easy to manipulate and then rid yourself of, I warrant."

Warwick took a threatening step toward her, but Mr. Burke approached with a stirrup cup of ale.

Jory wanted to fling the contents in Warwick's dark face, but thought better of it. *I'll be damned if I'll give him the satisfaction.* She smiled her thanks at the steward, raised the cup to her lips, and drained the ale without pausing for breath. With a regality she had learned from Princess Joanna she walked over to her horse, took the reins from the groom, and mounted with fluid grace. "I bid you *adieu,* until we meet again, Frenchman."

"Haughty little bitch!" he muttered between his teeth. He spoke to the groom. "Saddle up and give the lady safe escort until she is back on de Warenne land."

■ ■ ■ ■

PART TWO:
DEVOTED WIFE

■ ■ ■ ■

CHAPTER 10

Jory stood before the altar in Hedingham's chapel arrayed in the de Warenne colors of azure and gold. She had not been able to bring herself to wear the exquisite green gown she had planned to wear when she wed Guy de Beauchamp. The flames of the tall thin tapers mesmerized her as she remembered other weddings that had gone before. She wondered if all brides felt as she did on their wedding day: uncertain, apprehensive, and poignantly vulnerable.

When she vowed before God to obey Humphrey de Bohun, to serve him, love, honor, and keep him, in sickness and in health, a wave of guilt washed over her. *I do not love Humphrey, but I promise to try.* She closed her eyes. *What about the rest of it, Jory? I have forsaken all others!* she assured herself adamantly.

Jory was distracted from her distressing thoughts when the priest asked, "Who giveth this woman to be married to this man?"

"I do." The Earl of Surrey placed her hand in Humphrey's.

Jory felt her hand tremble slightly and she wondered wildly if this was the mistake of a lifetime. By sheer dint of will, she stilled her hand and stiffened her resolve.

The reception began in the early afternoon. It was the last time the de Warenne men-at-arms and Lynx's Welsh archers could indulge themselves before they left for France. Trestle tables had been set up outside to accommodate the castle's fighting men plus the household staff.

The newlyweds stopped at every table to join in a toast and accept congratulations before going inside to the hall where their noble guests awaited them. Jory, already merry with wine, decided it was a very good way to keep a smile on her face.

Joanna said. "You are the *second*-most beautiful bride England has ever known. Even Gloucester here is half in love with you."

Gilbert grinned. "I've learned to never contradict a woman who is breeding. Promise you'll save me a dance, Lady Marjory?"

"It will be my pleasure and a great honor,

my lord earl."

Jory's godmother embraced her warmly. "My dear, I am so proud of you today. I hope you will be very happy."

"Thank you, Lady de Bruce. I hear your men are in Scotland."

"His Majesty appointed the Bruces as Governors of Carlisle as a sop. All know Bruce should have been appointed king, rather than our enemy Baliol. By pitting one against the other Edward thinks to keep them in line." Marjory Bruce winked. "The king is getting six for the price of one," she said, referring to her husband and five sons. "They went a fortnight ago and left me lumbered with the baggage train. Typical selfish male behavior. Anything that puts them within spitting distance of their Scottish lands suits them down to the bloody ground." She turned to John de Bohun. "You're all alike. You'll be off to Wales to quell uprisings and leave this lovely young bride to her own devices."

Jory glanced at Humphrey and saw that his face looked grim. "Is something wrong?" she murmured.

He quickly shook his head. "Talk of war is out of place at a wedding celebration. I don't want you filled with apprehension."

Jory squeezed his hand. "Sylvia is signaling us to take our places so she can give the order to serve the food."

The meal was a credit to Lady de Warenne. There were six courses, each with its own selection of *vin de marque.* Jory did not have much of an appetite, but she forced herself to eat a little so she would not become flown with wine. The wedding cake was decorated with swans to represent the de Bohun device and it was cut with Humphrey's sword. Finally, the tables were cleared and moved back for dancing. Jory danced every dance, first with her new husband, then with her brother and her uncle. Young Henry who was already on the road to intoxication danced with her numerous times, then moved on to Joanna. This gave Gilbert de Clare the opportunity to claim his dance with the bride.

"Are you happy, Marjory?" he murmured.

"But of course," she said quickly, then glanced into his eyes.

"He did not answer your letter," he guessed, omitting a name.

"No, he didn't offer for me." She forced a smile. "Don't worry. I shan't hold it against you that you are his friend."

He smiled back. "I have a fool for a friend."

The music and dancing, the laughter and drinking went on into the night. Jory was enjoying herself and didn't care if it went on until morning. Joanna had other ideas, of course.

"Darling, I think you should escape while you have the chance. Maud, Blanche, and Eleanor are ready to go up with you."

"Why do I need them?" Jory asked owlishly.

"Because there's to be a *bedding* — go while the going is good."

"For the love of Christ, Joanna, how could you?"

Eleanor de Leyburn took Jory's hand and urged her to run. She gathered up the voluminous folds of her wedding gown and as her steps quickened, she realized that Maud and Blanche followed.

"Joanna didn't have to suffer the indignity of a bedding!" Jory remembered that Sylvia and Lynx had been subjected to a bedding, though Jory had been forbidden to join in because she was too young. But she had attended other beddings when Court ladies had wed, so she knew more or less what to expect.

Jory ran to her own bedchamber, since this was where she and Humphrey were to spend their wedding night. Eleanor picked up her white silk night rail and robe, while Maud and Blanche began to remove the azure wedding gown edged with embroidered gold leaves. Joanna and Sylvia rushed in and firmly closed the bedchamber door. Sylvia took the robe from Eleanor, and Joanna said, "Hurry . . . I can hear them coming!"

As Jory stood nude and vulnerable, Sylvia said, "There's no time for the night rail, slip on the robe."

Joanna poured her a goblet of wine and thrust it into her hand.

Jory had taken only one gulp of wine when over the rim she saw the door fly open and half a dozen males stumble into the chamber carrying the naked bridegroom. Behind them their noble guests, at least those still able to climb stairs, crowded into the room.

Sylvia, with amazing sleight of hand, wafted the silk robe open and closed, allowing everyone a moment's glimpse of one naked arm, leg and part of her back. The ancient custom was observed to show that the bride came to her marriage bed unblemished. Jory was thankful the wine had blurred the edges of the ordeal for her.

Humphrey was tossed naked onto the bed amid shouts of drunken laughter and much lewd advice, accompanied by graphic gestures. His brother, Henry, the ringleader, began a bawdy song, and many of their guests, both male and female, joined in the chorus. Jory, clutching her robe, was pushed into bed by the women, who then crowded round to ogle the groom. Amid raucous laughter the males filled the chamber pot with wine and handed it to Humphrey. "Drink! Drink! Drink! Drink!" they chorused.

Jory, feeling helpless, glanced about the room looking for Lynx, her uncle, or any authority figure to whom she could appeal. Then she saw John de Bohun elbow the others aside.

One glimpse of his new daughter-in-law's face was all he needed to galvanize him into action. "Out! The lot of you! The little bride is a gentle-born lady, delicate as a flower!" He brought his hamlike fist down on Henry's skull, then took him by the scruff of the neck and bodily removed him from the chamber. The others slowly and with much reluctance followed.

Weak with relief, Jory sprang from the bed, took an iron key from a chest drawer, and firmly locked the door. She rested her head against its oaken panel and took some deep breaths to expel the dizziness the wine had produced. One nightmare was behind her, and she said a quick prayer that another was not before her.

Jory turned, and as she approached the bed she stared in disbelief. There lay Humphrey in all his youthful, naked splendor with the empty chamber pot balanced on his belly. The bridegroom was in a deep sleep, dead to the world.

Cautiously, she lifted the china pot and set it on the floor. Satisfied that he was not about to waken up, Jory stared curiously at Humphrey de Bohun's body. He was tall and could be described only as slim, in spite of his youthfully smooth muscles. His chest was covered with fine golden hairs and his shoulders were dotted with freckles that matched the ones on the bridge of his nose. Her gaze moved lower to the apex of his long legs. His pale cock lay limp; his sac was nestled amidst a thatch of silken hair, somewhat darker than the sun-bleached hair on his head.

Jory's eyes moved up to his face, completely relaxed in slumber. She could hardly credit how impossibly young he looked. *He's just a boy! There is absolutely nothing to be afraid of.*

Jory snuffed all the candles and slipped into bed. Even as she was wondering how she would ever be able to sleep with another person taking up half the sleeping space, she began to yawn. Morpheus claimed her the moment her lashes touched her cheeks.

When Jory awakened in the morning, she found Humphrey sitting on the side of the bed with his head in his hands. When he heard the covers rustle, he turned to face her with an abject apology.

"Marjory . . . please forgive my disgraceful behavior last night. I imbibed too much and remember naught after being carried in here."

"It is no wonder you don't remember. They made you drink a chamber pot full of wine." She smiled her understanding. "I'm sure you don't do that every night, Humphrey."

"If the throbbing pain in my head remains, I shall never drink again." He winced. "I didn't assault you, did I?"

"Of course not!" She rubbed her temple. "I too have a headache."

He glanced worriedly at the door. "What the devil will we do if they come barging in here demanding evidence of —" He flushed. "You know what I mean."

"I locked the door as soon as everyone left last night."

Humphrey sagged with relief. "Would you mind if . . . that is, would it be all right if . . . we wait until tonight?"

"I thank you with all my heart for your consideration." Jory was quite willing to take the blame for the delayed consummation of their union. "No one needs to know."

Humphrey groaned his thanks.

"Would you like to go back to sleep for a while? I'll make sure we're not disturbed."

He nodded bleakly and lay back down.

Jory slipped from the bed and went to look out the window. The purple foxgloves were already going to seed. *The flowers will be gone with the first touch of frost,* she thought sadly. *That's not the end; they'll be back next year more beautiful than ever.*

She heard a low knock, glanced over at the bed, saw that Humphrey was asleep, then ran lightly to the door. "Who is it?"

"Your breakfast, Lady de Bohun."

"Leave it outside the door please. We are not ready yet." She heard the dishes rattle as the tray was set on the floor. "In an hour's time, I would be most grateful if you would order my slipper bath and plenty of hot water. Thank you."

She waited a few minutes, then brought the tray inside and relocked the door. She set the tray in the stone recess of the window and left the silver covers over the hot food. She spooned blackberry preserves onto a fresh scone and poured herself a cup of honeyed mead that the thoughtful cook had put on the tray.

Lady de Bohun, she mused. *My name is now Marjory de Bohun.* It sounded strange; she had never anticipated such a name. *Marjory de Beauchamp, how often my thoughts whispered that name. Life is filled with surprises, twists and turns that I never dreamed of.* Gilbert de Clare's question came back to her: *Are you happy, Marjory?* She thought about it as she sipped her mead.

You shouldn't rely on another for happiness, she realized. The people surrounding you could certainly add to your joy, or to your misery, but the ultimate responsibility was yours. Jory saw clearly that marriage had placed her at a crossroads. Her common sense told her to take the path that offered hope rather than despair. *I shall choose happiness — I have quite made up my mind!*

When the servants arrived with the bath, she let them in and as they were pouring in the steaming water, Sylvia slipped into the chamber carrying clean sheets and towels. Jory knew a moment of panic. She quickly touched her finger to her lips and pointed to her sleeping husband. "The bed is still occupied. We are not done with it yet." She gave her sister-in-law a coy look. "When we are quite finished, I'll put the fresh linen on myself."

Lady de Warenne looked disappointed that she had been deprived of her chatelaine's morning-after prerogative, but she handed over the linen. "You have a newfound confidence and authority, Marjory, so I will allow you your privacy." She ushered the servants from the chamber and closed the door after her.

Jory carefully relocked the door, set the linen down, and glanced over at the still sleeping Humphrey. She quickly slipped off the white silk robe, stepped into the tub, and slid down into the deliciously hot water. She picked up the lavender-scented soap that Sylvia had made and sniffed with appreciation. *It is the little things in life that give us pleasure.* She vowed to live in the moment, without dwelling on the past or anticipating the future. *Why borrow trouble from tomorrow?*

As she bathed, she contemplated what she would wear today. She glanced over at the bed and was surprised. Humphrey was awake, his blue eyes watching her intently. She smiled tentatively.

"Forgive me, Marjory. I didn't mean to stare at you."

"Humphrey, there is no need to keep apologizing to me. If you stare at me, I won't melt into a pool of mortification. There is food over on the window ledge, if you can face it."

He looked green around the gills. "I can't, but my throat is dry as —"

An Arabian desert. Jory heard the echo of the first words she had ever heard Warwick utter, and she was horrified.

"Dust," Humphrey finished.

"There is ale and honeyed mead. Help yourself."

"I — I'm naked."

"Me too. I warrant we will have to get used to each other."

"I don't wish to offend you, Marjory."

It doesn't offend me — I've already had a good look at it. Jory couldn't bring herself to say it aloud. *He's treating me like a gently bred lady . . . like a virgin bride, which indeed I am; yet I'm no innocent babe who is shocked by the naked state.*

"I believe a robe and some of your garments were brought to the chamber yesterday." She pointed to the wardrobe and then modestly averted her eyes to give him a chance.

Humphrey sprinted from the bed, grabbed his robe, and donned it quickly. He poured himself ale and drank thirstily. "We will be expected downstairs." The idea made him look miserable.

"Lynx has organized a hunt for the men. It will fill Hedingham's larders before they leave for France. You won't be expected to join them. It will be taken for granted a bridegroom will remain with his bride on the first day of their marriage."

"You are right." The knowledge didn't lessen his misery.

"Why don't I dress and go downstairs to brave the inquisitive females. That will allow you to bathe and dress in private."

He looked so relieved, Jory had to mask her amusement. She stood up and reached for a thirsty towel. Humphrey's gaze was drawn to her as she stepped from the slipper bath, and she hoped he wouldn't start apologizing again. He followed her every movement as she selected stockings, a peach-colored underdress, and an amber surcoat decorated with golden pheasants to go over it. She sat to draw on her hose and saw that his look was devoid of lust, or even a healthy male appreciation. *He looks dismayed — daunted really.*

When she was dressed she walked to the opposite side of the bed from where he was sitting. "Help me make the bed, Humphrey. That way, no curious eyes will be able to examine our sheets."

He glanced down. "I must have spilled some wine last night."

"That's all right. I'm sure it's dry by now." *There'll be more than wine spilled on them tonight. Stop it, Jory. Your young husband would be scandalized if he could hear your thoughts.*

Humphrey's hand emerged from the pocket of his robe. "I forgot to give you my wedding gift," he said with dismay. He held out his palm to offer her a jeweled brooch.

"Oh, it's a diamond swan! Thank you. It is exquisite." She waited for him to pin it onto her gown and was relieved when he made no move to do so. She was reminded of other fingers that had pinned on another brooch. She quickly fastened it herself. "I shall wear it downstairs. The ladies will be green with envy."

Joanna and her ladies, who were amusing themselves with Tarot cards, greeted Jory.

She held up *the lovers,* a card from the major arcana. "I suppose your husband *served* you with the traditional morning-after breakfast of sausage and eggs?"

Jory gave her friend an enigmatic smile. "Do you never tire of suggestive innuendoes?"

"No, and I never shall," Joanna said, still laughing. "Since the queen and her ladies have returned to Windsor, we can behave outrageously." She turned over another card. "*The world.* How prophetic. I have the world at my feet and I'll keep it that way." Joanna turned over another card. "*Three of cups,* that refers to my child, the result of one and two. Cups mean love and joy."

She turned over the next card and her hand froze in midair. It was key thirteen, *death.* Joanna threw down the cards and pushed them toward Jory. "It's the bride's fortune we want to know."

Jory shuffled the large cards, dropping a few because her hands were small. She gathered them up and chose five. "*Two of cups,* the beginning of a new romance." Jory smiled. "So far so good. *The wheel of fortune,* that means the turn of events in one's life, from elation to despair to elation. The only constant thing in life is change. That's true for all of us," Jory added. She got a two, which was a time card; then she turned over *the devil.*

Joanna rolled her eyes. "We both know who that is. You had a miraculous escape."

Suddenly, the fun had gone out of it for Jory. She decided not to turn over the last card, so Joanna did it for her. Her face fell when once more *death* was revealed.

"It's all nonsense! I'm not even superstitious," Joanna declared, making a surreptitious sign of the cross. "Let's go into the garden. The cold winter wind will be here all too soon."

Jory was determined to speak of something joyful. "Have you picked any names for the baby yet?"

Joanna slanted a brow. "You mean other than Edward and Gilbert? At one time I rather fancied Roger, but one look at Roger Bigod ruined that for me."

"What if it's a girl?" Jory asked.

"God forbid," Joanna said irreverently. "Actually, I rather like Margaret. It's close to Marjory."

Jory smiled her secret smile. Joanna was a good friend.

The hunters were back in time for the

evening meal. Sylvia once again was in her glory, catering to her guests. Marjory and Humphrey were seated in the place of honor and when dinner was over, the newlyweds were encouraged to withdraw, amid assurances they would be left in peace tonight. With a show of gallantry, the groom took the bride's hand and led her from the hall.

When the couple entered the bedchamber, Jory turned the key in the lock. She felt little fear, yet she was apprehensive about the unknown. She and Humphrey were about to become intimate, and she knew that blood and pain were integral parts of the hymeneal rights. "May I pour you some wine, Humphrey?"

"I've sworn off the stuff, but let me get you some." He immediately filled a goblet and brought it to her.

Jory took a few sips and set it down on a bedside table. Humphrey took her left hand and brought it to his mouth. "I can hardly believe how tiny you are, Marjory." He hesitated, then blurted, "I'm so afraid of hurting you."

That's the reason he acts so formal! Jory felt relief. "I'm not the least bit fragile. I promise I won't break."

His arms went around her gently and he touched his lips to hers in a tentative kiss.

"You smell like flowers."

"It is a new rose perfume that Sylvia concocted in her stillroom. Scents can be most provocative." *That's why I've stopped using freesia.* "Would you help to unfasten me?"

"My hands are so clumsy, and the material of your lovely garments so delicate, Marjory, I'm afraid of ruining them."

She took his hands and looked at them. "They're not clumsy. They're long and shapely. You're in no danger of ruining aught. Just undo the buttons at the back and I'll manage the rest."

He did as she asked, then moved to the other side of the bed and began to remove his own clothes.

Jory was mildly surprised — she thought he would continue to undress her. She took off her tunic and then lifted off her soft underdress. She put on the white silk night rail that she had not worn last night and sat on the edge of the bed to remove her hose. Since Humphrey seemed awkward and shy, she avoided looking at him as she hung her garments in the wardrobe, then went to her dressing table, sat down, and began to brush her hair.

She was well aware that most males found her silvery-gilt hair fascinating, and tonight proved no exception as her young husband was drawn inexorably across the room to touch it.

"You have the prettiest hair I've ever seen. In the candlelight it looks like a halo . . . and you look like an angel."

She threw him a mischievous smile. "I hope you won't be disappointed, my lord husband, but I'm not angelic in the least."

Though he was wearing his robe, she saw in the mirror that he was aroused and guessed it was the result of touching her hair. She set the brush down, stood up, and went into his arms. Though he held her very gently, she could feel his hard erection against her soft flesh. He snuffed all the candles save one, took her hand, and led her to their bed. When she slipped in, he went around the other side, removed his robe, and joined her.

He began to caress her breasts through the slippery silk material of her night rail and was soon groaning with arousal. "Marjory — I'm going to have to — Marjory, please?"

"It's all right," she murmured.

He loomed above her, pulled up her gown, and lowered his body to hers. "Open for me," he urged.

Jory knew she was not ready for him, yet

she did as he bade her. When he thrust into her quickly, she gasped from the sharp pain. Humphrey didn't seem to notice as he moved in and out with a rapid rhythm. She clutched a handful of sheet and was about to ask him to move more slowly when he collapsed upon her with a long moan, and she felt wetness between her legs. She feared it was a gush of blood, but as he withdrew and rolled over she saw in the dim light that the wetness was only lightly streaked with blood.

"I'm so sorry I hurt you. I feel like such a brute. You were so small and tight — are you all right, Marjory?"

"I . . . yes, I warrant I am," she said shakily.

"Thank God!" He kissed her temple. "Good night, little bride."

Jory lay quietly, assessing exactly what had just happened. She heard Humphrey's breathing slow and was shocked at how quickly he had fallen asleep. She felt a bit sore, but that is not what disturbed her. She had not felt the least bit aroused or sensual in any way, and yet, and yet, the encounter had left her yearning, longing, desiring something — she knew not what. It was too ephemeral to put a name to the feeling. She sat up in the bed, picked up her goblet, and began to sip slowly. *Mayhap the wine will ease the craving deep within me.*

CHAPTER 11

When Jory awoke, she was alone. She slipped her robe over her stained night rail, removed the soiled bed sheets, and remade it with the clean linen Sylvia had provided. She ordered her bath, and as she lay in the fragrant water, she forced her thoughts away from last night and instead focused on what she would wear today.

Humphrey strode into the room and when he allowed the door to bang close, Jory knew he was agitated about something. He paced to the window and paid scant attention to the fact that his bride was sitting naked in her slipper bath.

"What is it, Humphrey? What has upset you?"

"Gloucester made a promise to his wife that they would remain at Hertford for a month, so de Clare has asked Father to take our men-at-arms to Wales in an effort to nip the uprising in the bud. Naturally, the constable agreed immediately."

Her husband was so upset he was cursing. She dried herself quickly, slipped on her robe, and closed the distance between them. She slid her arms around him, hoping she could assuage his anger. "If it means we must travel to Hereford immediately, don't worry about me, Humphrey. I will be ready."

He stroked her hair. "You are an angel — it's so unfair!" Suddenly he gathered her up in his arms and carried her to the bed; he fumbled with his chausses, then with feverish hands he opened her robe, lifted her nightgown, and lay between her legs.

Jory braced herself to accommodate his sexual needs. She felt him press into her, but he did not penetrate her as she expected. She held her breath as he muttered a frustrated curse and her hand came up to caress his sex. Humphrey was flaccid, his cock limp.

He rolled off her. "I can't . . . Marjory, I'm sorry."

"It's all right, Humphrey." Jory was at a loss.

"I'm not afraid!" he asserted.

Afraid of what . . . afraid to make love? Suddenly, Jory understood. *He's afraid of war!* "Of course you're not afraid. You are thinking only of me. I was so looking forward to

216

our spending time at your lovely Midhurst Castle and refurbishing it." She leaned over him and kissed him. "You are very gallant."

She went to the wardrobe and pretended that choosing a gown was important. *Perhaps it is for what I have in mind.* "What do you think — the red or the blue?"

"You look exquisite no matter what you wear, but the pale blue is very pretty, Marjory." He stood and straightened his garments.

She donned the delicate underdress and pulled on a short, midnight blue tunic, embroidered with silver moon and stars. She pulled on stockings and matching slippers, then brushed her hair and threaded a pale blue ribbon through her curls.

Downstairs, the first person they encountered was Henry. Humphrey's brother could not hide his excitement. "Did he tell you, Marjory? We're off to fight in Wales!"

"Of course he told me. We share everything."

Henry rolled his eyes. "More than once, by the time of day you finally manage to come down," he teased.

"Have you seen Lynx anywhere?" she asked.

"He's readying his men to leave tomorrow. He and Father are in the armory. Your brother gave me a chain mail chainse with flexible links. Wait till you see it, Hump. You'll die of envy."

"My godmother, Lady de Bruce, is leaving today. I must go and say my good-byes to her." Jory headed toward the solar, then made a detour outside to search out her own brother and de Bohun. She noticed that the wind had turned cold and was glad of the warmth from the braziers when she entered the armory. She paid no attention to the de Warenne men-at-arms who stared at her.

"You shouldn't be here, Minx, among all these rough men, especially in such a costly gown," Lynx admonished.

John de Bohun beamed at her. "You are such an ethereal beauty. They will think you the moon goddess descended from on high."

Lynx gave a mock groan. "Don't encourage her, Hereford. The she-devil will wrap you around her little finger."

She gave the earl a dazzling smile. "As if I could." Jory tucked her arm beneath her father-in-law's and sent Lynx a signal that she wished to be alone with de Bohun.

Brother and sister could communicate without words. "You two go ahead. I want a word with my sword smith." Lynx turned back.

"My lord earl, do you know what a honeymoon is?"

He laughed aloud. "It's so long since I had one, I've forgotten. What is a honeymoon, my dear?"

"It is a period of one month following a marriage, set aside so that the newlywed couple can establish harmony and share love."

He nodded. "Yes. It's a romantic idyll."

Jory sighed. "Mine is to be cut short because of war."

"My dear, we hope to stop the unrest before it grows into war."

"But still, if I could have a wish, it would be that Humphrey and I could go to Midhurst for our honeymoon month, and then we could hasten to Goodrich Castle in Hereford and Humphrey could then join you in Wales to help stop the insurgency."

"Well, my dear, I don't see any reason why you cannot have your wish. A bride as lovely as you should be indulged." He squeezed her hand. "Never let it be said I stood in the way of harmony and love. You shall have your romantic idyll, Lady Marjory."

"I thank you with all my heart, John." She used his first name deliberately to show that she thought of him as a man first, then a father-in-law. Jory knew she had manipulated the earl, but did not feel much guilt because she had done it on Humphrey's behalf.

She sought out her godmother and found Marjory Bruce packing her clothes. "May I ask you something personal? Was your first marriage arranged or was it a love match?"

"Arranged by King Alexander of Scotland. He wed me to the Earl of Carrick, who owned vast estates in England and Scotland."

"Did you grow to love him?" Jory asked anxiously.

Lady Bruce smiled sadly. "There was hardly time. I became a widow almost before I had a chance to become a real wife."

"Please tell me that your second marriage was a love match."

Marjory Bruce's smile turned radiant. "Yes indeed! Robert de Bruce was a wild young devil. I encountered him hunting on my estates and our attraction was immediate. Since he had no title, we knew the king would not give his consent to my marriage, for that would make Robert the new Earl of Carrick."

"You wed without the king's consent?"

"Robert kidnapped me and forced me to wed him. He swept me off my feet; I was ready to do aught he asked. He took me into hiding and when we emerged as man and wife, I told the king that I had instructed my men to abduct the Bruce. So, yes, my second marriage was definitely a love match." Lady Bruce bent close and lowered her voice. "Now that I am older and wiser I often suspect that the shrewd devil set a marriage trap for me to gain the earldom and the vast lands. Yet I don't regret a day of it."

"That's the most romantic story I've ever heard," Jory said with a sigh. "I shall miss you. Go with God, my lady."

Later that day, Gilbert de Clare and Joanna were supposed to depart for their castle at Hertford, but a courier brought a message from Windsor that the queen had been taken ill with a congestion of the chest. Since Eleanor's health had not been robust for some time, Gilbert persuaded his wife to return to Windsor until her mother recovered.

Joanna embraced Jory. "Why don't you manipulate Humphrey to stay at your castle of Midhurst for a month instead of rushing to the godforsaken Borders of Wales? Then we can travel together."

"I wouldn't dream of manipulating my husband."

Joanna's eyes sparkled. "You little hussy. You are one step ahead of me, as usual."

"Nay, I simply follow your lead," Jory assured her.

That night, when she and Humphrey retired to their bedchamber, he was elated. "Marjory, you won't believe it. Father says it wouldn't be right to deprive a bride of her honeymoon. We are to have a month at our castle of Midhurst before we go to Hereford."

"I am indeed fortunate to have wed into such a kind and thoughtful family. I am proud to be a de Bohun."

Humphrey had no trouble becoming aroused, yet as Jory tried to prolong the preliminaries, hoping to kindle her own desire, she almost ruined things. Her husband became so excited when they fondled each other that he barely had time to glove himself in her tight sheath before he spent. He groaned with frustration.

"It was almost over before I began. Next time you mustn't tease me, Marjory. I want to stay inside you longer."

When her husband slept, Jory lay staring

into the darkness. She knew the feeling she was experiencing was akin to hunger.

The next day the de Bohuns and their men-at-arms departed, and two hours later the de Warennes were ready to leave for the coast, where ships would take them across the Channel.

Jory was determined that her farewell with her brother and uncle would not be a tearful one. Though she was terrified at their going to fight a war in France, she was resolved not to show her fear. She snuggled into her fur cloak. "Good-bye, Lynx. I hope Gascony will be warmer than England when you arrive."

Lynx enfolded her in his arms. "Take care of yourself, Minx."

She kissed John de Warenne's cheek. "I know the king chose the right man to win back his English possessions. I am confident the de Warennes will emerge victorious and win many honors."

During the next two days Jory directed the packing of her and Humphrey's personal things as well as the many wedding gifts they had received for their household of Midhurst. The master bedchamber was to be refurbished with the couple's new bed and bedcurtains and the walls hung with

Jory's own tapestries.

Finally, the beautiful linens she had received from Sylvia were lovingly packed and sent downstairs to be loaded on the wagons. Jory descended the stairs and, for the last time, she looked about Hedingham, fighting the tears that suddenly threatened.

Don't be a coward, Jory. Face your future with courage!

She and Sylvia went outside to the courtyard, where Humphrey was waiting to help her into the saddle. A messenger bearing Gloucester livery rode up and handed Humphrey de Bohun a letter. "It's addressed to you, Marjory. It's from Joanna."

Jory smiled. "She's probably wishing us bon voyage." She opened it and scanned the note. Her smile faded and she raised sad, incredulous eyes to Humphrey. "Queen Eleanor is dead!"

The nobles who were still in England gathered at Windsor for Queen Eleanor's funeral. Humphrey escorted his bride to the Royal Castle, where Jory immediately sought out Princess Joanna.

"You must be in shock. How are you holding up?"

Joanna allowed Jory to take her hands. "I'm so glad you came. Gilbert has been like a rock for me. With Father away fighting in France, I didn't know what to do."

"Do you feel well? Is the baby all right?" Jory asked.

Joanna nodded. "My husband has made me rest each day. Mother's ladies-in-waiting have done all that needs to be done."

"We brought my sister-in-law with us. Sylvia is devastated. Lynx had already left for France when we received your letter. I don't know how she will cope without him."

"Her father arrived at Windsor this morning."

"I'm glad Sylvia will have her father's strong arm to support her. Your brother must be desolate over the death of his mother, especially with his father being absent."

Joanna's dark eyes glittered. "Edward's been drunk ever since he arrived. De Clare tore a strip off him last night for his inappropriate behavior, yet in truth the queen was not an overly devoted mother to any of her children. The king was her sun and her moon, the center of her universe."

"She was married to Edward for almost fifty years, since she was a child of ten. The queen's devotion is understandable."

Joanna bent close so that only Jory would hear her words. "And yet I am willing to wager that the King of England will not tear himself from his war with France long enough to bury her."

Jory was shocked at her friend's cynical words, yet she realized Joanna likely spoke the truth. "You and Prince Edward will represent His Majesty at Queen Eleanor's funeral tomorrow."

"With my sallow skin, I look haggard in black, while the mourning color will flatter you beyond reason."

Jory shuddered. She could not deny that black made her look ethereal. "I beg you go and lie down. Tomorrow will be a long, emotionally exhausting day. I'll go see how Sylvia is faring."

Sylvia de Warenne was ghastly pale and her eyes were red from weeping. She patted the hand of Alicia Bolton in an effort to console the distraught lady-in-waiting.

"There, there, my dear. It is difficult for all of us."

"Lady de Warenne, I nursed the queen night and day and followed the directions of her physician implicitly. When her cough worsened, I applied mustard clysters to ease her suffering."

"None could have served Queen Eleanor more devotedly than you, Alicia. Take consolation in knowing you did all that you could."

"Whatever will become of me, my lady?" Alicia moaned. "Lady Catherine Percy and the queen's other ladies-in-waiting have great families to return to. I was a ward of Eleanor's because I have no family. I know not what will become of me."

"Surely a young woman as attractive as you has marriage prospects, Alicia?"

"Alas, without dowry I stand little chance of marrying well. My only hope will be to find a position of lady-in-waiting in a noble household . . . like yours, Lady de Warenne."

"After serving Her Royal Majesty here at Windsor, surely it would be a step down to become one of my ladies?"

"It would be an honor to serve you and become part of the de Warenne household at Hedingham Castle. Someday you will be the noble Countess of Surrey."

"Then consider it settled, Alicia. We will help each other get through this tragic time."

"Thank you for your gracious generosity, Lady de Warenne." Alice Bolton, who had renamed herself Alicia, lowered her lashes lest Sylvia see the triumph in her calculating eyes.

A knock on the door prompted Alice to

say, "Allow me to get that. If you're not up to seeing anyone, I'll make your excuses." Alice opened the door and was surprised to find the newly wed Marjory de Bohun on the threshold.

Jory stepped into the chamber and spoke to both women. "You have my heartfelt condolences. It is especially sad for you devoted ladies who were in the queen's service." She spoke to Alicia. "Please convey to the ladies-in-waiting that Princess Joanna is most grateful for all you have done for her mother."

Alicia dabbed her eyes with her handkerchief and departed.

Jory hurried to Sylvia's side and slipped her arm about her. "I am so sorry that Lynx cannot be with you."

"Men are little comfort when it comes to sickness and death. I remember when my own mother fell ill, how distant and short-tempered my father became. Women must rely upon each other for succor and solace at times like these."

"It's such a shock. The queen seemed well at my wedding."

"Actually, she began to cough that day we sailed on the royal barge before Princess Joanna's wedding. We all assumed she would recover from such a minor ailment, but her contagion must have gradually worsened. Eleanor forbade any from telling King Edward that she was poorly for fear he would not leave for France."

"Little danger of that," Jory remarked.

"You are very cynical for a young lady of eighteen."

"I'm sorry, Sylvia." *I'll soon be nineteen, but under the circumstances it will be inappropriate to celebrate a birthday.*

"Poor Alicia Bolton is racked with worry over what will become of her. Since she will lose her position here at Windsor and has no family to speak of, I have asked her to become one of my ladies and will take her back to Hedingham."

Joanna dislikes Alice Bolton intensely, but I'd best keep my tongue between my teeth before I say something cynical again. "That is most kind of you, Sylvia. Is there anything you need before the funeral tomorrow?"

"Take this money to the chapel to pay for candles for Eleanor from the de Warenne family. Westminster Abbey will be ablaze with wax tapers tomorrow, but Windsor's chapel must have them also."

"That's a lovely idea, Sylvia. I also will give money from the de Bohun family and ask that the candles be scented. Then I shall check on Joanna to make sure she is resting today."

"I envy her the child she carries. She is obviously a woman who conceives easily, as her royal mother always did."

Jory bit her lip. "Your time will come, Sylvia. Don't despair."

When Jory returned to Joanna's royal apartment, she found Gilbert busy at the writing table. "I hope I find you well, my lord. I've just come from Windsor's chapel. It seems all the flowers in England are withered; none can be found for Eleanor."

"I've sent to the Isle of Wight for whatever flowers can be found. They won't arrive until the last minute, I fear. Joanna's resting, but I know she will benefit from talking with you."

"Thank you." Jory opened Joanna's bedchamber door and sat down on the end of her bed. "Your husband has sent for flowers all the way to the Isle of Wight. He is very thoughtful."

"Gloucester has arranged the entire funeral. He said the king would expect no less of him. He has taken care of everything." Joanna sat up. "Do you remember when I did the Tarot? I got the *death* card, but I never dreamed it portended my mother's death."

"I too drew the *death* card in my layout. I hope there won't be another, though 'tis an old superstition that death comes in three. I pray that none die in battle." *Please, God, keep Lynx safe.*

Joanna shuddered. "Pull the curtains back and let some light in here. The darkness makes me feel morbid."

Jory went to the tall windows and drew back the drapes. "Oh, it has started to snow. How pretty it makes everything look."

"Good, I shall be able to wear my new black and white ermine cloak tomorrow. Be a darling and ask Maud Clifford to unpack it for me. Gilbert had it made for me to keep me warm when we journey to Gloucester. I am glad we will be close to each other. Gloucester and Goodrich castles are only fifteen miles apart."

I hope we can spend a little time at our own Castle of Midhurst before we go. Humphrey dreads going to Goodrich because he fears fighting in Wales. Still, we must go sometime. "Get some rest. Our rooms are in the Lower Ward; send word if you need me, Joanna."

Jory pulled up the hood of her cloak as she stepped out into the snow. She walked quickly from the Upper Ward, and as she entered the Middle Ward, she heard loud laughter and shouting as if pandemonium reigned. A gang of unruly youths was having a snowball fight, and when Jory peered through the veil of snowflakes she was shocked to see that Prince Edward was the ringleader. *What an unseemly display when his mother has just died. Edward is no longer a child. He should know better!*

Jory felt disgust rise up in her. He had six youthful attendants with him, all sons of noble families. Only one stood aloof, not joining in the roughhouse play. He was extremely dark, with a proud look about him, and suddenly Jory guessed who the youth must be. *I warrant that is Guy de Beauchamp's son, Rickard!*

Jory stood staring for long minutes. Then she skirted the Round Tower, keeping as far away from the elegantly garbed louts as she could. A commanding roar split the air. The youths stopped dead as if turned to stone. Jory gasped as she saw Warwick stride across the Middle Ward. She pulled her hood close and stepped beneath the sheltered portico of the Norman Gateway so that he would not see her. Her heart pounded in her ears.

She watched wide-eyed as, without preamble, Warwick closed the distance between himself and young Edward Plantagenet. He raised a powerful arm and smote the Royal Prince across the head. Warwick paid no heed when the youth fell to his knees from the blow. The earl then strode up to his own son and dealt out an identical punishment. Jory doubted any other noble would have dared to lay hands on the king's son. *That's why he's infamous!*

She stayed where she was until the Middle Ward emptied; then, on shaky legs, she made her way to the Lower Ward, where the de Bohun couple had been given accommodation.

CHAPTER 12

On the day of Queen Eleanor's funeral, the snow stopped, the sun shone brilliantly, and the temperature plummeted. The cortege from Windsor to London's Westminster Abbey plodded with a slow gait along streets filled with mourners. The men attending rode black, plumed horses and were led by Thomas of Lancaster, even though he was furious that the king had not made him regent in his absence. The less hardy mourners huddled in closed carriages.

The queen's flowers had arrived from the Isle of Wight at dawn and were taken directly to the Abbey. The Earl of Gloucester directed all the proceedings, and his wife, Joanna, sat with her brother, Prince Edward, in the front pew reserved for royalty.

Marjory and Humphrey sat with Sylvia and her father, Roger Bigod, Marshal of England. Archbishop Winchelsey began intoning the Burial of the Dead: "I am the resurrection and the life . . ."

Jory kept her eyes lowered, lest she find herself looking into the purple-black orbs of Warwick. She tried to think reverent thoughts, but each time she caught sight of the candle flames, her mind took flight, reliving Joanna's and her own arranged weddings. Though she tried valiantly to dispel the feeling of Warwick's powerful presence, she failed miserably. *I must not linger at Windsor or a meeting between us will be inevitable.* She whispered to Humphrey, "Can we return to our castle of Midhurst tomorrow?"

Guy de Beauchamp's attention also wandered during the service. He did not notice the small female until she removed the black fur hood from her silver-gilt hair. Then his attention became riveted. The candlelight of the Abbey seemed to form a halo about Jory's head that held him in thrall. *She is no bloody angel,* Warwick reminded himself. He glanced at the tall young man beside her and silently cursed Humphrey de Bohun to hellfire.

His mouth set in a grim line. *It's your own goddamned fault, Warwick. You gave her dire warning about becoming your wife.* He remembered his exact words: *Whether it be yes or no, I will honor your resolve. What horseshit! The minute Surrey refused your offer, you should have abducted her and carried her off.*

Everyone's attention was drawn back to Eleanor as the queen was interred in a crypt in the Abbey. Soon a bronze sculpture would be cast in her likeness to rest upon her tomb so that future generations could visit and pray for her soul.

After the burial service, Jory followed Joanna from the Abbey.

"We finally had word from Father in Flanders. He is grief-stricken at Mother's passing and has ordered stone crosses be erected between Lincoln and London at places Mother loved best."

"Will you and Gloucester stay here to oversee the work?"

"De Clare has asked Thomas of Lancaster to take on the task. The uprising in Wales is spreading and Gilbert feels he must return to Gloucester before the winter weather worsens."

Jory glanced at Humphrey and saw the blood leave his face at mention of more trouble in Wales. Sylvia de Warenne and her father joined them outside the Abbey. Jory's sister-in-law began to cough and held her handkerchief to her mouth. "Sylvia, you mustn't stand here in this bitter cold. Let us hurry back to Windsor. I'll come and see how you are feeling later."

Princess Joanna moved away from Lady de Warenne and pulled her ermine cape closer about her. "It seems that everyone has a cough. Did you hear all the people hacking inside the Abbey?"

In their carriage on the return to Windsor, Jory watched Humphrey with worried eyes. "I'll pack tonight. I want us to have a week at Midhurst before we make the journey to Hereford."

Jory's plans to travel to Midhurst were thwarted by Sylvia's illness. "Humphrey, I am afraid my sister-in-law has caught a contagion. I told her she should be abed, but she insists she will be better in her own bed at Hedingham Castle. Would you mind if we accompanied her? I'd like to see her safely home, and the sooner the better. I feel I owe it to Lynx."

Humphrey, glad of anything that delayed their journey to the Borders of Wales, capitulated. "Of course I don't mind, Marjory."

"Everything is packed. We'll leave at first light."

Jory felt slightly dismayed as Humphrey's eyes watched her hungrily as she undressed for bed. She was far from desiring a sexual encounter tonight, but hoped and prayed that wasn't because she had seen Warwick again. She pushed the disturbing thought from her mind and slipped into bed.

Humphrey quickly slid his arms about her and she forced herself to respond to him, masking her lack of desire. She was surprised at his enthusiasm after the solemnity of the past days, but was at least glad that for once he did not treat her as if she were too fragile to touch. Vague feelings of pleasure began in the pit of her stomach when he held her breasts, but before the pleasure could intensify, Humphrey spent and rolled onto his back.

"You excite me so much, Marjory. I wish I could draw it out to last longer, but the minute I touch you, I want to explode."

Jory curled onto her side, feeling conflicted. She didn't know if she wanted their lovemaking to be longer or shorter. She was acutely aware that their encounters left her dissatisfied. *It isn't really lovemaking . . . It's just a release for Humphrey.* She sighed, trying to ignore the deep ache within.

Jory did not fall asleep until long after her husband. Scenes from Westminster Abbey floated through her mind as her eyes finally closed and she began to dream.

She was back in Westminster Abbey, but this time it was not for a funeral, but a wedding. She was garbed in her white silk night rail and inside she was bubbling with excitement. As she floated up the long aisle of the Abbey, she could see Guy de Beauchamp standing at the altar, waiting for her to reach his side. It seemed to take forever, but finally she arrived and gave him a radiant smile. His black eyes devoured her and he took her small hand and squeezed it. She closed her eyes as she felt Warwick's great power flood into her and she heard the words: "I now pronounce you man and wife." Jory opened her eyes and to her great dismay, Warwick had vanished and Humphrey de Bohun had taken his place. "Noooooooo!" she cried.

Humphrey took her by the shoulders. "Marjory, what is amiss?"

She blinked into the darkness. "A nightmare," she said softly.

Once Jory de Bohun and her husband escorted Sylvia de Warenne to Hedingham, another nightmare began to unfold.

"She has coughed the entire thirty miles," Sylvia's tiring woman declared as Jory helped her sister-in-law from her carriage.

"She must go straight to bed. I believe she has a fever."

Alicia Bolton, who had ridden in the de Bohun carriage, approached Jory. "I'll get someone to unload all the baggage while you concentrate on making Lady de Warenne comfortable."

"Thank you, Alicia, but you can leave all that in the capable hands of my husband. As soon as we get Sylvia settled, I'll ask the housekeeper to find you a comfortable chamber in the castle."

Jory helped Sylvia undress and then she tucked her into bed. One maid ran for drinking water, while another brought a bowl of scented water to bathe Sylvia's hands and flushed face. "We will have you better in no time." Jory masked the worry she felt. "I shall ask the steward to brew you a syrup. When I was a child he made an elixir of horehound and liquorice that tasted wonderful and cured me of chest inflammation." Jory knew Lynx had taken his physician to France to tend battle wounds, so they would have to rely on the apothecary skills of Hedingham's steward.

Jory gathered the household servants. "Lady de Warenne has developed inflammation of the chest and she is fevered. With good nursing and medicine we'll soon have her on her way to recovery."

A sennight passed slowly, but Sylvia showed no signs of recovery. Jory had a trundle bed set up in Sylvia's chamber so that she could be with her through the nights, in spite of Humphrey's objections that his wife was exposing herself to the contagion. Sylvia's eyes were now swollen closed and her breathing was so labored and shallow that Jory had begun to fear the unthinkable. She remembered the death card when she had done the Tarot cards and began to feel hopeless.

An hour later, Sylvia de Warenne took her last excruciating breath and her tiring woman burst into sobs. Finally, she said to Jory, "There is nothing more we can do for her, Lady Marjory."

Jory turned glassy green eyes on the woman. "She's sleeping. She will be fine."

Half an hour later, Humphrey came into the chamber and lifted his wife into his arms. "Sylvia has passed. You need to rest."

"Put me down! I cannot leave her! Sylvia must not die! She is the mother of Lynx's future children!"

The letter that Jory wrote to her brother was the most difficult thing she had ever done. She told him about Queen Eleanor's sudden death and explained that Sylvia had caught the contagion while attending the queen's funeral.

My heart is torn asunder, she wrote, and her teardrops stained the parchment of the letter. Jory did not dwell on Sylvia's illness and suffering, but focused instead on the beautiful spot she had chosen at Hedingham where Lynx's wife was laid to rest.

Sylvia's father, stoic and truculent as ever, bemoaned the fact that he would never have a grandson. He stayed until after his daughter's will was read by the castle steward. She left everything to her husband, Lynx, with the exception of her jewels. These she left to her firstborn, but in the event she died childless, they were to go to Marjory, since the de Warenne emeralds and diamonds had come to her upon her marriage.

Today is my birthday, Jory realized. *It is as though Sylvia is giving me a birthday gift.* She felt agonized with guilt, especially when she told Alicia Bolton of the bequest.

"Those jewels should go to Lynx de Warenne's wife when he remarries."

"Remarries?" Jory was deeply shocked at her words.

"Your brother is a widower now," Alicia remarked.

Jory froze. "You bitch! Are you licking your lips over him, Alice? D'ye dare fancy yourself the future Countess of Surrey?"

"Such remarks are unseemly and unfounded, Lady Marjory."

"Forgive me my trespasses and I will try to forgive you yours." Jory sought her husband and found him in the stables.

Humphrey put a proprietary arm about her shoulders. "There is little more we can do here. Let's go to Midhurst."

"How can I do that? I want to be here when Lynx returns. He will need me to comfort him in his devastating loss."

"Lynx de Warenne won't return from France until Gascony is irrefutably in English hands. The death of a wife cannot be placed before duty to King and Crown."

"Damn the King and Crown, and to lowest hell with all wars!"

Humphrey sighed. "I agree. War will be the death of us all."

Jory's eyes flooded with tears. "Please don't say that."

He wiped a tear from her cheek. "Let's go home. When Lynx returns from France, you may come back and visit with him."

Jory packed their belongings. She unlocked the jewel casket and looked at the precious emeralds. "I never saw you wear these gems, Sylvia. Why did you keep them locked away? For some special occasion that never arrived?" In that moment, Jory resolved to wear them often. *Jewels are meant to be displayed, and display them I shall. I have quite made up my mind!*

After dark that same night a courier arrived from Gilbert de Clare. The rider was cold and mud-stained as he gave the message to de Bohun. Humphrey opened the letter and read:

The Welsh uprising is greater than anticipated and I am preparing to leave immediately for Gloucester. If we are to travel together, as arranged between our wives, there can be no delay. I await your reply.

Gilbert de Clare

Jory saw the color leave his face and his freckles stood out sharply on his pale skin. She took the paper and read it.

"Joanna told me of the trouble in Wales and suggested we travel together. Our plans changed when Sylvia took poorly and I didn't want to upset you further. What will you do?"

"I have no choice, Marjory. Gloucester is not only England's most powerful earl, he is now the king's son-in-law. We will journey to Gloucester together and then go on to Hereford. I am sorry. Your honeymoon was marred by two deaths and now you are to be deprived of your stay at our Castle of Midhurst."

"Don't worry about me, Humphrey. All is packed and ready."

That night when they retired, Humphrey was eager for a sexual encounter. Try as he might, he could not maintain an erection. Frustration roiled his temper and he flung from the bed and sought to drown his sorrows with whiskey. Finally, he slept deeply.

Jory lay awake. She realized that her husband's behavior fell into a pattern. Fear aroused his need to couple, but it also made him impotent. She herself was in mourning and had neither desire nor inclination for bed sport. *I warrant we are a sorry pair.*

The huge party that traveled west numbered almost one hundred, since Gilbert de Clare was taking his fighting men from Clerkenwell and his castle of Hertford. Jory shared Joanna's coach. "As soon as we arrive, our men will go into Wales."

"Men are always away somewhere fighting their wars and there is nothing we can say or do to stop them. My father is a warrior, as is my husband, and though both are advanced in years, they will remain warriors until they draw their last breath."

Jory thought of Humphrey. "Not all men enjoy fighting."

"My brother hates martial arts. He is expected to follow in Father's footsteps, but he will never make a military leader."

"Perhaps when Edward becomes king, there will be no more wars."

Joanna began to laugh. She placed her hands on her belly in a protective gesture. "Not only will my princely brother make a lousy warrior, he will make a piss-poor king. The thought fills me with mirth. Some males are not man enough to fight battles."

"I like your husband, Gilbert, very much." Jory bent close so she could speak confidentially. "Does he ever have trouble . . . does he ever have difficulties . . . in bed?"

"It happened only once, the night of my mother's funeral. Actually, he's a far better lover than any young noble I've lain with, so save your pity."

Not for the first time Jory wondered if Joanna had lain with Humphrey. And if she had, was it not possible that he was the father of the child she was carrying? *Don't go down that path,* her inner voice warned. *That way lies anguish and misery.*

Jory shivered in spite of her fur-lined cloak and the wolfskin throws. "Tomorrow I intend to ride to keep myself warm."

"The least you can do is get Blanche, Maud, and Eleanor to take your place. Their collective body heat will help warm me."

The following day, Jory was transformed from a shivering, pale wraith into a laughing nymph with pink cheeks and windblown hair. Though the winter solstice was upon them, the Cotswold Hills were beautiful, dotted with herds of sheep and bubbling streams not yet frozen. When the River Severn came into view the travelers heaved a collective sigh of relief because Gloucester lay on its banks.

Joanna toured the castle with Jory at her side. She marveled at its size and the vast number of de Clare fighting men. She stood warming herself at a massive slate fireplace that rose up to touch the beams. "This is quite an eye-opener. I imagined it to be the back of beyond, but I believe I'll be quite happy here."

"It is a kingdom of its own and Gilbert its ruler."

"You are right, Jory, and I shall be *queen of the castle!"*

Humphrey and Marjory were given a spacious chamber with a curtained bed to stave off the drafts. He removed his hauberk, rubbed the back of his neck, and groaned. "The damn thing has goaded me all day. My muscles are sore down my entire left side."

"Let me help you, Humphrey. Lie down on the bed and I will rub it for you." Jory took a flacon of perfumed oil and warmed it over the brazier while her husband stripped off his clothes.

Jory came to the bed and removed her velvet surcoat. Wearing only her fine underdress, she climbed onto the bed and poured the warm oil into her palm. Starting at Humphrey's neck, she drew her hands down across his muscles with long, slow strokes.

"Christus, that feels so good, Marjory. Your hands are magic."

Pleased that she was able to help, Jory massaged the knotted muscles in his neck and back until he groaned with pleasure. Her touch aroused him and his cock stood up like a ramrod. Suddenly, he arched his back and ejaculated like a fountain.

He laughed, slightly shame-faced. "Your

touch always has that effect on me. It makes me lose control."

Jory had no idea if he was complimenting her or blaming her. She moved away from the bed and sat down to brush her hair. She knew she had very little carnal knowledge and limited experience with men. She had only ever been alone with Humphrey, other than her encounters with Guy de Beauchamp.

Always when she thought of Warwick, she quickly pushed that thought away. Tonight she did not. Tonight she explored the feelings he had provoked in her. She remembered how hearing his name quickened her heartbeat. Just a glimpse of his dark face excited her. His slightest touch physically aroused her, compelling her to respond to him eagerly, wantonly.

Guy, what made you reject me? Why did you change your mind about offering for me? The answer was clear: *I was not woman enough for you, and you thought me too young to be a mother to your son.* Jory lifted her chin in defiance. *I will learn to be a woman in every way and vow to be the best mother who ever lived.*

She picked up the scented oil and moved toward the bed. "Humphrey, would you like to return the favor and massage away my aches? I warrant my bottom would benefit from a good rub."

Jory removed her underdress and lay facedown on the bed.

Humphrey poured oil into his palms and gingerly rubbed his wife's back. Her skin seemed so delicate, he was afraid of marring it. When he touched her buttocks, he felt his cock stir and hoped he would become aroused again. When he couldn't achieve another erection, he cursed under his breath in frustration.

When Jory felt warm hands caressing her buttocks she thought of Guy de Beauchamp and a frisson of desire rippled up her spine. Then she heard Humphrey's murmured curse as he moved away. She wished she hadn't asked her husband to perform the intimate favor, for now she was left once again with a yearning for fulfillment.

"I can hardly credit it, but Gloucester's army is ready to march tomorrow," Humphrey told his wife. "His second in command, Ralph Monthermer, keeps the fighting men of Gloucester ready for battle at all times. They will ride with us to Goodrich Castle; then I will cross into Wales alongside them to join my father."

That will be much safer for you, I hope. Jory had more good sense than to voice her apprehension for her husband's safety. "Will Gilbert leave a force here to guard Princess Joanna?"

"Aye, his troops number in the thousands. He has a standing guard of de Clares to protect his castle."

"Do the de Bohuns have a standing guard at Goodrich Castle?"

"We do, Marjory. Have no fear; it is a secure fortalice."

She searched his face and saw how vulnerable he looked. He also looked impossibly young to be heading into battle. *I wish with all my heart that I could take away your fear, Humphrey.*

The following day when Goodrich Castle came into view Jory could not believe her eyes. It was massive and ancient, with a twin-towered gatehouse. As well, it had three imposing round towers with spur buttresses. It was protected by a thick curtain wall and a rock-cut moat filled with water from the River Wye.

Humphrey had grown progressively more silent as they approached Goodrich, and Jory took pains to include him in their conversation. "I didn't realize the castle was built on the River Wye."

It was Gilbert who replied. "The Wye is the ancient dividing line between England and Wales."

Jory glanced at her husband and saw his mouth tighten at the mention of Wales. "The vista of mountains fills me with awe, as does this ancient fortalice. When was it built, Humphrey?"

"In the eleventh century," he said shortly.

"The Normans are such magnificent builders. It has stood for two centuries and will likely be here for many more," she said.

The skin around Gilbert's eyes crinkled in a smile. "It will be here long after we are gone, I warrant."

Oh dear, another reminder for Humphrey of his mortality.

They clattered across the drawbridge and into the open bailey, and the hooves of the mounted men who followed them made such a thunderous noise that conversation was no longer possible.

De Clare and Monthermer had their hands full billeting their scores of fighting men for the night, but Humphrey assisted his wife from the saddle and took her inside the fortalice to introduce her to the servants and castellans.

When they had all gathered in the ancient

Great Hall, Humphrey took her hand. "It is a great honor for me to present my bride, Lady Marjory. This castle has not had a chatelaine for many years, and I hope you will make her welcome and grow to love her as the de Bohuns do. Tomorrow, I go to join my father in Wales, so it will be up to you to make her feel at home and watch over her."

The steward, David Bridgen, came forward and made his bow. He carried a great ring of iron keys that he offered up to her.

Jory smiled. "I would appreciate it if you would keep them for me, Master Bridgen."

"I would be honored, my lady."

He had a lilting Welsh accent and Jory took a closer look at the dark servants who were assembled and realized a large number were probably from Wales. He presented the only two female servants, Morganna and Rowena, who were dark as Gypsies. They stared at Jory's silver-gilt hair before they made their curtsies.

"I shall have your baggage brought up to your tower, my lord."

Humphrey took Jory's hand and led her toward the tower that he and his brother occupied. "Don't mind them staring at you. They likely imagine you've just stepped down from a cloud."

"I've only just realized a lot of the people

here are Welsh."

"They are hard workers and loyal too. A great many of the de Bohun fighting men are also Welsh. They are amazing archers."

Jory gazed about her. "Well, they certainly keep everything clean and well polished. All the fires are lit and the bed linen is spotless." She refrained from criticizing the threadbare furnishings. "Did your father mean what he said about hoping I would refurbish the castle and that money was no object?"

"I know it's asking a lot of you, Marjory, but it will be deeply appreciated if you make the place inviting and comfortable. Spare no expense; the de Bohun coffers overflow, I assure you."

"Then it will be my pleasure. Acquiring beautiful things is one of the tasks that make a lady happy."

Humphrey's face settled in grim, determined lines. "You'll have to excuse me, Marjory. I have to see that the men I am taking with me on the morrow are prepared. My father will also expect a fresh supply of mounts and plenty of fodder."

"Oh, please don't worry about me, Humphrey. I know you must have a score of things to do before darkness falls."

When the steward and his helpers brought

up the baggage, Jory realized there were no wardrobes; the de Bohun men kept their garments in trunks. Also, there was no bathing tub anywhere in the tower. Master Bridgen informed her that the stone bathhouse in the bailey was no fit place for a lady. She accepted the bowl and jug of water with a gracious smile.

When darkness fell, the steward brought her dinner on a tray, explaining that Lord Humphrey and the Earl of Gloucester would eat with their men in the great hall tonight. David, as Master Bridgen asked her to call him, brought her a flagon of honeyed mead and a jewel-encrusted goblet of Welsh gold. She had plenty of time to sip it and reflect before the fire; then she undressed and got into bed. Humphrey did not join her for three hours.

He set a stone jug of whiskey on the mantel and then without a word he removed his clothes and climbed into bed. When he reached for her, Jory went into his arms willingly. She knew it would be their last night together for some time. He was eager to mount her and couple, but after a number of frustrating, futile attempts, he flung himself from the bed and reached for the whiskey.

"Humphrey, don't!" Jory cried.

He stared at her with cold blue eyes that were icy with fear.

"Whiskey won't help." She held out her arms. "Come to me."

His legs seemed to move of their own accord, drawn back to the bed by the intangible feminine allure she possessed in abundance.

He climbed in beside her and she enfolded him in her arms and held him tightly. "You need warmth and comfort. Let me help you, Humphrey. Together we will banish the darklings."

He clung to her like a man drowning and buried his face in her perfumed hair. "You have no notion what it is like."

"I do!" she insisted, conjuring up Warwick's words. "War is bloody, brutal; the enemy is vicious. It is not cowardice to fear it. You go to your duty in spite of your misgivings and to me that is courageous beyond measure."

She stroked his back and nuzzled her lips against his throat offering him strengthening words and holding him secure in warm, loving arms. Jory had no idea what war was like, but she knew exactly what it was to feel vulnerable. Being held was a sure antidote. She wanted his fear to melt away like snow in summer.

Humphrey's grip on her was so tight, she had difficulty taking a deep breath, but gradually his arms slackened, and finally he drifted into blessed, peaceful sleep.

Jory smiled into the darkness. She did not ache tonight. By fulfilling her husband's needs, she herself was fulfilled.

CHAPTER 13

When Jory awoke she found herself alone. "Humphrey?" When there was no answer, she left the bed and ran to the window. The bailey was empty except for castle servants. It took a few moments for her to realize that her husband and Gilbert de Clare must have taken their fighting men into Wales at first light.

I'm alone in an unknown world was Jory's first vulnerable thought. Her second thought was braver: *Better get used to it.* She poured cold water from the jug and washed herself. Then she opened one of her trunks and, knowing that beautiful clothes gave her confidence, chose a warm velvet dress in vivid rose.

She met the steward at the bottom of the tower steps. "Good morning, David. I shall eat breakfast in the Great Hall," she said decisively, "and then you can show me around."

The stone walls bristled with weapons and armaments of every ilk presenting an intimidating display to the faint-hearted. She decided to keep everything as it was with the addition of banners and de Bohun coats of arms. When the steward brought her food, she asked, "David, do we have any artisans in the household?" When he said there were many, Jory told him her plan. She decided that the de Bohun arms, the great winged swan, should be painted on a huge wooden shield and that its supporters would be a lion for England and a dragon for Wales.

"Draig." David nodded and looked pleased.

"Draig means dragon?" Jory laughed with delight. "I've learned my first Welsh word!"

When she finished her breakfast, she toured the vast kitchens, where all the cooks were Welsh. "Make a list of all the utensils they need to make their jobs easier. I myself need a bathing tub. David, where can I buy all the furnishings this castle needs?"

"Merchant ships sail into the Bristol Channel and up the River Severn. They carry goods from many parts of the world, my lady."

"Oh, that's wonderful. I'm receiving an

education — apparently civilization does not start and stop with London."

"Gloucester is a thriving town, as is our own Hereford. They supply most of our needs."

"I thought the de Bohun castle was in Hereford. I didn't realize Goodrich was a dozen miles from the town."

"Goodrich is often referred to as Hereford Castle. It can be confusing to an outsider."

"I want to be an *insider!* Why is the castle called Goodrich?"

The steward's eyes twinkled. "For centuries the Welsh marcher barons have held more power than any other lords in England. The three most powerful families are Mortimer, de Clare, and de Bohun, who've been allowed to keep any land they conquered in Wales. The earl owns everything between here and Brecon. Power means wealth, my lady — hence *Goodrich Castle*."

"I see." *So I really can spend money without feeling guilt.* "Being Welsh, do you not resent these Norman English conquerors?"

"What does resentment profit us? Far more expedient to freely give our allegiance to one of the most powerful and wealthy

English barons than to be beaten into submission."

Jory was aghast. "That's terrible —"

"It was decided ages ago, not by me and the present de Bohuns. Prince Edward Plantagenet, long before he was king, spent his youth conquering Wales. Trouble is, it won't stay conquered. Beyond Brecon and the mountains there are wild men who would rather fight and die than join civilization."

What he said dredged up words that Gloucester and Warwick had exchanged: *"We invade France or Wales out of political ambition or revenge, then try to plant our seeds of law and government in some very harsh soil. Cultures can be changed, but it takes years, not months. Look at Wales — how many years?"* Warwick had replied, *"Most of my life."* Jory shuddered. She prayed the fighting would not last most of Humphrey's life.

Two days later Jory, accompanied by her steward, David Bridgen, purchased carpets, wardrobes, high-backed padded settles, quarion stands that held square candles, and dozens of cushions. The pièce de résistance, however, was a black marble bathing tub carved in the shape of a swan. Its beak was gold; its eyes were orbs of golden amber. Since the swan was the de Bohun device, Jory could not resist it.

All her purchases were then brought to the castle on their own oxcarts. The first thing she did was ask that water be heated, and she took a long relaxing bath in the exotic tub, which she vowed to keep in her bedchamber.

Before the week was out, she visited Joanna, and the pair went into Gloucester on a shopping spree. Jory bought dozens of Flemish tapestries to cover the bare stone walls of Goodrich and she chose heavy bed-curtains in vivid jewel tones, not only for her own use, but for all the beds of the castle, including those in the guest tower. Joanna bought furnishings for her expected child's nursery, but refrained from adding a cradle since the de Clare castle already boasted half a dozen. Jory bought the baby a carved rocking horse with silver bells plaited into its mane.

"That's just like the white palfrey Warwick gave you," Joanna said, tinkling the tiny bells.

"Really? I had forgotten," Jory lied.

The following month Jory and Joanna attended the wedding of Roger Mortimer at the castle of Wigmore.

"He is scandalously young," Jory whispered to Joanna as they sat in the church.

"Ha! Wait until you see his child bride. Mortimer's uncle of Chirk is extremely ambitious for his nephew. Little Joan de Glenville is an heiress who will bring the town of Ludlow as well as Ludlow Castle to the Mortimers."

The wedding was attended by many of the important nobles who owned castles in the Welsh Borders. Jory met the parents of two of Joanna's ladies, Eleanor de Leyburn and Maud Clifford, who lived at Tewksbury and Clifford respectively. There were more females than males at the wedding. Many a noble baroness and countess were wintering alone because their lords were fighting in Wales, and all accepted invitations from Jory to visit her at Goodrich.

What Marjory had expected to be long lonely months turned out to be anything but. Guests arrived on a regular basis, and Jory enjoyed entertaining them, relishing her role as chatelaine. She discovered the rich musical talent of the Welsh members of her household. Their singing voices were beyond compare, and she encouraged them to play their Welsh harps for her guests.

Jory grew confident of her abilities. She became adept at discouraging overtures from lusty males who found her irresistible. She set the fashion with her beautiful clothes and jewels. She took an interest in everything and could converse on many diverse subjects, and she was also learning Gaelic.

Spring weather arrived in April, yet still there was no sign of the de Bohuns' return from Wales. Joanna's baby was due in May and Jory worried that Gilbert de Clare would miss the great event. When May was half over, Jory packed her trunk and was about to depart for Gloucester when she suddenly heard a great rumble of thunder. She ran to the window, and only when she saw that the sky was clear, did she realize the sound was hoofbeats.

She hurried up to the castle ramparts and her heart lifted with joy as she saw the brave pennants fluttering in the breeze and the sun glinting off the men's breastplates. She saw chevrons belonging to Gilbert de Clare's army. Then she saw the de Bohun swan device and knew that the Earl of Hereford had come home.

"Humphrey . . . Humphrey." Jory stopped breathing as her eyes searched frantically among the mounted men. Then she saw him and her legs went weak with relief. "Lord God Almighty — he is safe after all!" She took time to compose herself before she went down to the bailey. *He must never know I doubted.*

Jory waited quietly beneath the twin towers of the gatehouse. John de Bohun was the first to see her and he strode to her side.

"Ye are a vision of loveliness. To be welcomed home by our very own lady warms the cockles of my heart."

"My lord earl, I thank God for your safe return."

John winked. "God had nothing to do with it!"

Suddenly she was picked up and swung around, and to her surprise realized it was Henry who was kissing her. Humphrey shouted his protest and his brother set her down before her husband.

She slipped her hand into Humphrey's and they moved away from the others for a private greeting. She smiled into his eyes and murmured, "I told you that you would be safe."

He squeezed her hand and gazed down at her with gratitude. "You are my talisman, Marjory . . . my lucky, magic touchstone."

"Nay, it was your own courage that

brought you through."

Gilbert de Clare rode up to them. "I won't dismount, Lady Marjory. I'm eager to get home. Has my wife been well?"

Jory was shocked at how tired he looked. "Joanna is blooming with health, though impatient to get the birthing over and done. She will be happy you returned in time for her accouchement."

The concern on his face eased as he bade them a hasty farewell.

Suddenly Goodrich Castle was no longer a quiet haven. It was immediately transformed into a noisy beehive of activity. Men, animals, and wagons were everywhere. Weapons, campaign tents, and supplies were unloaded; horses were unsaddled and put to pasture. The men-at-arms waded into the River Wye to cleanse away the sweat of travel, while the three de Bohun men made use of the bathhouse.

When the de Bohuns saw all the improvements Jory had made to the castle's comfort, she was showered with praise. She basked in their approval, happy that her father-in-law was not the least concerned with what she had spent.

At dinner Lady Marjory sat in the place of honor between the Earl of Hereford and her husband, Humphrey. She wore a violet velvet gown and Humphrey's wedding gift, the diamond swan brooch. She left her hair uncovered because she knew it was her most arresting feature. The Great Hall was full tonight, and every male's gaze was riveted upon the castle's prize possession, the exquisite Marjory de Bohun.

When the singers arrived, accompanied by a harpist, her father-in-law's jaw dropped. He elbowed Henry and said, "Did ye ever think to see such refinements in a de Bohun castle?"

Henry jested, "Have a care or Lady Marjory will civilize you."

When everyone laughed, Jory reached for Humphrey's hand. He reacted as if he had been burned. "Don't touch me," he whispered urgently. "You must know how you affect me."

When the music was finished, Marjory arose. "I bid you good night, gentlemen, so you will be free to talk without a lady's presence to inhibit you."

The other men urged Humphrey to retire with his wife and, needing no further encouragement, he arose from the table and accompanied her to their tower. He was in a fever to get his wife undressed and Jory, understanding his need, helped in their disrobing. Humphrey had no time for foreplay and once he got her inside the curtained bed, he mounted her and began to thrust like a man obsessed. He was carried along on a great surging wave that nothing on earth could hold back. He arched his neck and cried out as his release came; then he collapsed onto her, spent.

Jory lay still, clenching her teeth. She had been unprepared for the onslaught, yet knew she should have known better — she should have expected it. "Humphrey . . ."

When he heard his name, he rolled his weight off her. "Sorry."

Things cannot go on this way, Jory thought desperately. *I must say something . . . do something to make him aware.*

She touched his arm to soften her words. "Humphrey, when you rush through making love to me, it leaves me feeling . . . I need more time . . . I need you to go more slowly . . . I need . . ."

"You don't understand how it works for a man. A delay can make a male lose his erection. It is better when I am in a fever of need. Downstairs tonight I became aroused just looking at you. When you touched me, I almost came out of my skin." He brushed his lips across her forehead. "Marjory, my love, you have made me feel sated, completely satisfied. Now do you understand?"

After he slept, Jory got out of bed and poured wine into her favorite goblet. As she sipped, she had to push away the memory of Guy de Beauchamp. Lingering thoughts of Warwick haunted her constantly. Jory moved slowly about the chamber admiring the stags and the leopards displayed in the beautiful tapestries that hung on the walls. It calmed her restless spirit and helped her to focus on Humphrey and devise a plan that would overcome their sexual incompatibility.

A week after her husband's return to Gloucester, Joanna was safely delivered of a beautiful daughter. There was no prouder father in all England than Gilbert de Clare, who promised his wife that he would make their daughter, Margaret Eleanor, his heiress, if they failed to produce an heir.

All the de Clares, the de Bohuns, and the other nobles who lived in the Welsh marches gathered at Gloucester for the christening celebration. Joanna proudly showed her daughter to Jory.

"You need a child of your own; then we can be mothers together. Now that Humphrey is home again, you have no excuse."

"I would love a baby of my own. I am green with envy."

After the toasts the men's talk turned to the Welsh campaign.

"When we first arrived, we won every battle," John de Bohun told the Earl of Tewksbury. "Then the wily devils became elusive and most of our time was spent searching for them."

Gloucester took up the tale. "They withdrew into their mountain hideaways and set traps for us, hoping we'd follow. Then the snows came and blocked every passage. Yet still they came like phantoms in the night to steal our supplies."

"When the thaw came, the skirmishes started again," de Bohun continued. "The numbers of Welsh fighters dropped off steadily as they fled north. We tracked them until our supplies ran out; then we came home. At least we quelled the uprising in the south."

Gilbert de Clare warned, "We all know they will raid the northern marches from their mountain strongholds this summer."

Young Roger Mortimer spoke up. "It has already begun. Last week my uncle of Chirk was raided of sheep and cattle."

As Jory listened, she realized with dismay that it had not been a decisive victory. All too soon the men would be returning to Wales. Her time with Humphrey might last for only weeks. If she wanted a child, she must carry out her plan.

The de Bohuns returned home, and the next night, when Humphrey came up to their tower, Jory had her plan laid. *He is an immature boy. I must take the leading role and fashion him to my liking. If I am clever enough, he will be malleable clay in my hands.* She awaited him in a silk night rail with scented oils set out by the bed. When she tried to undress him, he stayed her hands.

"You know what happens when you touch me."

"Of course I know." She kissed him. "You need immediate release, and I intend to see that you get it. Once you have spent, I will massage you with oil until you spend a second time."

Eager for his beautiful wife's ministrations, Humphrey allowed her to help with his disrobing. "You excite me to madness, Marjory, but once I ejaculate I fall into a heavy sleep."

"I promise you won't fall asleep tonight, Humphrey." She allowed her gaze to play over his naked limbs. "You have the muscles of a warrior. Stretch out on the bed for me."

Jory lay down beside him and firmly took

his hard cock in her hand. "You are bigger everywhere, it seems." Humphrey could not wait for her to move her fingers. He began to thrust his erection in and out and within a minute he was arching his body up off the bed and crying out as his orgasm exploded. She pumped him until he was completely finished, then gently wiped it all away.

"There, now we have got that out of the way, I will attempt to arouse you again." She poured a small amount of oil into her palms and starting at his feet, stroked up his long legs.

His member lay flaccid. "It's soft. It won't happen again."

Jory smiled her secret smile. "Not only will it happen again, but your cock will be twice as hard." Slowly, she bent over him and allowed her hair to trail across his nakedness, teasing his groin until it became sensitive and alive. Then she removed her night rail and straddled him. Starting at his rib cage, she stroked her perfumed palms down across his belly; then she cupped his sac and watched with sparkling eyes as his cock stood up like a ramrod. She felt the first stirrings of her own desire, and knew it was nothing her husband had done — she had aroused herself.

She licked her lips. "I want a baby, Humphrey," she whispered sensually. "Make a baby in me."

He rolled her beneath him and buried himself in her tight sheath. Feverishly, he surged in and out, driving frantically to reach his goal. His hands clutched her roughly and much to Jory's surprise and chagrin he again spent quickly and collapsed on her.

Humphrey was asleep in no time. As she lay beside him, fighting her disappointment, she cautioned herself to exercise patience. Perhaps with practice, Humphrey could learn to slow his ejaculation until she became aroused. The thought of practice daunted her. *I'm so small. Perhaps it will always hurt.* Jory curled over onto her side and escaped into a dream where she was held secure in Guy de Beauchamp's powerful arms.

Within a month, all the de Bohun weaponry and armor was repaired and their supplies replenished. Hunts were organized to fill the castle's larders and just as it seemed that Goodrich was back to normal, the powerful Earl of Chester arrived.

Jory spoke with the steward to arrange a lavish meal. She asked the Welsh harpers to entertain at dinner and even planned for a dramatic recitation of the epic *Beowulf*. Garbed in an elegant gown of primrose silk that set off her emerald and diamond jewels, she curtsied to Chester and gave him a radiant smile.

Chester kissed her hand. He took his seat beside John de Bohun. "Heaven sent you a treasure when Lady Marjory consented to wed your son Humphrey."

The Earl of Hereford beamed. "We are indeed blessed. She is our prize possession."

Jory's heart lurched as their guest explained what brought him.

"The Earl of Warwick has gone to Gloucester to recruit his friend Gilbert de Clare while I have come to beg aid from you. Our northern marches are being raided every night by hundreds of wild heathens. They are burning and pillaging entire villages and we must mount a force large enough to ride into Wales and beat them into submission. We also intend to post a patrol along the entire Border from Chirk to Chester to protect our landholdings."

"As Constable of England, I am sworn to protect the marches, but patrolling the entire Border will take a great number of men. The devils know our armies are fighting in France."

"The Earl of Surrey is returned. His army has succeeded in wresting Gascony back from Philip of France."

A joyful cry erupted from Jory's throat. "I had no idea my brother was back in England!"

"The de Warennes are on their way to Chester. The Welsh bowmen they command will prove invaluable to us."

"Any word of the king's progress in Flanders?" the earl asked.

"Aye. His Majesty plans all-out war with France. He is returning to recruit the largest army England has ever known. We'll hammer the Welsh; then we'll put the French to the sword."

Jory glanced at her husband and saw that he was deathly pale. Her heart went out to him. That night she turned all her attention to Humphrey, who once again plunged into anger and depression brought on by his deep-seated fear of fighting. His behavior fell into the old pattern. His physical need for her became insatiable, while his fear of war made him impotent.

All Jory could do during the nights that were left to them was hold him secure and bolster his courage with words that were strengthening. *Dear God, I would do anything to take away your fear and dread.* "I am your talisman, Humphrey. My love will surround you and protect you until you come back to me."

By the second week of July, Jory was once more alone at Goodrich Castle. She made the best of it, and made plans to refurbish the chambers in the towers. She purchased bolts of vivid velvet to make padded seats and cushions for all the chairs; she bought Turkish carpets, Italian chandeliers, painted screens and polished silver mirrors. She visited warehouses filled with dyes, wines, spices, and perfumed oils, where she selected the things she knew would turn Goodrich into a haven of gracious hospitality.

Marjory entertained guests on a weekly basis, organizing hawking parties, flying the hunting birds that the de Bohuns had brought from Windsor and housed in a newly established mews. Though her days were filled with people and activities, her nights were unbearably lonely, and she sometimes felt the castle walls closing in to stifle her very soul. At these times Jory found the ache deep inside could only be assuaged by soaking in hot water in her lovely black swan bathing tub.

Each and every night she got on her knees. *Please God, take away Humphrey's fear and give him courage.* Then, when she slept, she fell into a recurring dream. She was safe and secure in a man's powerful arms. The way he touched her and kissed her was so sensually passionate and so fulfilling, she knew she loved this man more than life. She whispered his name breathlessly. "Guy, Guy . . . I'm madly in love with you!" She awoke with a start the moment she realized the man in her bed was not Humphrey. "I must be mad! I don't love Warwick; I *hate* him!"

CHAPTER 14

"Baby Margaret adores you!" Joanna lay upon cushions on Gloucester castle's lawn, watching her daughter chortle and lift her arms to Jory. "You need a child of your own."

Jory lifted Margaret and kissed her freckle-strewn nose. "I'd love to have a baby, but how the devil am I supposed to get with child when my husband has been in Wales for more than a year?"

"I can think of a solution," Joanna said slyly. "You could have any man who looks at you — a husband isn't necessary."

Jory flushed and lowered her lashes. *Perhaps not necessary for you. I've often suspected this could be Humphrey's child.* She glanced up. "Here comes Gilbert. I'm so glad his leg wound has healed." De Clare had returned home to Gloucester when he was wounded and left his men-at-arms in the capable hands of his first lieutenant, Ralph Monthermer.

"Papa!" Margaret cried gleefully and reached out her arms.

"My little rosebud. I shall miss you when I return to Chester."

"My lord, if there is any chance you will see Humphrey, will you give him my letter? My anxiety over him never lessens."

"There is a very good chance. The barons who've been on Border patrol for months will rotate with those who've been doing battle in Wales. The constable and his sons have done their fair share of heavy fighting and are due to return to patrol the marches. They'll be housed at Chester Castle, which is palatial."

"Eleanor de Leyburn tells me it is even larger than this castle," Joanna added. "Her mother has taken up residence there so she can spend time with her husband."

Jory's eyes widened. "Wives are allowed to reside at Chester?"

"Aye. Roger Mortimer's bride arrived just before I left. The Countess of Chester holds court every night." Gilbert grinned. "She extends her hospitality to wives and mistresses alike."

"Then I shall go to Chester!" She searched Gilbert's face anxiously. "May I travel with you, my lord earl?"

"Of course. I return in two days, unless you need more time."

"Are you sure you want to leave your own castle where you reign supreme for a few stolen hours with your husband when he returns from night patrol? It's a big sacrifice, Jory."

If I can be with Humphrey I will try my utmost to give him comfort and relieve his fear. I'm sure my presence will bolster his confidence and give him courage. If we can be together, even for brief intervals, it will help get him through this dark time.

"I shall go to Chester. I've quite made up my mind!"

Jory packed her trunks, said her good-byes to the household staff, and finally spoke with the castle steward. "David, I know I can leave everything in your capable hands. You ran Goodrich Castle long before I came on the scene. The Earl of Hereford has complete faith in your ability and knows he is lucky to have you."

"You have the courage of a dragon, Lady Marjory."

"Nay, it is the men who do the fighting who have the courage. I am *eager* to be at

Chester. I cannot wait to spend time with Humphrey and I know the earl will welcome me. I'll also get to see my brother and my uncle. It will be a joyful reunion."

With Gilbert de Clare and a dozen fighting men as escort, Jory rode through the beautiful, lush Border country with its abundance of wildlife. She was amazed at the multitude of game birds and felt a thrill of delight each time she spotted a herd of deer. The travelers made overnight stops at the Mortimer strongholds of Ludlow and Chirk and finally saw the spires of magnificent Chester Cathedral long before the castle came into view.

The Countess of Chester made Jory welcome. "I shall put you in the chamber just vacated by Lady Joan Mortimer. She returned home when Roger went back into Wales. It's a constant juggling act to provide private accommodation for the nobles fortunate enough to have their ladies visit them. I have a dozen in residence at the moment, so you won't lack for company."

"Thank you, my lady. I deeply appreciate your kind generosity."

Jory unpacked and took special pains to look her best. She chose a lavender underdress and surcoat edged in silver. She brushed out her hair and threaded ribbon through her curls before she went down to the castle's Great Hall for dinner.

The place was thronged with men, and as Jory moved among them searching for a familiar face, they openly stared at her, and the babble of their voices momentarily ceased until she passed by. Her glance traveled along the far wall and she let out a little scream. The tawny head was unmistakable. "Lynx!"

As she hurried to her brother's side, the crowd parted to ease her way. When Lynx saw her, he opened his arms and she went into them. Tears flooded her eyes and she pressed her face against his heart. "I feel overwhelming relief you are back in England, though it was a sad homecoming. I am so sorry about Sylvia."

"When I got your letter, I was in shock and covered with guilt because I couldn't be there. In the months since, I've slowly come to terms with it. I know you did all you could, Jory." He lifted her chin and gazed down at her intently. "You look extremely elegant. Your husband is a lucky man."

"Where is Humphrey? I can't seem to find him."

"He's not here yet. Tomorrow, John and I

take the de Warenne men-at-arms into Wales to relieve the de Bohuns. Humphrey will ride hell-for-leather when he learns you are here." He took her hand. "Come, you'll dine with us. Uncle John will be surprised."

As Lynx led her toward a long trestle table, Jory stopped in her tracks. "Alice Bolton! What the devil is she doing here?"

"I brought her — she's here with me."

"My God, I knew she fancied being the next Lady de Warenne, but never thought you gullible enough to fall into her marriage trap!"

"Don't worry your head about Alice. She's attractive and amenable, but marriage is the last thing I have in mind."

She's your mistress! Jory was momentarily shocked. *Joanna is right — men are all alike.* "Then I shall stop worrying," she said faintly and went to greet her uncle John.

"Minx! What a delightful surprise. You grow lovelier each time I see you. Marriage has made you thrive." He made a place for her beside him and slipped his arm about her fondly.

"Hello, Marjory." Alice Bolton's eyes narrowed. She was unsure of Jory's acceptance and expected an unkind remark. She was ready to unsheathe her claws at the least sign of a snub.

"Hello, Alicia." Jory smiled warmly. "We meet again under happier circumstances." *Poor lady, constant husband hunting has given her a lean, predatory look.*

Jory enjoyed her evening in the rare company of her family. They would leave at dawn, and she had no idea when she would see them again. The Countess of Chester was a comfortable hostess, providing good plain food and encouraging the men to enjoy themselves with a full tankard and a game of dice or gambling while the women indulged in gossip until they retired to bed.

Two days later, Jory stood atop the ramparts of Chester Castle eagerly watching for the first glimpse of the de Bohun banners. She had decided to wear her lovely azure and gold wedding gown and she couldn't wait to see the look on Humphrey's face when he saw her. As the breeze played with her hair, tossing it about her shoulders, she was aglow with anticipation. *The wait will be worth it. This time it will happen. I feel it in my bones. The time is ripe for me to have a child.*

The sound of horses coupled with the first glimpse of a banner took her breath away. "Humphrey!" She picked up her skirts and ran lightly down four flights of stone steps until she reached the ground floor of the castle.

The Countess of Chester cautioned her. "Don't go rushing out, my dear. The sight of the wounded can be most upsetting."

"I'll stay on the castle steps overlooking the courtyard," she promised and hurried outside to watch the cavalcade arrive. The Welsh bowmen marched in first; then the Earl of Hereford rode in at the head of his mounted men-at-arms. Jory's heart swelled with pride at the brave figure he made.

Her glance traveled over to the man riding abreast of him and her heart lifted as she recognized Henry de Bohun. Her eyes moved to the left, seeking out the tall figure of Humphrey. When she didn't see him, her glance traveled slowly and carefully over the men who rode in the vanguard. Then she saw that some of the horses were pulling litters and realized these were the wounded men. Jory's hand flew to her throat. "My God, Humphrey has been wounded!" Her feet moved of their own volition as she ran down the steps and out across the wide courtyard.

John de Bohun raised his arm toward his son. "Keep her back!"

Henry was out of his saddle in a flash. He

grabbed Jory and held her tightly to keep her from reaching the litter.

She fought him with fingers and nails. "Humphrey's been wounded! He needs me! Let me tend him, damn you!"

"Nothing more can be done, Marjory. My brother is dead."

She stared into Henry's eyes as if his words were incomprehensible. "You are lying! Let me see him!"

"No! His body bears fatal wounds, unfit for your eyes."

"He is my husband!" She wrenched herself from his arms and fell to her knees beside the litter. With a determined hand she lifted off the deerskin. Three arrows pierced his chest. The feathers had been broken off, but the thick shafts were still embedded in the wounds. As well, his skull was caved in.

When Henry saw that she had begun to tremble all over, he picked her up, carried her to the castle steps, and sat her down gently. He knelt down and clasped her hands. "Humphrey is a hero. It was a surprise attack and we were badly outnumbered. He held them at bay so that Father and I could escape. We fled until we ran into the de Warennes. They took their men in and annihilated them. Your brother brought

Humphrey's body out."

"I must see to his wounds." Her lips were bloodless.

"His men will tend his body — it is their right. Then you can take your husband home for burial."

The Countess of Chester came out and helped the young widow to her chamber. She knew there were no words to ease her suffering.

Jory went through the motions of removing her wedding gown and hanging it in the wardrobe. Then, clad in her shift, she sat numb, feeling nothing, thinking nothing. Detached and unaware of her surroundings, she had withdrawn to a safe place within. An insistent knock on her chamber door roused her from her trance. It was full dark and she wondered where the day had gone. She lit the candles and turned to the door as it opened.

John de Bohun slowly advanced into the room. His armor and weapons were gone. He wore a leather tunic and boots. The earl looked lost, stunned, disoriented, and weary enough to drop.

Jory's heart immediately went out to him. Here was someone who needed her ministrations. Helping him tonight would fully occupy her and blot out the horror of her own loss.

He raised dazed eyes. "My son, Humphrey —"

"My dearest lord, you are exhausted." She sat him on the bed and knelt to remove his boots. De Bohun stared at her. "I have come to —" He lost track of his words.

Jory sat down beside him and took his hand. His eyes flooded with tears and he began to sob. Her arms went around him and she held him tightly as he choked out his sorrow. She pressed his head to her bosom and rocked him back and forth, like a mother with her child. She encouraged him to pour out his anguish and his grief and, though her own emotions were still rigidly locked away, her face became wet with tears of commiseration.

When his sobs turned to dry heaves, Jory eased him back onto the bed, and then she lay down beside him and enfolded him in her arms once more. It was the only way she knew how to show him that he was not alone.

Eventually the bereaved father sank into blessed sleep. Jory did not remove her arms from John, but kept him anchored to her. She closed her eyes and lay quietly. She did not dare to sleep for fear that her nightmares would consume her.

At first light, John de Bohun roused and sat on the edge of the bed, dry-eyed. He looked at his daughter-in-law for long minutes, noting her wraithlike appearance. She looked fragile as a delicate cobweb that could be destroyed with a touch, ethereal as a ghost that would vanish like a puff of smoke at a harsh word. She had been his bastion last night. Now he must be strong for her. He spoke softly so he would not startle her.

"Let's take our lad home."

Jory nodded, blessedly relieved that he could function enough to make decisions. For of a certainty, she knew that she could not. Not yet.

They buried Humphrey next to his mother, beneath a magnificent copper beech. The funeral was attended by the entire household of Goodrich Castle and the townspeople of Hereford. All genuinely mourned the loss of the constable's firstborn son and heir.

Jory looked at the dark-haired Celts who paid their respects with tears in their eyes. *How strange that the Welsh mourn him, yet it was the Welsh who murdered him.*

The earl spoke with his daughter-in-law

after the ceremony. "I left Henry in charge of our men-at-arms. In all fairness I must return and share the burden of night patrol of the marches. I warrant you are still in shock, my dear. You will mourn in your own time and your own way. In the peace and tranquility of Goodrich, the floodgates will open. Good-bye, Marjory. I love you like a daughter."

Jory walked about in a trance, not allowing herself to think or feel anything. She knew it was the only way to keep pain at bay. About certain things her mind was a complete blank. She could not remember anything about the journey from Chester when she and John de Bohun had brought Humphrey home to be buried.

Goodrich Castle and its people were in deep mourning. Everyone followed Lady Marjory's lead, walking softly and speaking in whispers. It was obvious that she wished to be left alone. A letter came from Joanna, inviting her to Gloucester and assuring her that a visit would help to dispel her sadness. Jory sent no reply and when another letter arrived, she left it unread.

Slowly, gradually, her grief and guilt ate their corroding way through the iron carapace that Jory had built to protect and deaden her emotions. Finally, the introspective thoughts began.

It's my fault. Humphrey thought I was his talisman, his lucky touchstone, and I could keep him safe. But I failed to protect him. I encouraged him to think foolish thoughts by telling him that my love would surround him and protect him until he came back to me.

Jory felt so much guilt that she could not bring herself to visit Humphrey's grave. She picked flowers for him every day, but asked David Bridgen to take them to the hallowed place beneath the copper beech tree.

She began to ride out alone through the lush Borders on a sure-footed Welsh pony. She suspected that a groom followed her, but if he did she was thankful that he kept enough distance between them to give her privacy.

"Why did I continually urge him to be courageous?" she asked the trees. "He acted the hero because I insisted upon it. It's my fault that he was killed!"

That night, Jory awoke with a start after her recurring dream about Guy de Beauchamp, the infamous Earl of Warwick. She jumped from bed and lit the candles to dispel the darkness. Resolutely she faced the demon that had been devouring her for months.

"I didn't *love* him enough!"

A tear rolled down her face, and then another. Soon she was sobbing uncontrollably and it went on and on throughout the long night and into the next day. Jory castigated herself, holding nothing back, confessing all her shortcomings and admitting to all her faults. When she had cried herself out and her tears finally stopped, she felt chastened. She knew there was only one thing left to do. She must go to Humphrey and beg his forgiveness.

Jory bathed her swollen eyes, brushed her hair until it fell into silken waves, and pinned on her diamond swan brooch. With firm, purposeful steps she left the castle bailey and made her way to the giant copper beech. When she came to the wooden cross, she went down on her knees and gazed at his name. As she knelt in silence, a profound feeling of peace filled her heart, and finally truth dawned, pure and simple. It was a revelation.

"Humphrey, *I did love you!* Oh, not at first. When we married, neither one of us was in love. But we comforted each other and grew to care deeply even though we were apart for much of our married life. In the end I was ready to make any sacrifice if it would help stave off your fear and bring you comfort."

Jory traced his name with her fingertips. "Rest in peace, Humphrey, knowing full well that you were loved."

As she walked back to the castle her heart felt considerably lighter. A poignant sadness lingered, but the heavy burden of guilt had been lifted. *I felt guilty because I survived him, not because I didn't love him.*

By the time the insurgency in Wales had been put to route and the de Bohuns were on their way home to Goodrich Castle, Jory had begun to pick up the pieces of her life.

David Bridgen received advance notice of their arrival, and Lady Marjory and her steward were determined to give them a worthy homecoming celebration.

"Henry!" Jory stared down into the bearded face of the man who had lifted her from the floor. *You have been away so long, you are like a stranger to me.* He swung her about and set her feet to the floor of the Great Hall. *I remember a boy, but you are a man.*

John de Bohun's massive arms came about her, preventing her from curtsying to him. "My lord earl, thank heaven you look

293

exactly the same." Some of the disquiet she had felt evaporated.

"Nay, it is I who thank heaven for the treasure he sent us when you wed Humphrey. You are a wonder! You are flying a victory flag atop our castle, you have welcome banners here in the hall, and I can smell meat roasting on the spits for a feast tonight."

Jory took extra pains with her toilet. She was aware that she had grown wan and pale, so she rubbed her cheeks with rose petals and set aside her black surcoat. She donned a gray silk gown and put on a matching head veil, befitting a widow.

Though Jory had arranged for singers and harpists to entertain at the homecoming dinner, it soon became evident the men were more interested in drinking and dicing and fondling the women they hadn't seen in over a year. She withdrew early so that everyone could enjoy the celebration without worrying about offending her.

Jory sat up in bed, awakened by the sound of scratching on the door. She threw back the covers and went to investigate. Her eyes widened in disbelief at the sight of Brutus. Then she was swept up in powerful arms and her heart almost burst with joy that Guy de Beauchamp had come home to her, jubilant with victory.

Guy carried her back to her warm bed, threw off his clothes, and joined her. He gathered her to his heart and she lifted her mouth eagerly as a surging wave of hot desire swept through her veins. His lips met hers in a kiss that unleashed her fierce yearning. His kisses deepened and roughened with his mounting need until Jory was weak with longing. His strong fingers splayed through her hair and held her captive for his mouth's ravishing. His lips traced a hot trail, seeking the pulse points on her temple, behind her ear, and at the base of her throat. She saw his face harden and his nostrils flare with a carnal desire that she shared. His insistent hands slid her night rail from her shoulders, freeing her breasts for his mouth's pleasure. Heat leaped between them, arousing a smoldering need that cried out to be quenched.

Jory opened her eyes and saw that she was alone. She moaned softly, frustrated beyond all endurance. *Why couldn't my dream of Guy play out to its passionate conclusion?* She knew the answer, of course. She had no experience of passionate lovemaking. How could she dream of fulfillment if she had never known it? *Damn you, Warwick, will I*

It took only a fortnight for things to get back to normal at Goodrich. Jory sat in the place of honor and if the earl had guests she acted as his hostess. As each day passed, more of her sadness melted away and she started to come out of her cocoon.

John de Bohun followed her up into the mews one afternoon. "Marjory, my dear, I long to see the roses back in your cheeks. I want to know honestly how you are feeling. Are you able to talk about it yet? Are you over your mourning?"

She smiled at her father-in-law. "Yes, I believe I am finally over my mourning and I am quite able to talk about Humphrey without the lump in my throat choking me. There are things I will always regret, of course . . . things that will forever make me sad, but I am coming to terms with it all."

The earl frowned. "What things do you regret?"

"That Humphrey and I never got to spend time at our Castle of Midhurst in Sussex. I regret we didn't have a child — I am sorrowful that I never made you a grandfather, my lord."

"My dearest Marjory, you are a young woman of little more than twenty. There is a way that Midhurst can still be yours. Henry is now my heir. I have signed the castle over to him and his firstborn child. You can still make me a grandfather. You are the perfect daughter-in-law. I want no other, now or ever."

Jory felt cold fingers steal about her heart. *He cannot mean what I fear he means.* She licked suddenly dry lips. "My lord earl, you are not speaking of Henry and me?"

"Indeed I am. Marriage with Henry is the ideal solution."

"My lord," she explained gently, "it is against English law for a widow to wed her husband's brother."

He waved a dismissive hand. "There is a way around that impediment. All it takes is a dispensation from Rome — a mere formality." John de Bohun smiled at his own cleverness. "I think it is safe to say you can start to make your plans."

She stared at him in horror. *Unless I wed Henry, I am to be cheated out of Midhurst. I put my trust in you, John de Bohun, and you have betrayed me.* "I . . . I am speechless, my lord."

He placed his big hand over hers and squeezed. "I'm glad we had this little talk. I was worried that it might be too soon."

Marjory recoiled mentally and withdrew back into her cocoon. When she arrived at her chamber she locked the door securely and sat down to think. *Humphrey's father has proprietary feelings for me and for Midhurst, but there is no way on earth I will marry my husband's brother to gain a castle. I am a bloody fool! Men cannot be trusted. John de Bohun is not the first earl of the realm who has betrayed me, but I vow he will be the last!*

She felt as if she was being snared in a trap that was fast closing in on her and pure panic rose up in her. Jory jumped up from the bed and began to remove her garments from the wardrobe. She packed her clothes, all her personal articles, and her jewels.

Jory sought out the earl and gave him a disarming smile. "My dearest friend Joanna has invited me to visit Gloucester. Now that my mourning period is over, I have accepted her invitation. I'm sure you have no objection, my lord."

"Of course not, Marjory. Just come back to us soon."

She asked David Bridgen if he would see that all her things including her bathing tub were loaded on a wagon and asked him to escort her to Gloucester. Before she left, Jory made her way to her husband's grave.

She knelt down and spoke to him in earnest.

"I have come to say good-bye, Humphrey. And to make you a sacred promise. I will never, ever marry your brother, Henry."

■ ■ ■ ■

PART THREE:
MERRY WIDOW

■ ■ ■ ■

CHAPTER 15

"Jory, you look ghastly!" After a warm embrace, Joanna held her at arm's length. "Whatever has happened to you?"

"My mourning for Humphrey took its toll. It took a long time to work through my grief and my guilt. When the de Bohuns returned, I thought I was recovered, but the truth was that I was still in a half trance, sleepwalking through the days and nights."

"You have absolutely nothing to be guilty about. You were a most devoted wife. I'll awaken you from your trance in no time."

"My sleepwalking is over, Joanna. I've had a rude awakening. John de Bohun wants me to marry Henry!"

"Are you being serious?"

"The Earl of Hereford is certainly serious. Henry is his new heir and he has signed Midhurst over to him for his firstborn son. The constable still wants me for his daughter-in-law. I am still to have Midhurst and still give him a grandchild. Everything is to be the same except I am to substitute Henry for Humphrey."

"You were right to escape the madhouse," Joanna declared.

"I *have* sometimes feared for my sanity this past year."

"All that is about to change. You need fun and games and laughter and, by the looks of you, a brand-new wardrobe. We shall have a lark burning these hideous widow's weeds. Father is on his way to Gloucester and the barons and nobles within a hundred miles will flock here to him. It will be a perfect opportunity to practice your feminine wiles and beguile them with your wit, charm, and exquisite beauty. Jory, you are about to learn that a woman is at her peak of attraction and power when she is a widow."

When Eleanor de Leyburn, Maude Clifford, and Blanche Bedford welcomed her back into the fold it felt like old times, and Jory's wan demeanor soon vanished and was replaced by a natural vitality. Her new clothes brought back the confidence she had lost.

When King Edward arrived with his entourage, Joanna's ladies were all atwitter, but it was Jory who received the lion's share of attention from the courtiers and she became adroit at luring them while at the same time keeping them from crossing the line in their games of dalliance.

"You have the earls of Tewksbury, Lincoln, Derby, Percy, Stanley, and Clifford along with their sons and nephews to choose from," Joanna told Jory. "All are wealthy and powerful and ready to worship at your shrine. You need a lover."

"I quite agree." Though Jory had been transformed on the outside, the empty longing on the inside needed to be assuaged. "I haven't yet found the man who takes my fancy."

"I have," Joanna confided, as her gaze lingered on Gilbert de Clare's first lieutenant. "He has the body of a young warrior. Look at those rippling muscles; they make me feel quite faint."

"I suppose there's no harm in looking, so long as you don't touch," Jory warned.

"Ralph Monthermer is too damned noble to even acknowledge the invitation in my eyes. He has pledged his loyalty to Gilbert and nothing will induce him to break it. Believe me, I've tried."

Jory laughed. "You are behaving outrageously right under the nose of your husband and your father."

"They are so engrossed in their plans for

this full-scale war with France, they wouldn't know if I dined naked. Just listen."

"I want every earl and baron to spend the winter recruiting. By spring I expect to be able to muster five thousand horse and thirty thousand foot soldiers. The de Warennes will recruit and train men from Suffolk, Essex, Surrey, Kent, and Sussex," King Edward declared. "Guy de Beauchamp will be responsible for Warwickshire, Leicester, Northampton, and Cambridge."

"I'll recruit from Gloucester to Hertford, though I already command more men-at-arms than any other," Gilbert added.

"I want you and your forces to remain in England. You're the only one I trust to keep the country safe. Train any new men you recruit for France with the longbow," Edward advised. "French archers still use those inferior crossbows."

"De Bohun and his son will go to France, but what about Bigod? Will the Earl of Norfolk refuse again?" Gilbert wondered.

"I have Bigod by the short hairs this time. His daughter died and left him without an heir. If he doesn't want his castles to revert to the Crown, the marshal will ready his men for France."

Jory shuddered. *Poor Sylvia is a pawn even in death.*

Her patience at an end, Joanna threw down her serviette and stood up. "My ladies and I will retire, I warrant."

Gilbert protested. "No, no, my dear Joanna. You must have the hall for your dancing. Call in your musicians. His Majesty and I will repair to the war room."

The older earls and barons followed the king. The younger men, save one, remained in the Great Hall. Joanna sighed loudly when Ralph Monthermer arose and followed Gilbert de Clare.

The winter months were mild and when the Yule season arrived Jory, Joanna, and her ladies took great delight in gathering holly, ivy, and mistletoe from the woods to decorate the castle. Little Margaret was the center of attention. Her happy laughter was a joy to hear as they taught her songs, dances, and festive games.

A week before Christmas, after a long day of instructing recruits in the use of the longbow, Gilbert de Clare lifted his little daughter for her ritual good night kiss. The moment he set her feet back to the carpet, he grabbed his right arm and the excruciating pain drove him to his knees.

Joanna ordered him to bed and sat with him for two days to make sure he stayed there. Gilbert was a good-natured patient who seemed to recover from his bout. On the third day he grinned at his wife. "I refuse to stay abed unless you go and rest. Ask Marjory to come and sit with me for a while."

Jory took Joanna's place and sat down beside the bed. "My lord, I hope the pain has left your arm."

Gilbert smiled ruefully. "It's not my arm, Jory. It's my heart — it is worn out. I know I won't recover this time." He saw her eyes widen. "Don't be upset. I need you to be strong for Joanna. I would like to confide in you, if I may?"

Jory gathered her composure and nodded.

"Joanna is young and she will marry again. Margaret is my heiress and will get my landholdings, but since we have no son, Joanna's next husband will inherit my title, Earl of Gloucester. Every self-serving noble in England will seek after the king's daughter and the avaricious bastards named de Clare will lead the pack. I don't want Joanna to be a pawn; I want her to be happy."

Jory knew there was more and leaned forward.

"I have chosen her next husband. Ralph Monthermer is the only man worthy enough to rule Gloucester. He's been my right hand for years and knows how to lead men. He has sworn an oath to me that he will look after Joanna always." Gilbert grit his teeth until the gripping pain in his chest subsided. "You must not tell her that Ralph Monthermer is *my* choice. She must think he is *her* choice. On our wedding night I vowed that she could choose her next husband and rule her own destiny."

"I am Joanna's friend. You must know, my dearest lord, that I will do all I can to ensure her happiness."

Gilbert de Clare died shortly after Christmas and everyone in the realm mourned his passing. The funeral was attended by a score of nobles, including the de Bohuns. The constable paid his condolences to the widow and took Marjory aside.

"My dear child, I am overjoyed to see that you have regained your strength and vitality. But your presence at Goodrich has been sorely missed. I have come to escort you home."

"My lord earl, I am Joanna's best friend. In all conscience I cannot desert her now. She would be devastated. Perhaps I will be free to return sometime in the new year."

Early in the new year, Joanna felt the first

stirrings of love. Ralph Monthermer had been like a solid rock when the aging Earl of Gloucester died. He took care of all the burial details, and not only did the men-at-arms look to him as their natural leader, he conducted the castle business with competence and saw to it that the household continued to run smoothly.

Joanna's gratitude soon turned into something deeper, and though Ralph kept a respectful distance between them and conducted himself with reserve, she saw the yearning in his eyes in unguarded moments. She recruited Marjory to act as go-between and the couple's relationship began to change, at least in private.

Jory became caught up in the delicious intrigue of secret messages and private meetings. Joanna shared her thoughts and feelings with her dearest friend and coconspirator.

"Jory, I am in love! For the first time in my life, I am head over heels in love. I live for the stolen moments we share. When I see him, my pulses race. When I hear his voice, my heart melts. If he as much as touches my hand, I shiver and tremble. Yet the cruel devil refuses to become my lover!"

"He is protecting your reputation, Joanna. That is gallant of him. You are ready for a romantic interlude, but Ralph is thinking of your future."

"Ralph *is* my future. I want him to live with me and love me."

"That could only be possible if you were married. If you do not marry quickly, the king will find you another husband."

"Dear God, I hadn't thought of that. The king is all-powerful. I would have no choice but to obey him. What will I do, Jory?"

"Put your case before Ralph. Explain to him that you must wed secretly. Through this marriage he will become possessed in his own right of the earldoms of Gloucester and Hertford. It is a perfect solution. Once it's a fait accompli, all will accept it."

"You don't know my father!"

"He's a man. You were the one who taught me there isn't a male breathing who cannot be manipulated."

"Here comes Margaret. She adores Ralph as much as I do."

Jory embraced the little girl and kissed her freckled nose. Margaret had the exact same coloring as Jory's late husband and suddenly her curiosity got the better of her and she threw discretion to the wind. "Was it Humphrey you lay with before you wed Gilbert?"

"No!" Joanna denied quickly. Then she

flushed guiltily and confessed, "It was Henry."

Jory didn't know if Joanna was lying to protect her feelings, but suddenly it didn't matter. Margaret was a beautiful child who was loved and adored no matter her sire. Jory began to laugh. "Joanna, you are absolutely outrageous!"

"Of course I'm outrageous — I am a Plantagenet!"

"Then do it! Take charge of your own destiny and secretly wed Ralph Monthermer."

On a beautiful spring night in late March after most occupants of the castle had retired, Marjory, acting as decoy, met Ralph for a midnight stroll through the gardens. When they slipped into the chapel, a heavily veiled Joanna was already at the altar with the priest. They exchanged their holy nuptial vows quickly yet solemnly. They signed their names in the church register and then the priest and Lady Marjory signed as legal witnesses.

Hand in hand, Jory and Ralph left the chapel and made their way to her bedchamber. They were fairly sure that none saw them, but if anyone had observed the couple, it would be Jory's name that would be bandied about — Jory who had indulged in dalliance.

An hour later, Guy de Beauchamp made an appearance in Jory's dream. "Don't you dare come near me, Warwick! Thoughts of tonight's romantic wedding have conjured you and you are nothing more than a figment of my imagination."

"If you are just imagining me, why do you fear my nearness? It is *your* dream; you can control every element, including me."

"Liar! You always take control. They call you the Wolfhound because you are a notorious womanizer and a lecherous swine. Once I let you make love to me, I will never see you again."

His dark eyes licked over her like a flame. "Tell me to leave and I will. It's *your* dream, Jory." He held out his hand with his fingers closed.

She had an insatiable curiosity to know what small treasure it held. She felt her determination waver and lifted her chin. "I shall allow you one kiss only. I've quite made up my mind!"

In the morning when Jory awoke she found a white rosebud on her pillow. She refused to let her imagination take flight. *It must have come from Joanna's bouquet.*

It was inevitable that Joanna's ladies learned of the secret marriage within the first two weeks. The princess was radiant, her glance languid, her words soft and gentle, her smile sweet, and her sighs blissful. Joanna walked on a cloud and it was obvious that she had fallen in love.

Their idyll was shattered when Ralph's first lieutenant came to him with the news that the de Clares had learned of his clandestine nuptial vows and had sent a messenger hotfoot to the king demanding that the marriage be declared null and void.

"I'll ride to Newcastle," Ralph declared, "and put my case before your father. Surely the king will listen to reason."

His words threw Joanna into a panic. "Dear God, Father is not a reasonable man. He will have you arrested and order our marriage set aside. Then he'll be off to France to fight a bloody war that could last for years. I must get a message to him before he leaves England."

"Joanna, write him a letter that will tug on his heartstrings and I will take it to him and plead your cause," Jory suggested.

"But he is in Newcastle, gathering his invasion forces."

"I'm ready for an adventure. What better place to find it than Newcastle, where every earl and baron in England will be gathered? John de Bohun will take his men-at-arms to join the king. I'll ask him to give me safe escort. He will be eager for my company."

As Jory rode through the Midlands and then the Northern shires, she knew there was no more beautiful country than England. The meadows were blanketed by the wildflowers of April and the hills were dotted with newborn lambs. Jory was in her glory in the vast company of warriors all overeager to do her bidding and see to her safety and comfort. They paid such homage to her beauty, they appeared ready to barter their souls for one of her smiles.

The northern air was crystal clear, like fine wine, and Jory drank it in, feeling as if she could breathe deeply for the first time in years. Excitement bubbled inside her. She had just witnessed two people fall hopelessly in love and she had become caught up in the breathless romance of it all. Jory was ripe for a love affair of her own and the thought of the adventure that lay ahead filled her with giddy anticipation.

Jory threw back her crimson hood and swept into Newcastle's Great Hall. She immediately spotted Lynx and knew she would have to diffuse his anger that she had dared to come.

"What the hell are you doing here?" Lynx demanded with a frown.

"The de Bohuns brought me. I have an urgent letter from Joanna for King Edward. 'Tis a delicate matter she has entrusted to me."

"Newcastle is bursting at the seams. My men are camped outside the walls. You may come to my room while you explain yourself."

Jory stood warming her legs before his fire as she told him about the secret marriage of Joanna and Ralph Monthermer.

"Christ Almighty, you actually intend to tell Edward Plantagenet that his daughter has married a bloody squire?"

Jory raised her chin in defiance. "Ralph Monthermer is no less than the Earl of Gloucester and Hertford."

"Bones of Christ!" Lynx suddenly realized the consequences of the secret marriage. "The king will be incensed. You are a pair of willful little bitches! I forbid that you seek him tonight. Edward is in a towering rage over the Scottish situation."

"I thought the army was gathering to invade France."

"King Baliol of Scotland was ordered to

bring his army. He has refused. He also has dismissed all English office holders and confiscated all lands and castles held by Englishmen. Is it any wonder the king is in a mad rage?"

The look of defeat on Jory's face and the mauve shadows beneath her lovely eyes had their effect. "You may have my chamber. I'll have my squire bring you a tray, then you must get some rest."

Jory slept until noon the following day and awoke refreshed. Anticipating an audience with the king, she bathed and took special care with her appearance. She donned a pale green gown that matched her eyes and wore a cabochon emerald that swung in the valley between her upthrust breasts. She slipped a gold chain around her waist decorated by another emerald that rested in blatant invitation upon her mons. She brushed her silver-gilt hair until it formed a cloud about her shoulders.

Her afternoon was spent in frustration when Lynx's squire informed her that the king was closeted with his generals. It was early evening before John de Warenne emerged with Lynx.

John looked down at her with appreciation. "Hello, Minx, your beauty grows lovelier each time we meet."

"Don't indulge her, John. She is embroiled in deep trouble."

"All I did was bring a letter from Joanna to the king."

"You shouldn't be here," John admonished. "There is trouble in Scotland. We are taking the army there tomorrow."

"Then after I speak to the king, you can give me safe escort to Carlisle. I shall go to visit my godmother, Marjory de Bruce."

"No!" Lynx growled. "Carlisle Castle will be overrun with the Earl of Ulster's Irishmen any day now — no fit place for a lady."

"Then I shall go to our de Warenne castle of Wigton." Jory smiled triumphantly. Wigton was only eight miles from Carlisle, where the Bruces were governors.

"Good." Lynx hid a smile. "You will be company for Alicia. I will save a place for you in the hall tonight for dinner."

An hour later, when Marjory entered the Great Hall she held the attention of every male eye. As she passed down the rows of barons and earls, she had a radiant smile for each of them and sweetly declined when they offered to make room for her.

She glanced at the king's carved chair on the dais and was disappointed to find it empty. Lynx was there however, and he sent his squire to get her. As she climbed the steps she saw that Lynx was talking with another man, who had his back to her.

Jory stopped in her tracks. Her eyes widened and her pulse began to race. *Warwick!* Her eyes lingered on the long, coalblack hair; then her glance swept over the impossibly wide shoulders and the ramrod-straight back. She clutched the squire's arm, fearing she might faint from being in close proximity to the powerful devil who had the ability to steal her senses.

The man turned to look at her and she felt her heart sink as she realized it was not Warwick. She recovered quickly; the young, darkly handsome male piqued her curiosity. His eyes glittered with interest, but it was not until he grinned that she recognized him. "Robert Bruce! I haven't seen you in years."

"Even at seventeen you played hell with the hearts of all the Bruce brothers, including mine." His hot glance licked over her.

"You were a wild devil who teased me unmercifully." She was openly flirting with him and felt the sparks ignite between them. He was no longer a youth, but a powerful Scots earl whose attraction was almost magnetic.

Lynx purposely sat between them. "I'm

sorry you did not get to see the king, Jory. He has declared war on Scotland. He and the entire army will leave at dawn."

Her glance met Robert's. "For whom do you fight, my lord?"

"Robert Bruce fights for himself," he admitted frankly.

"He stands with us," Lynx interjected. "He governs Carlisle Castle and will keep it secure for King Edward."

"I return there now, but when the fighting starts I'll be over that Border to take back my Annandale lands and castles that Baliol confiscated and gave to my enemy Comyn."

The corners of Jory's mouth lifted. "Since you go to Carlisle, could I persuade you to give me safe escort to Wigton Castle? My family has banished me there and I'm in sore need of protection."

"I warrant you could persuade me to anything, Jory." His dark eyes smoldered at the thought of assuaging her sore needs.

"Have a care. She is a willful little filly who will take the bit between her teeth at the first opportunity," Lynx warned.

"I'll handle her reins with a firm hand," Bruce promised.

Marjory's imagination went wild at the thought.

■ ■ ■ ■

Jory paced her chamber waiting for the hour of midnight. This would be her only chance to seek out King Edward and beg him to view his daughter's marriage in a favorable light. Her pulse raced at the temerity it would take to enter his bedchamber and try to bend Edward Plantagenet to her will. *If I think of him as a king, I will be lost. I must treat him as a man, and beguile him with my femininity, soft words, and sweet smiles.*

Jory slipped Joanna's letter into her bodice; then she rubbed perfumed oil in the cleft between her breasts and positioned the cabochon emerald so that it would draw his eye to her bared cleavage. She brushed her hair until it shone like silk and covered it with a transparent veil.

Jory picked up a small silver dish of sweetmeats and ascended to the high tower where the king slept. The guard on the door proved no match for her. "I am expected," she murmured softly. "His Majesty has a taste for something sweet when he retires."

"I received no orders to admit a wench."

"He told me how vigilant you are . . . and how discreet. Here, let me give you a taste of what he likes." She picked up an almond flavored sweetmeat and lifted it to his mouth. At the same time the tip of her tongue traced her lips. While his focus was distracted she opened the oaken door and slipped inside.

Edward Plantagenet turned his leonine head toward the intruder. "Who is it? What do you want?" he demanded.

She advanced into the chamber. "Your Majesty, it is Marjory de Warenne. I bring you a letter from Princess Joanna."

At mention of his daughter's name, he glared at her angrily. "I've ordered this Monthermer thrown in irons! The swine has taken gross advantage. Gilbert de Clare has been dishonored and his family is outraged! The marriage will be set aside."

Jory went down before him in supplication and let the veil slide from her hair. "Sire, Joanna begs your forgiveness. She wants you to know the truth before others poison your thoughts." She raised her lashes and saw that his eyes lingered on her breasts, then lifted to gaze at her hair. She saw his resolve waver and pressed her advantage. "Gilbert de Clare took me into his confidence when he knew he would not recover. Ralph Monthermer was his choice to succeed to the Earldom of Gloucester. He was his most valiant warrior who led the fighting men to victory in battle after battle. Gilbert trusted Ralph with his life and made him swear an oath to look after Joanna always."

As Jory reached into her bodice and took out the letter, she saw that the king's eyes followed her fingers. "Joanna is deeply in love with Ralph Monthermer. He reminds her of you, Sire. All those he commands hold him in the highest respect." She handed him the letter. "Her greatest wish is that you give Monthermer a chance to show you his mettle and his loyalty."

Edward reached out and raised her from her knees. Then he opened the parchment and read his daughter's words.

The moment he finished reading, Jory said fervently, "Tomorrow you go to war, Sire. Do not go into battle without forgiving her. Your love is so precious to Joanna."

"Your loyalty to my daughter is commendable. I shall send for this Ralph Monthermer and judge his worth for myself."

Jory dipped her knee and lowered her lashes to mask the triumph she felt. "Thank you, sire." She knew she had tipped the scales in her friend's favor and truly believed that Edward Plantagenet would now accept Joanna's marriage.

As she readied herself for bed she felt as if

a great weight had been lifted from her shoulders. She caught herself humming a merry tune and was amazed at how light-hearted she felt. The corners of her mouth lifted. Her encounter with Edward Plantagenet was behind her, but she knew very well there was another underlying cause for her mood to soar.

"Robert Bruce." She whispered his name. Jory was ready for more than a flirtation. She was ready for a full-blown romance.

CHAPTER 16

On the ride from Newcastle to Wigton, Lady Marjory and the Bruce indulged in a daring game. He treated her with rigid respect and in return her manner was cool and distant. This, of course, was a pretense they feigned in the company of others. The Bruce made certain they rode alone together every few hours so that they could secretly indulge in an outrageous flirtation. The things they said were seductive, intimate, and even shocking. They teased and toyed with each other, exchanging suggestive innuendos designed to titillate and provoke a sensual response. The game was doubly delicious because it was a secret they alone shared.

At every rest stop he was there to lift her from the saddle. Since they were surrounded by others and did not wish to arouse suspicion, they exchanged only a few polite words. His touch, however, clearly told her that he wanted her. His daring fingers touched the sensitive underside of her breasts as his eyes, smoldering with lust, promised he would soon take what he wanted.

Whenever his bold hands touched her intimately and his powerful arms lifted her from the saddle, she could feel the scalding heat from his palms seep through the material of her riding dress, and she became weak with longing. By the time they reached Wigton their days of foreplay had reached the point of culmination.

Jory ran up to the ramparts, knowing the Bruce would follow. He strode to her side, his arms bare, his chest covered by a metal breastplate. Her head fell back as she looked up at him. "You look like a conqueror."

He reached out and wrapped a silver-gilt tress of hair about his fist. "Conquest is in my blood."

"Robert!" Jory was breathless with desire.

His mouth swooped down and took possession of her lips. He felt her quiver, felt her arms entwine about his neck to keep her from falling. "Wrap your legs about me," he urged.

In a fever of need he carried her from the crenellated roof and swept her into the chamber she indicated. His arms felt so strong, she wanted them about her forever. The ache inside her spread from her belly, to her heart, and into her throat. She was filled with a raging desire to be mated, something that had never ever happened with her husband. With eager hands she removed her clothes while he stripped before her. She reached out hungrily to touch the musculature of his chest and found it as hard as if he were still wearing the breastplate.

His upthrust cock was hard too, and she reveled in the feel of it as he rolled her beneath him and thrust up inside her to the hilt. He filled her with so much sexual energy, she went wild, clawing and arching and crying her pleasure with abandon. The Bruce's mating was hard and savage and selfish, and Jory relished every passionate moment. In frenzy she bit his shoulder and the tide was turned instantly. From drowning in need she soared on the crest of a towering wave; then she shuddered uncontrollably with liquid tremors. With a hoarse cry, he spilled his white-hot seed up inside her. He rolled with her until she lay above him in the dominant position, her disheveled hair spilling to his chest.

"I'm sorry I behaved like a great rutting stag, throwing you on your back and having my way with you."

She gazed down into his eyes. "Liar, you are not sorry at all. You are triumphant!"

He lifted her off his body, laid her beside him, and came up on his elbow. "Do you know why I am triumphant? I've lusted to fuck you since you were seventeen."

"Robert!" she protested. "We made love."

"Love? Nay, it was lust, pure and simple." His fingers touched the delicate golden curls on her mons. "You have the prettiest cunny I've ever seen. I've imagined it for years."

Jory smiled a secret smile. This mating had given her a sense of power and confidence. *I will make you love me, Robert Bruce. I'll have you eating out of my hand before I'm done with you . . . and I'll never be done with you!*

He took her again, and Jory marveled that she had aroused him so quickly. She exulted in the power she had over him. The moment he slaked his lust, however, he quit the bed and dressed.

"Take me with you to Carlisle," she tempted. His hand caressed her bottom and she thought he would take her. Then he slapped her bum and said, "Can't be done."

Jory couldn't believe her ears, and then realization dawned. "You won't be staying at Carlisle, will you, Robert?"

"Not for long. I'm off to topple a king from his throne. I'll take back my castles and then Annandale and Carrick."

His ambition and hard resolve were so palpable they filled the room, blotting her out. She stood on the bed, forcing him to look at her. "You won't stop there — you'll try to take Scotland!"

"You're a clever wench, wheedling my secrets from me. I should know better than to let a woman close enough to read my heart."

Jory soon learned that she did not wish Alicia Bolton for her friend. They took their meals together, but spent their days in different pursuits. Alice attended her wardrobe and her person, embroidering petticoats, dying her hair, and drinking vinegar to keep off fat and make her lean. Jory also discovered that Alice hoarded a supply of pennyroyal, an herb that induced abortion. *Alice is a bloody fool! Doesn't she realize that Lynx would marry her if she gave him a child?*

Jory much preferred being outdoors, riding through the foothills of the Cumbrian Mountains or flying a hawk in the forest. She thought about Robert Bruce every day and knew with a certainty that he would be back. Her femininity would draw him like a lodestone. They may be disparate in size and in coloring, but under the skin she fancied they were birds of a feather . . . two of a kind . . . a perfect match.

Robert Bruce's thoughts were occupied elsewhere. He recruited fighting men from Northumberland to march across the Border into Scotland. When word reached him of King Edward's massacre of Berwick, he knew that his enemy Comyn, who commanded the Scottish army, would retaliate by attacking Carlisle. So Bruce set a trap.

Comyn's army crossed the Border and began to ravish England. They destroyed Hexham, then looted and burned their way through Redesdale and Tynedale, drawing ever closer to their goal.

Comyn rode into the walled City of Carlisle with three thousand, relishing the surprise attack. When most of his army was inside, he was the one surprised as the Bruce's men attacked from four directions. They were trapped like fish in a barrel, and by afternoon more than one thousand Scots lay dead in the streets of Carlisle. Comyn escaped through the city gates and urged the commanders and clan chiefs outside the walls to attack, but they caught wind of the massacre and fled back through the dales.

It was only after the Bruce had achieved

victory and was washing the dust from his throat with a tankard of ale that he thought of Marjory de Warenne. He suddenly realized that Wigton was unsafe and knew he must go immediately and bring her to the safety of impregnable Carlisle Castle.

"I knew you would come," Jory said.

He heard the note of triumph in her voice and grinned wickedly. He bent his head close so that Alicia could not hear. "We've no time to fuck, sweetheart." He raised his voice to include Lynx's mistress. "The Scots army is fleeing and looking for a refuge like Wigton. Pack your things. I'm taking you both to Carlisle."

Jory ran upstairs to do his bidding, excited to be going to Carlisle, but she discounted the danger and privately thought it was an excuse the Bruce had decided upon to get her to his castle.

Marjory Bruce kissed her goddaughter. "Welcome to Carlisle. 'Tis an ugly castle to look at, but it is massive and impregnable."

" 'Tis impregnable because the Bruces govern it," Jory declared.

She bribed a steward with a coin and a smile to give her a chamber apart from the ladies' quarters. After she unpacked, she went down to the hall for dinner and was introduced to young Elizabeth de Burgh.

"This is Elizabeth, the Earl of Ulster's daughter. Her father has placed her in my care while he takes his Irishmen to fight for Edward Plantagenet. Poor child thought she was going to France, but finds herself stuck on the Border of Scotland."

"Don't we all?" Alicia Bolton said caustically.

Jory engaged the fourteen-year-old in conversation, and by the end of the meal it was clear to all that the girl had fallen under the spell of the fascinating lady with silver-gilt hair who wore the most elegant clothes Elizabeth had ever seen.

When Jory retired she sat daydreaming before the fire. It was the eleventh hour before the Bruce came.

"Why aren't you abed, my beauty?"

She smiled up at him. "I thought you'd enjoy undressing me."

"You didn't know I'd come," he protested.

"Of course I knew you'd come . . . I am your obsession."

He grinned. "Aye, you are my folly. But I spoke true at Wigton when I said there was no time for bed play."

She stood and unfastened her own gown. "Then we'd best dispense with the play and get to the heart of the matter."

With a low curse he threw off his clothes and tossed her onto the bed in her petticoat. He dived after her and laughed as she wrapped her legs tight about him and arched her mons so that he could glove himself in her honeyed sheath. The mating was cataclysmic. She had always feared that she might be sexually inadequate, but her response to Robert proved to her that she was a sensual, feminine creature who could be aroused in an instant by the right man. Her heart soared with her newfound knowledge.

"I'm coming," he cried as he thrust wildly. "I won't wait."

She arched her body up to him and shouted joyfully, "I'm there before you!"

They spent together and clung to each other laughing. His face sobered and he said earnestly, "I'll make it up to you next time." He grabbed up his clothes and strode naked from the room without a backward glance.

The Bruce set out immediately to rout the Scottish invaders from the English dales and chase them back across the Border. So many flocked to the Bruce banners that he soon had control over his old territories in Scotland.

Ensconced in his stronghold of Lochmaben at the head of the Annandale Valley, Robert sent a message with his brother Nigel to John de Warenne who commanded the English army:

At Carlisle we won a victory over half the Scots force. The Bruces will hold Annandale, Galway, and Carrick secure for Edward Plantagenet if he reconfirms our lands and castles in our name.

John de Warenne sent Lynx back with Nigel to persuade the Bruce to join forces.

When Lynx arrived at Lochmaben, Robert seemed averse to the plan. He rode out with his friend across Annandale visiting the Bruce castles and showing him the two thousand acres that had been granted to his ancestor by William the Conqueror. When they visited Dumfries Castle, Lynx could not help coveting the place.

"Dumfries isn't mine; it's a royal castle that lies in my territory." Each time Robert looked at Lynx he was vividly reminded of Lynx's sister, Jory. Their green eyes were identical. "When we defeat Comyn, ask the king to make you Governor of Dumfries; then we can be neighbors."

Lynx searched his face, wondering what prompted his change of heart. "I'm glad you'll join the fight; you won't regret it."

John de Warenne's military strategy worked like a charm. As his forces swept down on the main body of the Scottish army, Bruce's men came up behind to trap them between the two deadly forces. The battle that ensued was a crushing defeat for the Scots. Comyn was captured along with a hundred Scottish earls and knights and Dunbar Castle surrendered.

The king arrived from Berwick, well pleased with his commanding general. Edward promised to reconfirm Bruce in his lordship of Annandale once Baliol was captured. He needed Bruce to watch his back to keep the Scots from regrouping behind the English army. He did not trust Bruce, however, and knew sooner or later he would make a bid for the Crown of Scotland.

John de Warenne convinced the king that the next strategic goal should be Edinburgh. On the way they would force the surrender of every castle they encountered. John ordered Lynx to garrison Dumfries Castle to keep the supply route open for his army. "The king wants an eye kept on Bruce activities. As his friend, you are least likely to arouse his suspicion."

Robert Bruce returned to Carlisle for a brief visit. He wanted to quench the thirst that Marjory de Warenne had set up in his blood, but his main purpose was to learn where his enemies lay. He'd set a trap with a baggage train of supplies so he could learn where on the route the wagons and pack-horses would be raided.

Jory was elated when she saw him and believed she was the sole reason he had returned. They wished to keep their liaison a secret and arranged to meet outside the town gates at twilight. The weeks they had been separated felt like months and the long hours of keeping their eyes and hands from each other throughout the day made their desire mount to such a peak, they could think of nothing but assuaging their passion when they met.

Robert galloped past her, but she soon closed the distance between them and they rode neck and neck into the countryside. They came to a long stone wall that humped across the landscape like a dragon's back. "Hadrian's Wall, built by the Romans a thousand years ago to keep out the barbarian wildmen."

She threw back her head and laughed.

"That describes you exactly. The Scots are still uncivilized louts!"

He lifted her down, her hair brushed his face, and he shuddered with longing. He kissed her deeply and groaned as she pressed her breasts close and kissed him back with sensual abandon. "Not here! I want to make love to you in the land I intend to rule." He vaulted to the top of the wall, then reached down to help her. He dropped down on the other side and held up his arms.

Without hesitation, Jory flung herself down, knowing he would catch her. Hand in hand they ran through the tall wild grasses until they came to a stone lookout tower. Inside, Robert laid his cloak down on a thick bed of bracken and, as he'd promised, he completely made up for their last hurried coupling. He undressed her slowly and for the next two hours worshipped her body, lavishing her with kisses from her temples to her toes.

They were reluctant to end the tryst, knowing it could be their last for months. "Do you think you could be happy in Scotland?"

Jory felt apprehension. "You fight for King Edward. You would have to betray him to get the Crown."

"He would betray me without a moment's hesitation." He wrapped her cloak about her shoulders. "I shall become King of Scotland one way or another. It could be as simple as outliving Edward Plantagenet. He grows old. His son is a weakling who could never hold this land, even if his father wins it for him."

Her apprehension passed. Robert believed in his destiny and so must she. *This is more than a flirtation . . . he is courting me!* Happiness bubbled inside her even when he escorted her back to the castle and kissed her good-bye. *I must not cling to him — he would hate that.* She smiled bravely and whispered, "Godspeed!"

It was five months before Jory saw Robert Bruce again. He came into his mother's solar to give them the news. "Baliol has been taken, stripped of his crown, and sent as prisoner to the Tower of London. Edward Plantagenet has called a parliament at Berwick for the last day of August and has ordered every landholder in Scotland to appear there to reaffirm his allegiance to England." He looked at his mother. "I want signed and sealed documents that state officially that Annandale and Carrick have been taken back from Comyn and returned to the Bruces."

"Then the king will appoint another to govern Carlisle," Lady Bruce declared. "I shall return to our English estates. Will you return with me Jory, Alicia?"

"Oh, no, thank you, my lady. I shall go to Berwick. Everyone of importance will be there to celebrate the king's victory."

"My father will be there." Elizabeth de Burgh begged Lady Bruce to let her go with Jory, who immediately promised to take the girl under her wing and appease the Earl of Ulster if he objected.

"What if Lynx de Warenne objects and sends you all packing?"

"Alicia shall be our secret weapon." Jory carefully kept the sarcasm from her voice. "How could Lynx possibly resist her?"

Lynx de Warenne's demeanor was glacial as he stared at Alicia with icy green eyes. "You should not be here! This parliament has been called to conduct important business of the realm."

"It was Jory's idea. She insisted!"

Jory saw his eyes warm as he looked down at her. "Don't be angry, Lynx. History is being made here in Berwick."

His laugh rang out. "As if you give a damn

for history! You couldn't resist the victory celebrations. You'll flaunt your beauty before the Scots nobles and dance till dawn every night."

Lynx found them accommodation, making sure that Alicia's chamber was as far from his as possible and that Jory's was close to his own. He brought his sister wine, and found her unpacking. "I have a deal of news to tell you. Six months ago I garrisoned Dumfries Castle. It's in Annandale, about eight miles from the Bruce stronghold of Lochmaben."

Jory's pulse raced. "I shall love living in Scotland."

"I went through a handfast ceremony with a young woman by the name of Jane Leslie. She is the daughter of Dumfries's steward."

"Isn't that an agreement to live together for a year and a day, then decide whether to part or to marry?" Jory puzzled.

"If she conceives a child, I will wed her immediately."

"You'd marry your steward's daughter when you could have any noble lady in the land? You must be madly in love with her!"

"Splendor of God, we hardly know each other. Two days after the ceremony, the king recalled me to the army. That was six months ago — half my year is gone."

"Won't flaunting convention raise eye-brows?"

"To hell with convention. What matters to me is a child. The Leslies are prolific breed-ers. Jane has nine brothers and sisters. When I told Robert Bruce and John their eyebrows stayed in place. I don't give a damn about the rest. It's my life."

When Alicia finds out she'll run mad!

"The king is about to install our uncle as Governor of Scotland, while he goes to fight in France. I'm sick to death of war. All I want is the domestic peace of Dumfries."

Jory's eyes widened in astonishment. "John is to rule all of Scotland?" *What on earth will Robert Bruce think of that?*

On the journey to Dumfries, Jory occasion-ally left the company of Alice Bolton and Elizabeth de Burgh to ride alongside her brother and Robert Bruce. She did not intrude in their conversation, but instead listened to what they had to say.

"John de Warenne earned his governor-ship, but Edward should not have made Cressingham the treasurer. He should have given it to a Scots noble. It could come back and bite him," Lynx declared.

"He thinks Scotland crushed, but it won't

stay conquered. It will rise and fight again," Bruce predicted.

Jory caught her breath. *Dear God, it will be just like Wales. The fighting will go on forever!*

"Christ, Robert, let's enjoy our castles in peace, at least through the winter. Then in the spring, many of the Scots nobles will accompany Edward across the Channel. They've accepted the king's offer to fight in France in exchange for their freedom."

"Let's see . . . This is October; there should be peace until spring." He threw Jory a conspiratorial wink. "I'll be happy as long as he keeps my enemy Comyn locked up."

Jory let out a sigh of relief. Spring was five or six months away. She and Robert would have plenty of time to indulge in a long, delicious winter romance.

When the cavalcade neared Dumfries, the Bruce bade them good-bye. "We are for Lochmaben. I'll be back to visit soon."

"Bring your brothers," Lynx invited. "My castle is yours."

"It will be one day," Robert said, laughing.

Both Lynx and Jory knew he was deadly serious.

CHAPTER 17

When Jory met Jane Leslie in the stables at
Dumfries she saw how innocent and completely unspoiled the young woman was.
She was also six months' gone with child
and Jory was overjoyed that her brother
would marry the lovely, sweet-natured girl.

Lynx de Warenne was over the moon when
he saw that Jane was having his child. That
night he made a proud announcement in
the Great Hall. "Raise a cup with me and
drink a toast to Dumfries." Hundreds of
hands were raised. "I am about to become a
father!"

The whistles and shouts of joy were
deafening as all but one person at Dumfries
celebrated the event. Jory saw that Alice
Bolton was filled with jealousy and hatred
and she immediately vowed to protect the
mother-to-be against the vitriolic woman.

When Jane revealed her innermost worries to Jory that Lynx cared only for the

child she carried and was oblivious to her as a woman, a close friendship began to blossom between them. "Oh my dear, we shall indulge in the most fascinating game in the world. I will tutor you in infallible ways to attract the opposite sex. I shall thoroughly enjoy transforming you into *Lady Jane!*"

The lessons began, and Jane proved to be an apt pupil as Jory taught her airs and graces she had never known. Jory impressed upon her that she was the most important lady at Dumfries, and showed her how to put her domineering sisters in their place.

Jory taught Jane to be saucy and mischievous and not to jump to obey her husband when he issued his high-handed demands. "Men don't want meek, submissive women. They like vixens who will lead them on a merry chase. They love nothing better than a challenge."

Lynx took it for granted that Jane would marry him, but at Jory's urging she temporarily refused. "We are handfast for a year and a day. When that time is up, you may ask me again."

Though Lynx had severed his relationship with Alicia, it occurred to him that perhaps the presence of an ex-mistress prevented Jane from becoming his wife. He sought Jory's advice about how to rid himself of the woman.

"Send Alice Bolton to Edinburgh, where John de Warenne has his headquarters. She'll flaunt her connection with the governor of Scotland and will soon find a wealthy noble to take care of her."

"Thanks for the advice, Minx. I'll pack her off today."

Robert Bruce was a frequent visitor. One day he arrived when Lynx had gone hunting and Jane found herself trapped in Jory's wardrobe as the lovers shared an afternoon of shameless passion. When Jory discovered her, she feared Jane was deeply shocked, but instead she revealed her secret longing. "Oh Jory, what you have with Robert . . . that's what I want with Lynx."

Jory recruited Robert and his two brothers to aid their cause. They promised to pay the little mother-to-be every attention and drive their friend Lynx mad with jealousy.

As the time for the birth of his child drew near, Lynx was in a fever to persuade Jane to marry him, but though her words were soft and gentle, she always postponed the reckoning. By this time Jory realized that Jane was deeply in love with her brother and she would not consent to marry him until

Lynx loved her in return.

Jane gave birth to a healthy boy and Jory knew that her brother was the happiest man alive. He was humbled by Jane's generosity and, because she had given him his heart's desire, she could do no wrong. Jory worked on Jane with a vengeance, designing a new wardrobe of beautiful gowns to show off her newly slim figure, and advising her to unplait her lovely red hair so that the long curly tendrils fell to her waist.

"During the upcoming New Year's celebrations you must exercise your newfound power as chatelaine of Dumfries. Let him see your fine hand in everything. Lynx will see you through new eyes and will not be able to resist you. Men want what they cannot have. Refuse him and he will turn over heaven and earth to get you."

The Bruces arrived from Lochmaben loaded down with presents and a determination to indulge in festive fun and games. Nigel appointed himself Lord of Misrule and mayhem ensued for an entire twelve days and nights.

Jory watched Lynx become enamored of Jane right before her eyes. The pair became intimate again and it was obvious to all at Dumfries that Lynx de Warenne was falling in love for the first time in his life.

Jory too was filled with happiness. She savored every moment of Robert's long, ardent wooing and knew without doubt that the time she'd spent at Dumfries had been the most joyful of her life.

At the end of January the castle and townspeople gathered to christen the baby in Dumfries's chapel. Robert and Jory stood as godparents and the name Jane chose was Lincoln Robert de Warenne.

After the baptism, the Bruces departed for Lochmaben. Lynx watched Jory dash away a tear and slipped his arm about her. "Don't wish for his child. It would be disastrous. The scandal would ruin you and bring shame on the de Warennes."

Her eyes widened. "We've been so careful. How did you know?"

"There's little about the Bruce that I don't know. He'll not wed you, Jory. His driving ambition to be King of Scotland stands in the way. The people would never accept an English queen."

"You're speaking of the future. I live for today; I'm not greedy enough to want tomorrow also." Though her words were deliberately light, her heart was suddenly heavy. That night she studied her reflection in her mirror. *I don't want him to marry me!*

Being a widow suits me far better than being a wife. I want things to remain exactly as they are between us. She stared defiantly at her reflection. *I could make him wed me if I chose — he is madly in love with me!* She believed it with all her heart.

In February, a Scot called William Wallace started a rebellion and John de Warenne summoned Lynx and Robert Bruce to Edinburgh. Bruce, incensed that Edward had freed Comyn, ignored the summons.

"The king has ordered me to reassemble the army. We are to sweep through the Lowlands from the Border to the Firth of Forth. He wants this rebellion nipped in the bud and he wants Wallace."

Lynx sent Bruce a message telling him the king was testing his allegiance. If he refused, his English estates would be forfeit.

Bruce brought five hundred from Annandale and pledged another thousand from Carrick. "I would have ignored the call if you hadn't warned me. My spies tell me Comyn is in league with Wallace. Once Edward sails to France, all hell will break loose."

By the end of March, de Warenne, Bruce, and Cressingham had marched through the entire Border region. Treasurer Cressingham became adamant that the exercise was wasting the Crown's money and sent reports to the king that the back of the Scots resistance had been broken. As a result, Edward Plantagenet sailed for France in April and left the governing of Scotland to John de Warenne.

Just as Bruce had predicted, William Wallace joined with Comyn and the clan of William Douglas. The Scots marched on the sacred town of Scone and took it back from the hated English.

John de Warenne ordered Lynx to march on Scone and retake it, and the Bruce agreed to secure the surrender of William Douglas.

Outside Scone, at a strategic place called Irvine, Lynx de Warenne prepared his men for battle. At dawn he led the charge as always and by dusk his army had won victory for the English and defeated the enemy, but not without a horrendous cost. His lieutenants found Lynx de Warenne on the battlefield close to death. He had sustained a massive belly wound and his lifeblood was almost drained away. Even his Welsh bowmen who practiced healing arts feared they would lose the race with death before they could get him home to Dumfries.

When Jory saw them bring her brother in on the litter, she was in despair. On the journey home the flesh had melted from his body and he was emaciated. It stirred graphic memories of Humphrey and convinced her that Lynx's wound would prove fatal.

Jane, strangely calm, looked at her husband's wound without flinching, then firmly took over as chatelaine of Dumfries. "Carry him to our chamber in the master tower. Fetch the priest quickly." Under her watchful instructions they lifted him onto his own bed. Jane took her beloved's hand and nodded at the priest. Solemnly he began to give Lynx de Warenne the last rites.

"What in the name of God are you doing? I sent for you to marry us. Get on with it; he is in agony."

The priest began the Solemnization of Matrimony. "Wilt thou have this woman to be thy wedded wife? Wilt thou love her, comfort her, honor and keep her, in sickness and in health; and forsaking all others, keep thee only unto her, so long as ye both shall live?"

Lynx's green eyes glittered and all agreed that he nodded.

The priest then repeated the vows for

Jane, adding, "Wilt thou obey him and serve him?"

"I will," she vowed solemnly, and her father stepped forward to give his daughter to Lynx de Warenne.

Jory, who had been hovering tearfully at the door, stepped into the chamber. "I will plight my brother's troth." She placed her hand on Jane's, which in turn covered Lynx's, and said the words that bound them together as husband and wife.

Jane, who had an abundant knowledge of herbs and their healing powers, seldom left her husband's side in the weeks that followed. She had other Celtic powers, including the ability to take away pain, and though his life hung by a thread she believed that if she loved Lynx enough, she would save his life.

His punctured bowel stank with putrefaction, but with the use of strong herbs and meticulously clean dressings it slowly began to heal. The problem was that Lynx could keep nothing in his stomach and the total lack of nourishment threatened his life.

Jane solved this by tenderly feeding him her breast milk and finally the danger passed and Lynx began to regain his strength.

The Bruces came to Dumfries, overjoyed

that Lynx had cheated death and that his fighting strength was steadily being restored.

After the Bruces' visit, Jane told Lynx of a dreamlike vision she'd had about Robert. "I saw him surrounded by a brilliant light with a golden crown upon his head."

"Bruce is the rightful King of Scotland, Jane. I won't oppose his bid for the throne, but he'll need more than my cooperation."

"But the lady beside him was not your sister, Jory — it was young Elizabeth de Burgh!"

Lynx laughed. "If Robert could get the power of the Earl of Ulster behind him, he'd soon be wearing the Crown of Scotland."

Jory could see that the bond between Jane and Lynx strengthened with each passing day and night. Jane had become a part of him, wife, lover, friend, nurse, and his trust in her was absolute. Jory lay abed, remembering that Jane had once said she wanted what Robert and she had. *What we have pales beside the selfless love and adoration these two now share.* Jory could not help but wish that Robert loved her with his whole heart. "I once teased him that I was his obsession," she whispered into her pillow, "but I was wrong. The Crown of Scotland is his obsession. I fear I will never hold first place in his affection. Perhaps he doesn't truly love me. Perhaps all he feels for me is lust, pure and simple."

Jory felt deeply conflicted. Part of her wanted to believe that Robert Bruce loved her, but the other part was filled with questions and doubts and fears.

The Bruce visits continued throughout the summer months as Lynx gradually regained his fighting strength.

"The news from John de Warenne is all bad. His forces lost Stirling to Wallace and Comyn, and Treasurer Cressingham was killed. The king signed a hasty peace treaty with France and has returned to organize his army to reconquer Scotland. He has the levies of Warwick, Bohun, and Ulster's Irishmen," Lynx told Robert.

"When the army moves north of Edinburgh, it will find only blackened fields and burned farms. Edward's soldiers will find no food, nor fodder for their horses. My country is being torn asunder by both the English and the Scots," Bruce said bitterly.

"Poor Robert, you wish the English out of your country completely, do you not?" Jory asked with heartfelt sympathy.

"In truth I do," Robert acknowledged.

"What about the Irish?" Elizabeth de Burgh asked with a blush. It was plain to all that she hero-worshiped the Bruce.

Robert ruffled the young girl's hair. "The Scots hate only the English, not the Irish. We share Celtic blood."

"Elizabeth is excited because her father will be accompanying the king," Jane said. "We should invite him to Dumfries."

"I suppose I'll have to house some of Edward's forces at my castles if I hope to keep them in my possession," Robert said.

When Lynx took the Bruce to the armory, Jory and Elizabeth rushed to their chambers to don prettier gowns. Jane followed Jory. "I cannot bear the thought of Lynx going to battle again."

"Darling, never let him know you are afraid for him. Let him think he is omnipotent. It frightens me out of my wits that Robert will someday make a bid for the Scottish Crown. But he believes it's his destiny and because I love him, so I must too."

"Do you want to become his queen?"

"I would love it, but that is impossible. Though I hate to admit the truth, the Scots would never accept an English queen."

"Yet you still want him to become king?"

"Yes! I'd do anything to help him achieve his goal."

"Do you love him enough to make a great sacrifice? With the Earl of Ulster's power behind him he could gain the throne. If Robert offered to betroth de Burgh's daughter Elizabeth and make her his queen, it would induce Ulster to help Robert become king."

Marjory's eyes widened with shock and the blood drained from her face so quickly, she looked as waxy as a corpse.

During the evening meal she was unusually silent and pensive and the candlelight showed dark smudges beneath her eyes. Hours later as Robert lay spent, cradling Jory, he remarked on her mood.

"You are as ferocious as a tigress tonight."

" 'Tis the fear of losing you," she confessed.

"I'm needed to patrol the marches against Wallace's raiding parties. I likely won't be fighting any battles."

"I'm not talking of losing you in battle." She took a deep breath and dared say the words. "You know our parting is inevitable." *Please deny it! Please tell me you cannot bear to part with me, now or ever, Robert.*

He looked into her eyes. "You've never had trouble before embracing the present and pushing away the future."

Tell him, Jory. See if he's willing to push away the future. "There is a way to speed your bid for the Crown," she said intensely, "if you induce the Earl of Ulster to back you."

"De Burgh owns half of Ireland. What could I offer him?"

Once he hears the words, you won't be able to take them back. Jory's heart constricted, but something inside drove her. She had to know what choice he would make. "You could offer to make his daughter your queen. It's an offer few fathers would refuse."

"Enough!" He covered her mouth with a silencing kiss.

Jory's heart soared. *He wants no part of it! Robert loves me too deeply to sacrifice me, even for the throne of Scotland.* "You won't even think about it?" she asked breathlessly.

"Jory, my heart, you know me well enough to know that I will think of little else."

She gave him a radiant smile, then bit her lip. It prevented the scream that was building in her throat from escaping.

Edward Plantagenet received a message that Wallace's army was encamped at Falkirk and ordered his commanders to march. On the first night out, as the king slept on the ground, his horse rolled on him and crushed some ribs. He tried to carry on but saw that the Bruce's report of blackened fields was correct and there was no fodder for the horses. John de Warenne came down with ague, coughing up his lungs and Edward knew that both his own and his general's health were failing. He ordered the Earl of Warwick and his men to Falkirk and withdrew to Carlisle on the English Border.

Warwick arrived at Falkirk and joined his forces with those of Bigod and Bohun. Wallace's Scottish army of *schiltrons* with their long spears and Comyn's cavalry awaited them on the field. The moss was wide and dank and the Scots had chosen this place so that the impact of the English cavalry would be lessened.

Retreat and cover were not in Warwick's vocabulary. His men were under orders to wear their armor at all times. He led the charge at full gallop to rout and trample the enemy. His heavy, steel-mounted attack was too much for the cowardly Comyn and his Scots cavalry melted away. The thousands of *schiltrons,* however, stood firm.

Guy heard the arrows of his Welsh bowmen whistle through the air and thunk into soft flesh. His nostrils were filled with the hot metallic stink of blood and sweat and vomit and panic. He closed his ears to the moans and screams of the dying on the battlefield and fought on fiercely, savagely, until his sword arm was numb and his voice rough and gravelly from shouting orders.

When the light began to fade from the day and the battle ended, ten thousand Scots lay dead on the moss and Warwick knew he had dealt the enemy a fatal blow. The land behind the hillside at Falkirk was heavily wooded and the beaten Scots who were still alive fled. Warwick knew he would not pursue them; the slaughter sickened him. He dismounted and began to search the blood-soaked field for his own men. He would leave no man behind, wounded or dead.

At the end of the month Robert Bruce rode into Dumfries with news. "The Earl of Warwick saved the day and won the Battle of Falkirk. Wallace escaped, but Comyn betrayed him and turned him over to the English. Edward has taken him to London for trial."

"So your enemy Comyn is once again enjoying royal favor."

"Not so. Baliol died recently and Comyn is claiming all his possessions. So we are both out of favor at the same time."

"Mayhap the time is ripe to make your move," Lynx said quietly.

"If I take up arms against the king, will you oppose me?"

Lynx shook his head. "I am returning to my lands in England. John is upstairs in bed with an ague. He asked Edward to appoint a board of commissioners to govern Scotland — one man cannot do it. John and I know the Scots will never accept English rule."

Jory, who had been tending her uncle, came downstairs. She searched Robert's face, wondering if he had reached a decision.

"I cannot stay. Will you see me out, Jory?"

She courageously swallowed her fear and smiled with delight.

In the stables, she told him that Lynx was making plans to return to England. She held her breath, daring to hope he'd vow that he could not live without her and beg her to stay.

He wrapped his arms about her and held her enfolded against him for long minutes. Then he reached into his doublet. "Will you give this letter to Elizabeth? It is from her father."

He has chosen the path of destiny! He has betrayed me — not for another woman, but for Scotland. "Go with God, Robert."

With a brave face she returned to the castle and found Elizabeth with Jane. She delivered the letter quickly.

When Elizabeth read its contents, she was ecstatic. "My father is visiting the Bruces at Lochmaben in a sennight and wants me to join him there." Her cheeks blushed a pretty pink. "Oh, I will need a new dress," she said breathlessly.

"You must have more than one new gown," Jory insisted. "Don't forget that Robert Bruce is Scotland's most eligible bachelor."

When the young girl ran off to find her serving women, Jane looked at Jory with shining eyes. "How selfless and generous you are. I don't think I'd have had the courage to do it."

"Nonsense. I learned courage from your glorious example."

A week after Elizabeth de Burgh left to visit Lochmaben, she sent Marjory a note to tell all her exciting news.

The Earl of Carrick asked my father for

my hand in marriage and in a midnight ceremony, Robert Bruce plighted his troth to me. I am returning with my father to Ireland tomorrow for a quick visit. I'm happier than I've ever been and can never thank you enough for your generous friendship.

Elizabeth, Countess of Carrick

Jory managed to maintain a calm facade even when she passed along the fateful news to Jane and Lynx at dinner. Her face was serene and her manner unruffled as she bade them good night. Once she reached the privacy of her own chamber, however, she flung herself on her bed and the floodgates opened, drenching her pillow with the heartbreaking tears of what might have been.

It was a large undertaking for the de Warennes to vacate Dumfries and return to England, so they planned it in stages. When John was well enough to travel, he left first with his men. A few days later, the Welsh foot soldiers began their long trek back to England, and the next day Lynx took his sister aside.

"Jane is having another child, so I think it best to put her and our son on a ship in the

Solway that will take them to Chester. I know you're capable of riding and keeping up with my knights, but I want you to go with them and watch over Jane."

"She told me her wonderful news about the baby. You're right. It will be less rigorous to go by ship. Don't worry about Jane. I'm a wonderful sailor; I'll take good care of her."

The next day, as Lynx began to load the wagons with the mountain of baggage that Jane and Jory were taking to England, Robert Bruce, with two of his men on his heels, rode hell-for-leather into Dumfries's bailey. Lynx saw his grey pallor and agitation and knew there was trouble. "What has happened?"

"Comyn and I made a pact. The swine betrayed me — he dispatched our signed bond to Edward. We caught his messenger with the incriminating documents on him."

"The fool must have a death wish, to betray you!"

"Then he got his wish. I just stabbed him by the high altar at the Franciscan monastery where we held our secret meetings. I am riding to Scone immediately to be crowned. I have no alternative — they will arrest me for treason."

"You killed him on holy ground — you

will need absolution!"

"I have the clergy on my side. Don't worry about me. Look to your own safety, my friend. Get out of Scotland *today!*"

CHAPTER 18

Before the ship was out of the Solway Firth, Jory was clinging to the rail, retching up everything she had eaten that day. With a gentle arm, Jane led her down to her cabin and put her in her berth. Jory groaned. "I'm supposed to be looking after you."

"This bistort will make you feel right as rain."

"Jane, I'm amazed you have no nausea. Are you certain you are having another baby?"

"I'm certain. My monthly courses have stopped, my breasts are extremely tender, and I have to pee every few minutes." Jane saw a strangely rapt look come over Jory's face as she listened to the telltale symptoms. "You don't think you could be . . . ?"

"I have reason to hope," Jory whispered.

"Oh my dear, Lynx was right, you *are* headstrong!"

"Don't you dare to tell him. I want to keep

my secret as long as I can before his terrifying ranting and raving starts."

"Lie down and try to get some sleep," Jane urged. "I'll be back in a little while to check on you."

As Jory lay in the ship's bunk, fighting nausea, conflicting thoughts tumbled about in her mind. Two weeks ago when she had missed her monthly course, she had dismissed the notion that she could be with child. For years she had wished for a baby to fill the void of loneliness, but it had never come to be. After hearing Jane describe her symptoms, however, Jory realized she had conceived. For one moment the thought of having Robert Bruce's child seemed like a dream come true. *For one moment only!* Then the reality began to dawn and she realized it was a nightmare! Lynx's words after the christening of his son came rushing back to her: *Don't wish for his child. It would be disastrous. The scandal would ruin you and bring shame on the de Warennes.* The thought of Lynx's reaction filled her with dread as the dire consequences of her predicament fully sank in.

Her nausea passed off and was replaced by fear and anxiety. Jory sat up in a panic. "I should never have let Jane know. She's far too unworldly to keep a secret from Lynx!"

Jory washed her face and brushed her hair and as she did so, she wrapped herself in a facade of serene confidence. She had no immediate solution to her problem, but until she decided what she would do, she was determined to mask her emotions and show a calm face to the world.

Jane opened the door and peeped in. "Oh, you look so much better, Jory. Did the bistort take away your nausea?"

"Yes, thank you. It also took away my wishful thinking about having a child. You having another baby made me long for one of my own, but 'twas no more than a bout of seasickness." Jane looked so relieved that Jory laughed and quickly changed the subject.

A few days after they arrived at Chester Castle, Lynx and his men clattered into the bailey and he told them of his plans to take Jane to the magnificent cathedral.

"I want us to be married in England and more than anything I want to be able to pledge my own vows to you."

As Marjory sat in the front pew of Chester Cathedral, sudden panic threatened to choke her. As she stared at the flames of the

366

long, tapered candles ablaze on the altar, she became dizzy thinking of the disastrous mess she had made of her life. Until now she had managed to hide behind a mask of serenity, her emotions buried deep, concealed from the unforgiving light of day that would expose her to a shameful scandal of her own making.

As much as I would like to blame Robert Bruce for my predicament, I cannot. I can blame only myself. I am a grown woman, a widow for God's sake, and know the risks involved in taking a lover. Almost from the beginning I knew he would never wed me. He demonstrated over and over that he was selfish to the core, but I willfully blinded myself to his faults. He never lied to me — he admitted the Crown of Scotland was his obsession. I knew the Bruce would sacrifice anything and anyone to become king.

For the hundredth time she went over the limited options available to a woman in her condition. An unwed mother could rid herself of the baby, or give birth in secret and pay another to bring up the child. Jory knew she could never do either, so she moved on to a third possible solution. She could brazen it out and flaunt the rules of society.

If I had a home of my own, that is exactly what I would do! But her father had left her no property — and her marriage had brought her no castle. She would be forced to live on the charity of her brother, and how could she do that if she brought shame to the de Warenne name? On top of everything, her child would be a bastard. *Dear God, I cannot do that to my baby. I love it too much!* Her hand brushed across her belly, and her face softened with tenderness. Her child was a miracle; she would do anything to give it a happy life.

To avoid the stigma of bastardy, I need a husband. Once again her options were pitifully few in number. She pictured Henry de Bohun and her mind recoiled. *I gave my sacred vow to Humphrey that I would never wed his brother.* Fleetingly, she thought of Guy de Beauchamp. *Do not wish for the impossible, Jory. That road leads only to heartbreak.*

She saw Lynx kiss Jane and knew that the wedding ceremony was drawing to a close. She had time for only one quick prayer. *Please, Lord, I ask only that my baby be healthy.*

At the wedding feast in Chester Castle's

vaulted Great Hall, Lynx laid out the travel plans he thought would be best for Jane. "When we get to Kenilworth Castle, we will stay and rest for a few days. It is the halfway point on our journey home and the place where we will meet up with John and his men-at-arms. You will like Kenilworth, Jane. It is a royal castle with every amenity, belonging to Henry Plantagenet, a son of the king's late brother. It lies on the banks of the lovely River Avon in Warwickshire."

The name of the county caught Jory's attention. *Kenilworth lies close to Warwick Castle. I have always been curious to see what Beauchamp's castle looks like.* "I hope John's health has improved. A week at Kenilworth will be good for all of us."

Three days later, the de Warenne cavalcade crossed over into Warwickshire and the square, sandstone towers of Kenilworth came into view. When they rode closer, Jory saw the water.

"How beautiful! The castle sits in the middle of a lake."

"It is a man-made mere, dammed from the River Avon to make the castle impregnable. The only entrance is over that earthen causeway and through the portcullis," Lynx explained.

Jory smiled at the surprised pleasure she saw on Jane's face. "If we are staying for a week, we'll need at least part of our luggage." When they reached the bailey, two de Warenne knights rushed forward to help Jory dismount while Lynx lifted Jane from her saddle. "Come, I'll help you find the wagon with Lincoln Robert's cradle and his toys." Jory smiled at the knights. "I'm sure these gallant gentlemen will carry whatever we need up to our chambers." She raised her eyes to the top of a square crenellated tower and saw two figures gazing down at them. The sun came from behind a cloud and momentarily blinded her. "Lynx, I believe John is here before us." She pointed to the tower; then she and Jane, with the knights in tow, walked over to the baggage wagons.

When John de Warenne and his men had arrived at Kenilworth the previous day, he was weary from the long days in the saddle since they had left Scotland. He was infinitely thankful for the tower chamber the steward had plenished for him, and after he'd been fortified by a good meal, he sat down to write a note to the Earl of Warwick, asking if it would be convenient to come and give him his heartfelt thanks for saving the day at Falkirk.

Guy de Beauchamp was aware that the head general of the royal army, as well as the king himself, had been unable to fight due to a bout of bad health. That was the reason he'd been ordered to Falkirk to defeat Wallace's army. Since Kenilworth was less than five miles from his own castle, Warwick had replied to John de Warenne's note, telling him he would ride over to see the earl.

Guy remembered the last private meeting he'd had with Surrey, when he had offered for Marjory de Warenne and been turned down. Though the encounter was almost five years ago, Warwick still recalled the angry words he had exchanged with her guardian. He shrugged — since then they had fought together in Wales without animosity. Yet it still rankled that the exquisite beauty had passed him over in favor of a young noble her own age.

The following day when Warwick saw Surrey, he was shocked to see how much de Warenne had aged in the years he had been governor of Scotland.

John de Warenne poured ale for his guest. "Warwick, I am deeply grateful that you pulled victory from defeat at Falkirk."

"There is no need to thank me for fighting. That we won the battle was satisfaction enough. Last week Edward Plantagenet offered me a place on the board of commissioners to govern Scotland. I suppose that was his way of thanking me." Ever blunt, Warwick said, "I declined the offer. Trying to govern Scotland is a thankless task, as you have learned to your sorrow."

"My fighting days are over. Administering my own estates will occupy me full-time from now on. I am turning my army over to my cousin by marriage, Aymer de Valence, Earl of Pembroke."

"What of Edward Plantagenet's fighting days?"

"At the risk of uttering treason, I tell you that if he tries to fight another campaign, it will be his last."

Warwick nodded. *As I thought, the king's days are numbered.* "I'm frankly relieved I had no hand in capturing Wallace. He was a brave knight and did not deserve the brutal treatment he received at the hands of Plantagenet. It was beneath contempt."

"Lynx and I agree it was unspeakable butchery, especially when Edward has pardoned the Scots nobles again and again for their treachery. My nephew also is returning to England and bringing his wife and son. Our plan is to meet here at Kenilworth. I'm expecting them today."

"I hear riders thundering along the causeway. Perhaps they are here." Warwick opened the door that led out to the tower's parapet walk. "We can watch them ride in."

"Yes, it's Lynx. They are flying the checkered azure and gold pennants of de Warenne."

Warwick narrowed his eyes. It was not the pennants that had caught his attention, but the female riding in the vanguard. She was small, erect, and her scarlet hood had fallen back so that her silver-gilt hair streamed in the sunlight like a shining banner.

The physical impact of his first glimpse felt like a heavy blow to his heart. Her visual impact mesmerized him to such a degree, he found it impossible to take his eyes from her. Her mental impact set his brain to plotting ways to make her his woman.

With difficulty he looked away and broke the spell. "I'll be off so you may greet your family and spend time together."

Back at his castle, Warwick unsaddled his horse and led it to its stall. Then he went to the armory where his knights were busy repairing their weapons and reshoeing their mounts. They had been home from Scotland for only a month and there was much to do.

As he often did when Warwick Castle had no guests, Guy invited his steward, Mr. Burke, to join him for supper. "I have it on good authority that the king is likely living out his final months."

"Edward Plantagenet has had a long reign and England has prospered under his kingship mainly because of the strong support he received from powerful barons like yourself, my lord."

"Though we have disagreed many times, mainly about taxes, and I have always spoken my mind, he has ever held me in high esteem." Warwick shook his head with regret. "When young Edward succeeds to the throne, he will need much guidance, I warrant."

"You were wisely thinking of the future when you placed your son Rickard in the prince's household at King's Langley, my lord."

"It never hurts to have a Warwick in high places, Mr. Burke."

When Guy de Beauchamp retired to his chamber that night, he was unusually restless. He paced to the window of his high tower a dozen times, seeing nothing but the blackness of the night without, yet seeing a multitude of vivid pictures that lit up his mind within. He relived asking for Marjory de Warenne's hand in marriage, and for the hundredth time he cursed himself. He addressed Brutus, who sat quietly watching him. "The minute Surrey refused my offer, I should have abducted her and carried her off!"

The black wolfhound nodded his agreement.

Warwick's mind flew back to Chester. He had been in Wales when Humphrey de Bohun was killed. He was aware that Jory had come to visit her husband at Chester Castle. "She arrived an eager wife and left a widow." He thanked God that a dose of cold common sense had come to his rescue at the last minute and stopped him from rushing to her side and making a bloody fool of himself. What noble lady would entertain a proposal of marriage when she had just lost a young husband she loved?

"My timing was always wrong!" He smote the stone windowsill with his fist. A year after she was widowed, his friend Gilbert de Clare had died. He traveled to Gloucester to pay his respects, intending to seek out Jory at Goodrich Castle, but he learned from Joanna that the beautiful young widow had no desire to remarry. She was enjoying her freedom and had ridden north to Newcastle.

Slowly, Warwick raised his eyes and looked in the direction of Kenilworth. "Finally, we are both in the same place at the same time." He flung from the window and tried to dismiss the reckless plot that had jumped full-blown into his mind. Yet his imagination would not let the idea die. It stole back to him again and again as he paced across his chamber. It was a simple enough plan. If he wanted her, all he had to do was go and get her, then hold her captive until she agreed to wed him. He looked at Brutus. "Am I willing to risk all on one throw of the dice?" The answer came back a resounding, "Woof!"

Warwick threw open his chamber door. "Mr. Burke!"

His steward answered the summons without delay. "My lord?"

"I want the empty chamber above mine to be fitted out with every amenity. I want it plenished with the finest furnishings that Warwick Castle has to offer."

"Do you want rugs on the floor and wall hangings?"

"I want silken carpets and the tapestries that are woven with mystical beasts. I want gold plates, jeweled goblets, and Venetian crystal bowls. Make sure the bed curtains and window drapes are plush velvet to keep out the drafts. It will need at least two mirrors, a bathing tub, and a modesty screen. I also want the chamber filled with flowers. There are early roses blooming against the garden walls, but that can wait until tomorrow so they will be fresh."

Mr. Burke's eyebrows rose slightly. "You want the high chamber plenished *tonight,* my lord?"

"Yes. Now. I want to create a lady's bower, and your help is imperative. I'll rouse the servants and, if necessary, some of my knights to assist you. Lead on, Mr. Burke."

The Warwick staff worked throughout the night, transforming the sparsely furnished master tower room into a luxurious chamber that would appeal to a noble lady with delicate sensibilities. By early morning the bed was freshly made with woodruff-scented linen and sable fur covers. A small games table inlaid with mother-of-pearl held a set of carved ivory chessmen. Bowls of fragrant early roses and lillies enhanced the delicate atmosphere, adding to the chamber's romantic allure.

Guy de Beauchamp's discerning glance swept about the room with approval. "Perfect, Mr. Burke. All I need is the key."

The steward handed him the iron door key. "Thank you, my lord."

Jory, who had arisen late for once, luxuriated in the lovely hot bathwater until the aches from three days in the saddle were eased away. Though she was insatiably curious about Warwick Castle, she decided it could wait until tomorrow. Today would be perfect for a long, solitary stroll about Kenilworth's lake. Not only would a walk allow her to stretch her legs, it would allow her mind the unfettered freedom to seek a solution to her problem.

She gave the guard in the barbican tower above the portcullis a radiant smile, then walked along the causeway until she reached a grassy expanse that led down to the lake's edge. Small frogs plopped into the water as she approached, and an occasional trout jumped up to catch an insect. Ducks swam among the bulrushes and tiny, iridescent dragonflies hovered above purple water hyacinths.

As she began to focus inwardly on her problem, the scene before her faded and she became unaware that her slippers and stockings were becoming soaking wet. She resolutely put aside what might be best for her and thought only of her baby. *Perhaps I will have to confess all to Lynx and ask him to offer compensation to one of his knights if he will wed me and make my child legitimate. Perhaps the marriage could be in name only.*

Guy de Beauchamp, astride his favorite stallion, had been slowly circling Kenilworth's mere since dawn, hoping that Lady Marjory would be drawn by the lake's beauty. If she failed to leave the castle he was fully prepared to go in after her, but his instincts told him that if he was patient, Jory might come outside to explore her surroundings.

Jory was distracted from her reverie by the sound of a horse in a slow gallop. She looked up and saw the dark outline of a rider. She thought her imagination was playing a trick on her, because the man reminded her of Warwick. As he rode closer, she became more certain that the rider was indeed Guy de Beauchamp. And yet she did not trust her senses. The vision before her seemed unreal, as if she were caught in a dream. *Perhaps I conjured him.*

That thought was immediately dispelled as the dark rider swept her up in powerful arms and set her before him on the saddle. She gasped for breath as she found herself staring into purple-black eyes. "Warwick! It *is* you! What the devil are you doing?"

"I should think that is obvious, *chéri*. I am abducting you."

"You are too old to play childish games," she said coldly.

"Alas, I am older, but not wiser where you are concerned, Jory." He spurred his mount and it sprang forward into a full gallop.

Amazingly, Jory was not afraid. The infamous Earl of Warwick, whose reputation with women stank to high heaven, had snatched her from the edge of a lake with brute force. Yet held secure between his powerful arms she had never felt safer.

"Where are you taking me in such a bloody hurry?" she demanded.

"To Warwick Castle's highest tower."

"Oh my God, you're serious. You *are* abducting me. Guy de Beauchamp, you are a madman!"

CHAPTER 19

"At last my curiosity regarding Warwick is about to be satisfied."

He dismounted and lifted her down from the saddle. "Your curiosity about Warwick the man, or Warwick the castle?"

"Don't flatter yourself." She moved away from him across the courtyard and studied the massive fortress with interest. The grey stone castle was dominated by a magnificent circular tower.

He turned Caesar over to a groom and joined her. "That's the Master Tower."

"Where you intend to imprison me, I warrant," she said lightly.

"Jory, I am delighted that you have decided to cooperate and act in a civilized manner."

She swept him a mocking glance. "One of us has to be civilized, and since you insist on the role of raptor, that leaves only me." She had pretended an air of serenity for so long, it came easily.

"Jory, I'm deadly serious," he warned.

She laughed up at him. "You expect me to take you seriously when you insist on playing *Beauty and the Brute*?"

He ignored her taunt and took hold of her hand. "Shall we go inside, Lady Marjory?"

"By all means, Lord Warwick." She took a deep breath and explained with cool disdain, "Just filling my lungs with fresh air before my incarceration."

He hid his amusement. She was trying her damnedest to annoy him, but in truth everything she said bemused him. Looking at her, hearing her voice, having her here with him at Warwick filled him with joy. *She makes me feel young; she makes me feel alive. As always, she holds me spellbound!*

She kept pace with him as they climbed the tower's stone steps and somehow managed to look both unhurried and unconcerned. The lower level held servants' quarters and above those was a large kitchen. As they climbed higher, Jory saw a spacious dining room above the kitchen, and then they arrived at what was obviously Warwick's private chamber. It was furnished in an overtly masculine style with a black oak desk, a map table, black leather chairs before the stone fireplace, and a massive bed curtained in gold and black. The circular room exuded power, reflecting the personality of its owner and creating the impression that it was a haven, safe and secure from the outside world.

Jory's pulse quickened at the thought of being alone with him in this intimate room of the aptly named master tower, where Warwick undoubtedly ruled the roost and his word would be law. When he gestured toward more steps that led upward and murmured, "My lady's chamber," Jory experienced a moment of acute disappointment, then chided herself for the absurd emotion.

The room above was in such stark contrast to Warwick's she was startled at how feminine it was. The pink and blue silk carpet was the last word in luxury and the mythical unicorns, satyrs, and griffins that gamboled among the wildflowers of the tapestries were designed to pique a lady's imagination. The symbolism of the bowls of flowers, early English roses combined with the fleur-de-lis of France, was not lost on her. She found every detail of the chamber delightful. The corners of her mouth lifted in a mocking smile. "How could I have forgotten that Guy de Beauchamp is a romantic at heart?"

"Your slippers are wet. Have a seat before the fire."

Jory glanced down in surprise. She hadn't been aware of her feet, yet Warwick had not missed the small detail. She wondered what else he had discerned about her.

He went behind the screen and came back with a towel. Then he went down on his knees before her and removed her slippers. Without asking permission he proceeded to fold back the damp hem of her skirt and draw off her stockings. His eyes met hers in an intimate glance. "You made no protest," he murmured.

"I wasn't aware a captive was allowed to protest any indignity her captor perpetrated upon her person."

He patted her feet dry with the towel, then took one bare foot between his large palms and began to massage it. Then he did the same thing to her other foot.

It felt warm and wonderful and she stretched sensually. "So, tell me, my lord, what is your plan?" Obviously, the arrogant devil had dalliance in mind, and she was going to revel in leading him on and then totally rejecting him.

"It's an ingeniously simple plan." He took the iron key from his doublet. "I intend to keep you locked up in this chamber until you give in and surrender to my demands."

Her eyes sparkled with mischief. "And if that doesn't work, what diabolical method of persuasion do you intend?"

"I intend to woo you, Jory," he said simply.

"Woo me?" Her playful air evaporated. "I don't understand."

"I intend to keep you here until you agree to marry me."

"Marry you?" She jumped up from the chair in a fine fury. "You are nothing but a whoreson!" She slapped his face. "You dragged me through this ridiculous charade more than four years ago, surely you don't think I'll fall for your lies a second time and give you the opportunity to do it all over again?"

Warily, he got to his feet. "Do what all over again?"

"Betray me with lies and break my bloody heart, you cruel bastard!" She stood panting, staring at him in outrage.

"I never lied to you, Jory. I told you that dark rumors of murder swirled about me. It was probably best that an innocent eighteen-year-old maiden marry a young noble her own age, but now that you have been widowed for some years, I see no reason why we should not marry. You must know how I feel about you, *chéri*."

"No, I have no idea how you feel about me. Pray enlighten me."

"Please, sit. Let us at least be comfortable while we talk."

Jory sat down and tucked her bare feet beneath her. Warwick poured ale into a jeweled goblet and brought it to her; then he took the chair beside her and stretched out his long legs.

"I sat behind you in Westminster Abbey at Queen Eleanor's funeral service, shortly after you married Humphrey de Bohun. When you removed your hood and I saw your lovely hair, I cursed myself for a fool. I could not bear seeing you with him. Then and there I knew I should never have allowed you to wed him. I should have abducted you and carried you off. So you see, the idea came to me long ago and I have wanted to do it ever since that day."

"Clearly demonstrating that men remain boys forever."

"I was at Chester when Humphrey was killed. You will never know how much I wanted to come to you, to offer my comfort. Common decency made me realize how inappropriate that would be."

She sipped her ale. "Warwick, I doubt you

possess decency, common or otherwise."

He ignored her pointed barbs. "My timing was cursed once again when Gilbert de Clare died and I traveled to Gloucester to pay my respects. I fully intended to ride to Hereford to ask you to wed me, but Joanna impressed upon me that you had no desire to remarry. She told me you were relishing the freedom of widowhood and had ridden north to Newcastle."

"Ah, once again I had a miraculous escape."

His eyes narrowed. "But not this time, *chéri.* For once we are both in the same place at the same time. It is fate!"

"A fate worse than death!" she cried, pressing the back of her hand to her forehead in a mocking, melodramatic gesture.

He shot up from the chair and towered above her. "Jory, for Christ's sake, stop it! You are behaving like every selfish, spoiled, shallow, sarcastic noble bitch I've ever known. I thought you were different — nay, I *know* you are different. Stop this childish performance at once!"

"Me? *You* are the one who is playing childish games."

"Nay, Jory. I am laying my heart at your feet. I have never been more serious in my life. I'm asking you to marry me."

She dropped her pretense like a cloak and looked at him with regret. She successfully banished the tears that threatened to flood her eyes; tears were an unfair weapon. *I long to be your wife. I fell in love with you the day I first saw you, and even though you betrayed me, I have never stopped loving you.*

She raised her chin proudly. "I thank you for your offer of marriage, Guy de Beauchamp . . . but I cannot accept it."

He jumped to his feet. "You love another! You've made wedding plans. Once again I've waited too long." He flung away to the window and stared out with unseeing eyes.

Jory went to him and touched his shoulder. "Guy, I have no marriage plans. There is no man in my life. I swear it."

He looked down at her with renewed hope in his eyes. "Jory, we'll start again. Please forget that I abducted you. Let's pretend that I have invited you to Warwick to dine, as my guest. Will you do me the honor of taking supper with me, my lady?"

She rolled her eyes. "You smooth-tongued French devil, how can I resist such a gallant invitation?"

He raised her hand to his lips and kissed her fingers. "You have a generous heart, my love. I shall come for you in an hour."

Left alone in the circular bower, she walked to the window and saw the spectacular view. The round tower soared so high that she could see the River Avon for miles in both directions. When she looked north, she could just see the tops of the square sandstone towers of Kenilworth in the distance.

Jory's smile was cynical. Her family was so used to her independent ways, they wouldn't even know she was missing. She turned from the window and gazed about the chamber. She suspected that it had been newly furnished with her in mind. "Warwick *is* a romantic at heart, though no one else would guess it in a million years." Though she freely admitted to herself that she loved him, nevertheless, she knew deep down that she was furious with Guy de Beauchamp and had been since her days at Windsor. If he had offered for her, as he had solemnly vowed, they would have been husband and wife for years now. She sighed and for a moment allowed herself to dream of what it would be like to be married to the infamous earl.

When a lump came into her throat she had to stop herself from wishful thinking. *It can never be. What the devil is the point of fantasizing? I must face reality and make plans for my baby.*

She sat down to put on her stockings and slippers and her eye fell on the iron key. "Some bloody captor!" she mocked. "The man distrusts all women save me. He is an utter fool." She picked up the key and slipped it into the neckline of her gown, then pushed it down to lie hidden in the valley between her breasts.

When Guy de Beauchamp arrived to take her to his private dining room for supper, Jory decided to abandon her false air of serenity. She had always found him easy to talk with and she could see no reason why they should not enjoy their last meal together. He gallantly held her chair, meticulously kept his hands from caressing her shoulders, and took a seat facing her. When the steward brought in the food, she greeted him. "Do you remember me, Mr. Burke?"

"I do indeed. You are the lady who prefers ale to wine."

Guy removed the silver covers and carved a bird whose skin had been roasted until it crackled golden brown.

"Is it swan? I saw many on the River Avon."

"Nay, it is a humble marsh hen. Swans

mate for life — I would never separate a breeding pair to put food on my table."

"I approve your sentiments, though I warrant few men share them." As they ate, they spoke of many things. Jory told him how Gilbert de Clare had chosen Ralph Monthermer to become the next Earl of Gloucester by marrying Princess Joanna.

"It is too bad they had no son who could inherit the title, but at least his daughter Margaret will inherit his land and castles."

"You have no objection to a female inheriting landholdings?"

"Of course not. You must have inherited a de Bohun castle when Humphrey died."

Jory shook her head regretfully. "I own nothing, Warwick."

His dark brows drew together. "What the devil was your guardian thinking when he negotiated the terms of your betrothal?"

"Upon our marriage, John de Bohun deeded the Castle of Midhurst to Humphrey and thus to our firstborn child. When he died without issue, de Bohun made Henry his heir and reassigned Midhurst to him. I had no claim unless I was willing to wed Henry."

"But that is outright blackmail!" Warwick thundered. "When I made the offer for you, I promised John de Warenne that any child of mine, male or female, would be well provided with Warwick castles and land, as would their mother."

Jory wiped her mouth and set her napkin on the table. "Please do not tell me falsehoods, Warwick. We once made a pact that we'd never lie to each other. Unfortunately, you didn't honor that pledge. Instead, you told me what I wanted to hear. Please don't repeat the offense this evening; it would ruin our dinner."

Christ Almighty, that bastard Surrey never told her I made a formal offer for her! He told me she had chosen de Bohun over me and fool that I was, I said I would abide by her wishes.

He filled a crystal dish with strawberries and cream and set it before her. "Jory, did you marry Humphrey de Bohun because you were in love with him?"

She was tempted to lie, but found that she could not. "No. I wed Humphrey because my family and King Edward gave me no choice."

Warwick's heart began to sing. All the pangs of jealousy he'd suffered were for naught.

"Of course, I came to love him later." *At least, I hope I did.*

His jealousy came flooding back. He was cursed with it where Jory was concerned. He hoped and prayed that once she was his, the curse would be broken.

When they were finished dining, Guy helped her from her chair. This time, however, his hands cupped her shoulders possessively, and he dropped a quick kiss on her silvery curls. "Come, I shall escort you back to your bower. I have something to ask you." He enfolded her hand in his and led her back upstairs. He did not pause at his chamber, but took her back to her own.

Guy sat her down and knelt before her so that their eyes were on the same level. "Jory, you deserve a husband who will love you to distraction. If you will consent to be my wife, I will love you all my days. I want to make you the Countess of Warwick, and because I deem it unconscionable that you have no property of your own, I will deed you my castle near the village of Sutton, a day's ride from Warwick. Jory, will you marry me?"

It was the greatest temptation she had ever had to face. The powerful Earl of Warwick had created a magic haven just for her. Everything about his offer was enticing. It would be the easiest thing in the world for Jory to accept. *If I were not having another man's child, I would grab this chance for happiness.*

She reached out to touch his hand. "I thank you for your offer of marriage, Guy de Beauchamp . . . but I cannot accept it."

He shot to his feet, strode to the window, and came back again. "Damn you, Jory! You are more stubborn and willful than a dozen men-at-arms!" He paced to the window and smote the stone sill.

Jory stood up. "I must return to Kenilworth."

He turned toward her. The look on his dark face was incredulous. "What the hellfire are you talking about? I have abducted you. I intend to keep you until you agree to marry me. A few days at Warwick and you will be so compromised, you will have no other choice!"

Her voice was cool and determined. "Guy, I will not stay here."

He swiftly closed the distance between them and with powerful hands lifted her in the air. He began to shake her vigorously, deliberately. It was a full minute before he set her feet down. Then he bent and swept the iron key from the carpet where it had fallen. "Will you not, Lady Marjory? Then I give you no choice." Warwick strode from the chamber and turned the key in the lock.

Through the door, she flung his own words after him. "Damn you, Warwick, this is outright blackmail!"

Jory hoped he would return, yet deep down inside she knew he would not. *When Marjory Bruce told me of her abduction, I thought it the most romantic thing I'd ever heard. Ironically, now that it has happened to me, I am incensed!*

There was little point in railing against her situation since there were none to hear her, and in the end it would alter nothing. She prowled the circular room for a long time, walking off her frustration before she decided to conserve her energy, sit down quietly, and plan her best course of action. Until he unlocked the chamber door in the morning, she was virtually his prisoner.

Jory knew she must concoct a plan. She must use her wits against him — it was the only weapon she possessed. She and Joanna had always said there wasn't a man breathing who could not be manipulated. Jory reassured herself that it had worked on Edward Plantagenet, yet she was acutely aware that the Earl of Warwick was not so easily deceived. He was shrewd enough to know where she had hidden the key.

"To manipulate is to get one's way by unfair means, and the simplest way to do that is to use his own words against him." When her plan was finally set and she knew exactly what she would say, Jory removed her dress and hung it in the wardrobe to keep it wrinkle free. A female's appearance always played a paramount role when dealing with the male of the species. She climbed into the large, comfortable bed, knowing that a good night's sleep was the best beauty aid in the world.

As soon as the dawn light crept in through the east window of her chamber, Jory lay absolutely still until her morning queasiness passed off, and then she arose and went to the mirror. "I must appeal to his protective instincts. When I beseech him, I must remember to look feminine and helpless." She refrained from pinching her cheeks to add color; a pale ethereal look would serve her better. She washed and dressed, then used the silver brushes he had provided to untangle her hair and make it billow about her shoulders in a shining mass. Then she sat down to await him.

When Guy de Beauchamp unlocked the chamber door and stepped inside, he thought he had girded himself against any and all appeals Jory would make to him.

But this morning she looked as sweet and innocent as she had when she was eighteen, and it touched his heart. With an effort, he kept tenderness from his voice when he spoke. "Do you have something to say to me, lady?"

"Yes, my lord," she said softly. "I spent the night thinking of the things you said to me. I am half convinced that you told me the truth about the way you feel about me."

"Only half? Jory, every word I said was from my heart."

She looked at him solemnly. "You told me that you love me."

"I *do* love you. You are the only woman I have *ever* loved."

"If you truly love me, Guy, you will release me."

He stared at her aghast. She had cut the legs from beneath him. There was no argument he could make that would not turn him into a foul liar in her eyes, as well as a coward.

"Then I release you, Jory."

She saw that his face had gone paler than her own. "Yes, Guy, I knew you would," she said softly.

"Have some breakfast and I will take you back to Kenilworth."

■ ■ ■ ■

On the five-mile ride along the River Avon, Jory's heart felt strange. One moment it felt as if it was bursting with happiness and the next like it was drowning in sorrow. Guy de Beauchamp, the infamous Earl of Warwick, truly was in love with her. He was proving it beyond a shadow of doubt by returning her to Kenilworth, yet more than anything in the world she wanted to stay with him. Jory hardened her heart. *I must be mad! He was the first man to betray me — why would I give any man the chance to betray me again?*

She rode beside him across the causeway; then they drew rein before the portcullis. He dismounted from Caesar and lifted her down from the palfrey he had saddled for her at Warwick. He didn't release her immediately. His hands clung to her possessively while he gazed down at her. Finally, he dipped his head and brushed his lips across hers. *"Au revoir, chéri."*

When Jory passed her uncle's chamber on her way to her own, she decided to see how he was faring. Yesterday, when she saw him, he had looked worn out. She knocked and a servitor who had just brought the Earl of

Surrey's breakfast opened the door.

"Hello, John. I hope you are feeling rested today."

"Yes, I do feel better. Those long days in the saddle tired me out." He looked at her windblown hair and waited until the servant left. "Apparently, you don't have that problem. Where would you ride to at such an early hour, Minx?"

"Actually, I've just ridden back from Warwick."

"Warwick?" John's brows drew together. "He was here yesterday when you rode in. Did he invite you to visit his castle?"

"Something like that." Jory was curious. "Why was he here?"

"I wanted to express my gratitude for replacing me at Falkirk and to congratulate him on his victory. Without Warwick we would have suffered ignominious defeat. Is Warwick courting you again?"

"Something like that," she repeated evasively.

"He'd be a damn good catch for a widow, Jory."

"You've certainly changed your tune about the infamous earl."

"When you were eighteen, Warwick was not a suitable match. I made it plain to him at the time and he agreed with me."

Jory went very still. "Did Guy de Beauchamp offer for me?"

"Among others. We chose the young noble we thought best for you, Marjory," he said defensively.

"We? By *we* I suppose you are referring to you and Lynx?"

"I was your legal guardian. Warwick came to me, not to Lynx."

"But my brother knew about Warwick's offer of marriage?"

John de Warenne pressed his lips together.

"Devious old devil!" Jory rushed from his presence. At this moment she could not bear the sight of him. She went straight to her brother's room and hammered on the door.

Lynx opened it. "Jory, is something amiss? Is it John?"

She glanced at Jane, who was eating her breakfast in bed. "John is a lying swine, and you are no better!"

"What is this about, Marjory?" Lynx looked truly perplexed.

"It is about Guy de Beauchamp, the man I fell in love with. The man whose offer for me you refused, then concealed from me."

Lynx looked at Jory, shamefaced. "At the time, I thought it the right thing to do for your own protection. I had no idea what love was until I married Jane. Had I known then what I know now, I would have given you and Warwick my blessing."

My God, it wasn't Warwick who betrayed me; it was the men of my own family, the men who were supposed to love me!

Jory rode into the bailey of Warwick Castle. She slid down from Sheba and handed the reins to one of Warwick's men. "I have come to see the earl. Where would he likely be at this hour?"

"I warrant His Lordship is in Warwick's Great Hall, my lady." He pointed toward the square stone edifice. "Yonder, through the castle's main entrance."

"Thank you. Would you be kind enough to stable my palfrey?"

As she walked up the castle steps and through the massive oaken doors, Jory's knees began to tremble. Men-at-arms and household servants stepped aside and stared curiously at the elegant young noblewoman with the silver-gilt tresses.

When the hall suddenly quietened, Guy de Beauchamp raised his dark head to see what had caused silence to descend. He was stunned when he saw that Marjory had returned. He strode down the hall to meet her, his unruly heart hammering in his eardrums.

She went down into a deep curtsy before him. "My lord earl, I have come to offer you my abject apology."

He took her hands and raised her quickly. "Do not abase yourself to me, Jory. Come in here, where we can be private." With a firm hand beneath her elbow, he led her into a smaller map room off the Great Hall and closed the door.

"My uncle, John de Warenne, and Lynx have just admitted they lied to me and that you did indeed make a formal offer of marriage for me. All these years I believed you had betrayed me, and I have come to beg your forgiveness."

"There is nothing to forgive, Jory."

Oh God, there is . . . there is!

"Guy de Beauchamp, I have come to ask if you will marry me."

Warwick's face suddenly lit up with joy.

Quickly she reached up her hand to cover his mouth and echoed the words he had said to her so long ago when he had proposed. "Don't answer me now. You must think about this long and hard. Your life would be irrevocably altered forever. The wrong decision could make you hate me with a vengeance someday." Though she trembled, she looked into his eyes. "I am going to have a child."

Warwick's gut twisted with anguish. "Who is the father?"

She lifted her head proudly. "If you marry me, my lord, *you* will be my child's father."

He did not hesitate. What sort of man would hesitate when his beloved needed him? "I am honored to accept your proposal, Jory."

She swayed toward him. "Guy, I thank you with all my heart."

■ ■ ■ ■

PART FOUR:
NOBLE COUNTESS

■ ■ ■ ■

CHAPTER 20

Warwick caught Jory before she fell and lifted her to sit on a map table. "Would you like me to escort you to Kenilworth, so we can break the news to your family and collect your baggage?"

"No . . . I am not speaking to my family. We are estranged!"

"Because of the child?" he asked gently.

"God in heaven, they don't know about my baby. You and I are the only two people in the world who know my secret. Once we are wed, they will assume you are the father, unless you deny it."

"I won't deny it, Jory. I give you my word that I will do my utmost to think of it as my child." *Being needed is the next best thing to being wanted, I warrant.*

"You are all I need, Guy. Can you please send for my baggage?"

"I will take care of it. What about your ladies?"

"I don't have any ladies. I've always looked after myself."

He grinned at her. "A countess without ladies-in-waiting is a unique concept. Warwick should be able to provide you with a competent tiring woman or two, if that arrangement suits you."

"Can Warwick provide a priest?" Jory asked anxiously.

He cocked an amused brow. "You think us ungodly as well as uncivilized? Warwick not only has a priest but also a chapel. I'll go and make the arrangements. Is tomorrow too soon for you?"

Today would be better! "Tomorrow would be perfect, my lord."

"Up you go, then." He swept her into his arms from her perch on the table and lifted her high against his heart.

"What are you doing?" she asked breathlessly.

"Taking you up to your tower room."

"You mustn't carry me in front of your men. They'll think —"

"They'll think I cannot keep my hands from you and they will be right. Tomorrow you'll be the Countess of Warwick — they'll have to get used to it, and so will you, Marjory de Beauchamp."

Her smile was tremulous. "I've waited so

long to be Marjory de Beauchamp. Tomorrow you may carry me; today I'd rather walk." He kissed her ear and set her down. "Whatever you desire, love."

In midafternoon all her luggage arrived and was carried up to her tower chamber by Warwick's men. Mr. Burke led the way and brought an attractive older woman with dark hair and lively eyes.

"Lady Marjory, allow me to present Meg, who will help you unpack and is most eager to serve you in any way."

Meg bobbed a curtsy and said cheerfully, "Most eager to see your pretty clothes at any rate, my lady."

Jory laughed. "How delightful. A woman with a sense of humor and an eye for fashion is worth her weight in gold, I warrant."

Mr. Burke rolled his eyes. "If you don't keep Meg in her place, my lady, she will take untold liberties."

When the steward closed the door, Jory asked, "Have you lived at Warwick all your life, Meg?"

"I came with His Lordship's first wife, Isabel de Clare; then I was tiring woman to his second wife, Alyce de Toeni, and nursemaid to young Rickard until he grew too big for his boots. If there's aught you want to know about Warwick, ask me. I know *everything.*"

Jory hid her amusement. Clearly Meg wanted to gossip, and though Jory was curious about many things, she had more good sense than to listen to idle rumor from a servant about her bridegroom. She skillfully diverted the conversation to her elegant gowns as they were unpacked and hung in the wardrobe.

"Princess Joanna gifted me with the exquisite silk material for this gown when I was her lady-in-waiting. I've never worn it because I was saving it for a special occasion. I've decided to wear it tomorrow when I marry His Lordship."

"I've never seen anything as lovely." Meg held the pale jade silk so that its silver threads reflected the light. "It exactly matches the green of your eyes. You will easily be the most beautiful bride ever to be wed at Warwick, my lady."

"Thank you for the generous compliment, Meg. I am most flattered, and thank you for making me feel welcome."

Meg grimaced. "It's a man's world, Warwick Castle more than most places. Us women must stick together."

That night Mr. Burke brought a supper tray to Jory's room and she ate alone, wondering where Guy was and why he didn't join her. When it was full dark and she was about to retire she heard noises in the chamber beneath hers; then she heard him climb the stairs.

"I came to bid you good night, Jory." He looked at her quizzically. "Can you explain to me why you could not accept my proposal of marriage, no matter how I coerced you, yet you deemed it acceptable if *you* did the proposing?"

"It would have been so easy to say yes. But my conscience wouldn't allow it. The choice had to be yours, my lord."

He lifted her hand to his lips and kissed her fingers. "Tomorrow we will keep the promise we made to each other almost five years ago. *Bonne nuit,* my love."

An hour later, Jory lay wide-awake feeling both lonely and vulnerable. *Guy didn't hesitate . . . He made it plain he wanted to marry me even after I told him about the baby. I didn't dare tell him the father's name. He must never know.* She turned over. *Why wasn't he eager to exchange vows today? He must have needed time to get used to the idea.* She curled over onto her side. *I am so thankful he came to my rescue. I love him with all my heart.* She wrapped her arms about the pillow and clung to it. *Guy is the only* one I have now. Jory sighed. *Guy is the only one I need.*

In the chamber below, Warwick lay wide-awake. *She wouldn't tell me his name. I won't press her, but I will find out the name of the swine who did this to her, then abandoned her.* Raw jealousy flared up in him. He thumped his pillow. *I'll kill the whoreson!* A need to protect Jory and her child engulfed him. *You've been given a rare chance for happiness, Warwick. Don't squander it this time.*

Jory opened her eyes to a chamber filled with sunlight. When no hint of nausea threatened she smiled and stretched luxuriously.

"This is the happiest day of my life!" Her thoughts were suddenly shadowed by the estrangement with her family, but she vowed not to let it ruin her wedding day.

A nosegay of white roses decorated the breakfast tray that Meg brought, along with a note that read: *I count the hours until you are mine. Guy de Beauchamp, Earl of Warwick.*

Jory smiled a secret smile and sighed with happiness. "He is such a romantic devil."

"He can be a devil all right . . . I don't

know about romantic."

Jory laughed. "Meg, don't disillusion me on my wedding day."

After breakfast, maids carried in hot water for Jory's bath and Meg helped her wash her hair. "I've never seen hair like yours. It sparkles in the sunlight and makes you look like an angel."

"A devil and an angel — a perfect match, I warrant."

Two hours later Jory examined her reflection in the mirror and sighed with resignation that, garbed in the pale green silk with her hair falling to her waist, she looked no more than eighteen.

Jory picked up her roses and took a deep steadying breath. "You'll have to show me where the chapel is, Meg."

Meg pressed her lips together. "That honor has been claimed by Mr. Burke. I'd best hurry down and tell him you're ready."

Warwick awaited his bride outside the chapel rather than at the altar as custom dictated. "Thank you, Mr. Burke." Guy took her hand and waited until his steward went inside the church. "I will always remember the way you look today, Jory. The wait has been well worth it." He brushed her cheek with his fingers. "Please don't be angry with me when you go inside and find your family there. I could not bear to be a bone of contention between you and the people who love you. I went to Kenilworth yesterday and asked Lynx to give the bride away."

She looked up at him and felt like laughing and crying at the same time. "Oh, Guy, you have forgiven them to spare me distress."

"Nonsense. Two great noble families such as de Warenne and de Beauchamp should be allies, not antagonists."

Jory fought back tears. "Guy, you have made me so happy."

"From this day forward that is my sole purpose in life," he vowed with mock solemnity. He led her into the chapel, where her brother stood patiently waiting for her.

Lynx enfolded her in his arms. "I wish you happiness, Jory."

Brother and sister watched the bridegroom stride up the aisle and take his place at the altar to await his bride. Lynx bent to murmur, "Poor devil, I don't envy him the taming of you."

Jory floated up the aisle on her brother's arm, smiling radiantly upon the Warwick knights who filled the chapel and her heart filled with joy when she saw her uncle John de Warenne on the front row, standing beside Jane. "Lynx, you and I are truly blessed," she whispered. "We both got our heart's desire."

When Lynx stepped back, Jory looked up at Guy and saw his dark eyes were filled with adoration for her. The priest began the Solemnization of Matrimony, but she was so focused on the man who towered at her side that she barely heard the words. Pride was boldly stamped in every line of his face, and Jory gave thanks that she was marrying a mature man with a strong personality, who could be a law unto himself if the mood took him. That he was a powerful earl of the realm with both wealth and property imbued her with a sense of security, and his renowned fighting skills as a warrior made her feel totally protected from life's dangers.

Guy made his nuptial vows to her solemnly, seriously, and Jory offered hers sincerely, from the depths of her heart. He opened his large hand and she saw that nestled with her wedding ring was a perfect white rosebud, proving he was an unabashed romantic.

"With this ring I thee wed, with my body I thee honor, and with all my worldly goods I thee endow."

Jory was thrilled that the wide gold band fit her finger exactly, and she listened carefully as the priest said the final words:

"Forasmuch as Guy and Marjory have consented together in holy wedlock, and have witnessed the same before God and this company, and thereto have given and pledged their troth either to other, and have declared the same by giving and receiving of a ring, and by joining of hands; I pronounce that they be man and wife together, in the name of the Father, and of the Son, and of the Holy Ghost. Amen."

At the marriage feast, Jory insisted that Jane sit beside her so she could tell her the whole romantic saga that had begun almost five years ago between herself and the infamous Warwick.

Jane listened with fascination. "Obviously, you were fated to be together. It was written in the stars. Your husband's love surrounds you like an aura . . . I can see it, feel it."

"I'm so happy that Guy rode to Kenilworth yesterday and made peace between our families." Jory put her lips to Jane's ear. "He has such a tender heart, though he pretends otherwise."

"We will be journeying to Hedingham shortly. I suspect it is a grand castle such as this one. I would feel much more confident if you were going with me, Jory. I shall miss you terribly."

"Warwick's castle of Flamstead is close by Hedingham. Guy breeds horses there. It will be the easiest thing in the world to convince him that we should visit there soon." She gave him a tempting, sideways glance. "He can deny me nothing."

He gave her an indulgent grin. "Not tonight, at any rate."

When the tables were cleared, Warwick musicians provided music, but there was no dancing planned. "Wait until I take over as chatelaine," Jory teased. "We'll have dancing and singing, and none of your knights will be excused. I'll arrange lessons for them."

"If you can bring elegance or even a smattering of civilization to Warwick, my love, it will be a miracle."

The toasts to the bride began and Guy gallantly answered each one and then proposed one of his own that set everyone in the Great Hall to cheering. The hour was late when the de Warennes reluctantly got up to return to Kenilworth, and Guy and Marjory accompanied their guests out to the courtyard.

John wrapped his arms about Jory and kissed her brow. "My dearest child, I pray you find it in your heart to forgive what I did to you. My intentions were for your welfare — I only ever wanted your happiness. I hope you will find that with Warwick."

"I'm sure I will. I love you, John. Take care of yourself."

When Lynx wrapped his arms about her, she reached up and whispered in his ear, "I want the kind of love that you and Jane share and I intend to have it. I've quite made up my mind!"

Hands clasped, the newlyweds began to climb the stairs of the master tower, but Warwick, impatient to reach the privacy of his chamber, swung Jory up into his arms and did not set her feet to the carpet until they were over the threshold. He kicked the door shut with his foot. "Welcome to my life, Marjory de Beauchamp." He brushed the golden tendrils of hair back from her face, then cupped it with his hands as his gaze traveled from the gilt curls at her temples, to her green eyes, along her high cheekbones, and down to her pretty lips. "Your eyelashes are silver tipped with gold and your mouth turns up at the corners when you smile." When he brushed his lips against hers, she opened them as he hoped she would to invite and welcome his kisses.

A noise at the far side of the chamber by

the stairs made him lift his head. "Meg, what the devil are you doing here?"

"I was above, waiting for Lady Marjory in the special chamber you furnished for her, my lord."

"She won't be using it tonight, Meg, nor most nights for that matter. She will share my chamber from now on."

Meg looked surprised and muttered, "I reckon there's a first time for everything. I bid you both good night, my lord, my lady."

When Meg departed, Guy moved to the door and turned the key.

Jory laughed up at him. "What's this? You've never shared your chamber with a female before?"

"My previous wives expected and were given their own apartments. You are a different kind of woman, Jory."

"Different how?" she asked, bemused.

"You are earthy — a man's woman — the kind of female who will enjoy sharing a man's bed every night. Am I right?"

"I certainly intend to enjoy sharing *this* man's bed every night. Years of anticipation sharpen the appetite."

"They have made me absolutely ravenous." He began to unfasten the lacings at the back of her gown and shift to reveal the satin-smooth skin from her nape to the curve of her bottom. "The small of your back holds a sensual fascination for me." He bent his head and trailed tiny kisses along her spine until he felt her arch with pleasure. "So-o-o sensual."

Jory stepped from her gown and carried it to the wardrobe. "I want to keep this dress forever, not just because it's my prettiest, but because wearing it made me feel so special."

He picked her up, not caring that she still wore shift and stockings, and carried her to his bed. Then he disrobed, padded naked to his desk, and brought some papers back to the bed. Guy stretched out beside her on his belly and opened a folded document. He saw that she gave it a cursory glance, but her eyes showed far more interest in his muscular body than the paper. "Do wedding presents hold no interest for you, *chéri?*" he teased. "This is the deed to Windrush Castle near the village of Sutton. I have signed it over to you as I promised."

"Windrush is such a romantic name. Your gift means a great deal to me, Guy. It is the first property I have ever owned."

"It makes me happy to give you things." He picked up a second parchment and unfolded it. "*This* one was harder to come by."

Jory looked down at the paper. "Chertsey? This castle is in Surrey and belongs to my uncle John de Warenne."

"In the future it will belong to Marjory de Beauchamp. When I pointed out to Surrey that he had overlooked you when he distributed your late father's property, he was most contrite and rectified the omission by bequeathing you Chertsey in his will."

Jory's eyes sparkled. "Warwick, that was outright blackmail!"

"The power of guilt is a marvelous spur," he said solemnly.

She threw her arms about his neck. "You are my magic man!"

"Then let me see if I can make your shift and hose disappear." He lifted off the silk shift, then rolled her stockings down her legs, exposing her creamy flesh an inch at a time. He caressed her bare thighs with loving hands and when she sighed with pleasure he focused his attention on her enticing mouth. He kissed her for a full hour before his lips moved lower to caress her throat and tantalize her breasts, while his fingers played with her hair, stroking it, feeling its fine texture, curling it about his fingers and kissing the tendrils at her temples.

Jory felt as if she were melting inside. Guy's unhurried kisses and caresses made her feel cherished and languidly sensual. His sole intent was focused on giving her pleasure as he whispered love words and adored her with his eyes and his lips. Her senses of touch and taste and smell became heightened, and Jory knew her arousal was far more intense than anything she'd ever experienced before. She became flushed with passion and the desire to yield up everything to him.

Guy marveled at the marked contrast between their bodies. She was exquisitely fair, small, and delicate — ethereal as a faerie queen from some mythic tale. He was tall and muscular, and swarthy as a Gypsy . . . hard where she was soft, coarse where she was fine. Because they were physical opposites, it aroused a smoldering desire that cried out to be quenched. Guy enjoyed the foreplay as much as Jory, more perhaps, for she was writhing in uninhibited abandon when he plunged his marble-hard cock into her honeyed sheath. He held still until the throbbing fullness inside her set her whole body ashiver. Then he thrust slowly, deeply, with a rhythm that matched their heartbeats.

Threads of hot molten gold spiraled from her belly and spread up into her breasts and down into her thighs. She loved his dark, powerful maleness that made her feel feminine and feline and frenzied. His deliberate slowness told her that he savored every shiver and sigh, every tremor and cry of this consummate mating.

Guy's eyes glittered black with passion. His flesh was fiercely demanding, his blood sang in his veins, his pulse throbbed in his throat and his groin as he thrust deeply into the sleek heat of her silken flesh. He took complete control of her body, determined to make Jory feel that nothing else mattered but him inside her. He wanted to brand her as his, to mark her forever as his woman, to make every other man pale by comparison.

Jory shuddered with the bliss of it all. Whenever she thought of lovemaking for the rest of her life, this was the night she would remember. She cried out his name as heat leaped between them and the night exploded. She dissolved in liquid tremors and knew that this mating was achingly perfect. She clung to him sweetly, wildly, yielding her heart and her soul to him.

When he knew she was replete and not one moment before, Guy allowed his own body to take its release. His shout of joy was raw and elemental and undeniably triumphant. He enfolded her in his arms and held her against his heart as her body softened with surfeit. Guy, filled with life and love, felt completely satisfied for the first time in his life. Jory was like his other half, making him feel whole. He took his weight from her and stretched out beside her. He kissed her tenderly. "Jory, I love you so much. I can't believe that you're finally mine." He captured her hand and drew it to his mouth, kissing each fingertip with reverence. "You hold me spellbound."

Jory reveled in the attention he lavished upon her after they had made love. The experience was totally new to her. Exchanging touches, kisses, and soft love words thrilled her beyond measure. It was Guy de Beauchamp's way of showing that he cherished her. Later, as they lay curled together, she knew that he had changed her life forever. Her body was still vibrating to his touch and she realized how close she had come to never knowing what it felt like to be truly loved. She felt so safe and secure locked in his arms, entwined in the bed, warmed by her husband's powerful body. The heavy, strong, sure beat of his heart lulled her to sleep.

Guy's arms anchored her to him possessively. He had never felt so protective in his life. Now that she was finally his, he was determined to make her love him unconditionally and exclusively. The thought that Jory might share her heart with another knotted his gut. She had admitted that she had not been in love with Humphrey de Bohun, so he easily laid that ghost to rest. But somewhere there was a living, breathing male who must linger in her thoughts and Guy knew that curbing his raging jealousy would be the hardest thing he'd ever had to do. *Christ, being in love is the devil's own torment!*

CHAPTER 21

As dawn lightened their chamber, Jory opened her eyes and began to laugh. "Every morning for over two months I have awakened to find you gazing at me hungrily, as if you want to devour me."

He pulled her close. "I do. I'll never have enough of you."

"You are a compulsive madman, but I love it." She surrendered her lips to his demanding mouth and shivered with anticipation.

After their love play, Jory watched her husband shave before he went down to eat breakfast in the Great Hall. "I warrant your ardor will cool once I start to bulge," she teased.

"I doubt that, sweetheart. A woman with child blooms with a special, radiant beauty. Have you chosen a name for him yet?"

The blood drained from her face. "Warwick, don't say that!" *If I had a son and Robert Bruce found out, he could try to take him from me. Kings are obsessive about male heirs.*

Guy strode to the bed, thinking she was about to faint. "Are you all right? Did I say something that upset you?"

"I don't want a son!" She regained her composure. "I have my heart set on a little girl. I've quite made up my mind."

Guy saw that, though Jory smiled at him, her eyes were filled with fear. *Why does the thought of a male child terrify her?* "If you feel faint, sweetheart, I can mix you an herbal remedy."

"No, thank you. I've never fainted in my life," she assured him. "But it's good to know you have a knowledge of herbs."

"The castle has a stillroom well stocked with medicinal herbs and plants. It's right next to the brew house."

"Warwick is so vast, I haven't finished exploring yet."

He brought her a map of the castle and outbuildings from his desk. "This will help you. Just be careful, Jory." He opened the door to leave and Meg carried in her breakfast tray.

Jory studied the map. "I have a fancy to visit the stillroom."

"Do you dabble in potions, my lady?"

Meg looked alarmed.

"Nay, my knowledge is limited to bistort for nausea."

"Herbal potions can be *poisonous*," Meg warned darkly.

Jory remembered what Princess Joanna had once said: *Rumor has it that Warwick's first wife was poisoned.* She quickly changed the subject. "This map shows the castle and the River Avon, but what is this dark area marked Arden?"

"That is Arden Forest. The Earl of Warwick owns it outright."

"My husband has his own private forest? The close-mouthed devil never mentioned a word about it to me."

Meg pressed her lips together. "He has his reasons."

Jory held up her hand. "Save me from veiled hints and dire warnings, Meg. They won't deter me. After my bath I intend to seek the mysteries of the stillroom. Then, if I don't succumb to poison, I may even explore the deep, dark Forest of Arden."

When Jory entered the stillroom with Meg, she was surprised at its size. Myriad bunches of plants, herbs, flowers, and roots hung from the high beams to dry, and shelves held a variety of pots and jars that contained everything from ointments to seedpods. She greeted Mr. Burke, who was conversing with a pair of dairymaids churning butter. He left them and joined the countess. "I've been making wax candles for your chamber, my lady. The rest of the castle uses tallow."

"That's very thoughtful of you. I have much to learn if I am to be a competent chatelaine. It's much larger than I expected."

"We store sacks of hops and malt in here for the brew house, and those are barrels of vinegar made from fermented apples. Through this archway are the stone boilers where we make soap from rendered sheep fat. The smell is a little pungent today."

"More than a little, Mr. Burke. I'm afraid I need fresh air."

They followed her outside, where Meg asked pointedly, "Are you suffering from nausea, my lady?"

"It has passed. I'll be fine, thank you." Jory hid a smile as she saw Meg stare at her midsection with speculative eyes.

"I shall go for a short ride — the fresh air will do me good."

Meg looked alarmed. "Do you think you should be riding?"

Jory didn't want to confirm the woman's

suspicions just yet. "I'm used to riding every day. Exercise keeps me healthy, Meg."

When she entered the stables, Brutus padded up to her and barked his welcome. The young groom who tended her palfrey stepped forward. "Would you like me to saddle her, my lady?"

"Yes, thank you, Ned." She spoke softly to Sheba while he put on her harness; then he led her palfrey from the stall and helped Jory to mount. She waited for Ned to saddle his own horse, for Warwick insisted she take a groom whenever she rode. "Come on, Brutus, we'll take you for a run."

Jory led the way from the castle grounds, but today instead of riding along the river, she headed west toward Arden Forest. The wolfhound scented prey immediately and loped between the giant trees and into the thick green foliage of the underbrush. "Don't worry. I won't follow him, Ned. He'll go in too deep. I'll stay at the edge of the trees." She trotted forward beneath the canopy. "The forest is beautiful — it fills me with awe to think it has been here for centuries."

She had been gone from the castle for little more than an hour when she heard her husband's frantic voice shouting her name.

"Jory! Jory! Answer me, damn you!"

She trotted out into the open just as Brutus streaked past her, responding to Warwick's voice. "I'm here, Guy. What is wrong?" She saw that his face was dark with rage and felt alarm.

He was so angry, he could barely speak. "Home! Now!"

She flushed at his uncivil tone. "I didn't ride in deep."

"Not another word!" he ordered. "Home! Now!"

Jory wanted to fly at him and scratch his face. No one had ever spoken to her like that before. Fuming with suppressed anger, she raised her chin and urged Sheba into a gallop. When they arrived at the stables, the groom helped her to dismount.

Warwick loomed above her astride Caesar. "Never — *never ever* — ride into Arden Forest again."

Jory tossed her hair. "I have more good sense than to —"

"*Silence!* Seek your tower, madam!"

Jory fled. She had never seen a man enraged to the point of madness before. She dashed up the tower steps and when she reached his chamber, her feet did not even slow. When she arrived at her own room above his, she slammed the door shut and locked it with the iron key. "You are a monstrous *devil*, Warwick!"

Panting from anger and exertion, she sat down and pulled off a riding boot. Then she hurled it at the door. *Someone ran to him and told him where I was, and that someone could only be Meg! How dare he set spies to watch my every move! I won't be ordered to my room like a child, either. When he comes, I shall tell him so.*

Jory didn't have long to wait. By the time she had pulled off her other boot, she heard his footsteps on the stairs. She heard him try to open the door and held her breath through the minute of dead silence that followed when he found it locked against him.

"Open this door." His voice was low and controlled.

"Do not issue your orders to me, sir!"

There was another minute of ominous silence, followed by a loud thud and crash as the door burst open and swung on its hinges.

She told herself that she wasn't afraid of him, but her mouth went dry as she summoned the bravado to face him.

"Never lock a door against me again." His voice was implacable. His teeth and his fists were clenched tightly as he fought to control his fury.

Wielding her riding boot like a weapon, Jory defied him. "Don't you dare play the brute with me, you arrogant Frenchman!"

Warwick plucked the boot from her hand and, without a word, turned on his heel and quit the chamber.

Jory sank into a chair with relief and stayed there until her breathing calmed. Now that the confrontation was over, she was amazed that she had summoned the courage to fling defiant, insulting words at the powerful earl whose temper was infamous. She arose and on shaky legs walked over to the damaged door. With difficulty she managed to get it almost closed, but saw that it could not be locked to make it secure until it had been repaired.

She poured herself a goblet of wine and as she sipped it, her indignation increased. "I'll not speak to the arrogant swine until he comes and begs my forgiveness!"

As the afternoon shadows lengthened into evening she began to feel as if the room trapped her. The ridiculous part was that it was a trap of Jory's own making. She knew she was perfectly free to leave, but perversely, she vowed that she would remain aloof in her own chamber even if she starved to death.

Eventually, she decided she might as well go to bed. She undressed and hung her riding clothes in the wardrobe. Then she put on a night rail, covered it with a bed robe, and sat down to brush her hair. Her mouth curved with satisfaction as she heard a low knock on the unlocked door. She tossed her hair over her shoulders and shouted insolently, "Go to hellfire!"

"It's Meg, my lady."

Disappointment wiped the smile from Jory's face. She went to the door, opened it wide enough for Meg to enter, then closed it again. She was about to take the servant to task for being Warwick's willing spy, but thought better of it when she saw that Meg had brought her supper. Jory had more good sense than to bite the hand that fed her. "Thank you, Meg. Did *he* send you?"

"No, my lady. He left the tower hours ago."

"I've never seen anyone in such a mad rage."

"I warned you that he could be a devil, my lady."

"Yes, you did. And this morning I told you I didn't want to hear veiled hints and dire warnings . . . I'm sorry, Meg. I should have let you speak. I'm ready to listen now."

Meg set the tray down and took the chair that Jory indicated. "Lord Warwick's second wife died in Arden Forest."

Jory's hand flew to her throat. "I had no idea."

"They were riding in the forest and somehow she was trampled to death by a horse . . . *his* horse."

"God in heaven!"

"The de Toeni family accused him of murder. They contended that it was impossible for a superb horseman like Warwick to lose total control of an animal he was riding."

He's such a physically powerful man, no wonder they had doubts. "Was there trouble in the marriage?"

Meg pressed her lips together. "I warrant there's trouble in every marriage, my lady."

"I shouldn't have asked you that."

"His wife's death was ruled accidental. Lord Warwick was exonerated by the King's Court."

"Thank you for telling me, Meg. It helps me to better understand what happened today."

After the serving woman departed, Jory sat quietly as vivid memories filled her thoughts. She recalled Warwick's words when he had informed her that he'd had two wives and that both had died under suspicious circumstances: *Dark whispers of murder have swirled about me for years.* She had asked him if he denied the rumors and he had replied: *No, I do not deny them. Both deaths were rightly laid at my door and I accept full blame.*

Jory shivered. "Even though he was exonerated, Guy still thinks himself guilty. He carries the burden every day." Her heart went out to him. She could only imagine the horror he must have suffered, having his horse trample his wife to death.

She felt cold all over and drank the soup that Meg had brought in hope that it would warm her. She had little appetite for the other food, however, and set it aside. She went to the door and listened carefully for any movement in the chamber below. When silence told her Guy had not yet returned to the master tower, she climbed into bed and wrapped her arms about a pillow, hoping it would dispel the loneliness of the night.

Jory tossed restlessly for an hour, but eventually sleep overcame her and she drifted into a dream. It was tranquil at first as she wandered through a meadow filled with wildflowers. Then it changed and she realized someone was stalking her. She sought refuge in some nearby trees and suddenly her troubled dream turned into a full-fledged nightmare. A dark rider on a black horse was hunting her like prey. The trees became a thick forest and she knew there would be no escape. She cried out as her abductor swooped down and captured her, then carried her off.

Jory opened her eyes and recognized her captor. "Guy . . . no!"

"Hush, my honey love . . . Don't be alarmed. I'm carrying you down to our bed, where you belong. I refuse to sleep without you."

The candles were lit in his chamber, and she saw his eyes were filled with tenderness. He slipped her into the wide bed and propped the pillows behind her. Then Guy sat down on the edge of the bed and took her hand.

"My behavior was inexcusable today, but I do have an explanation."

"Meg told me what happened in Arden Forest. I'm so sorry."

His dark eyes searched her face. "Fear is a stranger to me, Jory. I've experienced it only once before. But today when I asked where you were and was told you had gone riding in Arden Forest, fear sank its fangs into my belly and threatened to tear out my heart. Raw fear turned me into a madman and I ask you to forgive me."

"I understand your anxiety. I won't go there again."

"When you married me, sweetheart, I endowed you with all my worldly goods. You are the Countess of Warwick and Arden Forest is as much yours as it is mine. You may ride there anytime, so long as I am with you to protect you from the dangers. My men and I hunt there often, and you are welcome to join the hunt, so long as I am at your side."

"Guy, I give you my word that I won't go there without you."

"This has nothing to do with your ability. You are an accomplished horsewoman and likely no harm would befall you in Arden Forest, but if it ever did, it would destroy me, Jory."

Guy snuffed the candles and joined her in the bed. He curved his powerful body around hers and tucked her head beneath his chin. He knew that he was overly possessive of her. She had eluded him once and it had taken almost five years to get her back. He silently vowed that he would never let it happen again.

A month later Jory sat on the dais beside her husband in the Great Hall. She had conspired with Mr. Burke to arrange music for the evening meal. To her delight she had discovered that two of Warwick's men-at-arms were accomplished minstrels. Just as they were taking their bows to great applause and whistles, Rickard de Beauchamp walked into the hall. The clapping was drowned out by shouts of welcome, and Warwick's son raised his arm in acknowledgment. Rickard bounded up onto the dais and father and son wrapped their muscular arms about each other.

Jory was amazed at the likeness between the two males. She had caught a glimpse of Guy's son at Windsor when he was about fourteen years old and had known who he was because of his resemblance to his father, but now that he was a man, he was a young replica of Warwick.

When Guy, with great pride, introduced his wife to his son, Rickard de Beauchamp brought Jory's fingers to his lips, displaying the same innate French charm and gallantry as his father. "It is a delight and an honor to meet you, Lady Marjory. When I received Father's letter telling me he had wed you, I wasn't sure he was telling me the truth."

Jory's smile was radiant. "And why is that, Sir Rickard?"

"He told me years ago that he was about to wed Marjory de Warenne, the most exquisite lady at Windsor, but alas, it never came to pass. Now I see with my own eyes that you are not a figment of his imagination, and I applaud his good fortune."

The steward set a chair and a place for him next to his father. "Congratulations on your knighthood, Sir Rickard."

"Thank you, Mr. Burke. It's good to see you again."

"How long can you stay?" Guy asked.

"Not long. I have much news. His Majesty's health is not robust at the moment, so he gave nominal command of the army to Prince Edward and we are moving north with all speed. We arrived with the cavalry at Kenilworth today; the men-at-arms should arrive tomorrow. I rode over to bring you the news."

"He gave his *son* nominal command of the army?" Warwick said with disbelief. "What prompted such a serious lapse of judgment?"

"It's a long story, Father. It all began when Prince Edward suggested that the Province of Ponthieu be given to his favorite, Piers de Gaveston. It finally dawned on King Edward that his son's relationship with Gaveston was immoral. His Majesty fell into a black rage and dragged Edward about the room by his hair. The king immediately banished Gaveston and told his son that he was negotiating to secure Isabella of France to be his bride. It is my conviction that Edward Plantagenet gave the prince nominal command of the army to make a man of him."

"Fat chance of that," Warwick said bluntly. "But why is the army moving north? Has rebellion broken out again in Scotland?"

"Didn't you hear the news, Father? The king received word that Robert Bruce was crowned King of Scotland at Scone!"

Jory's pulse raced as she listened intently. *Robert is King of Scotland, as he vowed! But for how long? The English will not rest until they hunt him down and pluck the crown from his head. There will be another war! Dear God, why do men lust for power?*

"The Bruce's timing is most expedient," Warwick declared. "The wily young devil knows Edward Plantagenet's strength is at its lowest ebb and his days as England's great warrior are numbered."

"Though His Majesty's health prevents him from traveling with all speed, King Edward fully intends to join us at Carlisle."

"Who did he name head general of the army now that the Earl of Surrey has stepped down?" Warwick asked.

"The Earl of Pembroke," Rickard replied. "The king has issued him orders that all who have taken up arms with the Bruce must be killed and all prisoners are to be executed."

Jory gasped with alarm. "Why is the king so vengeful?"

"It is open rebellion. It must be put down, my lady."

Guy glanced ruefully at his wife. "My son is eager to prove his skill as a warrior. He has not yet become jaded by war, as your brother, Lynx, and I have."

"You won't refuse the king's call to arms, Father?" Rickard asked with disbelief.

"As a leading baron of this realm, I've spent my life pledging my sword to Edward Plantagenet. If and when he issues me a call to arms, I'll consult with my fellow barons before I respond. I am in no hurry. My men and I have been back at Warwick for only a few months. I much prefer spending time with my wife than battling the Scots."

Later, when Guy and Jory retired, she

could not hide her apprehension. "You cannot be happy that Rickard is on his way to Scotland to fight this endless war?"

"I have few worries about his fighting skills. I trained him myself and he was a most adept pupil. Young knights need to prove themselves in battle and earn their spurs, my love."

"You once said that heroic and honorable war is an illusion. You said that war is bloody and brutal, the enemy vicious!"

Guy's eyes widened. "Is that why you are terrified of having a son, Jory? Because you dread him becoming a warrior?"

I am terrified that he will grow up like his father — obsessed with obtaining a crown!
"Yes! I hate the very thought of war. War is the reason I never knew my father. Guy, for many reasons I would be much happier if I had a daughter."

Warwick held her close to banish her fears and she soon fell asleep cradled in the security of his arms. In the middle of the night, however, Jory had a nightmare. She was running, running, determined to take the child she carried in her arms to safety. She desperately sought a place to hide and conceal herself and the baby, but there was no safe haven. Finally, she saw a tower and began to climb the stone steps. When she reached the top she found herself in a chamber standing between two dark powerful men. One was Warwick, the other was Robert Bruce. The King of Scotland, wearing a golden crown and wielding a bloody sword, spoke. "I have come for my son."

"Robert! No!"

Guy bent over his sleeping wife and shook her gently to awaken her. "Jory, sweetheart, you are having a nightmare."

Her eyes flew open. She clung to her husband, buried her face against his chest, and began to weep softly with relief.

"Hush, honey love, it was just a bad dream." Warwick's brows drew together. *Who the devil is Robert?*

CHAPTER 22

Early the next morning, when Jory looked from the tower window, she saw Rickard de Beauchamp strolling down to the River Avon. She realized this would likely be her only chance to speak to her husband's son privately and decided to join him on his walk.

She descended the tower steps as quickly as she could and took the path from the courtyard that led out to the riverbank. By the time Jory located him, he was on his way back. "Rickard," she said breathlessly, "this is obviously one of your favorite haunts and I am sorry to intrude upon your solitude, but —"

"Please don't apologize, my lady. I am delighted that you sought me out." Rickard took possession of Jory's hand and lifted her fingers to his lips. "I am so happy that you finally gave in and consented to become the Countess of Warwick. It must have taken a deal of courage to ignore the vile, baseless rumors."

Jory's eyes filled with compassion as she searched his face. "Your mother's death must have been an horrific tragedy for you, but I believe with all my heart that it was an accident."

Rickard's face became shadowed as if he were haunted by the memories. "It *was* an accident — but it was *my* accident, not my father's. He swore me to secrecy, and I've kept the secret for seven long years, but I think you should know the truth about the man you married." He took a deep breath and plunged in. "I was twelve when I heard rumors of my mother's faithlessness. I followed her into Arden Forest, where she went to meet her lover. When they saw me, the man fled, and my mother rode toward me. That's when all hell broke loose. A boar charged her horse and she fell from the saddle. My own horse reared up in fright and its hooves came down on her head. In a panic I tried to control my mount, but it continued to trample her. I feared she was dead and rode hell-for-leather to get my father. He ordered me to stay safe in the castle and went himself to aid my mother. He brought her body out and told everyone his horse had trampled her while they were hunting together. He swore me to silence, insisting I was too young to bear the stigma of killing my mother."

Tears flooded Jory's eyes, and she swallowed the lump in her throat as she slipped her hand in Rickard's. "Thank you for telling me the truth. I am infinitely sorry that such a nightmare had to happen."

"I beg that you never let my father know that I told you. What he did because of his deep love for me was noble and self-sacrificing, and we must never take that away from him."

"Rickard, you are truly your father's son. It is no wonder that he is so proud of you."

After the midday meal, Rickard de Beauchamp took leave of his father to return to Kenilworth. "Congratulations on your marriage, Father. I wish you every happiness."

"Thank you, Rick. Take care of yourself. It is a damn good thing Gaveston's hold on the prince has been severed. When Edward succeeds to the throne, you and the other young nobles who were in his service at King's Langley will likely be chosen to fill the highest offices in the realm." Guy heard his wife's step behind them. "Here's Jory.

I'll get your horse while you say good-bye."

Rickard took Jory's hand and kissed her fingertips. "I cannot fully convey how happy I am that you consented to become the Countess of Warwick. My father deserves a chance at happiness."

"I am most grateful that you do not resent me. Your father is extremely proud of you, and I am thankful that you feel so secure in your father's love that a new wife is no threat to you."

"No threat whatsoever, Lady Marjory." He gave her a conspiratorial smile. "I hope we can be firm allies and join our forces together to overrule the infamous earl if he proves unreasonable in the future on some point or other."

Jory laughed up at him. "As we are both certain he will."

As Guy led his son's horse from the stables, he saw Rickard and Jory laughing together, holding hands. He paused at the picture they made. She looked even younger than Rickard and they made a most attractive couple. Seeing them together made him aware of his years. His son's admiration for Jory was no threat to him. But other men were . . . men from her past . . . undoubtedly young, handsome men. One who had planted his seed in her, whose name she had called out in her sleep.

Jory and Guy watched Rickard until he rode out of sight; then her husband slipped his arm about her to gather her close. "How would you like to visit our castle of Flamstead? Several mares should have dropped new colts by now, your white palfrey Zephyr among them."

"I would love it above all things."

"We can spend the first night at your Castle of Windrush."

"I can't wait! How did you pick such a romantic name?"

"If I confess that it's named after the nearby River Windrush, will you promise to still think me romantic?"

"Ask me again after we spend our first night there." She stood on tiptoe and licked her lips in a tempting gesture that lured his hot, hungry mouth to ravish her with kisses.

Jory's head filled with plans. "When I visit Lynx and Jane, will you come with me?" she asked breathlessly.

"Absolutely. I'm looking forward to seeing Hedingham Castle." *I intend to find out if Lynx de Warenne knew what the Bruce was planning. The two families have been close friends for years. Surrey turned his fighting men over to the Earl of Pembroke, but if*

449

Edward Plantagenet issues Lynx de Warenne a call to arms to fight the Bruce, it will be interesting to see if he answers it.

"I can be ready to leave tomorrow if that is convenient."

"So can I. The only supplies we'll need to take are a few barrels of ale, since neither Windrush nor Flamstead have a brew house. You tell Meg and I'll inform Mr. Burke."

The following day, in the late afternoon, the small cavalcade arrived at Windrush Castle. Meg, who insisted she could ride, had stayed in the saddle for one hour only. She grudgingly journeyed the rest of the way in the baggage cart, pointedly ignoring the *I told you so* look on Mr. Burke's face.

The small castle sat on the bank of a tributary of the River Windrush surrounded by hills dotted with sheep.

"Oh, it is enchanting! Is it really mine, Guy?"

"Every woolly sheep and lamb," he declared solemnly.

"The flocks belong to Windrush?" she asked with excitement.

"They do, indeed. You are a woman of wealth, Lady Warwick."

Guy took Jory into the castle and asked the steward to assemble the household in the dining hall. When they gathered, Guy held up his hands for silence.

"I am proud to present my wife, Marjory de Beauchamp. I must also tell you that the Countess of Warwick is the new owner of Windrush. I gifted her with the castle as a wedding present."

A great cheer went up from the servants, the castle guards, and many of the shepherds who tended the flocks.

Guy lifted Jory onto a table. "Say something to your people."

At that moment, a territorial growling match broke out between Brutus and some black and white sheepdogs. Though the wolfhound was outnumbered, he soon had the other dogs on the retreat.

Jory smiled apologetically. "What can I say? Dominance runs in the family."

Everyone howled with laughter at the Earl of Warwick's expense and she captured their hearts with her first words to them.

"I smell something good cooking for dinner. Let me guess." She took an appreciative sniff. "Ahh, pig's dick and lettuce. His Lordship's favorite!"

Warwick joined in the laughter. "What can I say? Lewdness runs in the family." He

451

lifted her down and kissed her soundly.

Hand in hand they toured the small castle. "Windrush is in need of refurbishing. Why don't you do it over to suit your own taste, sweetheart? I think the Warwick coffers will permit me to offer you carte blanche."

"Will you teach me to speak French? Words sound so sensual when you say them *en Français.*"

"If you become any more sensual, Madame de Beauchamp, I'll be in a permanent state of arousal."

"Are you boasting or complaining, Frenchman?" Jory licked her lips and deliberately brushed against him.

"Little cock-tease," he murmured and pinched her bum.

Jory sensed eyes watching them and turned in time to catch a look of disapproval on her serving woman's face. "There's no need to unpack, Meg. We'll be here only overnight." She turned back to her husband. "Perhaps it was a mistake to bring her. She is not the least bit sociable and doesn't mix well with others."

"The Windrush Castle's household is made up of Midlanders. Meg is Welsh. People from Wales are a breed apart."

"She's an odd woman. She told me she was Rickard's nurse, yet she seemed to purposely avoid him when he visited us."

"They clash — after his mother died, Meg tried to take her place but Rickard would have none of it." He abruptly changed the subject. "Come, I want to show you the river before the sun sets."

They went outside and he took her down to a small boathouse where a couple of skiffs were moored. The water of the river was placid and slow moving. Ducks and a pair of swans glided by.

"I used to have a black marble bathing tub carved in the shape of a swan. I was exceedingly fond of it."

"Your words paint a provocative picture that is indelible. I am insanely jealous if it was a gift from a lover, *chéri*."

"Of course it wasn't," she denied. "I bought it for myself. Guy, you are the only man who has ever given me presents."

Are you telling the truth, or telling me what I want to hear? "That's good. How about a row on the river before dinner?"

"You have boundless energy. 'Tis one of the myriad things I find irresistible about you."

Guy handed her into the skiff and she reclined against the padded cushions. He removed his doublet and she watched the play of muscles through the fine material of his shirt as he picked up the oars and began to row. Jory trailed her fingers in the water and sighed with bliss. On their wedding day he had pledged that his sole purpose in life was to bring her happiness and, apart from the Arden Forest episode, he'd fulfilled that vow every day.

Before dinner, Jory made a point of mingling with the inhabitants of Windrush, learning their names and asking what duties they performed. Guy spoke with the sheep steward, who assured him the ewes were healthy and the lambs thriving.

After the meal, two women named Mary and Maggie came forward and presented the countess with a lambswool robe. "Thank you for such a lovely gift. You wove it yourselves; I will treasure it."

"Everyone loses their heart to you, sweetheart, and I am no exception." He rubbed the soft wool between his fingers and murmured intimately, "This will give pleasure to both of us."

When they retired, Jory saw that the bed was not nearly so wide as the one at Warwick. "We'll have to sleep very close tonight."

"Sleep wasn't what I had in mind. The thought of your naked flesh wrapped in lambswool has me randy as a Windrush ram."

"Perhaps it was the artichokes we had at dinner. They are rumored to be an aphrodisiac." She undressed and put on the robe, knowing the sight of her in the soft wool aroused his passion.

He sat on the side of the bed and pulled her between his naked thighs. "Since this is your castle, and your bed, and you are all-powerful here, why don't you make love to me tonight?"

Jory dissolved into laughter. "Warwick, you are deluding yourself if you believe you could take the passive role in anything, especially lovemaking, for longer than thirty seconds. Sex is a mating dance of domination and submission, and I warrant you are incapable of the latter. You are a master of control and you delight in driving me to the limit of my endurance. Your greatest pleasure comes when I yield and cling and shudder."

"Guilty as charged." He opened her robe and trailed his lips down her belly. Then he lifted her so that he could thrust his teasing tongue into her honeyed sheath. His hot, hungry mouth proceeded to devour her until she screamed with excitement.

In the dining hall the next morning before they continued their journey, Jory held up her hands for silence. "I have fallen in love with Windrush and promise to come back as often as I possibly can. I have quite made up my mind!"

Two days later the travelers arrived at Flamstead Castle. In the bailey, Meg shunned Mr. Burke's offer of help and descended from the baggage cart with a face like a thundercloud.

"Flamstead is just as beautiful as I remember," Jory told Guy. "I know it doesn't have soaring towers like Warwick Castle, but it is less intimidating and the graceful horses in the pastures make it feel serene and welcoming. Brutus looks happy; I'm amazed at his stamina. He kept pace with us all the way."

Guy lifted her from the saddle. "And I am amazed at your stamina, sweetheart. No one would guess your delicate condition."

Jory glanced quickly at Meg but didn't think she had overheard. "I'll be able to ride for months yet," she murmured to Guy.

"Nevertheless, I'd like you to rest tonight. Tomorrow will be soon enough to explore Flamstead's nooks and crannies. Meg will show you my living quarters and Mr. Burke will bring your luggage. As soon as I've stabled the horses, I'll join you."

When they entered the castle, Mr. Burke explained, "The Great Hall is far smaller than the one at Warwick, since Flamstead has no garrison of fighting men. There are guards, of course, and the castle household, but the rest of the inhabitants are horsemen, grooms, and stable hands."

Guy's living quarters were up only one flight of stone steps and consisted of two large chambers. Mr. Burke carried Jory's trunk into the bedroom and Meg lit the candles.

"Thank you both. I shall do my own unpacking. Go and see to your own needs, Meg."

"I shall bring you some hot water, my lady, then leave you to your own devices while I make sure the cooks provide us with a palatable meal." Mr. Burke held the door for Meg, who swept past him as if he were invisible.

By the time Jory had hung her clothes in the wardrobe, Guy arrived with his own luggage. After they washed and changed, he took his wife down to the hall for dinner. He led her up onto the low dais and grinned at the assembled household. "It gives me the greatest pleasure in the world to present my beautiful wife, Lady Marjory, Countess of Warwick. I know you will serve her well."

All raised tankards, cheered, and chorused, "To Lady Marjory."

Jory stood and lifted her goblet in a salute to the assembly. The six knights who had accompanied them, along with Mr. Burke, were seated at the first table below the dais. Beyond them were the castle servants and the horsemen, some of whom had wives. "Thank you for your warm welcome. Flamstead feels like home."

Later, when they retired, Jory put on her nightgown and knelt on the wide bed. "Guy, I need to discuss something with you."

"About which side of the bed you want to sleep on?" he teased.

"I want to sleep on your side, of course. No, be serious for a moment. When people learn I'm having a baby, my family for instance, everyone will congratulate you about becoming a father again and . . . it could make you feel awkward."

"My love, I *shall* be a father again. Their good wishes won't make me feel awkward in the least. I promise the baby won't be a problem, Jory. Stop worrying."

"Oh, Guy, I don't know what I would do

without you."

He cupped her face in his hands. "You'll never be without me."

During the week that followed, Jory and Guy spent every day together. Her interest and love of horses was almost as great as his and, like a sponge, she soaked up all the details of breeding and bloodlines that he taught her.

"This week has been heavenly. I was absolutely fascinated last night when I watched you deliver the foal. At first I was glad it was a filly rather than a colt, but when it managed to stand up and stagger toward its mother, all that really mattered was that it was strong and healthy."

"You discerned its sex, but can you guess its lineage?"

"Yes," she said with confidence. "It's a crossbred Anglo-Arab: delicate head, deep chest, short back, high tail, and long slender legs. They are reputedly spirited and intelligent."

"Rather like you. I believe I'll call her Jory."

She laughed, pleased at the name. "Do you christen them all?"

"I do. They have names from mythology, the galaxy, and upon occasion I resort to the names of plants and such."

"You mean like buttercup and daisy?"

"Good God, no! See that large grey stallion? I named him Phallus Impudicus, which is Latin for stinkhorn fungus."

Jory threw back her head and laughed with glee. "And for very obvious reasons. You have a wicked humor, Warwick."

"Do you consider that a virtue or a vice?"

"You have *virtues?*" she teased.

"Not many," he admitted. "Why don't we ride down to the river and I'll teach you to swim?"

"I know how to swim, but you can teach me a vice or two, my lord Phallus Impudicus."

They dismounted on the riverbank and tethered their horses where they could crop the sweet grass. Guy began to strip immediately and, not to be outdone, Jory followed suit.

"I feel like a pagan!"

His glance swept her naked beauty from head to foot. "Nay, pagans are swarthy-skinned, black-haired heathen devils, like me. You look more like an ethereal water sprite."

"But don't both indulge in sensual pleasures?"

"Let's find out." He picked her up and

460

carried her into the tall wildflowers that bloomed in profusion at the river's edge. He stretched out and pulled her down on top of him in the dominant position. "Let me teach you the art of *frottage*."

"Oh yes, please," Jory said breathlessly. "That is a delightfully sinful-sounding French word."

"You have no idea, English."

Toward month's end, Jory saw that her waist had thickened, but as she packed her stylish gowns for the visit to Hedingham she knew they would conceal her condition for the present. Even though it was not absolutely necessary to reveal to Lynx and Jane that she was with child, and she was slightly apprehensive about doing so, she felt a need to get it out in the open.

"Would you like to pick out a palfrey for Jane? I think that would make a splendid gift for your brother's wife."

"That is so generous of you, Guy! Jane has a mystical affinity for animals. She'll be thrilled with a palfrey from Flamstead."

That afternoon he showed her two dozen yearlings and allowed her to make the choice. Remembering that Jane had ridden a white horse in Scotland, Jory chose a filly that was the same color. "Since Meg has trouble in the saddle these days, I see no need to drag her to Hedingham; the castle boasts a dozen tiring women."

"Perhaps you can lure one away from your sister-in-law. Meg is woefully inadequate for a lady with your elegance and style."

Jory rolled her eyes. "Don't let her hear you, Warwick!"

"Mr. Burke won't be going either. I will leave him in charge here. Hedingham's not far; an escort of two should be adequate."

"If we're leaving in the morning, I should finish my packing."

Guy sought out two of the knights who had accompanied him from Warwick. "We will be leaving for Hedingham in the morning and staying at Lynx de Warenne's castle for a few days. Learn all you can from his men about the two years they spent in Scotland."

CHAPTER 23

"Jory, you look radiant." Jane, who had been standing beside Lynx to welcome the Earl and Countess of Warwick to Hedingham, ran down the castle steps in her eagerness to greet her dearest friend. " 'Tis obvious that marriage agrees with you." Jane watched avidly as Guy de Beauchamp lifted his wife from the saddle. Pride and love were etched in his face and, Jane also discerned, more than a touch of possessiveness.

The women embraced each other. "Jane, you are absolutely blooming. We brought you a gift." She took the reins of the white palfrey and led it forward. "It was Warwick's idea."

"Oh, she is a rare beauty. I thank you both with all my heart." Jane fondled the animal's nose and whispered something in her ear. "There isn't a chance in the world that Lynx will allow me to ride her now that I am starting my seventh month, but that will give us time to form an inseparable bond with each other."

Lynx joined them and shook hands with Guy. "Welcome to Hedingham. The gift for my wife is most generous of you." He took the palfrey's reins. "Come, I'll show you where you can stable your mounts. Then it will be the dinner hour. My wife is eager to show off her newly acquired skills as chatelaine, and we dare not be late for the meal." He winked. "You know how fiery redheads can be." Lynx beckoned a squire and asked him to show the Warwick knights to their sleeping quarters.

When the two men were alone, Guy asked, "How is John de Warenne, Earl of Surrey, faring?"

"Thank you for your concern. His health is much improved."

When Lynx offered nothing more, Warwick abandoned subtlety. "Surrey turned his forces over to Pembroke and now the king has made the earl head general of the army."

"Since Pembroke now commands the most fighting men, John and I expected him to be made head general."

"Did you also expect the king to order the army north?"

"What you are really asking is: *Did I know that the Bruce intended to seize the Crown of Scotland?*"

"Did you?" Warwick asked bluntly.

"Bruce, Earl of Carrick, is the rightful King of Scotland."

"Your answer tells me that you *were* expecting it."

"I was, though it came as a shock to Edward Plantagenet. He thought he had conquered the Scots and all he had left to do was appoint English administrators to run the country. As well as fighting in Scotland, I garrisoned a castle for over two years and know the Scots will never bend the knee to Edward Plantagenet. What he did to Wallace will only make them more determined."

"When Edward calls his barons to war, as he assuredly will, I would like to know who will answer the call and who will refuse before I make my own decision," Warwick declared.

"Well, I can tell you flatly that Roger Bigod, Earl of Norfolk, will refuse. When my first wife, Sylvia, died leaving him without heirs, the king declared that the Crown would claim the marshal's landholdings upon his death. On the other hand, I war-

465

rant that John de Bohun, Earl of Hereford, and his son, Henry, will answer the king's call to war. He takes his post as England's constable seriously and wants to pass it down to his son and heir."

Warwick nodded. "Will you answer Edward's call to arms?"

"Like you, I would prefer to know what the other barons will do before I make my decision. I am inclined to refuse, since I know it's a losing proposition, but His Majesty can be vindictive and I have a wife, a son, and another child on the way. In the end I will do what is expedient, as I am sure you will, Warwick."

"You may depend upon it. Shall we join the ladies?"

In Hedingham's Great Hall Warwick saw that Jory had changed her riding outfit for a gown of deep violet with a low-cut décolletage to show off her jewels. Her head was uncovered and her silver-gilt hair whispered about her shoulders in a most enticing way. His wife looked dazzling and he saw that he wasn't the only one to notice. He watched closely as she kissed one knight on the cheek and moved into the embrace of another handsome young devil. He strode over so that she would introduce her admirers. His gut knotted. *If one of these swines is Robert, he's a dead man!*

"Ah, Warwick my love, may I present my brother's squires, Taffy and Thomas? They have always been extremely protective of me."

With difficulty, Warwick managed to be civil to the pair. As he led his wife to the dais, she stopped to greet and bestow her smiles on so many of her brother's men-at-arms that he was grinding his teeth by the time they reached their seats. He made an effort to curb his jealousy and told himself that he had better get used to it — Jory was always at her loveliest when surrounded by admirers. "It appears that every de Warenne male has lost his heart to you, my beauty."

"They are just being polite. To a man, I warrant they have transferred their affection to Lynx's beauteous wife, Jane."

He glanced down at Jane, who sat next to him, and said gallantly, "Lady de Warenne, you grace your husband's hall with your beauty and warmth. He is a very lucky man."

Jane's face glowed. "Jory warned me about your fatal French charm, Lord Warwick."

Jory leaned forward. "Don't tell him that, Jane. His head will swell, not to mention other parts of his anatomy."

"Oh, how I've missed your saucy lessons."

She smiled at Warwick. "Your wife taught me the art of seduction. She knows everything there is to know about men and how to manipulate them."

"Indeed?"

Jory's eyes met her husband's and she tried to hide her dismay. "Jane was unbelievably innocent and unworldly."

"Desirable qualities in a bride."

Jory's dismay deepened. Need he point out that she had been neither innocent nor unworldly? She found the courage to answer his words with a jibe. "Warwick's an expert on brides," Jory said solemnly and saw the corner of his mouth twitch with amusement.

Over his wife's head, Lynx looked at Guy with commiseration. "I don't envy you the taming of her."

Jory smiled serenely. "Warwick wouldn't want me any other way."

Guy captured his wife's hand under cover of the table. "That's true, *chéri*," he murmured.

Jane's hand went to her belly. "Oh, my baby is kicking again."

Guy smiled down at her. "Are you hoping for another boy?"

"I am hoping for a girl this time, my lord."

"That is exactly what my wife is hoping

for," he confided.

"Jory, you are having a baby? Why didn't you tell us?"

Jory blushed. "I didn't want to be the center of attention."

Lynx choked on his ale. "You may be able to delude yourself, Minx, but we know better. Congratulations, Warwick. You already have a son, but I despaired of having a child until I met Jane."

Jory squeezed her husband's hand, silently thanking him for making it seem the most natural thing in the world that she was with child. *I feel so blessed to have this man.* She smiled at Jane. "Now it will be your turn to give me lessons. May I help with the wee lordling's bath in the morning?"

"If you can pry him from his nurse. Grace Murray rules the nursery here at Hedingham, as she did at Dumfries."

"I'm familiar with Edinburgh and Stirling, but not Dumfries," Guy remarked casually. "Is Dumfries Castle in the dales?"

"Yes, it is in Annandale . . . much wilder countryside than here, but it will always hold a place in my heart," Jane confided.

Annandale is Bruce territory. It is no coincidence that Lynx de Warenne garrisoned a castle there.

Before he retired, Warwick spoke with his knights. "What were you able to learn about the time they spent in Scotland?"

"Because de Warenne's uncle was governor, they were called on to fight in the front lines and chase down Baliol until the wily devil was captured. They said de Warenne persuaded the Bruce to fight on the side of the English many times, though he and his men were reluctant. The Bruce brothers often visited Dumfries, the castle de Warenne garrisoned. During the time de Warenne was recovering from his near-fatal wound, the visits increased. They became thick as thieves and even spent last yuletide together."

Warwick nodded. "Keep your ears open. Good night."

Next morning, Jory was up with the lark. "I'm off for some baby talk with Jane and her ladies. My nephew is the most beautiful child in the world — I can't wait to see how he's grown."

Guy touched her face with the back of his fingers. "Your cheeks have the soft bloom of rose petals this morning. It does me good to see you so happy."

"Thanks to you. All my apprehension about revealing my secret has melted away.

You have turned what could have been the most difficult time in my life to the happiest. You are my magic man."

Guy breakfasted in the Great Hall with Lynx and the de Warenne men-at-arms. Then Lynx took him to the castle's armory, where the blacksmiths were forging small metal links into chain mail shirts that were much more flexible than breastplates. When Guy admired them, Lynx made him a present of one.

As Warwick mingled with the de Warenne knights he found himself paying close attention to the names of those who were young and handsome. There was Giles, Bernard, Royce, and Harry, but as far as he could tell, none seemed to be named Robert.

They emerged from the armory into the bailey and saw a tall knight ride in with his squire.

"I don't recognize him," Lynx remarked to Warwick.

"I do," Guy replied. "It's Ralph Monthermer, who became Earl of Gloucester when he wed Princess Joanna." Warwick had met his friend Gilbert de Clare's first lieutenant many times over the years. "He's a good man."

Ralph dismounted and his squire took his horse. Guy greeted him warmly and introduced him to Lynx de Warenne.

"I have a message from His Majesty for you, Lord de Warenne, but I didn't know you would be here too, Lord Warwick. I shall kill two crows with one stone since the king's message is intended for all his premier barons."

Guy and Lynx exchanged a knowing glance. The call to arms had come sooner than either had expected.

"Come into the hall and refresh yourself, Gloucester. Did you ride in from London or Windsor?"

"Neither. King Edward is at my castle of Hertford. He summoned me to bring a force of fighting men from Gloucester."

They took Monthermer to the hall, and the three men were enjoying tankards of ale when Jory arrived on the scene.

"Ralph! Is that you? Oh, I cannot believe it!" She ran to him and the two friends embraced each other. "Are you at your castle of Hertford? Is Joanna with you?"

Warwick slanted a dark brow. "Is there no end to your conquests, *chéri?*"

Lynx threw him a wry glance. "I'm afraid there isn't."

"Yes, Lady Marjory, Joanna is at Hertford, as is her father," Ralph Monthermer confirmed.

"How wonderful! Will you take me to visit her, Guy? Hertford is within spitting distance," Jory declared.

Ralph looked from Jory to Guy de Beauchamp with speculation.

"I'm the Countess of Warwick. I wrote and told Joanna but sent the letter to Gloucester Castle. Oh what fun . . . I shall be able to tell her in person. Is baby Margaret well?"

"She is a baby no longer, my lady." Ralph grinned. "I congratulate you on your marriage, Lord Warwick. You must be the envy of every man in England."

Jory gifted him with a radiant smile. "How soon can we go?"

"Since King Edward has summoned our presence, we had best go today." Guy looked at Lynx for confirmation. "The sooner we get it over with the better, I warrant."

Jory glanced quickly at Guy and then Lynx. *Stop worrying. They'll both refuse the king's call to arms to fight in Scotland.*

"I shall go up and pack immediately. We can leave after lunch. Do you think Jane would like to come with us, Lynx?"

"I'll ask her, but I doubt she would enjoy a visit with the royal Plantagenets."

A few hours later, as everyone assembled in the hall for the midday meal, Jane brought her son to show him off to the guests. "He has his father's long legs and has begun to walk by himself," his mother told Guy proudly.

The boy staggered a few steps toward Warwick, who bent and picked him up. The laughing child immediately grabbed a fistful of Guy de Beauchamp's long black hair and chortled with glee.

"No, Lincoln Robert, that's naughty," Jane scolded. "I'm so sorry, Lord Warwick. His father encourages his antics."

"He's a strong, handsome lad." Guy asked casually, "Named Lincoln after his father, and Robert after a valiant de Warenne knight perhaps?"

"Nay, my lord. He's named after his godfather, Robert Bruce." She took her son from Guy de Beauchamp's arms and turned to see Jory enter the hall. "Here comes your beautiful godmother."

Warwick stood rooted to the spot. *Holy Christ, is it possible her lover was Robert Bruce?* He felt as if a boulder had smashed into his solar plexus. He stared at his wife. In the azure riding dress with her lovely hair billowing about her shoulders, she was exquisitely tempting. No man could see her and not want her. The more he thought about it, the more convinced he became that Robert Bruce was the whoreson who had seduced her. *How could I have been so fucking blind and obtuse?* He closed his eyes and saw a sea of dark crimson red. Warwick knew it was bloodlust.

The ride to Hertford Castle took little more than an hour. Jory rode beside Ralph Monthermer, who answered all her questions about Joanna and Margaret. She was completely unaware that Warwick, flanked by his two knights, rode in aloof silence totally immersed in his own private torment.

Raging jealousy almost consumed him. Robert Bruce, Earl of Carrick, was in his prime, no more than twenty-three years old, the exact same age as Jory. Moreover, he was now a *king* no less; apparently an exceedingly virile king, who had planted his seed without thought, then abandoned the lady shamelessly because of his driving ambition for a crown. *I'll kill the whoreson!*

They arrived at the castle, and Ralph helped Lady Marjory from the saddle. Filled with excitement, she lifted the hem of her riding dress and rushed inside to surprise Joanna. A servant directed her to a private walled garden, and as she stood on the steps that led out to a green lawn with a splashing fountain, she saw four ladies playing ball with a little girl, who could only be Margaret of Gloucester. The ball rolled toward her and she scooped it up and tossed it back to them.

"Jory?" Joanna shaded her eyes. "Yes, it is Jory!" She hurried across the lawn with open arms. "I thought you had dropped off the face of the earth." She embraced her friend, then stepped back to observe her from head to toe. "My God, I once predicted that someday you would exude sensuality and, lo and behold, that day has arrived."

"Oh, Joanna, it's so good to see you again and know that you still say exactly what you think."

"I warrant such a transformation must be the result of exploring and indulging your sexuality to the fullest. I cannot wait to hear all the details. Eleanor de Leyburn and Maud Clifford will be grass green with envy."

"Eleanor, Maud, how wonderful it is to see you both again."

"Jory, you look radiant," Eleanor declared.

"How do you always manage to look so elegant?" Maud asked.

The little girl ran up to her. "Are you an angel?"

Joanna hooted. "She does have angel tresses, but the resemblance stops there, poppet!" She took her daughter's hand. "It's been so long, I don't think Margaret remembers you, Jory."

"I remember you, Margaret. How could I forget the prettiest girl in the world?" *She still has the dear little freckles.*

Joanna turned and motioned for the other female in their group to come forward. "This is Catherine, youngest sister of Roger Mortimer, whom I'm sure you must remember."

"Of course I remember. We attended his wedding at Wigmore. I'm delighted to meet you, Catherine." *Her dark beauty is entrancing. She is so young and vividly lovely, I'm surprised Joanna doesn't resent her.*

"I remember you from the wedding, Lady Marjory. I was only ten at the time and completely in awe of you."

"Out with it, Jory de Warenne, you are fairly bursting to tell us your news," Joanna guessed shrewdly.

"My name is no longer de Warenne, nor de Bohun. I happen to be Marjory de Beauchamp!"

Joanna's jaw dropped. "Well, I'll be damned. I warrant the infamous Earl of Warwick is the source of your ripe sensuality."

Jory smiled. "If I look ripe, it is because I'm with child."

"At long last, you are getting your heart's desire for a child of your own. Marjory, I am so happy for you."

Catherine gazed at Jory with disbelief, and then she blushed profusely and lowered her lashes. "Is the Earl of Warwick with you today, my lady?"

Jory was slightly puzzled. The young lady looked lovestruck. "Do you know my husband, Catherine?"

"Oh no . . . I know his son, Sir Rickard de Beauchamp," she said breathlessly. "I met him at Westminster when he was being knighted along with my brother Roger and Prince Edward."

"Ah, you must guard your heart, Catherine. The de Beauchamp men have a fatal French charm that make them irresistible."

"Come, I have just the tower chamber to accommodate the Earl and Countess of Warwick," Joanna declared. "I warrant you have a mountain of luggage and I want to see every elegant garment. Catherine, gather some of those fragrant damask roses for milady's chamber."

When they entered the castle, Joanna dispatched a servant to locate the Warwicks' trunks and deliver them to the guest tower.

As they climbed the tower stairs Jory and Joanna each took one of Margaret's hands to help the four-year-old and all three took delight in counting the steps. "One two, buckle my shoe."

At the top of the steps, Joanna ordered, "Close your eyes." She glanced at Jory to make sure she complied. "Now . . . open!"

"Oh, my beautiful black swan bathing tub! You brought it from Gloucester Castle just for me."

"Well, not exactly. I had every intention of stealing it for my own use, but with my black hair and dark skin it made me look like a hideous Medusa."

The marble swan sat in a corner of the tower room beside a stone fireplace. The wide bed had royal purple curtains and the walls were covered with rich tapestries that depicted naked nymphs in various wooded settings. "This chamber is rather sybaritic — ideal for you and that dark virile earl you wed, I warrant."

Catherine put the damask roses in a vase beside the bed and their fragrant scent filled the air.

"I shall bathe in my decadent black swan tonight before I retire with the infamous devil. I've quite made up my mind!"

CHAPTER 24

"Come, we will dine in my private chambers tonight, rather than the hall. *I* can hardly bear to be in Father's presence, so I'm not about to expose *you* to His Majesty's murderous mood. Since he learned that the Bruce was crowned King of Scotland, he's been like a warhorse with a hot poker up its arse," Joanna warned.

"Robert Bruce is the rightful King of Scotland," Jory declared.

Eleanor and Maud gasped. Joanna's eyes narrowed. "Just because Marjory Bruce is your godmother, doesn't mean you owe your loyalty to a traitor. There isn't a man breathing who has turned his coat more than Robert Bloody Bruce!" Joanna beckoned her daughter's nurse and the woman led Margaret away.

"It is a fait accompli," Jory said flatly. "Why doesn't King Edward accept it and enjoy his declining years instead of calling his barons to fight another bloody, never-ending war?"

Joanna laughed. "It's a male thing. You know one male cannot bear another to have something he claims belongs to him . . . whether it's a country, a castle, a woman, or even a hunting bitch."

Jory went icy cold. *Dear God, never let Warwick know Robert Bruce was my lover.*

They arrived at Joanna's chambers and she informed a serving woman that the ladies would like dinner brought up.

"Joanna, your brother Edward is nominal head of the army and is already at the Border. Aren't you afraid for his life?"

Joanna laughed even harder. "My brother won't go into battle. He doesn't have the balls to fight. He's like a girl. I should have been the boy — I'd make a far better king and Edward would make a far better *queen!*" She laughed at her own jest.

"*He* may not fight, but he'll order others to do the killing and bloodletting for him — my brother, Catherine's brother, my husband, and your husband too, Joanna."

"King Edward Plantagenet did not fight all these years to conquer Scotland, then sit back and let the Bruce become king."

"Yes," Jory declared passionately. "He fought all those years to conquer Scotland so he could pass it on to his son. Once your brother is king, he will lose everything your father has won, and all the bloodshed will have been for naught."

Joanna sobered. "You're right, of course. Father realizes the only way my brother can hang on to any of our French possessions is to wed him to King Philip of France's daughter."

"Poor lady," Jory murmured.

"Isabella is only thirteen, little more than a child."

"Then my heart truly bleeds for her," Jory whispered.

"Let us talk of something more pleasant. I hope you realize you will become as big as a pig full of figs, my beauteous friend," Joanna said with unconcealed glee. "Ah, here is dinner. I cannot wait to see you gorge yourself, Jory. Before you're done, your hump will be as big as a camel's, I warrant!"

Jory went pale.

"Curse my tongue! I forgot your mother died in childbirth, darling. I'm jealous that you are so tiny — pay no heed to me."

Why is it Joanna cannot resist saying cruel things? Jory pondered. *It's in her Plantagenet blood, I suppose.*

After dinner, Joanna dismissed Eleanor, Maude, and young Catherine Mortimer so she could be alone with Marjory. "I'm simply dying to know how you ended up with Warwick after he betrayed your trust five years ago."

"As it turned out, it was my uncle who betrayed my trust. My family deliberately deceived me into believing Guy did not offer for me and coerced me to wed Humphrey de Bohun."

"It must have been a staggering blow to Warwick's pride that you turned down a powerful earl for an untitled, younger man."

"He's strong enough to withstand a staggering blow. It didn't deter him from pursuing me once I was widowed."

Joanna's smile was sly. "When he came to pay his respects after Gilbert died and revealed he still had a prurient desire for you, I took great delight in telling him the merry widow was relishing her newfound freedom and had not the slightest interest in marriage."

"What a thoughtful friend you are."

Joanna ignored the sarcasm. "So when did he finally catch up with you and propose?"

"I was the one who proposed and asked the infamous devil to marry me. To my delight, he couldn't resist the temptation."

"My hat is off to you, darling. You are an expert at male manipulation."

"I didn't manipulate him. I am deeply in love with him."

Joanna stared at her. "The sad thing is, I believe you. Why else would you marry a man who had killed off two wives? Jory, don't look at me like that — you know my tongue gets carried away."

Jory's smile was gentle. "I forgive you. I have a soft spot for people with flaws."

"Touché! Your barbs are far more subtle than mine."

"I should retire —"

"No, no. Before you go, I'd like to ask a favor. How would you like another lady-in-waiting?"

"I don't have any ladies. I have only a Welsh woman who is rather odd."

"You are the Countess of Warwick, for God's sake. You should have your own court. To start you off I'll give you one of mine."

"You want me to take Catherine Mortimer off your hands."

"Damn you, Jory. I'd forgotten how shrewd you are."

"If the young beauty is willing, I'd love to have her."

"You are a good friend." Joanna summoned a servant. "The Countess of Warwick needs hot water for her bath."

When Jory arrived at her tower chamber, she hoped her husband would be there before her. She feared that being closeted for hours with King Edward Plantagenet would be unpleasant, to put it mildly, and she was prepared to soothe and assuage Warwick's dark fury in any way she could. When she found the chamber empty, she began to worry. She caught a glimpse of her anxious face in the polished mirror and began to laugh. If any man on earth was a match for the King of England, it was Warwick.

A knock on the door brought servants with hot water to fill her marble bathing tub. She thanked them profusely and when they left she began to unfasten her gown. She heard another low knock on the door and when she opened it, there stood Catherine.

"May I speak with you, my lady?" she asked shyly.

"Come in, Catherine. I was just about to take a bath."

"Would you let me help you, Lady Warwick?"

"Thank you. That is most kind." She

turned her back to Catherine so that she could unfasten her gown.

"I would love to become your lady-in-waiting." It came out in a rush as if it took all her courage. "Princess Joanna has been most generous to find me a place among her ladies, but I don't fit in with Lady Eleanor and Lady Maude. They dismiss me because I am so young."

"So young and so vividly beautiful. You are a threat to them, Catherine. I shall have a word with Joanna and tell her that I would like to have you as one of my ladies."

"Oh, thank you so much, my lady. You are exceedingly kind." Catherine hung Lady Marjory's garments in the wardrobe, picked up a towel, and followed a naked Jory to her bathing tub.

Guy de Beauchamp opened the door and strode into the chamber.

Catherine gasped and flushed to the roots of her hair. She sank into a curtsy. "Lord Warwick," she said faintly and fled.

"You have a devastating effect on females, my love."

Guy didn't seem to hear her. He stood transfixed at the vision before him. His wife was reclining naked in a black marble swan. In the languidly sensual pose, her lush breasts seemed to float upon the bathwater.

Her golden-tipped lashes cast delicate shadows upon her cheekbones, and her full lips formed a little moue inviting his kisses. Her silvery hair cascaded over the edge of the tub to the carpet, tempting him to tangle his fingers in it and lift it to his face. He felt his cock engorge and begin to throb with desire. *You have a devastating effect on males!* Warwick was instantly, insanely jealous of every man who had ever glimpsed her naked beauty.

"Joanna brought my prized bathing tub from Gloucester. I refuse to leave it behind again; I shall take it home to Warwick."

"Only a besotted male would take on the task of hauling a bathing tub seventy miles across country."

Jory smiled her secret smile. "Let me besot you." She lifted the sponge and a rivulet of water cascaded down upon her upthrust breasts, making her nipples ruche into tiny pink pearls. She ran the tip of her tongue over her lips in blatant sexual invitation.

Warwick felt his control slip as his cock began to pulse wildly. His feet moved of their own volition and he was drawn inexorably toward the glistening wet nymph. All day his emotions had been in turmoil during his audience with Edward Plantagenet and he had made vows to himself based on those emotions. That his vows coincided with a pledge to the king was merely incidental.

The sexual lust he now felt was increased tenfold by the bloodlust for Robert Bruce that had goaded him all day. He held himself in check as he watched her raise a slim leg and stroke the sponge down its enticing length. Her relentless cock-teasing was producing more than the desired effect, and Warwick knew if she went much further Jory might have reason to regret the savage lust she was arousing.

Thinking to protect her, he moved away. When she reached for the linen towel that Catherine had dropped, however, he said, "I'll do that." It was not a request; it was a statement of intent. He picked up the towel, closed the distance between them, and held his arms wide. She swayed toward him and he wrapped her in the linen, lifted her from the water, carried her across the chamber, and stood her on the bed.

Jory watched him open the towel and lick the droplets of water from her breasts with his tongue. Its rough texture sent a delicious frisson of arousal spiraling from her taut nipples down into her belly. She watched in fascination as he twisted the towel into a rope. He reached up, wrapped it around her neck, pulled her face down to his, then ravished her mouth with his tongue. When he finally withdrew, she was melting with desire.

He slid the linen towel from her neck and twisted it tighter. "Open your legs, *chéri.*"

Jory was more than ready to obey him; she was eager for his bed sport. When he began to draw the rope back and forth between her legs she wanted to scream with excitement. She threaded her fingers into his long black hair to steady herself and arched her mons toward him.

Guy dropped the rope, cupped her round bottom with his palms, and slid his fingers into the deep cleft between her bum cheeks. He knew a raging need to devour her, but cautioned himself to give her pleasure, not pain. He dipped his head and blew on the golden tendrils that covered her mons. When she shuddered with longing, he thrust his tongue into her honeyed sheath.

She felt the scalding heat leap from his mouth up inside her woman's core and the fiery tendrils spread all the way up to her breasts like rivers of flame. His surging tongue ravished her with the same primal rhythm and hot sliding friction as his cock, and all too soon she was crying out her pleasure as she dissolved in liquid tremors.

Jory felt Guy slide his hands down the backs of her legs and grip her ankles. A quick tug brought her down to the bed, where she lay in a wanton sprawl, panting with anticipation at the passion she knew he was about to unleash. He stripped off his clothes and towered above her like a dark, powerful, and potent force of nature.

Guy felt like a raptor, ready to sink his talons into the soft flesh of his helpless prey. He closed his eyes and willed the fierce emotions that consumed him to have pity on the lovely, delicate female who lay before him, completely at his mercy.

His all-consuming love for Jory tempered his raging need. He wanted to bind her to him forever, and he was well aware that the surest way to do that was to focus on giving her a pleasurable experience. If he could delight, enchant, and *gratify,* not just her body, but also her mind and her senses, he stood a chance of keeping her.

Her silver-gilt tresses spread across the purple velvet created an alluring picture he would remember forever. He plucked a damask rose from beside the bed and crushed it. His senses were drenched with its fragrance and he opened his fingers and watched the delicate rose petals drift down upon her flawless bare skin.

Jory held up her arms in supplication. "Guy, come to me." Her hands slid over the polished muscles of his chest and shoulders and she reveled in the feel of his full weight as he covered her with his hard body. That he was a true flesh-and-blood warrior who had been victorious in many battles thrilled her. That he was dark and dominant appealed to her ultrafeminine nature. That he was the infamous Earl of Warwick enthralled her. She slid her arms about his neck and wrapped her legs high about his back, yielding her softness to his marble-hard length. Her tight sheath closed sleekly around him and she gave herself up to the hot glide of his thick shaft as he moved in and out in a tantalizing slow rhythm that played counterpoint to the powerful beat of his heart.

Guy de Beauchamp was drowning in need. Above all he wanted to obliterate her memories of Robert Bruce. He was fiercely determined to brand her as his woman and make her cleave only unto him. He wanted to possess her mind, body, and soul and was confident that he had the sexual energy and staying power to bind her to him forever. On top of all else he wanted to steal her heart and make her love him.

Her climax built to an unbearable peak, and she thrashed her head from side to side and bit the powerful column of his neck to keep herself from screaming. His body rose and fell in rampant splendor and a surging wave of passion engulfed her and she cried out her pleasure as the night exploded.

"Do you love me, Jory?" he demanded hoarsely.

"I adore you, Guy!" She sighed with pure bliss.

He crushed her in an embrace. "Will you love me always?"

"Forever and always!" Her heart sang with joy.

He held her tightly for a full hour after they had made love, his lips pressed to her silken skin, whispering love words that made her feel languorous, and lovely, and replete.

She clung to him sweetly, knowing she had never been happier in her life than she was tonight. Intimately entwined, she fell asleep with her cheek pressed against his heart.

Warwick lay awake, staring into the darkness as love and bloodlust warred within him. *Now I know why she fears having a son. Kings are always desperate for male heirs, and she fears if she has a boy, that whoreson*

Bruce will come and claim him!

When Jory awoke in the morning, Guy was dressed and ready to quit the chamber.

"Once I take my leave of the king, I will be ready to depart."

Jory was acutely disappointed that her visit with Joanna could not be longer, but sensing that Warwick wished to leave Hertford and His Majesty's presence as soon as possible, she did not demur. "I am taking young Catherine Mortimer as my lady-in-waiting. Her brother Roger was knighted with Rickard and I assume he too is with the prince's army."

Warwick assented with a brief nod, too preoccupied with his future plans to converse about trivial matters.

Jory joined Joanna and little Margaret for breakfast and when Catherine Mortimer arrived, she told her the news. "I asked Joanna if I could steal you for my first lady-in-waiting, and she has generously agreed, though she is most reluctant to part with you. Unfortunately, my husband has informed me that we must depart today and that doesn't give you much time to pack your things. Would you like me to help you, Catherine?"

"Oh, thank you, Lady Warwick. That isn't

necessary. I will be ready." She rushed off to gather her belongings.

"You do things with such finesse, Jory, trying to spare everyone's feelings. I warrant that is derived from your own vulnerability that you keep well hidden."

"I'm truly sorry that my visit could not be longer, Joanna. For some reason my husband has decided we shall leave today."

"And the infamous Warwick must be obeyed at all costs."

Jory smiled. "Though I did the proposing, I still promised to obey him when we exchanged marriage vows. I'm not afraid to challenge him, but I assure you that Warwick is master of his own household. And I wouldn't want it any other way."

"Well, 'tis obvious he gave you a thorough bedding last night. Warwick has no doubt taught you that men's mouths are good for more than kissing and their pricks for more than pissing."

"My doggie pissed on the carpet," Margaret declared.

"That's all right, darling. He'll soon learn better manners." Jory gave her friend a quelling glance. "For shame, Joanna."

She waved a dismissive hand. "Margaret's too young to understand. There's no need to apologize for leaving. The all-powerful, fire-breathing king has no doubt ordered him to ready his men for war. Edward Plantagenet is feeling his mortality and is impatient to reconquer Scotland and bring it to heel."

Warwick won't take his men-at-arms to fight in Scotland, no matter the king's orders! "Margaret, why don't you come with me while I pack? Perhaps I can find you a present among my jewels."

"I like jewels that sparkle," Margaret declared.

Jory smiled. "You thought she was too young to understand."

When they entered the tower chamber, Jory saw that her bathing tub had already been removed so it could be put on a baggage cart. She placed her jewel case on the bed and opened it up for Margaret's perusal.

The little girl immediately pointed to the black onyx brooch with its amber eye. "Doggie!"

"Yes, that's Brutus, my husband's black wolfhound. I'm rather attached to him."

Margaret soon lost interest in favor of more sparkling objects. She reached out and touched the diamond swan, which had been Jory's wedding gift from Humphrey de Bohun. "Pretty!"

"It is indeed. Would you like to have it, Margaret? A pretty jewel for a pretty young lady!" Jory gazed at the freckles that bridged the child's nose. *Who better to have the de Bohun jewels?* She pinned it to Margaret's dress.

"Go look in the mirror," Joanna urged her daughter. "Only you would be so generous, Jory."

"She's so sweet and innocent. It gives me pleasure."

Two hours later, when everyone was mounted and ready to leave Hertford, Jory said her good-byes to Joanna, Margaret, Eleanor, and Maud, while her brother thanked Ralph Monthermer for his hospitality. Catherine, mounted on her sure-footed Welsh Border pony, fell in beside Lady Warwick. After a few minutes, Lynx's squires rode up beside them and Jory introduced Catherine.

She urged her palfrey forward to ride beside her brother. "Tell me, Lynx, how did you get out of the king's call to arms?"

"Basically, I stalled for time. I didn't refuse his demands, nor did I accept them. I pointed out that John's de Warenne fighting men were now serving under Pembroke.

I confess I led him to believe I would consider sending my own men-at-arms, when in fact I will not consider it under any circumstances."

Jory gave him a smile of approval. "That was most shrewd."

Lynx observed his sister's smile with mixed emotions. At the moment she was happy, but he guessed that happiness would be wiped away when she learned that her husband had agreed to take his Warwick men-at-arms to reconquer Scotland and drag Robert Bruce from the throne.

Before they went to Hertford to the audience with Edward Plantagenet, Lynx had been almost certain that Guy de Beauchamp would refuse the king's call to arms. Warwick's abrupt about-face was puzzling, but it was his decision to make. Lynx worried about what Jory would do when she learned of that decision. He knew better than to take sides between husband and wife. He would never interfere in their private, intimate relationship. Would Jory acquiesce to her husband's will or would she rebel? Lynx knew his sister's mercurial temperament and feared that she and Warwick were about to collide.

CHAPTER 25

When the travelers arrived back at Hedingham, Jory watched her brother turn his
horse over to his squire Thomas and stride
toward Jane, who was awaiting him at the
castle door. It warmed her heart to see the
affection the two shared. Taffy helped her
and Catherine to dismount and gallantly offered to stable their mounts. Jory gave the
squire a radiant smile, then glanced quickly
at Guy to make sure he didn't mind, since
he usually enjoyed lifting her from her
saddle. Warwick, however, was speaking
with his knights and seemed oblivious to
her.

"Don't unpack the baggage cart. We will
be returning to Flamstead in the morning."
Guy led his horse into the stable.

Jory lamented his decision, since her time
visiting with Jane had been so short, but she
swallowed her disappointment and took

Catherine into the hall to meet her sister-in-law.

"This is Jane de Warenne, my brother's beautiful wife. She is without doubt the sweetest, kindest lady I have ever known. Jane, this is Catherine Mortimer, the youngest daughter of one of the most powerful Welsh marcher barons in England. Catherine has graciously consented to be my first lady-in-waiting."

"I am delighted to meet you, Catherine. Jory set me a glorious example of how to become a lady. She taught me everything I needed to know. It was most daunting to realize that someday I would become a countess, but she has instilled me with confidence and quieted all my misgivings."

"Little did I realize I would soon become a countess myself," Jory said, laughing. "Let's find Catherine a chamber. I'm afraid Warwick is planning for us to leave tomorrow. I would dearly love to stay longer, Jane, but I do understand Guy's longing to return to Flamstead Castle. His great passion is raising horses, and I know he doesn't get to spend nearly enough time there."

Jane threw them a mischievous smile. "Warwick's great passion is Jory de Beauchamp — 'tis plain to any who see them together."

"Finding and marrying the perfect mate is the most important thing we will ever do in our lives. Choose wisely, Catherine."

The ladies spent the rest of the day in Jane's lovely solar and never stopped talking. Both Jane and Catherine were from large families and had much in common. Grace Murray, Lincoln Robert's Scottish nurse, brought him to the solar, where he played happily with all his wooden toys, which Lynx's Welsh bowmen had carved for him. "Since this time I am hoping for a daughter, I trust they know how to carve dolls."

"I hope with all my heart that you get your wish, Jane."

"Thank you, Jory. I hope the same for you."

After dinner that night, Jory felt so sleepy she could hardly keep her eyes open. "I'm off to bed." She glanced ruefully at Guy and Lynx, who seemed absorbed in discussing battle tactics.

"I'm going up too," Jane decided. "They won't even miss us."

I'm tired because he kept me up all night making love. Where on earth does he get all that amazing energy? Perhaps I can steal an

501

hour's sleep before he comes to bed.

On the return ride to Flamstead Castle, Jory relived her good-byes with Lynx and Jane. The simple Scottish lass had taken to her role as Lady de Warenne as if she'd been born to the part. Jane had no misgivings about having another child, and Jory vowed that she would try to emulate her wise and courageous sister-in-law. When she left, Lynx had cast a few worried glances her way, which she assumed were because of her pregnancy. Jory knew no one questioned that Warwick was the father and all assumed she was about four months along, when in reality she was at least five.

When the horse pastures came into view in the late afternoon, Jory thought of Meg. "Catherine, you may put your trust in my husband's steward, Mr. Burke. He will accommodate your needs and answer all your questions, but I give you a small word of caution about my tiring woman. Meg can be quite moody. She arrived at Warwick many years ago with my husband's first wife, Isabel de Clare, and was nurse to Rickard de Beauchamp when he was a child."

Catherine blushed prettily at mention of Warwick's son, Rickard. "She must be Welsh. I have much experience with their dark secretive natures. My own nursemaid at Wigmore was Welsh."

"Ah, that eases my mind somewhat. Meg has been with the family so long that she tends to take liberties."

Jory yawned. Jane had warned her that she would become soporific as her pregnancy progressed. The thought of a hammock stretched between two shade trees with a view of Flamstead's grazing horses filled her imagination.

A black animal streaked past their horses and howled his welcome at Warwick.

"Don't be alarmed, Catherine. It's Brutus, my husband's wolfhound. Like Warwick, his bark is worse than his bite."

Guy dismounted, greeted his dog affectionately, and came to his wife's stirrup. "I hope the ride wasn't too much for you, Jory."

She went down into his arms. "Of course not. I'm happy to be back at Flamstead because I know it's your favorite castle."

"You should retire early. When I came to bed last night you were sound asleep and you didn't move a muscle until morning."

She gave him a saucy glance. "We both moved too many muscles the night before. I feel fine, darling; stop worrying."

Jory took Catherine inside and the first

person they encountered was Meg. "This young lady is Catherine —"

"Mortimer," Meg finished. " 'Tis not just the yellow and green Mortimer colors she's wearing; 'tis the strong family resemblance."

"How clever you are, Meg. I have invited Catherine to be my lady-in-waiting. I hope you will make her welcome."

"The Mortimers are second in importance only to the de Clares." The tiring woman's tone was condescending.

"We are not worried about pecking order, Meg."

"Pecking order is important to all marcher barons, my lady."

Young Catherine giggled. "She's right . . . It's certainly important to the Mortimer males. Their ambition knows no bounds."

"Most males suffer from that disease," Jory declared. "Since Mr. Burke is occupied with my husband, I'll find Catherine a chamber while you get her bed linen, Meg."

Jory left the two females furbishing Catherine's room and sought her own chamber. She sat down, pulled off her riding boots, and wriggled her toes. She was expecting a servant to bring up her luggage and was surprised when Guy opened the door and carried in one of her trunks.

"I hope you can make do with this. There's

no point in dismantling the baggage wagon since we are returning to Warwick."

"What on earth are you talking about? We will be staying at Flamstead for a few weeks."

"If you are well enough to travel, we will be leaving for Warwick tomorrow."

"That's ridiculous! We've only just arrived. Why on earth must we return to Warwick?"

"Because of my commitment to the king," he said shortly.

Jory jumped up from her chair. "Guy, please don't jest about such a thing. 'Tis not the least bit amusing."

"I am not jesting. Edward Plantagenet has called me and Warwick's fighting force to war."

Jory was outraged. "Why didn't you refuse? Or at least do the expedient thing and stall for time, as my brother did?"

"The decision has been taken." His words were curt, and his tone warned her to leave the matter alone.

Jory ignored the warning. She flew at him and pummeled her clenched fists against his chest. "*Your* bloody decision! What about mine? Do I have no say in this matter?"

He captured her hands and held them immobile. "No say whatsoever." His dark face was closed against her. "I'll have Meg bring you a tray. I suggest you get some rest."

When he released her hands and strode from the chamber, Jory gasped and sat down in disbelief. *This cannot be happening!*

Dismay slowly washed over her, leaving her limp. She could not understand why Warwick had made the decision to go to war. It was untenable. She knew she must find a way to stop him.

"I should never have flown at him in temper. That is not the way to persuade a dominant male to change his mind." She might as well have pummeled her fists against the castle walls for all the impact they had made.

Jory's worried expression vanished and was replaced by her secret smile. *When Guy comes to bed I will persuade him to my way of thinking. I will seduce the dark, dominant devil!*

She rose from the chair, suddenly bubbling with energy. She searched among her garments until she found a silk night rail that would conceal her slightly rounded belly while it revealed her lush breasts. "A little rouge on my nipples won't hurt either." The corners of her mouth lifted. *Warwick doesn't stand a chance!*

When Jory opened her eyes to sunlight, she felt slightly disoriented and it took her a moment to realize that she was at Flamstead Castle. "I must have fallen asleep waiting for Guy to come to bed." She glanced at the undisturbed covers and knew he had not come at all last night. *The devious devil purposely avoided me!*

Jory slid from the bed and dressed as quickly as she could. *When I find him, I'll tell him I feel ill. I'll convince him I can't possibly travel all the way to Warwick.* "I promised him I would never lie to him," she reminded herself. *I don't care; I have to stop him from fighting in Scotland. If I have to lie, I will do it gladly!*

Jory hurried down to the dining hall and when she didn't find him there, she walked across to the stables. Perhaps he had been up all night with a foaling mare. *It's autumn — too late for foaling.* Jory ignored the voice in her head and walked through the vast stables. Warwick was not there and neither was Caesar.

Jory retraced her steps and went in search of the steward. She found him in the kitchen. "I'm looking for my husband, Mr.

Burke, have you any idea where he might be?"

The steward gave her an apologetic look. "He has left for Warwick, my lady."

"Alone?" she asked in disbelief.

"Alone save for Brutus and a string of horses."

"When did he leave?" she demanded.

"He left last night, Lady Warwick. He insisted you must stay at Flamstead as long as you wished. The earl charged me with your well-being and gave me strict instructions to follow at a slow pace, whenever you felt up to traveling."

Jory dug her fists into her hips and lifted her chin defiantly. "I never felt better in my life. We will leave today, Mr. Burke."

Her anger gave her untold energy. She nimbly ran upstairs and encountered Catherine. "Pack your things and take them down to the bailey. We're leaving for Warwick within the hour!"

When she went into her chamber, Meg was there. She had brought up a breakfast tray for Jory.

The tiring woman indicated the bed. "There is no need for Catherine to take over my duties, Lady Warwick."

"She didn't make the bed. Pack your belongings, Meg. We are leaving for Warwick shortly. Put some pillows and blankets into a wagon. I may join you there for part of the journey. As you have probably guessed by now, I am going to have a baby."

"Are you pleased about the child?"

What an odd thing to say! "Of course I am pleased, Meg. I am a woman who longs for motherhood."

"You shouldn't travel on an empty stomach. Better hurry and eat your breakfast. The earl doesn't like to be kept waiting."

"The earl left for Warwick last night." Jory flushed.

Meg's eyebrows shot up. Then she gave Jory a pitying look.

"Damn you, woman! If you have something to say, say it!"

Meg pressed her lips together. "I warrant there's trouble in every marriage, my lady," she said smugly.

During the next two days, Jory had plenty of time to reflect upon what had happened. She was not afraid to travel without Guy, since she had half a dozen Warwick knights as well as Mr. Burke to guard her. She was, however, furious with her husband for leaving without her. *Why did the devious devil abandon me?* The reason was clear. *It's because I oppose his going to war to conquer Scotland.*

The travelers stopped at a stream to water their horses and Jory dismounted to stretch her legs. *The bloody infamous Earl of Warwick is too dominant, aye, and too arrogant to even consider a female's opinion or her wishes. He left so he wouldn't have to discuss it with me!*

Mr. Burke approached. "Lady Warwick, would you like to rest for the night?"

"The sun is still high. Of course I don't wish to rest. We can cover many more miles before dark."

The following day they arrived at Warwick. Guy de Beauchamp stared in grim-faced disbelief as the small cavalcade rode into the bailey. He challenged Mr. Burke immediately. "I gave direct orders that you were to travel at a slow pace!"

"The Countess of Warwick set the pace, my lord."

Jory saw that her husband's fighting force was making preparations for war. Baggage carts were piled with campaign tents, weapons, and food supplies and she knew she did not have much time to stop the madness. Yet she was far too wise to challenge him before his men. Guy de Beauchamp's unbending pride would never allow him to yield to a woman before witnesses.

Jory looked straight into his eyes and communicated without words that she needed to be alone with him. Then she lowered her lashes as if acquiescing to his authority. With Mr. Burke's assistance she gracefully dismounted and beckoned for young Catherine Mortimer to follow her into the castle. She asked Meg to plenish a chamber for the girl and told them she wanted her privacy and would not need their services again that night.

Jory knew Guy would not come for some time. At all costs he would avoid the appearance of rushing to her side like some fawning lapdog. It would give her a chance to change into something more feminine than a riding dress and make sure her face and hair were as pretty as she could make them.

Above all, Jory knew that she must not let her temper get the better of her. Flying at him and calling him names would put her at a distinct disadvantage with a man like Warwick. Rather, she must approach him as a supplicant. She must beseech him sweetly, gently, wistfully. The manipulation would have to be delicate.

Jory bathed and donned the pale green

dress in which she had been married to War-wick. She chose a jewel that would draw Guy's attention to her body. From a heavy gold chain dangled a cabochon emerald that swung in the valley between her lush breasts. She brushed her hair until it crackled, then threaded a pretty green ribbon through her gilt curls. She darkened her lashes and put on deep rose lip rouge. Finally she touched her earlobes and her breasts with her favor-ite fragrance of freesia, the alluring scent she had been wearing the first night she went to him at Windsor.

When Guy finally climbed the steps to her tower room he stepped inside and stood looking at her with guarded eyes. The way she had arrayed herself told him more than words that she was determined to change his mind about the decision he had taken and would use all her considerable feminine wiles to manipulate him.

Jory warned herself not to recriminate him for leaving her at Flamstead. She appealed to him in a soft, sweet voice. "Guy, I don't want you to answer Edward Plantagenet's call to war. You have served him enough years. You grabbed victory from defeat at Falkirk for him and that should be enough. But it will never be enough. The king is self-ish and demanding and without mercy.

Instead of enjoying the time he has left to him, he thirsts to crush the Scots once again beneath his heel. I want you to have no part in the senseless killing and the bloodshed."

As he gazed at her, he knew everything she said was true. But he was not doing this for the king. His lust for revenge was personal. Guy did not answer her harshly. He spoke low, but his deep voice was implacable.

"I have pledged my word to the king. My decision has been taken. Do not try to manipulate me, Jory."

Her eyes widened with apprehension and she took a tentative step toward him. "Guy, please, don't go . . . don't do this thing."

"Stop! Nothing will dissuade me!" His voice was now harsh.

In supplication she moved toward him and captured his arm. "Guy, please, I beseech you. *I beg you* not to make war on Scotland." Jory fell to her knees imploring him, pleading with him to listen, as she clung desperately to his arm.

"Get up off your knees," Warwick snarled through clenched teeth. "It sickens me that you would beg for your *lover!*"

Jory was stunned. She sat back on her heels and tears flooded her eyes. *In the name of Christ, how did you find out?*

"On our wedding night I vowed to find out the name of the whoreson who planted his seed and abandoned you. Robert Bruce is a dead man, Jory. Never doubt it!"

"Guy, no! 'Tis for *your* sake I beg. I don't want you to get wounded. I don't want you to die!"

Warwick's face darkened with fury. "*My* sake? How dare you imply my fighting skills as a warrior are inferior to Robert Fucking Bruce!"

Jory pressed the back of her hand to her mouth. "Guy, I didn't mean that!" Warwick's face was distorted by his towering pride and she feared he would never forgive her for the things she had said. Or the thing she had done. Because her lover was King Robert Bruce, Warwick was consumed by jealousy and bloodlust.

Jory sat alone long after Warwick slammed the door after he departed her chamber. "He won't go. He'll change his mind," she whispered. Yet in her heart she knew full well that nothing would prevent him from marching into Scotland and dragging Robert Bruce from his throne. If she had not begged on her knees, Guy might have listened. But her act of abasement obliterated any chance she'd had of dissuading him.

Jory was covered with guilt. She was the driving force behind Warwick's vengeful decision. She made the sign of the cross. "Dear Lord God, don't let them kill each other."

CHAPTER 26

"Don't have the men set up tents. If the king's vanguard fails to arrive by tomorrow, we will press on to Carlisle," Warwick directed Sir Hugh Ashton, his second in command. Guy de Beauchamp had been given orders by King Edward Plantagenet to await him at the royal castle of Kenilworth. But Warwick, not known for his patience, was countermanding those orders.

The following day, a dispatch from King Edward was brought to Warwick by one of Ralph Monthermer's lieutenants advising that Gloucester's army would be arriving at Kenilworth shortly. De Beauchamp cooled his heels for three days until the king arrived. The next three days were spent in Kenilworth's war room arguing battle tactics. At the end of six days Warwick's temper was foul.

Though Warwick argued vociferously against it, Gloucester was sent north with all speed, while Guy and his men-at-arms were ordered to accompany Edward Plantagenet.

Guy de Beauchamp stood on the ramparts of Kenilworth from which he could see the towers of his own castle. He had to banish pictures of Jory that taunted him day and night. Each time he saw her tear-drenched green eyes begging him to spare Robert Bruce, his fury increased.

"Why the hellfire has Edward commanded we act as his escort?"

"I believe he thinks Warwick invincible," Ashton replied.

"Then we think alike for once." Guy's dark humor was the only thing that saved him from going mad.

Finally, the king decided to advance and Warwick's small army rode north slowly, making camp at Leicester, Nottingham, and Sheffield Castles. The earl's patience was rubbed raw, and on the days when the king rested, Guy organized hunts for his knights in the dense forests that surrounded the great castles.

After Sheffield they traversed the Pennines, rested at Burnley Abbey, and progressed through Lancashire until they came to the enormous Lancaster Castle that was owned by Thomas of Lancaster, the king's nephew. Thomas, son of the king's late brother, Edmund, had the royal Plantagenet pride in abundance. Perhaps because he recognized Warwick's towering pride, the Earl of Lancaster had always held him in great esteem.

Thomas was the hereditary high steward of England and his lavish royal entertainments were legendary. On the king's first night in Lancaster's Great Hall, he was given the place of honor on Thomas's right, and Warwick was seated on Thomas's left.

"Allow me to congratulate you on your marriage to Marjory de Warenne. I warrant she is the most beautiful countess in the land and the envy of every baron in England."

Warwick glanced at Lancaster's richly clad wife, Alice de Lacy. She was no beauty, but because she was an only child of the Earl of Lincoln and Salisbury, Lancaster would inherit these two earldoms along with their wealth and property when Lincoln died. *I would not trade Jory for all the royal Plantagenet titles, wealth, and property lumped together!*

"I need to speak with you alone," Lancaster murmured.

Warwick nodded his understanding. He

waited until after midnight when he knew the king would be abed before he sought out Lancaster in his private chamber.

"I am alarmed at Edward's appearance," Thomas said quietly. "His Majesty's health has deteriorated since last I saw him."

Warwick was blunt. "This will be his last campaign, I warrant."

"This campaign will *precipitate* his demise." It was Lancaster's turn to speak his mind. "Prince Edward is ill suited to the role he will shortly be called upon to fulfill."

Warwick's dark glance took in the tall Plantagenet's physique, and not for the first time he lamented that Thomas had been born Edmund's son, rather than the king's son and heir to the throne. "Young Edward will benefit from your guidance and experience."

"He is a juvenile who resents authority, mine especially."

"The baronage will still be the dominant force in Parliament."

"Only if we stick together and form a powerful alliance. As a leading noble of the realm will you enter into a bond with me?"

"Yes — I will pledge you my support, when the time comes." Warwick paced Lancaster's chamber. "I chafe at the slow progress we are making. I am more suited to the role of warrior than bloody nurse-maid."

"Try to curb your impatience. He takes strength and courage from you. You are serving the purpose of prolonging his life."

The king remained for a full week at Lancaster Castle. Before he left, Edward ordered Thomas to gather his force from his northern landholdings and follow him to Carlisle.

From Lancaster, they followed the River Lune up through Kendal and the Cambrian Mountains. Warwick's men-at-arms made camp at Penrith while the king rested at Brougham Castle. Guy de Beauchamp had a horse litter made for the king so he could journey the final miles in comfort. Three days later the cavalcade finally arrived at Carlisle. An entire month had melted away since Guy de Beauchamp had set out from Warwick.

Carlisle Castle, the ugly red fortress on the Border of Scotland, bulged at the seams with English fighting men. Prince Edward and his entourage had not set foot across the Border since they had arrived at Carlisle more than two months before.

When Ralph Monthermer, Earl of Gloucester, had arrived a fortnight ago, he saw the crowded conditions and decided to cross the Border into Scotland to crush a reported uprising near Perth.

When Edward Plantagenet encountered Pembroke and his scattered army arriving at Carlisle Castle, he demanded to know the reason they had retreated from Scotland.

"Sire, we were ambushed at the Steps of Trool. We set up camp at the foot of Mulldonach Mountain and in the night an avalanche of boulders came crashing down on our campaign tents. We fled east around Loch Trool and ran straight into the Bruce's swords. They killed hundreds."

King Edward fell into a full-blown Plantagenet rage. "Whoreson! Dung Eater! Scab-arsed baboon! I'll hang the Bruce from the highest scaffold, then have him drawn and quartered!" The king's fair complexion became ruddy and mottled. "Get back across that Border, Pembroke, and bring Robert Bruce to me here!"

"Let *me* go, Your Majesty. My men are fresh and I am spoiling for a fight," Warwick volunteered.

"Why should you do Pembroke's job for him? He's the fool who bungled the raid. Pembroke is the head of my army. Let him prove himself worthy of the rank of general."

A frustrated Warwick sought out his son

who had been cooling his heels for two months. "Christ Almighty, it took a whole bloody month to get here, now my men are expected to stand about and pick the lice from their heads instead of marching into Scotland and capturing the Bruce."

"I understand your frustration, Father. I've tried to teach Prince Edward fighting skills, but he is inept and takes interest only in drinking, dicing, and playing youthful pranks worthy of a twelve-year-old. He insists that though Robert Bruce has been crowned king, all the Border strongholds are garrisoned by the English. He thinks the Scots are no threat whatsoever."

After a week of idleness, Warwick rode out alone every day through the Border country. He kept his mouth shut and his ears open, learning what he could about the Bruce's strength. His long black hair and swarthy complexion labeled him a Celt, so he could cross into Scotland without fear. An idea took root in his mind and began to grow. When it was fully formed he acted upon it.

Warwick rode to Dumfries Castle, which was garrisoned by English soldiers. When he identified himself by showing his bear and staff device and told the guard he was with the king's army at Carlisle, he was welcomed into the castle. Presently, he sought out Dumfries's steward, the father of Lynx de Warenne's wife, Jane.

"Well met, Jock Leslie. I've heard only good things about you from Lynx de Warenne." The two men clasped arms. "As a matter of fact, your lovely daughter Jane is now my sister-in-law."

Warwick saw the steward try to grasp the relationship and clarified matters for him. "I am Guy de Beauchamp. I wed Marjory de Warenne when she returned to England a few months ago."

"Congratulations, my lord. Jane and Lady Marjory became inseparable friends. Yer wife was extremely kind and generous to my daughter. Do ye know if Jane is well, my lord? When she left here, she was having another bairn."

"I visited the de Warennes six weeks ago. Jane was blooming with health and confided she would like a daughter this time."

"Us Leslies are prolific breeders — I'm father of ten."

"An amazing feat," Warwick declared. "I am trying to find Robert Bruce. I have a message for him."

"You and a thousand others." Jock winked. "We are castle keepers and try not to take sides, but now that the Bruce has been crowned King of Scotland, 'tis impossible to hide our pleasure."

"You think him Scotland's rightful king." It was a statement.

"I *know* he is. Any Scot breathing would agree — and half the English, if truth be told," Jock declared. "If ye want to get a message to the Bruce, seek out Black Douglas."

"I thank you, Jock Leslie."

Jock nodded. "I'd put my trust in any mon related to Lynx de Warenne. He's the salt of the earth. Give my regards to yer beautiful lady."

It was after midnight when Warwick gained his bed in Carlisle Castle. As he lay in the darkness, he probed the corners of his mind to see if he felt guilt over what he had done. He concluded that the end justified the means and promptly fell asleep.

At the end of the following week, messengers arrived from Pembroke with bad news. The army had met up with the Bruce's force and had been defeated in a brisk skirmish at a place called Loudoun Hill. Pembroke was sending his wounded soldiers back to Carlisle Castle, though he himself knew better than to return and face Edward Plantagenet.

In the war room at Carlisle Castle, the

king had foam on his lips as he raved and shouted. "I have assembled the largest and best-trained force of fighting men England has ever seen! It should be child's play for my fumbling, idiot fourth cousin to accomplish the complete subjection of these thick-headed Scots."

Warwick searched the maps for Loudoun Hill and saw it was at a place called Kilmarnock. His eyes followed a line directly east and there, not more than a dozen miles away was Douglas.

Edward Plantagenet was purple in the face. "By God's good grace, am I alone capable of leading this army to capture Bruce?"

Warwick was alarmed. The king had arrived here in a horse litter. How could he lead the army? "Sire, I will take my men to reinforce Pembroke."

"You and I together, Warwick. We will get the job done."

"I can be ready tomorrow, Your Majesty, there is no need —"

"There is *every* need. I will be ready at dawn. Do not keep me waiting, Lord Warwick."

Carlisle Castle was a massive fortress, but Guy de Beauchamp's men were billeted together and it didn't take long to put them on notice about tomorrow's departure. It took much longer to round up Prince Edward's troops, and Rickard told his father in confidence they likely would not be ready for two or three days.

At dawn the next morning, Warwick's men-at-arms were ready. His foot soldiers were armed and his knights were mounted. Edward Plantagenet, with much difficulty and plenty of aid, climbed into the saddle and insisted on leading the cavalcade.

The snail's pace he set in his weakened condition was mentally agonizing to Warwick and physically agonizing for the king. At the end of two days, they had covered only four miles. In spite of the monarch's protests, Guy de Beauchamp improvised a horse litter and persuaded King Edward to ride in it. At the end of the third day they reached Burgh-by-Sands from which the water of Solway Firth was visible. Beyond the firth lay Scotland.

Edward Plantagenet's pain was so severe he could go no farther. Warwick's impatience dropped away from him like a cloak and was replaced by heartfelt compassion. He carried the king from his horse litter to a large stone house where a bed had been prepared for him. The royal physicians and Warwick's Welsh healers shook their heads and could do nothing for the warrior king. Edward called his priest and his scribes and prepared himself for death. He dictated his will and composed messages of farewell for the members of his family.

When Prince Edward and his troops arrived, Warwick met him. "Your father is dying. He has orders he wants to pass on to you."

As the heir to England's throne knelt by his father's bed, all present heard the king's last orders:

"One hundred English knights must go to the Crusades and take my heart with them." Edward Plantagenet looked his son straight in the eyes. "Piers Gaveston is not to be recalled to England without the consent of Parliament." He struggled for breath. "Carry my bones before the army, so I may still lead the way to victory!" Edward the First had issued his last order.

Prince Edward looked upon the dead face of his father. "I am now Edward the Second, King of England!" He sounded amazed.

The young king issued immediate orders that everyone was to return to Carlisle. There, the old king's body was prepared for a journey and it was decided among the clergy that he should lie in state at the magnificent Minster in the great City of

York, which was the largest cathedral in England. Young King Edward, with all pageantry, would accompany his father's bier south.

The night before they were to leave, Rickard de Beauchamp sought out his father. "Edward has no intention of fulfilling his father's last wishes. Once we arrive at York, he intends to ride to London with all speed to bask in the adulation of the people he now rules. He has no intention of leading the invading army to victory. He harbors the old belief that a king can do no wrong!"

"The foolish lad has no concept that a king is no more than the representative of the ruling class. The baronage will remain the dominant force in Parliament whether he likes it or not." Warwick immediately pictured Jory and knew the news of Edward Plantagenet's death would sadden her. "When you reach Warwickshire, send word to Lady Marjory."

"Can I tell her when to expect you, Father?"

Warwick shook his head. "I have a mission." He embraced his son. "Go with God, Rickard."

As darkness descended, Guy de Beauchamp rode into a stand of firs and dismounted in a small clearing. He secured Caesar's reins, fed him oats, then lay on the ground to sleep. In place of his usual breastplate he wore the chain mail shirt that Lynx de Warenne had given him, and he carried neither sword nor battleaxe. He wore only his hunting knife tucked into his belt. It was the only weapon he needed to rip out the heart of Robert Bruce.

Bruce had been crowned king, but the English held every Scottish Border castle and he stood no chance of regaining the strongholds and actually ruling. *Until now.* Edward Plantagenet's death changed everything. The effeminate youth who now occupied England's throne would be no threat to the hardened and determined Scots. A steel bonnet would emerge from every thicket and clump of gorse. Eventually, Robert Bruce would emerge victorious and gain Scotland's independence from England. Warwick knew there was only one sure way to stop this from happening.

Guy de Beauchamp knew his horse would soon alert him if danger threatened and he fell asleep in an amazingly short time. It wasn't long before he began to dream and, as always, it was about Jory. Her exquisite beauty held him spellbound; her pale green eyes and silvery gilt hair took his breath away. But it wasn't just her looks that held him in thrall. He treasured her because she made him feel alive. If he could make her love him and no other, he knew his happiness would be complete, his life perfect.

Guy, please, don't go . . . Don't do this thing. Her voice was sweet, softly persuading. In supplication she moved toward him and captured his arm. *Guy, please, I beseech you. I beg you not to make war on Scotland.* Jory fell to her knees imploring him, pleading with him to listen, as she clung desperately to his arm.

Get up off your knees! It sickens me that you would beg for your lover!

Warwick woke with a start. Though the night was cold he was covered with sweat. Immune to physical discomfort, he lay still, listening for some sound that may have awakened him. He heard only a night owl and knew in his soul what had awakened him. He could not bear to hear Jory beg for her lover, even in a dream.

At first light he watered Caesar in a nearby stream and dipped his own head beneath the water to clear his brain and make him alert. He smoothed his wet hair back and secured it with a thong. Warwick had covered over sixty miles in the last two days. He mounted and rode the last few miles that led to Douglas. Mist still hung over Douglas Water, giving the place a sinister look, adding credence to the fortress's byname of Castle Dangerous. His plan was simple. The ruse had worked at Dumfries. If Bruce was at Douglas, and he wagered that he was, it should work again.

Warwick stopped at the gateway and told the guard he had a message for Sir James Douglas. The lone rider, assumed to be a Celt, was allowed inside the bailey. He dismounted and strode with confidence into the grey-towered castle. When a steward asked his business, he repeated that he had a message for Sir James Douglas. Presently, the Black Douglas descended the stone steps that led down from the living quarters.

"Sir James, I have a message for Robert Bruce," Warwick said.

"What makes ye think I can get a message tae the Bruce?"

Warwick lifted a dismissive hand. "Let's cut to the heart of the matter. I'll deliver the message myself."

"Who are ye and who is this *important* message from?"

"I am Guy de Beauchamp, Earl of Warwick, and the message is from Lynx de Warenne."

"A firkin' Englishmon!" Douglas shouted, reaching for his dirk.

"A firkin' Frenchman," Warwick corrected.

"It's all right, James." The voice of authority came from the gallery above. "The infamous earl risks much to seek me out."

Life had taught Warwick that a simple, direct plan worked best. He would stab Bruce to the heart and, when Douglas came to his aid, he would overpower him and use him as a shield and hostage until he was well away from Castle Dangerous.

As Robert Bruce descended the stone steps, Warwick schooled himself to patience till his quarry came within striking distance.

CHAPTER 27

Jory looked down from her tower window and saw a dark rider enter Warwick's bailey. She drew in a quick breath and proceeded downstairs with a racing heart. Her steps were measured because of her baby; she now took great care with any task she undertook.

When she reached the tower entrance and saw that it was Rickard de Beauchamp who had arrived, she was fraught with anxiety. "Your father?" was all she could manage to utter.

"Father is well," he reassured her immediately.

Jory let out a long, relieved breath and saw Rickard's eyes widen as he took in her condition.

"You are having a child." Rickard sounded bemused.

"Yes . . . your father didn't tell you?" she asked nervously. "You will always be first in his heart, Rickard."

"Lady Marjory, Father's love is all-encompassing. I harbor no fears that I will be replaced," he said, smiling to reassure her. "Let's go upstairs — I have news to impart." He followed her, ready to aid her if she misstepped.

When she was comfortably seated, Rickard said, "I know it will sadden you to learn that King Edward is dead."

She immediately thought of Robert Bruce and the war that Edward Plantagenet was waging. "Was he killed in battle?"

"No. The king was ill — he died before he reached Scotland."

Could it be divine intervention? Jane always said that it was written in the stars that Robert was destined to rule Scotland. "So Prince Edward is now King of England?" It was difficult for Jory to imagine such a thing.

"Yes. We escorted his father's bier to York, where his body is now lying in state at the cathedral. Soon he will be sent to Westminster Abbey for burial. Prince Edward — I mean, King Edward — is on his way to London. Father asked that I bring you the news."

"Thank you, Rickard. My friend Princess Joanna always insisted that her brother would never fight a war. Does this mean that there will be no campaign to reconquer Scotland?" Jory could not disguise the hope that had begun to blossom in her heart.

"The Earl of Pembroke and the army are still in the field, Lady Marjory, but the new king prefers to direct matters from the rear," Rickard said with contempt.

"Is Guy in York with the old king?"

"Nay — I left him at Carlisle. Father said he had a mission."

Jory went pale. She heard a low knock on the door and asked Rickard to answer it.

Young Catherine Mortimer blushed profusely when Rickard de Beauchamp unexpectedly opened Lady Marjory's chamber door. She stammered, "Sir Rickard . . . what . . . when . . . that is, how — ?"

"Catherine!" Rickard was as surprised as the young lady. "I had no idea you were visiting Warwick."

"Catherine has graciously consented to be my lady-in-waiting."

"This is marvelous news. Her brother Roger is my good friend," he told Jory. "We are at Kenilworth. I'm sure he would have accompanied me if he'd known you were at Warwick."

Jory looked from the handsome young man to the blushing maiden. "If you can

535

stay, Rickard, I'll have your old chambers plenished."

He took Catherine's hand and drew her into the room. "I would love it above all things if I could stay, ladies. But I am at the beck and call of a king who is riding to London with all speed." Rickard kissed Catherine's hand, then walked across the chamber and took Jory's fingers to his lips. "*Au revoir.* I deeply regret that I must take my leave. Catherine, I charge you to take good care of my father's beloved wife."

Jory guessed the couple would like a few minutes alone together. "Catherine, go with Rickard to the hall and ask Mr. Burke to fill a tankard of good Warwick ale to quench his thirst."

When she was alone, Jory whispered, "Guy, please don't slay Robert Bruce. There is no need. My heart belongs to you alone."

"You have news for me?" Robert Bruce descended the stone steps of Douglas Castle.

Warwick stared at the man who approached him. He was staggered at the contrast between this twenty-three-year-old Celtic warrior and the pitiful excuse of a king who was the same age and who now ruled England. What Bruce lacked in height, he made up for in the breadth of his shoulders. He was all sinew and rippling muscle. *Christ, Jory, you have superb taste in men!*

Guy de Beauchamp heard the echo of Lynx de Warenne's voice: "Bruce, Earl of Carrick, is the rightful King of Scotland." As the dark Celt drew close, Warwick knew in his bones that it was the absolute truth. *All that stands between this man and his rightful destiny is a knife thrust!*

"Edward Plantagenet is dead," Warwick declared. He saw the flare of ambition in the Bruce's eyes, but he also sensed his genuine regret.

"We will never see the like of him again, Warwick."

"Sadly, that is true."

"You are a close friend of Lynx de Warenne?"

"We are more than friends; we are related by marriage. Lady Marjory is now the Countess of Warwick."

Robert Bruce showed surprise. "You are a lucky man — I envy you, Warwick." His mouth curved. "I adored Jory. She was the most generous woman I have ever known. At her suggestion I wed the Earl of Ulster's daughter, Elizabeth de Burgh, a sure way to get him to support my bid for the throne."

As Warwick listened to the revelation he

realized that Jory had never truly been Robert Bruce's mistress. Ambition had been bred into his bones. The Bruce had only one mistress and that was Scotland. *The man has no notion that he got Marjory with child. She never told him. She wanted him to fulfill his destiny — that's how selfless Jory is!*

Warwick was at war with himself. He had come to kill Robert Bruce, but his instincts told him that Jory would never forgive what she would consider an act of treacherous betrayal.

You were given a rare second chance at happiness. Don't squander it, Warwick!

"I answered Edward Plantagenet's call to arms to reconquer Scotland," he said bluntly. "If we can reach an understanding, I pledge to take my men-at-arms home to England and never return." Guy de Beauchamp wagered that Robert Bruce would do the expedient thing, as always.

"An understanding?"

"Marjory is *mine*. Scotland is *yours*."

"Done!" A grin spread over the Bruce's handsome features as the two men clasped arms. "I am more afraid of the *bones* of the dead father, than of the living son!"

"Lord Warwick has just returned, my lady."

Jory let out a long, slow breath. "Thank you, Mr. Burke. Are the men-at-arms with him?" she asked anxiously.

It had been a month since Rickard de Beauchamp had brought her news of the king's death, and Jory felt as if she had been holding her breath ever since, waiting for her husband to return.

"They are, my lady, and they'll be thirsty. If I don't hurry to the hall, Meg will be there before me."

She watched the steward hurry off and wanted to follow, but she suddenly felt shy and self-conscious about her appearance. She had carried her baby for eight months and only in the last two had she been unable to conceal her pregnancy by wearing a loose, flowing gown. She carried the child high, her hands often resting on the small mound in a protective, loving gesture.

Jory closed her eyes and offered up a prayer of thanks that Guy de Beauchamp had not been killed in battle. Did she dare to pray that he had not killed Robert Bruce or would God think her greedy?

She left her own private tower room and went down one flight of steps to what she thought of as Guy's chamber. She went to the window and looked down into the bailey, hoping to catch a glimpse of the dark, infamous earl who held her heart captive. She didn't see him, but she caught glimpses of Brutus dashing about, wild with joy at his master's return. Just knowing Guy was there, issuing orders, stabling Caesar, and setting all to rights, comforted her and bolstered her sense of security.

Jory opened his wardrobe to make sure he had freshly laundered shirts and her hand fell on his black velvet bed robe. Her fingers traced the embroidered golden bear and the Warwick motto, *Non Sans Droit.* "Not without right." Jory shivered. In spite of the noble-sounding motto, she knew that Warwick and every other earl, including the Earl of Carrick, believed that *might was right.*

Jory heard servants moving about in the dining room that was below Warwick's chamber and she realized it was approaching the dinner hour. *Will he forego eating in the Great Hall tonight so the two of us can dine together?* The thought did little to quell her anxiety. Perhaps he wanted to be alone because he had distressing news to impart. Her baby kicked and she caressed her belly with gentle, soothing hands. She called down the stairs for a servant and asked that water be brought up so Guy could wash. It was Catherine who brought it upstairs.

"This is all so exciting, my lady. I think it marvelously romantic that you have a private dining room."

Tonight it doesn't feel romantic. It feels intimidating! "I think I had better change my dress. Will you help me, Catherine?"

Back in her own chamber, Jory chose a velvet gown in a shade of deep amber. It was low cut to show off her breasts that were now full and lush. She pinned on the black onyx brooch carved in the likeness of Guy's wolfhound, Brutus. Catherine brushed her hair and fastened an ornament of sparkling jet at Jory's temple.

They heard footsteps on the stairs. Jory licked lips that had gone suddenly dry, while Catherine retreated to a shadowed corner. The door swung open and Warwick filled the doorway. He was taller, darker, and far more powerful looking than she remembered. Jory tried to swallow and couldn't. *He sees only my belly!*

"Will you do me the honor of taking supper with me, my lady?"

Those are the very words he said to me when he abducted me. Jory remembered the reply she had given him: *You smooth-tongued French devil, how can I resist such a gallant invitation?* But tonight words failed her and all she could manage was a nod.

Warwick's hand rubbed his unshaven jaw. "I shall come for you in a half hour, *chéri.*"

When he turned and left, Jory remembered to breathe. She paced to the window and wondered when darkness had fallen. Below in the bailey, torches blazed as campaign tents and weapons were unloaded. She took it as a positive sign that they would not soon be returning to fight in Scotland.

She was still racked with worry, however. Warwick had been on a personal mission — to kill Robert Bruce. She understood that he wanted to obliterate Robert from her thoughts, and the only way he knew how to achieve such a thing was to obliterate him completely. *Did my husband accomplish what he set out to do?* Jory shuddered.

As Catherine chattered and hung up the dress the countess had changed from, Jory cautioned herself to not ask about the Bruce, even though his welfare was uppermost in her mind. When she looked at Warwick, she must not even question him with her eyes. She heard a noise at the door and gasped.

Guy strode forward and gallantly held out

his arm. "Are you ready to dine, Lady War-wick?"

"I am, my lord." Jory knew she sounded breathless and unsure.

Her husband held his hand at the small of her back as they descended to the dining room. "You are positively blooming tonight. I hope you have been well, Jory."

Blooming with child! "Yes . . . I cannot complain."

She looked at the table that had been laid for two. She saw that both Meg and Mr. Burke stood ready to serve them. She felt suddenly cold and moved to the fire to warm her hands.

Guy walked to the side table that held wine and goblets. "Where is the ale I brought from the brew house?"

"It's still down in the kitchen, Lord War-wick," Meg declared. "I'll run down and fetch it."

"Nay, I'll go. My throat is as dry as an Arabian desert and my lady prefers ale to wine, I warrant."

To Jory, the minutes dragged out endlessly until Warwick returned with a jug of ale. She lowered her lashes in an attempt to hide her impatience and her anxiety as her husband filled a goblet with ale and handed it to her.

He filled one for himself and raised it. "I met my full obligation when Edward Plantagenet called me to war. It is over and done. Warwick will not take up arms again against Scotland."

You are torturing me! What about Robert Bruce? Jory raised her goblet slowly as Warwick watched her closely. An unusual aroma filled her nostrils. She took a long, deliberate sniff in disbelief and raised accusing eyes to Warwick. "You cruel swine!"

She flung the contents of the goblet into the fire and heard the flames hiss. She was acutely familiar with the unique smell of pennyroyal. Her brother's mistress, Alice Bolton, had used the abortifacient to rid herself of Lynx's child.

The goblet fell from her fingers and her hands moved to cover her baby in a protective gesture. "You never wanted it! Oh, you wanted *me* all right, but not my *child.*"

"What the hellfire are you talking about?" Warwick demanded.

"Taste the ale. Do you deny that it has been dosed with pennyroyal? It won't affect you, of course, but it will effectively rid me of my child!"

Jory saw the shocked look on Mr. Burke's face and the fury on Warwick's. It did not deter her. "I will not live under this roof while you are in residence, Lord Warwick. I shall go to my own castle of Windrush, unless you want it back?" she challenged.

"I forbid you to travel in your condition," Warwick growled.

Jory laughed cruelly. "Because I might miscarry?"

Warwick's jaw set. "You *will not* leave tonight." His voice was implacable. "Tomorrow I will provide you with safe escort."

He watched her leave, then turned a bleak face to his steward. "I see Meg managed to slip away. Find the woman, Mr. Burke, no matter where she has run to."

"I hope you will come to love Windrush as I do, Catherine."

"The women of this castle are so kind and welcoming. They can't seem to do enough for us. I can understand why you like it here."

When they finished unpacking Jory's garments and hanging them in the wardrobe, the two sat down before the fire that the castle women had lit for them. "Catherine, I warrant you have many questions about why I suddenly left Warwick, but I thank you for not voicing them." Jory sipped on a cup of ewe's milk that one of the kitchen maids had brought her.

"I just worry about you having your baby away from Warwick."

"The women of Windrush are thrilled that I have chosen this castle for my lying-in and have assured me that Mary and Maggie are competent midwives. Catherine, are you afraid of childbirth?"

"Oh, no, Lady Marjory. The Mortimers are prolific breeders. I've been in attendance at all my sisters' birthings."

"That's comforting; it's a new experience for me." *She knows my mother died in childbirth — Joanna announced it with such glee.* "I confess I am apprehensive. Not about the pain. I am well aware there will be pain. I just want my baby to be all right."

"Would you like me to rub your back, my lady?"

"I'm not at that stage yet, Catherine. Let's go down to the River Windrush and feed the ducks. Ducks always make me laugh." *If I don't laugh, I'll cry. The lump in my throat is choking me.*

A few days later, when Jory and Catherine were sewing baby garments with the women of Windrush, a castle guardsman came up to the solar. "Ye have visitors, Lady Marjory."

Jory stiffened. "Is it Lord Warwick?"

"Nay, it is Lord Warwick's son, my lady."

Catherine pricked her finger and jumped to her feet, blushing.

"Rickard is supposed to be in London." Jory hurried down to the courtyard with Catherine in tow.

Rickard and Jory looked at each other and both said exactly the same thing: "What are you doing here?"

Catherine gave a squeal of joy, for the young man with Rickard was her brother Roger Mortimer.

Rickard led Jory away from the brother and sister so they could speak privately. "Is Father here?" His manner told her that Rickard hoped Warwick was not at Windrush.

"No. I came alone. When we married, your father gave me Windrush. Oh, I'm so sorry, Rickard. You didn't know. You too came here seeking refuge."

Rickard flushed because she was so perceptive. "Did Father return from Scotland?"

"Yes, he's at Warwick."

It was Rickard's turn to be perceptive. "There is trouble between you and Father."

"Yes — it's — a private matter, I'm

afraid." She watched his face closely. "Is there trouble between you and the new king?"

Rickard flushed to the roots of his hair and glanced quickly at Roger and Catherine Mortimer. "Edward recalled Piers Gaveston. Before his father is even buried, his favorite is back at Court."

"I am aware of their relationship, Rickard. You need not be embarrassed with me," she said gently.

"Gaveston can do no wrong. Edward piles honors, land and lucrative wardships upon the arrogant swine. He has made Roger, and Catherine too, wards of Gaveston until they come of age."

"But their uncle, Mortimer of Chirk, is their guardian."

"No longer, I'm afraid. Gaveston has a foul ulterior motive for wanting wardship of Roger. My friend was so outraged he refused to stay at Court another day, so we rode here to Windrush. I'm sorry to disturb your peace and quiet, Lady Marjory."

"You've told me Roger's reason for leaving — what is your reason, Rickard?"

He flushed again. "Don't ask. 'Tis unfit for gentle ears."

"I can guess. I warrant Gaveston has tried

to assault you." *Sexual assault would be my guess!*

"Fore God, Lady Marjory, I beg you keep this from Catherine."

"I won't speak of it. She's too young to know such things. Come to the hall. 'Tis almost dinner hour."

"No! Not tonight — I can't face her. I can't face anyone."

"I understand." She laid a comforting hand on his arm and felt tender compassion when he flinched. "Take whatever chambers you used in the past. I'll have the steward plenish them for you."

When Catherine and her brother approached Jory, Rickard disappeared into the castle. "Hello, Roger. I attended your wedding with Princess Joanna a few years ago and you were once at Goodrich when I was wed to Humphrey de Bohun."

"I could never forget so fair a face, Lady Warwick."

Jory tried not to stare at the pair. They shared a dark, brilliant beauty that caught the imagination. "I welcome you to Windrush. I willingly share my haven with you and Rickard."

Rickard remained apart for days, but gradually his sensitivity lessened and finally he joined the others in the hall for meals.

CHAPTER 28

A grim-faced Warwick stared at the woman crouched before him. "Explain yourself."

A three-day search of the immense castle for the Welsh serving woman had finally borne fruit.

"Lady Marjory asked me to brew —"

Warwick took a threatening step toward her and Meg immediately stopped speaking. "Start at the beginning. How did my first wife, Isabel de Clare, die?"

"My lord, I swear that she died by her own hand."

"I am quite familiar with the old tale that she could no longer bear me as husband," Warwick declared. "Now we'll have the truth! If you start to utter a lie, you will be dead before you finish your sentence." A crack of thunder added emphasis to his words.

"Isabel's best friend was Alyce of Angouleme — her brother's first wife. The foreign woman taught your wife all about potions and poisons."

"You were skilled in herbs. You also learned much from Alyce."

Afraid to lie, Meg nodded.

"What did my wife take?"

"Isabel was young and afraid of childbirth. She took an herb that Alyce told her would prevent conception."

"What did my wife take?" Warwick repeated grimly.

"It was hellebore," Meg whispered.

Guy closed his eyes and thanked the saints that Jory had only been given pennyroyal. Hellebore was a deadly poison. Meg had wanted Jory to lose her child; she had not tried to kill her.

"You are complicit in the death of my first wife. Let us move on to the second. You poisoned my son's mind about his mother, telling him of her faithlessness and urging him to follow her." He stopped himself before he said too much. *The tragic outcome of that makes you complicit in the death of my second wife.*

"I loved Rickard like he was my own son!"

"Aye. You coveted him, and that adds to your sins." Warwick glanced at Mr. Burke, who looked outraged at the revelations. "Now you will explain why you put penny-

551

royal in Jory's ale."

"Rickard is your rightful heir! Her child would soon replace Rickard in your affections. She'd set one son against the other."

"Your opinion of me is abysmal. I might be hard and cruel and insufferably arrogant but, before God, I am not evil."

"I don't think you evil. I love you! I too have de Clare blood. When Isabel died, you should have made me your countess!"

Warwick recoiled. *Holy God, you were jealous of my wives! Jealousy blackens the soul. No one knows that better than I.* "You cannot remain here. I am returning you to the de Clares in the Welsh Border. Pack your belongings."

That evening, the Warwick knight who had discovered Meg's secret hiding place in one of the castle's many turrets came down with a fever, and a tale quickly spread among the servants that Meg was a Welsh witch. Because she had been banished, the reasoning went, she had cast a spell on the unfortunate man, and his sickness was bound to spread throughout the castle like a plague.

Mr. Burke brought the tale to Guy de Beauchamp as everyone gathered in the Great Hall for the evening meal. Warwick cursed under his breath and held up his hands for silence.

"It has come to my ears that a tale of witchcraft is being bandied about. The serving woman, Meg, has been sent back to Wales on my orders. She was an odd female with strange ideas, but she was not a witch. Belief in spells is superstitious nonsense and I want none of it at Warwick! *Do I make myself clear?*"

Warwick's fierce glance swept over everyone in the hall. "John Montecute has a fever and a sore throat, most likely brought about by standing guard duty in the pouring rain. A dose of borage and clary will cure his affliction."

Guy gave orders to his steward. "Make sure Montecute is put in quarantine; if his fever spreads, witchcraft rumors will be rife."

At midnight when Warwick retired, he knew he would have another sleepless night. His worry about Jory was so intense, he feared it would drive him mad. His wife could not bear to be near him, but he could not bear for her to be out of his sight.

He flung back the covers and quit the lonely bed. He paced to the window and gazed out. Lightning still streaked through the dark sky, though it had moved off some distance. His thoughts were filled with Jory.

He knew she would be able to hear the storm at Windrush and hoped she wasn't afraid.

Of course she's afraid! Not of the storm, but of the ordeal she will soon face. She will not be able to banish the thought that her mother died giving birth to her. Neither can I.

He left the window and began to dress. *Christ Almighty, I can't go to her until I'm sure there's no contagion here.*

He heard a scratch at the door and opened it to admit Brutus. His wolfhound gave him a knowing look and Warwick went back to the window and smote his fist against the stone sill. He felt covered with shame that he had not eased Jory's mind about Robert Bruce.

"Don't look at me like that!" he growled. Brutus growled back. "I was going to tell her over dinner in our private dining room. I went down to the kitchen for ale so we could drink a toast." *Aye, you wanted to make a grandiose announcement that you'd decided to spare the Bruce, so Jory would think you noble.* "What a self-righteous swine I am!"

Brutus nodded his agreement.

She begged me, and all it did was fuel my jealousy. He clenched and unclenched his fists. *When I actually saw him and spoke to him, my jealousy disappeared and was replaced by a feeling of rightness — that Bruce was fulfilling his destiny.*

"Why did I let her leave without easing her mind? Why the hellfire did I let her leave at all?"

Brutus hung his head in remorse.

The next sennight crawled by as Guy de Beauchamp kept watch on the health of everyone at Warwick. Two servants who had come in contact with John Montecute came down with fever and they were immediately quarantined along with the knight while Warwick held his breath and strived to keep up everyone's morale.

If the days seemed to crawl, the nights seemed to stop altogether and the hours became endless tests of his endurance. A haggard Warwick looked into the mirror and finally admitted to himself that fear stared him in the face. Nay, fear was a pale thing beside the stark terror for Jory that was relentlessly building inside him. He vowed that if no others had fallen ill come morning, he would ride hell-for-leather to Windrush.

Warwick checked on his knight's health

just after dawn and, much to his relief, Montecute's fever and other symptoms had abated and no others had come down with the malady. He packed his saddlebags, told Mr. Burke where he was going, and admonished, "Keep Brutus from following me."

Rickard de Beauchamp was in Windrush Castle's courtyard when he caught a glimpse of his father riding in. He darted into the stables and joined Roger Mortimer, who was saddling up for a hunt.

"Father! He has the eyes of a hawk — I think he saw me."

Warwick thundered up to the stables, dismounted, and strode inside. "What the hell are you two doing here?"

Rickard avoided his father's piercing black eyes.

"Why did you leave London?" he demanded. Giving no time to answer, he shouted, "Why did you leave the king's service?"

Roger answered. "Edward recalled Gaveston. He took my wardship away from Mortimer of Chirk and gave it to his lover."

Rickard found his voice. "The strutting Gaveston and his friends from Gascony made it untenable. We left in protest."

"Then you can turn around and go

straight back to Court. You are the king's highest young nobles. You cannot leave the field to foreigners."

"I won't go," Rickard said flatly, demonstrating a deal of courage by defying his father. Though he tried to mask his embarrassment, his face turned crimson.

Warwick's eyes narrowed. "What exactly happened?"

"We brawled with the Gascons," Roger declared.

Warwick turned to Mortimer with raised eyebrows.

"Rickard was within a heartbeat of slitting Gaveston's throat."

"The cocksucker dared to touch you?" Warwick demanded.

"I fought them and had my knife at his gullet. I would have killed him if Roger hadn't stopped me," Rickard confessed.

"Edward would have thrown Rickard in the Tower and executed him if he had harmed his bedmate."

"Christ Almighty! Edward Plantagenet decreed in his last will and testament that Gaveston could not be recalled without the consent of Parliament," Warwick declared.

"Edward Plantagenet is dead, Father. England has a new king who rules by divine right and thinks he can do no wrong."

"The barons will soon disabuse the young cocksucker of his delusions of grandeur and rid him of his Gascon bum-fucker!"

Rickard changed the subject. "You have come to put things right between you and Jory, I hope."

"I should never have allowed her to leave Warwick. I've made some damned stupid mistakes. One was keeping Meg around all these years to create havoc in our lives."

"I've known since I was a boy that she couldn't be trusted."

"I sent her back to Wales. She dosed the ale with pennyroyal so Jory would miscarry. Fortunately she didn't drink any."

"Lady Marjory wouldn't tell me what the trouble was. She said it was a private matter."

"Jory thinks *I* did it because I don't want another child."

"She was right — it is a private matter. I hope you can resolve it, Father." Rickard hesitated, then warned, "Go gently. You can be very intimidating at times."

"Here, take care of Caesar for me. I've been worried to death about Jory. I want to see with my own eyes she's all right." He removed his saddlebags and strode purposefully toward the castle.

When he encountered the steward of

Windrush he greeted the man and moved toward the stairs.

"I should announce you, Lord Warwick."

"I'll announce myself."

"Begging yer pardon, my lord. Windrush belongs to Lady Warwick . . . I think it best that I announce you," he said bravely.

"So much for being intimidating," Guy muttered with irony.

The steward hurried upstairs and knocked on Lady Warwick's chamber door. Catherine Mortimer opened it and learned the rather alarming news. "Wait here," she admonished him.

Jory, who had been enduring a nagging backache on and off for the past twelve hours was sitting on her bed, propped up by pillows and sipping on a concoction of barley water and fennel that Maggie had brewed for her.

"Not only will it ease yer pain; it will increase yer milk. The babe will be here by this time tomorrow," Maggie predicted.

Catherine came to the bed. "Lord Warwick is here."

Jory's eyes widened. "I don't want to see him!"

"I'll tell the steward, my lady," Catherine murmured.

"No! Warwick will overrule the steward.

Go down and tell him that I don't want to see him."

"Me, my lady?" Catherine whispered with dismay.

"You stay here with Lady Marjory. I'll go and tell the earl," Maggie declared bravely. She opened the door and told the steward, "Lady Marjory won't see Lord Warwick. Come, we'll tell him together. I don't have the courage to face him alone."

The pair found the earl at the foot of the stairs. "Lady Marjory asked me to plenish a chamber for you, Lord Warwick."

Maggie, who knew better than to lie to the earl, cut the steward off. "She said no such thing, my lord."

"What *did* she say?" Guy asked quietly.

Maggie swallowed hard and raised her chin. "*I don't want to see him,* were her exact words, my lord."

"Is she well?" Guy demanded.

"As well as can be expected. Lady Marjory hasn't gone into labor yet, but there are signs," Maggie said cryptically.

Guy made an effort to control the panic that assailed him. "I'll take the chamber you offered," he told the steward.

The manservant led Warwick to a small room on the second floor, next to the ones that Rickard and Roger were occupying.

"I'll fetch you some water and towels, my lord."

"Can you get me a piece of parchment and a quill? I must send my wife a message."

"I can tear a page from the sheep tally."

"That will do fine. Hurry, please."

To Guy, the man seemed to be gone for an hour, when in actuality it was only minutes before he returned. Guy grabbed the sheet and the piece of charcoal and tried to convey the message in as few words as possible. He folded the note and handed it to the steward. "Would you be good enough to deliver this to my wife?"

Ten minutes later, Jory opened the note that Catherine brought to her. A lump came into her throat as she read Warwick's words:

Robert is alive and well. Bruce is the rightful king. I should have told you immediately to ease your mind.

Jory's eyes flooded with tears and she began to sob softly.

Catherine was alarmed. "What is wrong, my lady?"

"Nothing whatever is wrong . . . My husband seems to love me."

Jory's bout of sobbing precipitated the

onset of labor. Her midsection was gripped by an agonizing contraction that caught her by surprise. The pain was so severe that she cried out and pressed her hands to her rigid belly until the pain let go.

"I'm sorry, Maggie. I won't scream again," she promised.

"Don't make promises ye can't keep, my lady. I'll go and fetch Mary. Don't be afraid — nothing's going to happen right away."

"Thank you, Maggie. I know first labors are long and painful."

A minute after Maggie left, the door burst open and Warwick strode in. Catherine retreated to the bed in a futile attempt to protect Jory from the powerful male force that swept into the chamber.

"It's all right, Catherine." Jory looked up at the dark face towering above her and glimpsed fear in her husband's eyes before he could mask it. "The pain has gone, Guy. I won't scream again."

He covered her hand to reassure her. "You can scream Windrush down if it helps you get through this, Jory. Catherine, bring her a nightdress. She needs to get out of these clothes."

Happy to be given a task, the girl found a white cotton night rail and brought it to the bed.

Guy unfastened Jory's gown and helped her remove it. Then he lifted her shift over her head. Before he pulled the fresh cotton garment down over her shoulders, he gazed at her body as if he were spellbound. Her creamy skin was stretched taut and smooth over her rounded belly and her breasts were full and lush. He was amazed to see that her delicate beauty was enhanced by the changes it had undergone. He was gripped by an overwhelming desire to protect her, and the knowledge that he would not be able to keep her pain at bay filled him with frustration.

Maggie returned with Mary and the pair took the earl's presence in stride. He was the infamous Warwick, whose power was only slightly less than God's in their eyes. If the countess had changed her mind about wanting him at her side, they had no desire to deny her.

Mary asked, "How many pains have you had, my lady?"

"Just one." The words were no sooner out of her mouth than her midsection was gripped by another paroxysm. Jory gasped, and grabbed Guy's hands to keep from screaming.

"Half an hour apart," Mary estimated. "We've a way to go yet."

"Let's prepare by putting some extra sheets under her. As they get soiled we can remove them without changing the entire bed and disturbing her."

The women brought five large sheets and folded them in quarters, making twenty layers. Guy lifted his wife in his arms while they put the sheets on the bed. He held her against his heart and kissed her temple. Jory weighed so little he began to worry that she was too frail to survive the ordeal.

He took Mary aside. "She's so small," he murmured.

"Small is good, Lord Warwick. Big, fat women have a devil of a time in childbirth."

Mary urged Maggie and Catherine to go and rest because they might be needed in the night. When they left, Mary sat down before the fire and pulled a ball of lambswool and a crochet hook from her smock and started to make a baby blanket.

Christus! If the woman expects to finish a blanket for the baby, this is going to be the longest day of our lives.

Guy sat down on the bed. "Lean against me and get some rest, love. Close your eyes and try to let my strength flow into you."

During the next few hours, he was surprised that Jory did drift off to sleep between labor pains. Then he began to worry that it was taking so much out of her, she was becoming exhausted.

When darkness fell, her contractions came closer together and lasted longer. As she'd promised, Jory didn't scream and tried to not even whimper. It tore at Guy's heart. Between bouts of pain, he massaged her feet and her back, determined to distract her. He gave her drinks, but she could not face food so he stopped trying to tempt her. He bathed her hands and face every hour and told her tales about when he was a boy. He talked about breeding horses and she clung to him and listened with fascination.

At dawn, Maggie and Catherine returned, and shortly after Jory's water broke and she went into hard labor. The women immediately removed the wet sheet from beneath her and encouraged her to push.

Catherine found a linen towel in which to wrap the baby when it made its appearance and Guy reluctantly moved back, allowing the two experienced midwives to control the situation.

It took the better part of an hour before the child's head presented itself. To Guy, that hour seemed longer than the previous twelve that Jory had been in labor. Suddenly, she screamed and her baby was delivered.

"Oh, no," Mary whispered.

Immediately, Guy stepped forward, his face tense. He saw that the baby was blue because the birth cord was wrapped around its neck. His heart was in his mouth as he watched Maggie carefully unwrap the cord, and then Mary bound and cut it.

Guy snatched the linen towel from Catherine and took the child from Maggie's hands. "Take care of Jory." One swift glance into his wife's eyes revealed the stark fear that gripped her.

"My baby isn't crying!" Her voice was filled with anguish.

"Catherine, get whiskey from the steward. Run!" he ordered.

Guy carried the silent little bundle before the fire and carefully unwrapped it. His heart melted when he saw the tiny female. Though he was desperately worried about Jory, he knew the most beneficial thing he could do for her at this moment was make sure that her baby survived. When a breathless Catherine returned and handed him the whiskey, he poured some into his palm, warmed it at the fire and began to rub it directly on the baby's skin.

Guy began at the tiny rib cage and then turned the baby over and massaged its little back. With gentle fingers he rubbed his daughter's arms and legs, then massaged her tiny buttocks. Suddenly the baby began to choke. He quickly smacked her narrow little back, terrified that she had drawn her last breath. All at once a lump of mucus dislodged from the infant's throat. He wiped it away with the towel and immediately the baby began to wail. Guy felt weak with relief.

When Jory dispelled the afterbirth, Maggie and Mary once more removed the soiled sheet. They could see that though Lady Marjory was exhausted, she was overwhelmed with worry. They bathed her and propped her up against a large pillow.

Guy glanced over at the bed. Jory's face was ghostly pale, her green eyes wide with anxiety. Suddenly the little minx began to scream and Guy whooped with joy.

"Good girl . . . Daddy's girl!" He carried his little daughter to the bed and his black eyes minutely examined his wife to make sure she had come through the birth with no lasting harm. Jory's eyes were filled with gratitude for what he had done. She smiled tremulously and when she held out her arms, Guy placed the precious baby in them.

Catherine answered a knock on the door.

"Lord Warwick, it's your son, Rickard," she said shyly.

Guy strode to the door and grinned. "You have a sister. Go and find us a cradle."

He went back to the bed and stood mesmerized as he watched Jory suckle her baby. He knew in that moment that he had never seen a more beautiful or touching picture of love.

By the time the baby had been nourished and had fallen asleep, Rickard and Roger were dragging in a carved wooden cradle.

Guy took the baby from Jory's arms and gently laid it in the cradle. Mary covered the child with the lambswool blanket she had made, and after a few minutes everyone in the chamber quietly departed and left the little family alone.

Guy sat down on the edge of the bed and wrapped possessive arms around Jory. Suddenly she began to laugh and it was the prettiest, most carefree sound he had ever heard. He joined in her laughter, unable to contain his exuberance a moment longer.

"We got our wish, Jory. We got a little girl!"

CHAPTER 29

"I cannot believe how much she has grown in two months." Guy ruffled the baby's dark curls as her eyes closed and her rosebud mouth stopped sucking.

Jory passed her baby daughter to Guy. "I know you like to hold her, but we have important guests and I must dress for dinner."

"We've had guests since Christmas. I warrant everyone wants to be entertained by the exquisite Countess of Warwick."

"You smooth-tongued Frenchman, you know the earls and barons have gathered here because it's central. Call Mary for me."

As soon as Guy opened the nursery door, Mary hurried in. The midwife, who had delivered the baby in the first week of December, had traveled from Windrush with the Warwicks two weeks later, to be the baby's nursemaid.

The baptism had taken place at Yuletide

in Warwick Castle's own chapel and Jory, who had insisted that her daughter's name be beautiful, christened the baby Brianna de Beauchamp.

"I'll be back to feed her before I retire tonight. If I get Catherine to help me dress, it will be faster."

"I'll help you dress," Guy offered with a leer.

"Absolutely not. I've had a taste of your helping and we always end up in bed. Control your passion until we retire tonight."

"That will be at least midnight," he pointed out.

"I'm worth waiting for, Warwick. Cool your lust."

Thirty minutes later, Lady Marjory swept into Warwick's Great Hall on the arm of her husband. In scarlet velvet with diamonds blazing at her throat she was the most dazzling chatelaine most of the nobles had ever seen. There was not a male present, whether he be servant, knight, or baron, who did not envy Guy de Beauchamp his beauteous wife.

Mr. Burke's vigilant eye oversaw the pecking order of the seating arrangement he had worked out with the countess. Up on the dais, Thomas of Lancaster, High Steward of England, who had just returned from London, had the place of honor on Warwick's right and his brother Henry Plantagenet, who had ridden from Kenilworth, sat on Jory's left.

All the high-ranking earls sat below the dais, facing their host and hostess and the two royals. Thomas of Lancaster's corpulent father-in-law, the Earl of Lincoln, was flanked by the irascible Roger Bigod, Earl of Norfolk, and John de Bohun, Earl of Hereford, who had been Jory's father-in-law.

Jory signaled for the wine and ale to be served and at the same time the musicians began to play their lutes and lyres in the minstrels' gallery above the hall. Though her face was serene, Jory inwardly marveled at the important earls who were gathered here before her. Her eyes traveled over Hugh le Despenser, Earl of Winchester, who was on the Royal Council. *He is here because he fears the new king will take his office away from him.* Her glance moved on to the Earl of Pembroke, who had been made head general of the army. *Gaveston has nicknamed him Joseph the Jew because of his large nose.*

Baron Mortimer of Chirk had come to protest because his guardianship of the young Mortimers had been taken from him and given to the king's favorite, and even Joanna's husband, the Earl of Gloucester, who was now brother-in-law to the new king, had made the journey to show that he sided with the barons.

Jory smiled at her brother, who had come to support the barons and carried his uncle John, Earl of Surrey's, proxy. *My dearest Jane wanted a daughter, but I know my brother is well pleased that their second child was another son.* Jory lifted her goblet of ale and silently saluted Lynx. Her brother lifted his own goblet and winked at her. *You're winking because you know I love to be the center of attention!*

Marjory's mind flew back to the Yuletide celebrations when one by one the nobles began to gather at Warwick Castle.

"King Edward is on a rampage and won't be satisfied until he's swept us all out of office," the Earl of Winchester complained, "and replaced us with the relatives and friends of Gaveston!"

The Earl of Chester, who had allowed the late king's forces to use his castle to conquer and reconquer Wales, spoke up. "None of our lands and castles will be safe in this new reign. If Gaveston's avaricious eyes fall on a piece of property, Edward hands it to his lover on a silver platter!"

Henry of Lancaster had ridden in from Kenilworth. "Edward has bestowed on Gaveston the Earldom of Cornwall with its vast revenues from the tin mines. It's the last bloody straw! That earldom has always been traditionally reserved for *royals.*"

Lynx de Warenne arrived with more unbelievable news. "When Treasurer Langton objected to Edward lavishing huge sums of money on Gaveston, the king sent him to the Tower. The minute the treasurer was imprisoned, the thirty thousand pounds that had been collected for the new crusade vanished into the Gascon's pockets."

In January, the new king's uncle, Thomas of Lancaster, rode in from London. The proud-blooded royal was so furious he fell into a Plantagenet rage. "After all the diplomatic maneuverings I made to arrange for the young swine's marriage to Princess Isabella of France, he has put the Great Seal of England into Gaveston's hands while he is gone to Boulogne! I am the rightful Regent of England when the king is absent. He has deliberately and maliciously insulted me. Something must be done!"

"We will hold a consultation and make a decision. Edward's coronation is planned for February 25, three weeks after he returns from France. We must assert our authority before he is crowned king or it will be too late," Warwick declared grimly.

Lancaster said, "Gaveston calls Lincoln Burstbelly, and you, Warwick, he calls the Mad Hound of Arden."

"One day, I'll show him just how mad I am!" Warwick vowed.

That night, as Warwick and Jory were readying for bed, she voiced her concern. "Guy, the nobles are laying this burden on you. They secretly hope you will eliminate the king's lover. I know what they think: *What's one more murder to the infamous Warwick?* But I happen to know that you have never committed the foul deed of murder and I won't let you do it. Let them do their own dirty work!"

Guy lifted her in the air and kissed her soundly. "You know all my secrets. I am a romantic fool to share them with you."

"I love you with all my heart. I couldn't bear it if you were arrested and sentenced to death. Please, Guy, I beg you."

"No begging allowed." He pulled her against his heart. "We will lay the law down and have him banished. If the pervert returns anytime during Edward's marriage, then I won't be responsible for my actions, so don't ask it, Jory."

The barons made a plan and decided that Thomas of Lancaster, the highest noble in the land, would go to London and await Edward's return. He must confront his nephew and inform him that all the earls and barons in England were united. They would refuse to attend his coronation unless Gaveston was banished. They were giving him no choice. Without the nobles there could be no coronation.

Marjory's mind came back to the present and she saw that the food had been served.

"Have you no appetite, *chéri?*" Guy squeezed her hand.

She smiled up at him. "My mind was woolgathering."

He grinned down at her and teased, "That's what comes of owning so many sheep. Gathering wool makes you a wealthy woman."

Jory's glance fell on Rickard de Beauchamp, who was sitting with Roger and Catherine Mortimer. *She is certainly smitten with Rickard, and though he is polite, he still holds himself aloof from her because of what happened with Gaveston. It will be a long time before he feels at ease with a lady.*

When the meal was over, the servers cleared the tables. Jory had arranged no entertainment for tonight because Thomas of Lancaster was going to address the assembled nobles.

The Earl of Warwick got to his feet and held up his hands for silence. "Thomas of Lancaster is here to give us a report on his meeting with Edward, which took place two days ago, when the newlywed king arrived back in London with his bride, Princess Isabella of France."

The hall fell silent as those assembled were eager to hear if their alliance had borne fruit. Thomas Plantagenet, relishing drama, stood up and waited a full minute before he began to speak.

"First let me say that I awaited Edward at Windsor, where he was to bring his bride, Princess Isabella, to the apartments that have been furbished with every luxury for the future Queen of England.

"The day before Edward arrived, Gaveston's entourage of sycophantic relatives and friends paraded about Windsor Castle as if they owned it. Gaveston was actually wearing some of the crown jewels and conducted himself as if he were the King of England. I was treated with utter disrespect and my Lancastrian retainers were jeered at. I had to restrain them from committing violence on the Gascon interlopers."

Murmurs of outrage could be heard all over the Great Hall.

"When Edward arrived at Windsor, he summoned me immediately to voice his outrage that few of the nobility were at Dover to greet him. He informed me that his outrage had turned to fury when he arrived at Windsor with his queen and found no throng of earls and barons there to give him a triumphant welcome.

"I informed him in no uncertain terms that his baronage thought poorly of him from every standpoint and unless he changed his ways, we would *never* welcome him. In fact, I told him, the highest nobles in the land stand firmly together, and unless he agreed to banish Gaveston from Court, we would all absent ourselves from the coronation."

Shouts of *Hear! Hear!* reverberated around the Great Hall.

"When I presented the roll of parchment with all our signatures, Edward was taken seriously aback. He collapsed like a sail without wind when I challenged him and showed him proof that the nobility was solidly allied against Gaveston. Edward then assured me he would arrange matters to our satisfaction. When I flatly told him that wasn't good enough, he signed a pledge."

A great cheer rose up to the rafters of the castle's Great Hall. The Earl and Countess of Warwick stood and lifted their goblets and everyone joined in to salute Thomas of Lancaster.

After he had enjoyed the adulation for about ten minutes, England's hereditary high steward raised his arms for silence. "When we rid London of the Gascons, *we* must become the king's Court. Edward has no experience and is ill-fitted for the role of king that has been thrust upon him. He will need much advice and guidance in ruling this realm. We are the ruling class; we, the earls and barons, have a wealth of experience we must put to use for the good of the realm."

Lancaster drained his wine and continued. "It is easy to see why the future Queen of England is called Isabella the Fair. However, she is only thirteen years old, little more than a child. She is like a pretty little doll and will need a Court of English ladies to advise and guide her. I hope I can persuade the elegant Countess of Warwick and other noble ladies to take up residence at Windsor Castle to help this innocent young princess become a worthy Queen of England."

Warwick glanced at his wife and saw that the idea of joining the Court was not anathema to her. He would certainly have to rid himself of his tendency to jealousy if he was to have any peace of mind. *Everyone adores Jory, always have and always will. It is high time I came to terms with it. I love her just as she is and wouldn't change one beautiful hair on her head.*

All those gathered in the Great Hall spent the next two hours discussing the business of the realm, expressing opinions and exchanging ideas. Every man and woman present knew that united they would prevail and divided they would fall. It was in their own best interests to become a closely knit alliance.

The Earl and Countess of Warwick were the last to leave the hall. Both went to the nursery, where they found baby Brianna wide-awake. Guy picked her up and laughed when she wrapped her tiny fingers about his thumb in a grip that refused to let go.

"She's growing very attached to me," he teased.

"So am I," Jory said. "Go and turn down our bed while I feed her." She took the baby from her husband and cradled her against her breast. When Brianna fell asleep, she tucked her into her cradle and offered up a prayer of thanks that she was thriving.

When Jory entered the bedchamber she began to quickly undress.

"Let me do that," Guy insisted.

"I want to bathe my breasts before I come to bed."

"I'll do that, too. It will give me untold pleasure." He sponged her breasts with the warm scented water and gently dried them with the linen towel. Then he took infinite delight in removing her garments. "Every man in the hall tonight envied me. They think me a lucky swine to have such a young beauty for my wife — and they are right. Jory, you have made my life so special, sweetheart." He picked her up and carried her naked to their bed.

Guy de Beauchamp spent the next hour making love to his wife. He knew his feelings for her were akin to worship, but he didn't care. He had been without her too many years and on their wedding day when he had vowed to love and cherish her, he had meant every word. "I told you that I would devote the rest of my days to making you happy, but in truth, Jory, it is you who makes me happy." As always happened, Jory became flushed with passion and yielded up everything to him. *I am the luckiest man alive!*

After they were both replete, Jory lay prone between his powerful legs, her lush breasts cushioned upon his chest, so they could talk.

"The coronation will be here before we know it. I've been working on my gown for weeks. I am going to enjoy being at the Windsor Court for a while. From what I know of Edward, young Queen Isabella is going to need my protection. A poor little lamb to the slaughter, I'm afraid." She brushed her fingertips over Warwick's cheekbone. "I know you will sometimes hate being at Court, but whenever you begin to feel closed in, you can escape to Flamstead Castle and your horses."

"You'll enjoy spending time with Joanna, who will undoubtedly return to Windsor. And when you get tired of Court, you can visit with Lynx and Jane," he said indulgently.

"Ah, but when I truly get tired of Court and want to leave and return home to Warwick, I have a plan."

"And what is this diabolical plan?"

"I shall have another baby, of course." She moved against him sensually, fully aware of the effect she had on him. "And this time I shall have a *son.* I have quite made up my mind!"

ABOUT THE AUTHOR

Virginia Henley is a *New York Times* bestselling author and the recipient of numerous awards, including the *Romantic Times* Lifetime Achievement Award. Her novels have been translated into fourteen languages. A grandmother of three, she lives in St. Petersburg, Florida, with her husband.